THE BLACK SHEEP AND THE ROTTEN APPLE

K.A. MERIKAN

ACERBI & VILLANI LTD.

COPYRIGHT

Contents

CHAPTER 1

JULIAN

The cacophony of sounds filling Julian's head was unbearable. Had the tavern turned into a concert hall for drunken cats attempting to perform an opera, or was the floor about to crumble beneath his feet and send him all the way down to the depths of hell? He squeezed his eyes shut and hid his face in his sleeve when the door burst open, letting in the morning cold, and—worse yet—light to assault his senses.

And just when the noise turned into a dull yet pleasant silence that made Julian hope for a bit more time with his head comfortably resting atop the sticky wooden table, a tubal voice drilled its way into his ears.

"I knew I'd find you here, you wastrel," hissed Julian's father, and as the heavy click of his heels approached, Julian wished that hell had taken mercy on him after all. He'd take eternal flames over what was to come.

A sudden tug on the back of his coat pulled him up, and for a moment, Julian had no idea where the floor was anymore. The world spun around him as if he had become a spoke in the wheel of Satan's carriage. Nausea rose in his throat, and he hummed his displeasure, pressing his eyelids tightly shut. Why today? Why did Father seek him out so early? His skull was an empty shell, rattling only with echoing noise.

"Let's make haste, Father. We wasted enough time trying to find the damned drunk." So Horace, Julian's oldest brother, was here too? What in God's name could have possessed them to interfere with Julian's morning routine?

But he didn't have any time left for pondering as two pairs of strong arms hauled him up from the bench, causing upset to his stomach and mind yet again.

"Damnation! What is it that the two of you want from me?" he uttered, scowling at how hoarse he sounded.

"I see wine washed away all your memories of last night's conversation. Or was it gin that you drank with those mongrels you idle about with?" Horace said in a biting tone. Every word came out of his mouth accompanied by a squelch of his permanently moist lips, thundering through Julian's poor head like bugle calls. Julian already knew all the beats in Horace's repertoire.

Julian wanted to parry the blow, he really did, but with his mind still muddled by yesterday's gin, all he could think of was clean, lovely water to soothe his raw throat. "Yesterday?" he rasped.

"We spoke of your prospective engagement to Miss White. You promised me not to leave the house before the journey, and yet you fled like a rat. I cannot comprehend how you accomplished that with the footman guarding the doors," yelled Father into Julian's ears as he and Horace hauled Julian's poor body over the threshold and into the bright light of day.

Julian twisted in disgust and shook his head, feeling his feet drag through the expanse of mud outside. "Window."

"Ha. You damned clown," growled Horace, his damp lips slapping together so close to Julian's face, the tiny droplets of saliva misted his cheek. "About to marry into a title, and he's running as if you demanded he kisses a pig's arse."

"You must understand, Father. All I saw of this girl you intend for me is a damn miniature portrait, and you won't even let me say good-bye to my bachelorhood in the company of old friends?" Julian asked, forcing words through the thick leathery sole that was his tongue. When he managed to open his eyelids enough to see what was coming, the sight of a loaded carriage with Hunt, their driver, already waiting in the box seat, made him instinctively dig his heels into the mud, balking against this rape on his personal freedom. Hunt instantly looked away, as if Julian was to be ignored. He would not be ignored. He had a bright future ahead of him, one that his father and family intended to thwart, extinguish before Julian's talent could truly bear fruit.

"What do you see in that puddle, Hunt? Are the mud nymphs calling out to you?"

Hunt's jaw tightened, and he kept his eyes carefully turned away from Julian in such a blatant display of disrespect it burned the last threads of Julian's self-control.

Horace opened the door, and its dim insides started already sucking Julian in like the whirlpool that had taken Julian's cousin to the bottom of the river nine summers past. That was it, the marriage would not put him into a cold grave just yet, but it would be the death of Julian's ambitions and dreams, and those he needed to defend at all costs.

He put his hands on both sides of the door and recoiled, determined not to let himself be manhandled like a common thief, or worse yet—a silly girl who didn't know better—but with his powers so weakened, Horace and Father pushed him past the door after an embarrassingly short struggle.

"Don't make a further spectacle of yourself," hissed Father, looking inside the carriage with the flew-like skin around his mouth lifting to reveal several missing teeth—the result of over-consumption of sugar. A mistake Julian was wary not to repeat.

Julian moaned and shook his head, rolling back on the seat from the impact of the movement. "Father. I know the alliance has been made, but wouldn't the girl appreciate a longer courtship? I could stay in London and get to kno—"

"And lose all your funds on gambling and whores even quicker than you're doing at present? Out of the question. I want to be congratulated on your engagement by the end of this month at the latest," shouted Father. "You could do at least that for this family if you have neither the mind nor the work ethic to support the family enterprise in any other way than with your loins," Father growled like a bulldog and shut the door with a bang that sent Julian all the way to the floor between the padded benches. He let out a low groan and held on to the smooth leather of his valise, which one of the servants must have taken from his room. Maybe he could still stop Hunt once they reached the outskirts of town? Direct him somewhere else perhaps? Surely, there was a way out of this imprisonment.

His mind stalled when the other door of the carriage, the one he was facing now, opened and Horace carefully pushed his bulk inside. Julian could hear his plans spill into the gutter.

"And for God's sake, stop looking like a ruffian and wear your wig!" yelled Father before shutting the door.

The carriage rolled forward.

The sun was high up in the sky by the time the desynchronized orchestra left Julian's skull. There wasn't enough space to properly lie down anywhere in the carriage, but he managed to obtain a comfortable position by resting his legs up the wooden wall while his upper body occupied one of the benches. He still felt like the filling of an enormous rattle as the carriage bent in all possible directions on the uneven road leading away from the coast.

Horace didn't even make an attempt to hold back his disapproval, but after delivering several biting comments and a lengthy speech about duty, he at last leaned against the side of the carriage in the seat across from Julian and closed his eyes. It was difficult to say whether he was truly in need of a nap or if it was Julian's face that he didn't wish to look at.

With his headache out of the way yet not quite well enough to read, Julian opened the curtains in hope of amusing himself with the views, but so far, he merely got to see the side of a narrow gully—all dirt and grass.

He couldn't understand why Father was being so implacable about having his youngest son marry a title. Couldn't it wait a fortnight so that Julian could finish that new novel he came up with last night? This one could truly be the breakthrough Julian had been waiting for, the one that would make the Reece family known for more than fabric trade.

Inspiration was a moment in time when Julian's friend Martin emerged from the darkness of an alley behind the tavern. In that very second he had not resembled himself but a man made of bronze, dreamlike and yet of substance, with strong hands that could crush Julian if they wanted. The novel would start with a similar encounter somewhere in the narrow back alleys, just off the Colosseum. Haunted by the ghost of an ancient gladiator, the protagonist would be believed to be slowly descending into madness, when in reality his awareness of the supernatural would become a vehicle for truth.

Julian was not yet certain of the exact message he wished to convey, but the events would be presented from several points of view, through letters written by the protagonist, his friends, and an official of some sort who'd represent the stale world order.

He'd already had several beautifully evocative ideas for metaphors describing the gladiator himself, but they became somewhat blurry after a night of cards and drink.

Oh, if only he could travel to Rome to let the atmosphere of the city soak him all the way to the bone—without a wife fighting for his attention and pulling him away from work because of feminine fancies.

He looked out of the window with growing disdain. Who in their right mind traveled on Sunday, and so early at that? Julian would have much preferred listening to a sermon at church to spending the day in what was effectively a hearse carrying one of the brightest literary talents just waiting to be discovered.

Now that Julian was feeling better, he was upset with himself about not asking for a day's delay on religious grounds. He'd never been as devout about prayer as he was about his art, but if the Christian faith could postpone his commitment to a woman he never met, he would gladly kneel and pray. And Miss White wasn't even a woman but a girl of fifteen, quite pretty in the portrait Julian had been shown, and a viscount's only daughter at that, but surely as hungry for her intended's attention as the bawdy house wench who'd become sweet on Julian some years ago.

Back then, he still visited Madame Canard's establishment to do what everyone else did when they visited a school of Venus. These days, Julian had neither the overwhelming desire nor patience to handle a cunt, no matter how lovely the lady it was attached to. He still enjoyed having a drink with the harlots, and no card table within twenty miles was as lively as the one at Madame Canard's, but at twenty-five he'd much rather handle needs of the flesh in solitude.

Sweet perfume made his nose itch, the act itself made him unpleasantly sticky—with his sweat and hers—and while he would not dare to ask, it was his suspicion that the friends who usually accompanied him to the brothel were only whoring so much because of pride and bravado. It was a sign of status to be able to afford women and decent wine daily, and so fucking and gambling was the thing you did as a social activity.

Julian's eyes darted to Horace, who slept with his head thrown back and leaning against the side of the carriage. His wide-open mouth was asking for a distasteful prank, but Julian was far too upset to think of amusing himself at Horace's expense. So far, the day's joke was on him.

In the years past, he'd been mocked by his father and siblings over not taking on a profession that they deemed worthy of a gentleman, but with the family being very prosperous, Julian saw no reason to divert his focus from his one true calling.

Despite frequent threats, he'd hoped that Father—having four willing sons and three daughters—wouldn't push Julian into marriage, but it seemed a lost cause. Soon it would be a wife nagging Julian to stop wasting his time following intellectual pursuits and instead turn his attention to practical matters. As the head of his own family, maybe he'd even be pushed to join the family trade, one step farther from traveling abroad to meet the great artists of the continent.

The carriage started a steep climb up a hill, and Julian cursed, pushing the soles of his boots against the wall to keep his body from rolling off the narrow bench. How long would it take for them to reach London at this pace? It was over two hundred miles away, so a week perhaps? The last time Julian had made the journey, he was so intoxicated most days that he couldn't properly count them.

But out of nowhere, as the slope of the hill became gentler, the ugly dirt and grass that had been Julian's only source of entertainment for the last half an hour were replaced by lush greenery of tree tops. He grinned and glanced at Horace, but the fat sod was too busy snoring to notice the change in scenery.

A wicked plan was starting to take shape in Julian's head, and he quietly removed his feet from the side of the carriage and lowered them to the floor. Pulling himself upright was easy enough after that, and he stalled, eyes transfixed on the permanently flushed face of his brother that was an unappetizing contrast with the white wig he wore, and made him look like a man many years his senior. Julian might be less inclined to business, less sedate than his siblings, but at the very least he had good taste and flair most of Julian's family lacked, buried deep in the stern world of pretense and money.

Horace didn't even stir. The old pig was fast asleep, and if that wasn't Julian's chance to save his life, he didn't know what was. Careful not to make any sound, Julian gathered his valise and the coat he'd earlier taken off because of the heat, stilling when the carriage came to a halt. His eyes immediately darted to Horace, but his brother only smacked his lips in his sleep. Hunt could have stopped to relieve himself. What an opportunity this was!

Julian could feel his heartbeat in his throat when he softly pressed on the door handle. Still distinctly aware of his brother being close enough for their knees to touch, were Julian not careful enough. He opened the carriage and left it in a soft stride before closing the door with care.

A warm breeze combed through his hair, wiping away the unpleasant wetness of sweat, and his lungs filled with fresh air, but he didn't get to enjoy it.

The shining muzzle of a pistol was grinning at him from inches away.

Despite the warm weather, Julian's whole body was shaken by a chill when his gaze met a pair of eyes so dark they might as well have been lacquered coals. The man had a tricorn hat pulled low over his forehead, and a black scarf obscuring the lower half of his face.

This can't be happening.

"Don't try to scream, or I will blow your brains out." The man squinted and lowered his gun to Julian's pupil. "Through the eye."

Julian opened his mouth as his throat closed, robbing him of breath. He wanted to look back, suddenly wishing Horace weren't such an easy sleeper, but Hunt was nowhere to be seen either. Heat washed over Julian's body, making him stiffen as if he were made of clay. Had this man hurt their coachman? If so, where was the body?

"What do you want?" Julian whispered, resting his hand on the door handle when his knees softened.

"These." A hand in a leather glove gripped Julian's sweaty fingers and slipped off his rings. "And all your other valuables." The man didn't even blink, his voice dark as if dragged through tar.

Julian stared, and his mind finally came up with the answer for what this was. "You're a highwayman..."

"And you're cork-brained to travel on a Sunday when the roads are empty." The man's gaze drifted away to Horace for a split second, but he must have judged him as no threat, and when Horace snored from inside the carriage, the highwayman chuckled quietly.

Julian's lungs emptied, and a silly grin emerged on his face, encouraged by the highwayman's amusement. "Ah, I should have gone to church after all."

The smile died on his lips when the robber poked Julian's temple with his gun.

"Your valuables," he urged.

Julian clenched his teeth when they threatened to clatter. He needed to keep calm. His father believed his friends to be villains, so he could handle one. "I've been taken out of the tavern this morning with nothing but the clothes on my back. I lost everything at the tables. You should try my older brother. He's Father's heir. He should have a healthy sum on him."

The highwayman gripped the front of Julian's waistcoat and pulled him forward so hard Julian stumbled straight into the man's arms. He was much taller than Julian, with wide shoulders that were so strong their size couldn't be just padding. His clothes smelled of leather and horse sweat, and Julian found himself staring into the eyes above the black scarf.

Before he could say a word, the man turned him around, and pressed the gun to the side of his head.

"Go on, wake up your brother."

Julian breathed in and out, stiff with discomfort at the warm body pressed against his back as if the highwayman was seeking warmth. The gun provided some relief against heated skin. Its presence made Julian's blood speed through his veins. It wouldn't go off. Murder wasn't in the robber's interest, but if that was the case, then where the hell was Hunt?

Then an idea illuminated Julian's mind. "I have a proposition, Mister—"

The highwayman stilled. He'd be lying. Of course. "Noir," he said in the end. "What kind of proposition can you have, pretty boy? With no money in your pockets."

Something about Noir's tone sent a hot shiver through Julian's ribcage, but he ignored the condescending words and slowly looked back into the blackest eyes he'd ever seen. "I don't have much on me, but you must know my father. He's William Reece, the cloth merchant. You could take me and ask for ransom. We could split it between us like two gentlemen," he whispered and gave Noir a polite nod. Appealing to the highwayman's self-importance should do the trick. His kind were known for a love of opulence and status they didn't deserve.

He must have managed to surprise the thief, because Noir's grip on him faltered. "How much could I ask for a son who hates his father?"

Julian exhaled in relief when he felt Noir's aggression turn away from him. "A lot. He needs me. I'm worth more than you can imagine," he said with a small smile.

Noir stole another glance at Horace sleeping in the back of the carriage, and his gloved hand slid to Julian's neck, squeezing around his nape in a way that had Julian rising to his toes. "You better be. You scream, or try to run, and I *will* kill you."

Julian swallowed against the warm, soft leather. It felt surprisingly expensive. Might have been snatched from a gentleman. "I don't doubt that," he lied. "However, we share a common goal, friend."

"Call me 'friend' once this is all over." Noir shook his head and pushed Julian behind the carriage, where a gloriously jet-black stallion awaited its rider, and watched Julian with eyes as dark as Noir's.

"I hope you haven't hurt our driver. He's a good fellow," said Julian, smiling at the huge beast in front of him.

"He'll live. Your brother will find him once he wakes up."

Julian was sure there had to be a hint of a smile under that black scarf. When Noir put the gun inside his coat, Julian tried to assess the man more thoroughly.

The black leather riding coat was worn but of good quality. Could have been stolen too, but the clothes underneath, as black as everything the man wore, were clean, suggesting the highwayman wasn't sleeping rough somewhere. Unless he dressed up for robbery.

Julian opened his mouth to comment on the beauty of the horse, but Noir spun Julian around and pulled back his hands.

"Good heavens. We're partners," Julian whispered with distaste. Hot and cold sweats were hitting him in rapid waves, and he couldn't tell whether he was scared or excited about this new development. Once he got out of this, he could write a novel about the peril of travellers attacked by rogues while driving through a dark, rainy forest, and with a bit of poetic license, call it a true story.

"I haven't decided on that yet," said Noir, and a cold shiver went down Julian's back at the proficiency with which the man tied his hands. A former sailor perhaps? That wouldn't bode well, as those types rarely possessed the intellectual capability for complicated schemes. His speech was also far too refined to have been only recently acquired. Damnation!

"Mr. Noir. I'd much rather ride with my hands free. You see, I've been incapacitated by gin just this morning, and I don't feel secure enough without my hands to assist me yet. I assure you, I am harmless."

Once Noir had tied Julian's hands, he turned him around. "Now you are. Up." And just as Julian was wondering how exactly he was supposed to climb atop the tall beast, the scoundrel grabbed his legs and picked him up. Julian barely refrained from screaming. It was no way to handle a gentleman, and yet he couldn't help but be amazed by Noir's physical prowess.

Definitely a sailor. A naval officer, perhaps.

Julian's face flushed with heat when he imagined his bottom sticking out like a whore's ass at a party. Good grief, what had he gotten himself into? What was next? Being kidnapped by pirates?

His foot found the stirrup, and he exhaled with relief, pushing his other leg over the horse's hindquarters until he straddled its back. "I see no reason for this kind of treatment, considering it was I who came up with a most lucrative opportunity for you."

"Keep that up, and I will gag you." Noir was quick to get on the horse himself as soon as he'd attached Julian's coat and valise to the saddle. Julian felt completely overwhelmed when the man reached for the reins, all but embracing him.

Julian shuddered and curled his shoulders to not be in the way, though no matter what he did, the shape of the saddle brought them close together. "You're a scoundrel. Another man in your profession would have treated me right."

Noir laughed darkly. "You are correct, sir. How could I have forgotten." Even though the mockery had him exaggerate the polite accent, Julian was becoming certain that Noir's natural speech was not that of someone uneducated.

Before Julian understood what was happening, Noir pulled a burlap sack over his head.

"I will scream," whispered Julian, staring through the dots of light in the smelly thing. He squeezed his hands into fists and pushed them hard against Noir's stomach. His mind was rattling again, as if the drunkenness returned with full force.

"No one will hear you where we're going."

"Julian?" came a sleepy voice from the carriage.

Noir's thighs tensed, and he must have urged his mount to rush, as it went almost straight into gallop.

Julian screamed at the top of his lungs. "Horace!"

The stallion flew forward, and without the aid of his hands, Julian was forced to hang on to it with his legs alone, shaken like a rattle. The rapid gait moved him back and forth over the front of the saddle, making Julian stiffen and push back against the firm chest behind him. Without seeing where they were going, Julian tried to hold on to anything he had on hand, and as it happened, it was probably Noir's waistcoat. If the horse tripped, at least they would stumble and break their bones together. Or maybe the villain would cushion Julian's fall in a well-meaning act of God.

It *was* Sunday.

CHAPTER 2

EVAN

Evan sat on the cold floor, with his back against the heavy wooden door to the tiny room that used to house the most precious porcelain owned by his family but was now merely a shell with empty cupboards.

"Is anyone there?" Julian yelled out again from the porcelain room, his clear voice insistently drumming against Evan's ears. "It's very chilly in here..."

Evan put his face in his hands and let his fingernails cut into his forehead. What had he done? Did he really take a prisoner into the house that had been the pride of his ancestors for the last three hundred years? The highway robbery was supposed to be a clean crime that would leave no trace for the lawmen, a desperate measure to obtain the money he needed to pay his servants and purchase necessities. A one-time dip into lawlessness that was never to be repeated.

The faint light coming through the window was painting dusky green on the tiny pebbles underneath Evan's feet. He watched them for a moment to occupy his mind until yet another wail entered his ears. He was used to the house being completely silent at night, yet now he couldn't bring himself to walk away from this door and the noise his unexpected guest was making over and over.

No matter the circumstances, Evan was still Julian's host, and the complaints coming from beyond the door were becoming unnerving. He had covered his guest with blankets, but it was early spring. The room was not heated, and those old walls could become cold at night, even in the midst of summer. Evan knew of no man who'd die from spending a night on the floor, but then again, Julian did not seem like a man used to inconvenience. Would the lamentation go on all night?

Evan wished he could somehow reverse the flow of time and make a different choice than he had. It must have been the sheer bravado of his captive that made Evan go through with this ridiculous abduction idea instead of scavenging what precious items and money had been hidden away in the carriage. He had not considered details such as remaining anonymous when accepting the ransom money, as he should have done. After all, nothing good ever came from following the advice of a boy with pretty eyes.

Evan had tried to assert his position by tying Julian up, but now that he'd carried his captive away from the highway and his blood cooled down, he didn't even know where to start on the venture. He was still baffled that Julian wanted to be captured by a man he could only have seen as a common criminal, so he was either daft or desperate. But Evan wouldn't know until he talked to the young man and established what the issue with his family was.

A task he was not looking forward to.

What he *was* looking forward to though was pulling the sack off the man's face and having a better look at his harmonious features. Despite his reckless actions, he was clearly not a boy anymore, although Evan had difficulty placing an age on Julian's angular, genteel features. Dressed in a fine green suit embroidered with flowers, he was not something Evan was used to seeing around when living in a place as secluded as Tredele. This must have been what confused him and pulled him into this contorted plan in the first place.

Evan groaned and got up, feeling chilly himself. He opened the door loudly, to make himself known, and Julian, who was cooped up in the corner beyond rows of dusty shelves, stirred, pushing even deeper into the corner, as if he expected a strike. The burlap sack tied around his neck to obscure his eyes was an insult to the handsome features.

"Mr. Noir?" he asked breathlessly, the sound almost like a lover's whisper in Evan's ear. It could have been arousing if it wasn't the name of his horse.

He had to bite his lip to stifle the groan pushing its way out, because having this kind of power over a man was awakening demons that should be kept in their crypt.

"I heard you complain about your lodgings?"

Julian slowly rose, and the blanket fell off his shoulders. He exhaled. "All things considered, I expected fair treatment," he said in the end. "You could have gone away with a few pounds and rings at best, but you will be given much more in a few days because of my proposition. Don't I deserve a bed and some warm soup at least?"

The vision of Julian in his bed struck Evan's mind like an arrow shot straight from Julian's elegant hands. "I couldn't sleep with all your racket, so yes, you will sleep in a bed." Nothing wrong with putting Julian in his own. They were both men after all. Evan's bedroom was the only one being heated, and the bed itself was massive. Could even fit three men if necessary.

Julian's breath trembled, and he wiggled underneath the blanket, tied up like a pig for slaughter. "Thank you, Mr. Noir. I knew you'd be kinder in the end. My apologies if I cost you loss of sleep," he said, even though it was clear he was lying through his teeth. Men like Julian were not the least sorry about inconveniencing others.

Evan gripped Julian's arm and pulled him up in a movement that seemed abrupt even to him, but it was too late to amend that. He wasn't used to touching others.

"Let us go," Evan said in a voice he hoped sounded less threatening than before.

Julian's arm was thicker than he'd originally thought, pleasantly hard to the touch, and when his head turned toward Evan's voice, it was excruciatingly difficult not to stare at where the bright eyes should be underneath the sack. The rough cloth moved with each of Julian's breaths, sucked closer to his lips, only to be pushed away when he exhaled.

"Maybe you should reconsider this item on my head after all, Mr. Noir? It's so itchy against my skin. A few more hours, and I will look as if you've thrown me into an ant nest." Julian laughed without amusement.

Evan sighed as he led Julian up the stairs. The body next to him was stiff as a wooden plank, so he put one arm around Julian's shoulders and held on to his elbow with the other hand to steady him. Julian was wary of each step he took, carefully sliding his toes up each stair, and he must have gotten into a rhythm, because the moment they reached the second floor, he almost stumbled forward when his foot met the expanse of the wooden floor.

Evan held him up, enjoying the warmth of the other body molding to him in search for stability. Having intimate knowledge of every corner of this house, he didn't even need to carry a lamp with him to reach his bedroom, which now served multiple purposes and was cluttered with all the furniture Evan hadn't yet decided to part with. It was a place for sleeping, a library, a sitting room, and a dining room all in one. He hadn't been able to afford to heat the whole house for a while now, and so far, it hadn't mattered all that much that he lived like a barbarian, since no guests ever visited him, and those who came were sent away.

"It will come off." A part of him itched to apologize upfront for the living conditions that Julian would encounter, but he would not bow to conventionality. This was his home, and he would do as he pleased. Julian's presence had not been expected, and so he'd have to bear with whatever he was offered.

"That is good news indeed," babbled Julian, suddenly stumbling over the elevated threshold. Evan yanked at his arm and pulled him back to his feet, cursing beneath his breath as the other man pushed his body against Evan's side, moving his head about as if he were expecting the wall to charge at him next. "Shall we have that out of the way already?" he asked with hope clear in his melodic voice. "It really is most inconvenient."

Evan glanced at the steep stairs ahead and cringed at the accusatory glare of his grandfather, who stared him down from the portrait at the landing. He was just as Evan remembered him from his younger years—clad in stiff blacks and strong as an ox despite his advanced years. Grandfather wouldn't have approved of Evan's actions, even if it was desperation that put him in this position. He'd tell him that the mansion wouldn't have been in this state in the first place if Evan had managed it better. Or married well in these dire circumstances.

"No. We need to reach the room first." He slid his arm around Julian's waist, holding him even closer and telling himself that he only did so to save the man from breaking his neck, but lying to oneself was tricky when one knew he was being lied to.

Julian's body was of such a fine shape, exaggerated by the well-cut green coat he was wearing. If the quality of clothes on Julian's back was anything to go by, his family had deep pockets indeed. Fine wool and linen that was stained but of excellent thread. If Evan pressed down hard enough, he could easily sense the shape of the seductive valley between the shoulder blades, which he used to appreciate so much.

"Where have you taken me, Mr. Noir?" asked Julian, keeping his steps careful enough to slow Evan down. "A church, perhaps?"

"My lair," Evan said but frowned, scolding himself for the joke. This was no laughing matter. The man had been abducted, and Evan was his captor.

"Your *lair*?" asked Julian. "Sounds dangerous. Are your friends here, or are we alone?"

"You don't think I will spill all my secrets so easily, now do you?"

And there it was, the welcoming warmth of his 'lair'—because it certainly wasn't a bedroom. Cluttered with furniture and with little space for walking left, it was a shadow of the room Evan remembered from the happier times when his father was still alive, and the family-owned mines prospered. Evan refused to give up on this house, determined to restore Tredele to its former glory, even if he did it one room at a time.

Julian shuddered and took a deep breath of warm wood-scented air when Evan pushed him inside. "I suggest no such thing. It's merely curiosity about the man I call partner. I never met a highwayman before, and I dare suspect the stories about your lot aren't always true to the bone."

"What have you heard then?" Evan walked Julian over to the bed, which took up a good part of the space, and his body ached for him not to when he let go of the man. But candles needed to be lit, and he had to put on a mask if the sack was to be taken off Julian's head.

For now, the heat coming from the fireplace had to be enough to soothe Julian's bones, so Evan pushed him into an old armchair, which Julian sunk into with a surprised gasp.

"Forgive me if I am presumptuous, but are you new to the county? We have not heard of any highway robberies recently, and this chair is heavenly. Like it's been upholstered not that long ago," Julian said, shifting like an irritated squirrel.

Evan picked up the mask his brother had purchased in Venice years ago. Yet another trinket Evan wasn't willing to let go despite the misery his brother—may he Not Rest In Peace—had brought upon their family. The thing was simple enough to serve its purpose. Black, and wider at the bottom to hide his face.

And despite all the time he'd spent in Julian's company during the ride back home, he hadn't thought of a good story to tell him, too distracted with the youthful body in front of him. He decided on silence and leaned down to take the sack off Julian's head.

The thread tied around that graceful neck didn't come loose right away, and Evan almost let go when Julian's Adam's apple rubbed against his fingers, scratching him with afternoon stubble. Neither of them spoke, and as time stretched, Julian's breathing got louder, as if out of need to fill the silence with something. He'd been talkative so far.

"Cat got your tongue?" Evan grumbled in the end once he pulled off the sack and looked into those bright, wide eyes.

Julian blinked, his blond hair dishevelled, with many fine reddish threads defying gravity as he looked up from above that razor-sharp nose. He'd lied about the irritation to his skin, as the only imperfection there was on his cheeks was a faint spray of pale freckles that gave his handsome face a dose of roguish charm.

"Ah, is that from the continent?" Julian asked after a moment of silence. His mouth stretched into a wary smile, but the moment it happened, a slight dip in the middle of his lower lip beckoned all of Evan's attention.

Evan needed to get rid of Julian and his pretty face as fast as possible.

But he would not be doing so before he received the promised ransom money, no matter how long it would take.

"It's from Venice. Better tell me about your family. And don't lie, it won't do you any good if I find out you deceived me."

Julian sat back, and Evan could already see those sly, attentive eyes following the length of the tapestries covering the entire walls, all the way to the library of books at the mezzanine. Damnation. If Julian had told Evan the truth about his father, they were not far away from his home. Just a few hours of riding, and so he should have knowledge of Tredele, even if he'd never seen it. Evan should have taken him somewhere more inconspicuous than his own bedroom, or better yet—kept the man in the dark. In the stables maybe? No, that would have triggered too many memories.

"My family are the Reeces, Mr. Noir. Surely, my father needs no introduction if you live so close."

Evan waved his hand and settled on crossing his arms on his chest. "I'm not well acquainted with who is who." A lie. Of course he knew that if Julian hadn't lied about his identity, there was a lot of money at stake. "But if your father is a wealthy merchant, why are you running?"

Julian's chest fell, and the gloriously green waistcoat, just a shade lighter than the embroidered coat, clung to his body. "I am forced to be married, and I will not be degrading myself like this. Bachelorhood suits me just fine," said Julian with a small smile as he glanced Evan's way.

Evan paused when the story he'd made up in his head about Julian didn't line up with reality. Unless Julian was lying. "You'd rather spend time whoring and gambling than start a family. Up." Evan couldn't help that it gave him a thrill to tell the man what to do without the pleasantries necessary in any other situation.

Julian flexed the muscles of his thighs, outlined to perfection by his tight breeches, as he stood up. "I do enjoy card tables, just like any other man, but there is more to life than that. Do you enjoy whoring, Mr. Noir?" he asked, as if they were talking about the weather.

"I'm not fond of it, no. Neither am I of gambling. It's brought all too many men to ruin." Instead of asking, he just made Julian turn around, and worked on untying his hands. The man didn't seem like much of a threat, but most of all... if he were to change into a nightshirt soon, tied hands would prove to be a nuisance.

Even the back of Julian's head was pleasant to watch, with warm-hued curls tied into a tail that was now messy, the black ribbon halfway off.

Julian stiffened his shoulders but didn't protest and kept on talking. "I wholeheartedly agree. Gambling is not a sport for the weak. There's temptation, but playing safely enough to not be led into ruin requires strong will. I make sure never to stake higher than I've decided at the start of the night. Do you know of Madame Canard's establishment?" he asked and looked at Evan from over his shoulder. Just seeing him do that sparked long-forgotten memories in Evan's mind. He definitely needed to get rid of that beautiful, stupid creature. The sooner, the better.

"I don't believe I do. Though judging by the name, I can imagine what it is." While Evan untied Julian's hands, he couldn't help but notice how soft his fingers seemed and imagined what they would feel like to the touch. "Is this favorite bawdy house of yours the reason why you don't want to marry?"

Julian's eyes twinkled, as if this was a more agreeable topic of conversation. "It is true that I enjoy the company of whores more than that of honest women. The stories they have to tell! You can talk to one as you would to a man. The woman my father decided I should marry... she is just a child. I don't wish to settle down and look after my own household," said Julian, swiftly turning around, sandwiched between Evan and the chair. His knees brushed against Evan's as he looked up with a wicked smile. "But truth be told, I only visit Madame Canard's to gamble and dispute with friends. My life shall have a higher purpose than siring children or making women happy with my prick."

Evan took half a step back, overwhelmed by the closeness, and by how pleasant Julian's smell was even after the ordeal he'd been through today.

"Oh, is that so?" he mumbled, daring to meet Julian's gaze. "What higher purpose is that?"

Julian raised his chin, keeping his gaze steady. "I am a writer."

Evan squinted at him. "And what do you write about, Mr. Reece?" He reached out to Julian's vest, but stopped himself midway and turned around to a cupboard by the bed. "Take your clothes off."

Julian went completely silent, then, "I beg you pardon?"

Evan turned around, glad that his smirk wouldn't be showing. "Well, you will not be sleeping in your day clothes, now will you?"

Julian gave a bland laugh. "I'd think you want to see me naked, Mr. Noir. Surely, I can undress while you're back at your own lodgings."

Evan approached him with a spare nightshirt in hand. "I'm not letting you out of my sight."

For the first time since they arrived, there was honest confusion in Julian's eyes. He cleared his throat. "There is only one door. You don't need to watch me like a hawk."

"There is more than one door, and in fact, I do need to watch you if I want my reward. You seem confused. You start with the coat."

Julian's jaw set, and he frowned, stretching his slender yet solid form. "I'd need a valet. Are you up for playing that role, Mr. Noir?"

Evan's grip on the nightshirt tightened. Oh, what he'd now give for being a valet not a baronet. "Since when does a merchant's son need a valet?" he asked, already imagining unbuttoning the embroidered buttons of the vest, and leaning in for—

"Since he can afford one," said Julian coolly and stretched his throat, approaching the fire. "I am your guest, and yet so far I've been only offered discourtesy. Or do you not know that you are being rude?"

Julian was a spoiled idler, but it was himself that Evan despised most right now, because with all his attitude, and the outlandish idea to strip his own father of money, Julian was still the most beautiful creature that had graced this house in years. Standing there by the fire, the rich green color of his outfit complemented the flames as if he'd gotten dressed today, knowing he'd be here in the evening.

Evan lost patience. For Julian, for himself, for the whole situation dragging out and testing him.

He walked past the armchair, and approached Julian without a word. He pushed him at the warm wall by the fireplace, and his fingers went straight for the buttons of Julian's waistcoat.

A sharp gasp left Julian's lips, and he remained frozen, slim, graceful fingers trailing along the faded tapestry depicting the battle of Troy. He stopped resisting, as if Evan's impudence left him weaponless. He stared at the wall, possibly frightened but unresisting.

So Evan carried on. Pulled off the coat. Unbuttoned the waistcoat. When the shape of a stiffened nipple appeared where the shirt clung to Julian's body, Evan was ready to eat Julian alive. But he would not. He'd stay calm and move past all this.

Julian's breath wheezed, and he clawed his fingers into the tapestry, his body hot like nothing else Evan had touched in years. Even the fire burning so close couldn't compare to the warmth streaming from underneath the fine linens.

"How am I doing?" Evan asked when the tension became too much. He pulled on the silk of Julian's cravat, untying it from around his neck, and his heart was speeding up at the sight of the throat underneath the thin fabric.

"Dreadfully," said Julian through his teeth and still refused to look at Evan. "I wouldn't let you near me with a razor, but maybe you'd like to blacken my boots once you're done."

Evan backed away half a step and pulled on Julian's shirt. "Do you want to borrow my nightshirt, or would you rather sleep naked?"

The flush on Julian's cheeks darkened, and his nostrils flared as he finally met Evan's gaze with a fiery passion. "What was your profession before you chose this walk of life? Certainly not service." He frowned, glancing at Evan from head to toe. "The black... a rogue clergyman perhaps?"

Evan shook his head, proceeding to pull off the shirt. "Wrong, Mr. Reece. I am a sinner."

Julian didn't resist anymore and pulled up the stained shirt. When the fine fabric stretched over his face, the pale, flawless chest came into view. There was a pleasant definition to Julian's muscles, but his body was doubtlessly one that had never been forced to do physical labor, and had instead gained the harmonious shape through sports and other leisure activities. The short bristle of hair on his chest was a reminder that Julian wasn't a boy anymore, and as he stretched to finally untangle himself out of the shirt, his abdomen became a bundle of the most delicious muscle. Evan barely suppressed a moan.

"Sin is but a man's invention to keep the masses from straying off the path they're meant for, Mr. Noir," Julian said, bright red. He spun around and reached back his hand. "The shirt, please."

Evan took his time watching every inch of skin on show, but passed the garment to Julian. "Not in need of my services anymore, I presume?" He would not mind pulling off Julian's breeches as well and getting to see what a fine ass hid underneath, but that would have been a stretch for his patience.

"You're a worse valet than I'd ever be." Julian promptly pulled the linen over his head, obscuring his fair skin and shape, and only then did he begin unfastening his breeches.

Evan kept silent, anticipating the faint shape he'd get to see underneath the shirt, courtesy of the fireplace behind Julian. This sudden infatuation felt childish, yet he still couldn't resist the butterfly that got caught in his net instead of a grasshopper.

Julian pulled off his stockings, breeches, linen drawers, and there it was, the shadow of his graceful ass peeking through the nightshirt. Evan chewed on his lip, watching Julian storm through the room and climb into bed without a word.

Evan's heart thudded with bloodlust, as if he were a wolf following a deer. At this moment, he didn't even regret his robbery being a failure, because he hadn't felt this alive in years.

He took the bundle of rope from the stack of books on the way and approached the bed.

Julian turned his back to him, covering himself so tightly, only his mop of hair remained visible against the white pillows. He was motionless. A young animal knowing it would be apprehended by the hunter and without a way out. Evan could bet Julian's heart beat as fast as that of a rabbit.

He undid his cravat, and quickly pulled his shirt off as well, only now realizing that Julian's snotty retorts had ended.

The outline of Julian's body was slowly growing and shrinking as he breathed, silent as if this didn't affect him at all.

"How will we go about with the ransom?" Evan asked and pulled his boots off, pretending he was casual about the situation. That this wasn't his first robbery, and maybe even not his first abduction.

Julian curled up even tighter and pulled the top blanket closer to his neck. "We wait for my father's actions first. He will be searching for me soon. Maybe there will even be a reward for bringing me home safe."

"Maybe I should bring you home then." Evan shook his head at the idea. "Say I found you naked, without a penny to your soul, and tied to a tree?" He glanced at the tiny bit of Julian's hair still visible, and unfastened the front of his breeches.

Julian's head moved slightly, and just as Evan noticed the glint of his eye, he quickly returned to the previous position. *So shy.*

"Naked? Absolutely not. I would not support this."

"I would not bring you naked to your father. I'd give you... a sheet to cover yourself." Evan smiled under the mask and pulled off his breeches, already reaching for his nightshirt.

"Curse you. I never met a man so insolent in my entire life," grumbled Julian. He suddenly spun around, keeping his eyes firmly on Evan's face. "You should remember that this whole stunt depends on my compliance."

"Does it now?" Evan got up and pulled off his drawers, increasingly entertained by pushing Julian for a reaction. "Are you not my captive? Can I not demand ransom?"

Julian bit his bottom lip, and that tiny groove was begging for Evan's tongue. It was hard to focus on anything else.

"I came here of my own will. If you cross me, I will find you and have you brought to justice!"

Evan pulled on the nightshirt and looked into the angry blue eyes. "You don't even know where you are. I could kill you and bury you under the nearest tree. No one would ever find you." He wouldn't do that, but if he wanted to keep Julian under his thumb, threats were a necessity.

He kneeled on the bed and grabbed the rope he'd earlier left on the floor.

Julian's breath rasped. "No," he said firmly. "This is my final warning."

"You didn't think I would sleep next to you and just believe to find you there in the morning, did you?" Evan inched closer, taking a deep breath to fight his excitement over tying up an almost naked man in his bed. If it made him deviant, then so be it. Julian didn't need to know his most private thoughts, and Evan did have a legitimate reason to tie Julian's hands.

"Stay back," whispered Julian, slowly emerging from the covers, his body tightening like a dog's waiting for its master to strike it.

The words only felt like a challenge, teasing Evan's senses and urging him to pounce on his prey. He unwound the rope.

Julian hunched his shoulders, staring straight into his eyes, pushing him away and drawing him closer at the same time. There was a fire pit burning in Evan's chest, and as the heat of it warmed the joints of his fingers around the rope, he inched closer, close enough to smell the remainder of spirit on Julian's skin.

Julian moved with savage speed, and Evan leaned forward to push him down on the bed when sudden pain made him see red. Julian cried out and shoved Evan, trying to rush for the door.

He looked at the rattling metal flask on the floor, unable to comprehend that all while pretending to be frightened, Julian must have stolen the weapon-to-be from Evan's drawer.

Evan threw his arm forward with a growl and grabbed the hem of Julian's nightshirt. The linen ripped at the collar with the impact of the pull, but it was enough for Evan to yank Julian back to the bed.

"You rotten cockmongrel!"

The tug was like a carpet pulled from underneath Julian. He slid to the floor with a bang that would have made Evan wince if he weren't so furious. The bloody rat wouldn't flee this time.

Julian tried to crawl back to his feet, but once Evan's much sturdier body was atop his, it was a lost cause. He was still struggling, his firm ass pushing between Evan's spread thighs as he straddled the cocky beast, this time intent on taming it without playing nice.

"Help," Julian cried out in a high-pitched shriek. "Somebody!"

"Shut up!" Evan grabbed his cravat from the chair where he'd left it, and pushed it into Julian's wide-open mouth when the bastard was about to scream again. What did Evan do to deserve this unbearable suffering?

Blood trickled from under his mask and fell on the back of Julian's nightshirt. Somehow, the contrast of the bright red against white gave him a rush of strength, and he pulled on Julian's head with the cloth, as if he were really taming a horse with a bridle.

Julian moaned something that could be *let me go*, or pretty much anything else, but this time Evan would not show him mercy. He tied the cloth around Julian's head, only to force his hands back so hard Julian cried out and stiffened under him, finally motionless.

"Will you be a good boy now, or should I carry on handling you as if you were a maiden?" hissed Evan straight into Julian's ear, and once again, Julian stayed still.

Evan huffed, half-surprised the struggle finally ended, but every single hair on his body bristled at the sudden rattle at the door. He froze, and instinctively pushed Julian's head down, flattening his cheek against the floor, but finally realized they were still alone, and no servant of his would enter without permission.

It was bound to be Frederick, always eager to anticipate Evan's needs even when told that his services would not be needed for the rest of the day.

"Sir?" called Frederick from beyond the door. "Is something the matter? I overheard someone shouting."

Julian moaned but immediately quieted down when Evan pushed on his head hard.

Evan took a deep breath, and peeked out from behind the bed so that his voice would carry better. "Everything in order. I just had a nightmare and tumbled out of bed. Truly, Frederick, you should rest." Couldn't the man just give himself peace when asked to do so? Frederick's sense of duty would be the death of Evan one day.

"Very well, sir. Have a good night," Frederick said in the same polite voice Evan remembered him use since Evan was still a very young child. If there was a constant in his life, it was his old butler and his never-ending loyalty.

Silence stretched, and Evan slowly became aware of how shapely were the buttocks he was now mounting. The torn shirt on Julian's back showed a shallow dip where the parting between them should be. It would have been so easy and so wrong all at once to pull up the shirt, slip some oil in there, and ram his cock in hard and fast. Fuck, what he'd give to tame this frisky colt like that.

Evan needed to act fast, because he knew all too well what the spike of excitement in his veins would lead to, and his cock was too close to Julian to allow himself to express his arousal in any way. He shouldn't even be aroused by Julian. Period.

"Aren't you a naughty buck?" Evan whispered and pushed Julian's arms over his head to tie them.

Julian wasn't resisting anymore and let himself be led back to the bed, which he obediently climbed with the help of the movable steps. It was clear to Evan that his captive was finally resigned to his fate, and the ripped fabric on his back was the sole reminder of the struggle. Julian lay down without a word and looked away when Evan leaned over him to fasten the cords to the bed.

Evan pushed the covers away to crawl underneath and let his gaze settle on the exquisitely spread out body before him.

"Will you scream again?"

Julian pressed his eyes tightly shut but slowly shook his head.

"Good, because I don't want you to accidentally choke at night. I still need you, as we've established. Your dead body won't do." He pulled the cravat out of Julian's mouth, and promptly pushed it up, fastening it over Julian's eyes instead.

Julian opened his lips wide, gasping for breath. He slid his tongue along his lips, and it was almost as if he were inviting Evan for a kiss.

"Water?"

Evan took his time shamelessly ogling Julian now that the man couldn't see it. He took a glass of water from the side table and gently pushed it up to Julian's lips.

"Next time you hit me, I *will* strike you back."

Julian stayed quiet and arched off the bed, greedily sipping from the cup. As soon as he was done, he slumped to the pillows and turned his head away.

Evan sighed and rotated the glass so that when he drank the rest of the water, his lips touched the same place Julian's had. The glass was still slightly warm against his mouth.

This would have to do for kissing.

They were all too close already.

Chapter 3

Julian

The bedding smelled of herbs. The thread of the pillowcase felt softened, as if slightly worn, less crisp to the touch than Julian was used to. It should have been as pleasant as any morning without the aftermath of drinking, but he couldn't breathe properly. It was too hot, his limbs too tangled up in the covers. Something was sitting on his chest like a nightmare, stealing his air and tickling his cheek with its hair. Soft strands were tangled around Julian's head and pressing on his eyes. It was all shoving him out of his sleep.

Julian awoke as the reality of last night dawned on him with its full weight. He opened his eyes wide to the blur of light coming through the cloth that Noir had used to blindfold him the night before. He blinked, scratching the white muslin with his lashes while panic boiled within his ribcage. Now that his mind was slowly becoming untangled from sleep, he understood what it was that had suffocated him all morning.

The weight, the heat of it, the shape. It was a man's arm.

Noir's arm.

Heavy. Hot. The pulsing of the arteries inside his elbow pressed against Julian's nipple.

Julian clenched his teeth, trying to calm his breathing, to not awaken his captor. Gently, he tugged at his hands, but they were still securely fastened to the headboard. Noir's proficiency at tying knots suggested he could have worked at sea, but the fact that the man had a servant, and one so politely-spoken, smashed every bit of the image Julian had built up in his mind.

Who was the highwayman with burning black eyes and an affinity for cruel smiles? Certainly not a common criminal, yet not a gentleman either. The room Julian saw last night was a clutter of furniture and trinkets from the olden days, with dusty tapestries covering all walls and cheaply whitened walls peeking out from under them, and yet the number of books gathered in the library at the mezzanine on one end suggested that a learned man lived here, but maybe Noir simply had taken over someone else's property and moved into the storeroom?

When the arm on top of Julian's chest shifted, he held his breath so hard it felt as if his chest was about to implode. Noir pulled him closer, and wrapped his leg over Julian's, making him freeze in the heat of the embrace. It felt nothing like the legs of women. Muscular and thick, with prickly hairs. But it was something else that had Julian exhale just as violently as he'd inhaled.

A stiff, hot prick pushed against his hip.

Noir might have as well touched him with a hot poker. Julian stiffened even further, his mind empty except for a tangle of thoughts he could not unwind. Now that Noir pressed closer, Julian could sense with his whole body how big and sturdy his ungrateful host was. His was the body of a man who could stop a bull with his bare hands, like those of some men Julian knew from the Black Crab. Like his friend Martin, who frequently took Julian home when he'd been too weak with drink to drag himself back to his own lodgings in the middle of the night.

He slowly sucked in a lungful of air and waited, but the prick wasn't going anywhere. It was petting Julian's skin through the thin linens, and even without it dragging over bare flesh, it was a violation of the most embarrassing kind. He could call Noir out on the impropriety and make him stop this nonsense, but the man's breathing was calm and steady. Julian's cock stiffened in his sleep just like any other fellow's, so this was not anything out of the ordinary, and he was on the fence about whether it should even be mentioned. Julian might be vulgar in the eyes of his father, but he did not like to consider himself so.

He tried to simply ignore the insistent heat at his side, but the man's erection remained a constant presence in Julian's mind. He chewed on his lip when his body tingled in that way he loved and detested at the same time. It reminded him of his whoring days, when he'd frequently awakened with a cacophony of bells ringing in his head and a woman spread out on top of him. Maybe it had been too long since he put his hands on a woman? Maybe his body needed something less familiar than his own fingers every once in a while?

He turned his head toward the warmth blowing softly against his cheek and suppressed a shudder when Noir's breath danced over his nose and lips. How close was his face now? If only the damn blindfold came off, Julian could identify the man and make him pay for all the indignities that brute had made him suffer through.

Gently, Julian rubbed his temple against the side of his bound arm, and his heart fluttered when the cloth obscuring his eyes shifted slightly.

Just inches away, Noir slept without the mask he'd worn last night, and the sight of him was overwhelming at first for reasons Julian could not understand. A straight, elegant nose divided the symmetrical face in half, and unexpectedly pretty pale lips were slightly parted in his sleep. Noir's eyebrows were as dark as his name, and even now seemed drawn together in a permanent frown, as if his dreams didn't agree with him. Another feature Julian didn't expect and hadn't noticed before despite looking into those dark eyes many times already, were the black, long eyelashes of the kind to promise smoldering looks from ladies.

Julian pressed the tip of his tongue into the dip in the middle of his lower lip and stared, unsure how he could possibly untangle himself from those arms. Just a slim ray of light came in through the curtains that Noir had drawn around the bed last night, but it was enough to uncover the color of his skin beneath the linen shirt. Noir's bare leg rested on top of Julian's thigh, muscled like an ancient sculpture, yet there was dark hair dusting the tan skin.

Noir's face belonged on a statue as well. The man could model for Hercules himself with that strong chin and those high cheekbones, only his body was nothing like cold, unforgiving marble. It pressed against Julian so shamelessly he was rendered mute at the impropriety of it. Touching another person's flesh was not a luxury Julian allowed himself often, and now that it had been thrust upon him, he did not know how to deal with it.

Noir let out a deeper breath, and pushed his nose against the pillow, bringing more detail into light. Julian saw dried blood in the unruly dark hair, and a smudge of it running down Noir's temple and jaw. Despite believing with all certainty that Noir had deserved the strike, Julian still regretted marring the perfection of this man's face. What if he had broken Noir's nose?

Julian's attention was back to the hard prick when he sensed moisture on his skin through the nightshirt. He gasped, shifting his thigh, but it only made matters worse, as the prick slid farther up his thigh and left behind a smear of fluid that was now both burning and cooling on Julian's skin.

He should rouse Noir from his sleep and make him pull away, but that wouldn't spare him the indignity of having been spent on. The heat inside his skull rivalled that of a forge fire, and he could not come up with any solution to his current predicament, because of the strange sensation that fluttered inside his body. His own morning stand did not help matters, and when Noir shifted his leg again, Julian fretted the man's knee would eventually rest on his prick. This wouldn't be good at all.

Noir groaned and opened his eyes halfway, but they instantly widened when he noticed Julian watching him from under the blindfold. He pulled away as if burned by charcoals, but the heat of his body remained present on Julian's skin. Noir's breath sped up, and his whole body heaved with yet unspoken fury.

Julian's words—which had always been at his side—were failing him again as he watched a flush spread across the handsome face. His morning stand was gone.

"Is this all a game to you?" Noir hissed through his teeth, yet Julian couldn't deny that in his rage, with the black hair reminiscent of a nest and in only his nightshirt, Noir was still handsome. If not more so.

Julian shook his head and stayed limp on the bed, to not enrage the brute any further.

Noir pulled back the curtain around the bed and began walking from one stack of books to another, almost stumbling over a marble-topped table on the way.

"There is no need for all this anger, Mr. Noir," said Julian, finally finding his tongue. "I mean you no harm."

"Since you've seen my face, let us be done with this charade. My name is Evan Penhart, and you've put me in a most inconvenient position." His eyes focused on Julian, and he ran his fingers through his hair.

Julian stalled as bright red shock penetrated his brain, picking up scraps of information he'd just gotten. "You can't be serious... you're Sir Recluse, the Ghost of Tredele?" he choked out, staring at the handsome villain, who was nothing like the man he'd imagined based on the stories he'd been told about the local baronet. Those painted Noir... Evan (because he refused to think of the criminal as '*Sir* Evan') as a monster who chose the life of a recluse after a horrifying accident at sea. Now that Julian looked at Evan with his own eyes, he knew that the tales held no truth whatsoever.

Evan frowned and stalled, as if time stopped, then kicked over a huge stack of books, sending them to the floor in a flood of paper. His roar of fury made Julian's flesh itch, yet he still stole a glance at Evan's backside, all too visible when the man turned toward the window, his shoulders rising and falling.

"I take it you are not aware of the gossip about you, sir" Julian said in the end.

"I do not gossip," Evan hissed, not even turning around. He didn't have the manners a baronet ought to possess, that much was sure. On the bright side though, at least Julian was almost certain where he was kept prisoner. Tredele had belonged to Evan's family for generations, but while the world around them developed, the old house had not, which was painfully obvious from the condition of the furnishings gathered in this warehouse of a room. None of them would have satisfied contemporary tastes. Tredele was a relic of an era gone by, standing on a remote hill in the woods, an hour's ride from the closest gathering of people that could be called a town.

"Oh, but it is necessary... sir," said Julian, keeping to the social convention instead of treating Evan with the lack of respect the man's criminal act last night had earned him. "Knowing gossip is the modern man's shield."

All Julian got in answer was an angry snarl that reminded him much of a boar's. Rejecting all propriety, Evan took his nightshirt off.

Julian stiffened, watching his strong silhouette in front of the uncovered window. He couldn't miss the shadow of Evan's prick, which still hadn't completely softened despite the outburst of anger.

Julian swallowed hard, tracing his gaze over the broad back and thick arms that belonged on a well-fed worker, not someone who had men in his service and owned many acres of land.

"Why the robbery? You could hang... sir."

Evan washed his face in a basin by the window and started putting on his clothes quickly and efficiently, as if he didn't need a valet.

"I enjoy the thrill. You better watch your words."

Julian frowned. "I merely question your motives, sir. This house, while old, is still worth a healthy sum. Why risk disgracing your family name and your own life, like a rogue from the streets?"

"Do you wish death upon yourself?" Evan said darkly, and approached the bed in just his breeches. "You have no idea about my family and this home, nor my name. I want for nothing, and everything that happens here in Tredele happens for the very reason that I wish it to."

Julian sighed. "You're no criminal to murder a man in cold blood. And I knew your brother, Sir Peter. I spent a great deal of time in his company in my younger years. It's a pity he hasn't introduced us in friendlier circumstances."

Evan sneered. "Of course you knew him. That is beyond appropriate. Did he teach you how to lose at cards, or what to do when paying for three whores at once?"

Julian frowned. Poor Sir Peter had never been a careful gambler, but every man was allowed a weakness, and he'd been a great fellow, always more than accommodating to his friends. "He showed me what to do with one whore," said Julian, daring Evan with his gaze.

Evan shot him a dark glare once he was done fastening his breeches. "Mention his name again, and I will have you hanged in my garden." He began untying Julian's hands in haste.

Julian pressed his lips tightly together and watched the stern face above him. Those black eyes were burning again, but now that he knew who his captor was, he felt safer to question the threats. "You could have learned a thing or two from him, sir. About the polite way to treat your allies."

The slap to Julian's face was so harsh and unexpected he could hardly believe it even as heat spread down his jaw. But the afterburn on his cheek was there to confirm it.

Evan took the rope off Julian's hands and threw it to the ground before walking back to the washstand. He carried on with his morning ablutions, as if he'd forgotten to finish them earlier. "I said, do not mention him again!"

Julian grabbed the covers and pulled them up to his chin, watching his host dry himself. No wonder Evan would be furious to hear kind words about Sir Peter. In comparison to his gallant older brother, he was a brute, not much different to the men who got into fights at the Black Crab or at Madame Canard's. "You should go out more. Being here with servants as your only companions made you forget how to act around your equals."

Evan put on a fresh shirt, which was of a dated cut, the fabric mended in one place and rough-looking from age. Maybe it was his lack of manners and style that had made him become such a recluse in the first place.

"Get up, get dressed, and let us write the ransom letter so I can be rid of you and your pestering advice as soon as possible."

Julian sat up, ignoring the burning sensation in his cheek. He wouldn't give Evan the satisfaction of showing it had affected him. "All my fresh linens were left at the carriage."

Julian saw Evan's lips curl into a smile. He'd seen that kind of smile in his eyes before, but now here it was, in all its cruel glory.

"Would you rather be naked then? I could add more wood to the fire."

Julian gave him a hard stare. "Your brother owned a beautiful red banyan, as I recall. I could wear it over my shirt," he said, purposefully mentioning Sir Peter again, just to dim the self-satisfaction on Evan's face.

And just as quickly as the smirk had appeared, it crawled back down Evan's face.

He walked over to a coffer which must have dated back centuries and opened it with a screech of the hinges. Evan proceeded to disembowel it of precious garments, showing no regard to the expensive silks and meticulous embroidery. Julian itched to pick them off the floor. Each one of the colorful pieces had much more class than Evan.

"There." Evan gritted his teeth and pulled up the glorious banyan, its red as impressive as a robin's breast in the spring, but enhanced by the masterfully embroidered branches and birds.

Julian took care sliding out of bed in just the thin night shirt. The wooden floor creaked under his feet, as any old wood that should have been replaced long ago, and he exhaled with relief when he stepped on the faded Persian carpet that provided some warmth.

Evan's lips barely had any color when Julian accepted the banyan, gently stroking his fingers over the fine fabric, which had come here all the way from faraway China. "Magnificent," he said and picked up one of Sir Peter's old shirts off the floor.

"Go on, why not. Take it all," Evan said bitterly and backed off to put on a waistcoat as black as tar and nothing like the bird of paradise wardrobe of his late brother.

Julian frowned. "I see no reason for anger. They are wasting away in those wooden coffins."

"Everything wastes away. And then it dies. Don't think a red banyan will save you from death. It hasn't saved Peter either." Evan walked over to the far end of the massive room and sat by a desk, arranging inks and papers.

Julian gently rubbed the expensive fabric, looking down at all the finery so carelessly tossed to the floor. Sir Peter's wardrobe was magnificent, even more so than Julian's, who was limited by the allowance granted by his father. He slowly looked up, not quite understanding the disgust Evan expressed toward his brother. And yet, despite all the hate, he had not disposed of the man's personal possessions either. Was it jealousy that drove Evan so mad?

"It would not save my skin, but it would absorb the blood, or make a beautiful contrast with my skin, if you chose to hang me after all."

"You don't believe I would. You are wrong," Evan muttered, barely audible from where he sat.

"You are mad, but not that mad," said Julian, taking the clothes to the bed, to change out of Evan's sight. He could sense the burning gaze on his back but he chose not to comment on it and moved with as much grace as he could.

"My only moment of madness was when I decided to bring you here."

Julian laughed despite his better judgment. "I'm happy you're finding humor in our situation," he said, relaxing once the night shirt was off. Sir Peter's linens smelled a bit stale, but that was nothing unexpected considering they'd spent the last five years in a trunk. As least it wasn't stained with food and sweat, like his own shirt, or blood—like the one he'd slept in.

"I couldn't be more serious. Now come over and write the ransom letter. I cannot have my handwriting recognized."

"You sound like my father," said Julian, pulling the stiff fabric over his body. Next came the banyan, a bit too large for him in the shoulders but it still made Julian feel like the Chinese emperor. He combed his hair with his fingers and walked out from behind the bed, watching the bright fabric trail over the floor. It was exquisite. And when he looked up to see himself in a large mirror, he set his shoulders, for a moment unable to look away. The garment truly made him look regal. He wondered if he'd get to keep it if Evan was letting it rot anyway.

There was no frown on Evan's handsome face when Julian noticed him staring in the reflection. The longing in Evan's eyes came as a surprise.

Maybe he did miss his brother after all.

CHAPTER 4

EVAN

The banyan made the reddish hue of Julian's hair more apparent. The candles—real wax, not tallow tonight—made his bright eyes appear even livelier. Evan could not explain why he'd asked the maid to use the better set of porcelain plates instead of the simple dishes he used every day. But he did enjoy seeing Julian appreciate them. He kept glancing across the table at Evan as he ate the mushroom broth, and whenever his mouth was vacant, it spewed words as if he were a vicar on Sunday.

"Did you think about maybe refurbishing at least the interiors? They are so gloomy as they are."

Evan clenched his teeth. There was no denying that someone as wealthy as Julian wasn't used to eating his meals in the same room he slept and leisured in. Not at a tiny table that forced them both to constantly bump their knees. It served Evan just fine when he was alone, so he couldn't wait to have it back that way. He refused to bring a bigger table into the room just for Julian's comfort, as that would imply the change was to be more permanent.

Evan calmly ate his broth, as he decided to bear the indignities and insults. Together with Julian, they had crafted the most exquisite ransom letter, so all he needed to do for now was survive Julian's company and keep him pleased. This way he wouldn't have to remain tied up all the time. Even if seeing Julian tied up was a much more appealing prospect than listening to his sermon about the lack of modern conveniences in Evan's home. Preferably naked and tied up. And begging for cock.

"I like it the way it is," Evan said. Yet another lie to keep up appearances. As soon as he reaped a fresh harvest of money from the ransom, he would renovate the roof, not the interior.

Julian sighed and leaned back, sipping some of the tea served with their supper. He'd complained about the lack of wine or ale already, but it seemed he'd taken Evan's sobriety as yet another eccentricity. "I'm not surprised Sir Peter preferred spending his time elsewhere. He liked bright colors, and this is like a medieval manor. It suits your personality," he added, raising his cup toward Evan.

Evan let go of his, as the sudden burst of anger made him clench his fist, and he didn't want to crack the porcelain. "The Ghost of Tredele after all," he muttered bitterly. Knowing of the things people said about him only made him less inclined to venture out and talk to anyone. He did like seeing the flush on Julian's cheeks from drinking the hot beverage though. Evan briefly wondered if his unwanted guest would fall asleep more peacefully if he had some wine after all, but quickly dismissed that idea.

Julian smiled. "I once wrote a short story about you. What a coincidence that I got the dubious pleasure of meeting the man of my fantasy in the flesh."

Evan struggled with swallowing his broth. "A story? About me?"

"Yes—well, about the Ghost of Tredele," said Julian, making a light gesture with his hand. "I'm afraid I got it all wrong. You are many things but not horribly disfigured."

Evan couldn't help a sneer despite having promised himself to stay polite, forget past arguments, and be done with this charade once he received the ransom within a few days. After all, in his letter, Julian begged his father to comply, citing his captor as a cruel man, who only fed him bread and water, and kept him in a doghouse.

"What did you write about this... ghost?" Evan shook his head. Knowing that silence wouldn't help the time go by any quicker, he figured conversation was the best way to keep Julian less anxious.

Julian's face brightened, as if the candle lent its fire to his eyes. "He used to be a proud young man, afraid of nothing. One night, he went for a walk in the moonlight and followed the loveliest-sounding laughter all the way down the hill. In the river, a group of women was bathing, completely bare to his eyes. They didn't know he was there, or so he thought when he hid behind the bush—"

"Sounds like a book for tossing off."

Julian blinked, but then burst into a generous laughter that for once sounded sincere. "That was implied. Lewd words don't belong in books. Their place is in private correspondence."

Evan squashed a flutter in his chest and stuffed some bread into his mouth. "I don't appreciate you tarnishing my name this way."

"Tarnishing? Me? You should hear what they say about you in the Looe taverns."

Evan flinched and couldn't even bear looking at Julian's handsome face anymore. "I don't want to hear."

Julian stayed silent for several moments, then his hand suddenly closed over Evan's. The searing heat of that touch sent Evan's hand back, and his elbow smashed against the teacup, which wobbled and fell to the floor before Evan could catch it. Evan sighed in relief when it didn't break and instead rolled over the old rug. This set of china was an heirloom of his late grandmother.

Julian cleared his throat. "I wanted to say... that the gossip is being spread around because of your insistence to never leave Tredele. No one sees you anymore. People always weave stories when they don't know what to think."

"I have no interest in mingling with strangers. It is a waste of valuable time." Evan could hardly believe he was so rattled by the little gesture that has been surely meant as an expression of support.

Julian snorted. "Well then, you need to be prepared for people like me making mermaids cast a spell on you."

"Why would you write about such nonsense? And since I was a disfigured ogre in your story, did they make me handsome?"

Julian finished his wine. "No. They were the ones to make you disfigured and blind for taking pleasure in their bodies without their consent. I write about what speaks to my heart. Have you not walked through the woods and felt a presence around you?"

"I can't say I have." Evan raised his eyebrows. "And you say I'm the one who is mad."

Julian shrugged. "It's not madness. Not everyone is open to perception of things that cannot be noticed with ordinary senses."

"And you are? Do I understand this correctly?"

"Well, certainly. I think there's more to this world than what we can see with our eyes and hear with our ears. Country folk haven't yet cut the ties human beings have to nature, but for men like us, looking past what is obvious proves difficult sometimes. Particularly the men need to consciously open up to it, as the female kind is naturally inclined to perceive such things with much greater ease."

Evan shook his head. "I assure you I will be opening up to no such thing." Opening Julian's legs would have been another matter entirely.

"You're too set in your ways. This house is a testament to that," said Julian.

There was a knock on the door, and Esther's quiet voice cut into the little world of the cluttered room. "Sir, I've come with the second part of the meal."

Evan called her in, hoping that it would be now easier to change the conversation to food, or the weather. "Right on time, Esther."

She walked inside with the tray which held a course of meat and pudding, rushing to the table in the tiny steps she always took, gaze cast down. Unruly dark hair kept slipping out from underneath the cap on her head, its color matching the cloud of freckles dotting her cheeks, but with her constantly looking away from him, he didn't feel like he should stare either and found comfort in pretending she wasn't there.

"Miss, do you believe in fairies?" asked Julian.

She looked up, flushing so intensely Evan felt he needed to defend her from his captive's inconsiderate inquiry.

"That is enough. This question is beyond appropriate. My friend has been spending too much time reading fairy tales, Esther, do not fret."

"Why will you not let the girl speak?" asked Julian, taking the plate off Esther's tray, which seemed to agitate her further, and she promptly put the other plate in front of Evan.

"Fairies, Mister?" she asked, and cast a nervous glance at Evan, as if she feared that whatever she'd answer, her master could hold it against her.

Evan shook his head and counted to ten in his mind. "Answer only if you wish to, Esther."

Esther pressed the empty tray against her chest, her dark gaze trailing over the tabletop as she chewed on her lip. In the end, she spoke, "Fairies took me brother when 'e was still a babe, sir. Better not to go out alone at night in certain parts."

Julian shot Evan a glance radiating his triumph. "Ha."

Evan put his face in his hands. "Thank you for the insight, Esther."

She curtseyed and shot out of the room, closing the door almost too loudly.

"Women have it in their blood," said Julian, happily cutting into his chicken leg.

"You should have married one then."

Julian waved his hand, dismissing the notion. "Maybe I will fall in love someday. She would have to be special."

Evan looked out the window. It had started raining again. Of course. "I bet she will. To handle a personality as big as yours."

It wasn't a compliment, but Julian still smiled. "I'm glad to have made an impression. How about you? Scared a wife would not like your house and change everything? Imagine blue or yellow wallpapers on those walls instead of dusty, old tapestries."

"I despise the idea," Evan muttered, unwilling to specify if it was the idea of a woman, or new wallpaper that he hated so much. In truth, it was both. The house was a legacy of the Penharts who came before him, not a trifle to be toyed with and painted over like an Easter egg.

Julian smiled like the spawn of the devil but quietly ate his meal, watching Evan in the flickering light of the candle.

To fight his agitation, Evan focused on the food. What did the smile mean? Did Julian know that Evan hadn't been asleep when he'd taken the liberty to touch Julian in the morning? Did he suspect that Evan had an interest in men? Could he possibly... share that kind of inclination?

Julian's voice was soft, almost dreamlike when he spoke again. "My father doesn't understand my feelings. I don't think anyone around here does."

"Oh." Evan choked out, watching Julian intensely and trying to read him to no avail. "What are the feelings your father does not comprehend?"

Julian played with the fork and exhaled, looking at Evan. He was so incredibly beautiful, like a foreign prince in the expensive, wasteful fashions of Evan's late brother. At this moment, Evan was ready to forgive him for being such an insensitive wastrel.

"I don't think I belong in a family of merchants," said Julian in the end, his gaze serious. "Sir Peter told me about so many things he'd seen on the continent, in Italy. Back there, antiquity is still alive in its ruins. I want to see all that and savor it with my senses. I know that once I'm there, I will meet people who think the way I do. That is what I need the money for."

Evan's hope for Julian professing his lack of interest in women faded, and he instantly scolded himself for even lighting that flame in his own heart. The persistent mention of Peter despite threats of death made the food bitter, and Evan pushed his plate away.

Of course everything Peter did was amazing to Julian. Peter had been loud, colorful, impossibly insufferable, and his frivolous Grand Tour emptied half the family's coffers. But Peter had *wanted* it. So he got it. As Evan was sure Julian would eventually.

"You want to spend all that ransom money on travel?" Evan asked, just to make sure he wasn't imagining things.

"Not travel. I want to establish myself there."

"Right. And write your books, I presume."

Julian picked up his cup and clinked the porcelain against Evan's as if he were making a toast. "A novel to represent my philosophy. I truly believe the written word has the power to change our world, and the time has come for something new."

Evan shook his head, but as he was about to answer, question Julian's power to save the world by writing a toss–off book about fairies, Esther burst into the room without even knocking.

"Sir, I am so sorry to disturb yewr mealtime, but something dreadful 'appened." Her whole body trembled, and she twisted her apron as if trying to drain it of water. "I hate to be the bearer of bad news, but it's no use to ignore it."

Evan got up quickly, with his heart in his throat. Was something wrong with his horse? "What is it, Esther? Choke it out already!"

Esther gasped. "Smoke is pouring into the kitchen, sir. Mrs. Merryn believes the chimney is clogged again, and both Mr. Merryn and Jory are gone for the evening. We don't know what to do."

Evan glanced at Julian. Could he trust the man to stay here? They had argued terribly both yesterday and in the morning, but then again, Julian *was* counting on the ransom money to fund his fancy trip.

Evan composed himself and took a deep breath, using the fake name he used to introduce Julian to his servants. "I shall be back soon, Mr. Berry. Feel free to browse my library."

Julian shot to his feet. "Nonsense. I am well acquainted with a chimney sweeper, and he tells me stories of his work from time to time. Surely, something can be done quickly to amend the troubles of your servants," he said, and Esther curled up her shoulders, as if scolded.

"Your involvement is really unnecessary," Evan said through clenched teeth, wordlessly urging Esther to lead the way. The last thing he needed was to have Julian witness the disarray in other parts of his house, but of course the cockmongrel followed him downstairs.

As they rushed through the sequence of rooms and corridors, the smell of smoke was starting to penetrate Evan's senses, and he coughed, rushing after Esther's small form, into the most remote part of the house. All windows were open, but he could already hear his cook, Mrs. Merryn, cough and move about.

The size of the kitchens, smaller than in many of the modern estates and with low ceilings, was not helping matters. When they entered the space with the hearth, the dusky air started making Evan's eyes water even before he reached the source of the problem.

"Mrs. Merryn, step aside, I will deal with this." Evan pulled his sleeves up, hating that Julian was there to witness him getting down to his knees on the kitchen floor, but at least Evan knew what he was doing, since this wasn't the first time the chimney had failed.

Mrs. Merryn made room for him, but she was still attempting to sweep out the tainted air with her apron with so much fervor that some of her long gray locks escaped the white cap on her head.

"I am so sorry, sir, but my husband took Jory to town to buy supplies, and they haven't returned yet. Perhaps your guest should retire to *his own* room after all," she said, watching Evan lean over the hearth. He still needed to be careful of the hot embers, but with a wet piece of cloth pressed against his mouth, he could at least have a look up the chimney. Truth be told, he believed the problem lay in the upper part of it, but stepping on the roof right now, with the rain so heavy, would have put him at risk of death. It too needed repairs. Just as Evan needed that ransom money.

"That's not necessary," said Julian without a worry. "I have some knowledge about those matters. Maybe I could assist your master."

"You can most definitely not," Evan growled, accepting their makeshift chimney-sweeping brush from Mrs. Merryn. The tool had been cleverly designed by Jory, the stable boy and all-around help, but he was much more proficient at its use than Evan. "Please, retire, Mr. Berry."

Julian ignored him and pulled up his shirt to cover his nose. "Have you tried spraying some water with vinegar inside? The vapors should help with the mass inside the chimney, I heard."

The indignity and humiliation of this whole situation was killing Evan on the inside. He'd have to wash himself whole after dealing with the bloody chimney, too. Spreading his feet over the hearth, he pushed his hand into the shaft above, trying to ignore the heat of the stones and the air as he twisted his hand to put the brush into motion.

"Sir, I am so sorry—." As if things weren't bad enough, Esther broke into a sob before finishing her sentence.

"It's not your fault, Esther. You best leave, or your clothes will smell of smoke for days." Evan was already filthy anyway, and each upward push with the tool sent more hot, dark dust and mud his way. Nothing would save his shirt, or his face for that matter, but at least what he was doing worked, because the smoke eased.

"Esther, really, go to your room. We will be fine here, girl," said Mrs. Merryn, swiping the maid out of the room much more effectively than she had the smoke. But Julian was still there, leaning down with his head crooked with interest.

What would he say next? 'You should get one of those modern hearths, and make the chimney wider'? If Evan had the money to do so, he would.

"I think it would have been ideal if at least one of your male servants were at home at all times," said Julian in the end. "Will they be able to wash the sadza out of your clothes?"

"We will manage," said Mrs. Merryn curtly. "Please, Mr. Berry. I insist you return to your rooms," she tried again, only reminding Evan that he'd refused to have her and Esther prepare a separate room for Julian under the pretense of conserving wood when in reality it was all about his frustrated desires.

"Most of my clothes are black anyway," Evan said grimly, as he pulled away from the hearth, dreading to think how dark and sticky his face was. To someone as refined as Julian, he was bound to seem as dirty as a miner after a whole day's work.

"Sir Evan is only joking," Mrs. Merryn must have felt obliged to say. "All clothes are thoroughly washed, as often as necessary."

"I believe this time it is his skin that needs a thorough wash," said Julian, grinning at the sight of Evan's front. At least someone found Evan's suffering amusing.

"I shall get Esther to draw a bath right away!" Mrs. Merryn said.

"Please, Mrs. Merryn, it is unnecessar—"

"Oh, I assure you, sir, it is most necessary," she told him, and it sounded more like a mother scolding her child than a servant addressing her master. Most times, he didn't even notice when her tone got this way, but with Julian here, it made Evan shrink on the inside.

He gave up. His utter humiliation was complete.

Chapter 5

Julian

Julian had no choice but to look at Evan undressing in front of the bathtub. After all, for some inexplicable reason Evan demanded they use only one room out of the many that the manor surely consisted of. Taking baths in one's bedroom was nothing out of the ordinary, but with all the other furniture piled up in the same location, hardly any walking space remained. Julian had visited houses of the less fortunate in the past, but their cottages, so much smaller than this single room, only contained necessities when Evan kept his brother's things that he never used.

And since Evan would bathe here, where else was Julian to look if they talked every now and then? Nothing odd about a fellow seeing another naked. Nothing genteel about it either, but Evan was a barbarian anyway.

Last night, Julian hadn't seen all that much of Evan, but now that his host removed the tar-stained clothes, the planes of his broad, strong back and thick, steady thighs were a testament to the man's strength, the same that allowed him to handle Julian with such ease.

Julian browsed through the trunk full of Peter's unused clothes, but as he was touching the fabrics, his gaze kept straying across the room, where Evan stood in front of the fireplace in his naked glory. The flames made the copper sides of the tub turn into liquid fire, so unlike the tan skin of Evan's shoulders, which only absorbed the hot blaze.

Julian swallowed, touching silk breeches against his face when Evan chose to step into the hot water. There was something casual about his nakedness, yet nothing ordinary. When he stood inside the tub, chest gleaming with dark hair, legs slightly spread and presenting all of his flesh without an ounce of shyness, Julian found himself captivated by the uninhibited nature of the display.

Evan let out a long breath once he sat in the water, and Julian regretted that the herculean body wasn't on show anymore. Maybe it was the harmonious way Evan was built that made it so pleasant for the eyes. Even the gooseflesh that dotted Evan's skin from the chill could not mar his beauty. As a lover of antiquity, Julian always found enjoyment in admiring the handiwork of classical artists and their love for perfect bodies, so why would appreciating Evan's physique be so different? As all things, the man was the work of God and Nature.

"You surprise me," Julian said, slowly opening the button at the top of his banyan. Evan looked his way, and as he stretched inside the tub, the lower part of his arm gleamed with wetness, beckoning Julian to stare. "It's almost as if nakedness is your natural state. Maybe you did play with the fairies in your younger years."

Evan stalled, but his intense gaze settled on Julian, even more fiery with the blaze behind him. "Nakedness is everyone's natural state."

Julian smiled, approaching the bed with a whole bundle of Peter's clothes, but his eyes were firmly trained on Evan. It was a thrill to see him watching Julian back. "You are so very right. I reckon the modern man forgot all about it. Have you read Rousseau?"

"I have. The modern world must have spoilt you completely, because you didn't seem comfortable to undress yesterday..."

There was an undertone to Evan's words that Julian didn't truly understand, as if he didn't possess the right key to the secret Evan was trying to convey.

He opened the banyan, remaining only in the shirt once he gently placed the outer garment on the mattress, and his heart thudded faster for no reason at all. "Maybe you are right. Maybe

I should be more open to practice what I preach. But can you blame me? A man wants to have friends, not be cast out for his eccentricities."

"No one wants to be the Ghost of Tredele." Evan's back slid down the end of the tub, and he submerged his chest in the hot water, before rubbing his dirty face with soap and water.

"You seem to," said Julian, choosing an especially fine suit of Peter's, emerald with birds embroidered at the front of the coat and the waistcoat.

"Until earlier today, I didn't know I was a ghost. I haven't decided yet if I want to be one or not." Evan poured water over his head as well, and Julian's gaze drifted to Evan's nape.

Water painted paler lines on the tar-blackened skin. It was a fascinating picture, but Julian wasn't comfortable staring at it too long and pulled up the breeches. They were a very tight fit, but he managed to button them up after some fumbling with the fastening at the back.

"I'm afraid that your servants will not tell you the truth of what is being said about you, no matter how much you fraternize with them."

Evan let out a long groan. "Oh, so that's why you're here? To tell me the truth? I hope your father pays up quick then, and we can both be on our way."

Julian put on the waistcoat, admiring the fine decorative stitching. "You are being unreasonable, really. You do need friends of a similar social standing. Even a ghost needs company, but it should be someone he can talk to on the same level."

"A ghost is dead. He needs no company." Evan leaned back in the tub, his handsome face clean again. Droplets of water shone in the light of the fire as they slid down Evan's neck.

"You're not playing that game with me," Julian said with a small smirk. He found it amusing just how unwavering Evan was in his attempts to push away an offer of friendship. After all, the man *was* a gentleman, even if rough around the edges from spending too much time away from polite society. He was, in fact, like a rough diamond, smooth and shiny underneath layers of dirt that Julian would polish. It would be an interesting development in Julian's life to become friends with the Ghost of Tredele, introduce him to more suitable company, remind him of proper manners. Yes, that would be very interesting indeed. "You would not have taken me with you if you hated company so much."

Evan barked out a laugh and Julian's heart sped up when Evan's gaze settled on him once more. It had to be the aura of being around a man from such an ancient family that had him so jittery.

"You have to be joking. I agreed to your mad proposition out of boredom, and you've made me suffer for it since we agreed on the ransom."

"You have not made me silent yet," said Julian, parading in front of the tub in the emerald suit, which—while of a slightly outdated fashion—still looked impeccable. "So better tell me what your real purpose is. What do you intend to do with the ransom? Purchase another fine mount, perhaps?"

Evan's gaze followed him like that of a wild cat, still deciding whether to pounce or retreat. "I have always wondered what else is out there in the world that we have never heard of. With enough money to spare, I could fund, an... exploration venture."

Julian stood at the feet of the tub and watched Evan's face, which stuck out of the now muddy water that obscured everything beneath the surface. There was something odd about the air, as if there was a storm coming soon, with lightning bolts about to strike right in front of Julian's toes. He swallowed.

"What is it that you intend to explore?"

"Have you ever been to the Isles of Scilly?"

"I can't say I have," said Evan and brushed his fingertips over the warm copper edge of the tub, which oddly reminded him of Evan's skin. Julian's eyes strayed to Evan's knee where it emerged from murky water, glistening with moisture. "Tell me."

Evan sat up straighter, and Julian couldn't help but notice the droplets of water sliding down the black hairs on Evan's chest, all the way to his dark nipples.

"I've been there years ago, and it's the farthest I've ever travelled off the coast. The place was like a different world parallel to ours. I sat down on the sandy beach, and for the short stay there, I did not feel tied down to anything or anyone. Not even to England. The sea was vast, warm, and I could breathe as freely as nowhere else in the world."

Julian brushed the tip of his tongue along his lower lip. "Can't you breathe freely out here?"

Evan looked thoughtful while he stared into the dark water. "Sometimes it's difficult to know whether possessions are something to treasure or a burden."

Julian watched him with an intense burning sensation blooming in his chest. He took slow, careful steps and had the rim of the copper tub to guide him closer to Evan. "The estate. Is there no one else to care for it in your absence?"

"There is no need for anyone to do so. It is my heritage." Evan licked his lips, not even blinking.

Julian sighed and leaned his hip against the tub, sitting on the rim with one buttock. There was some kind of oil in the water, and its fresh scent penetrated Julian's lungs. "But you wish to explore, don't you? We're not as different as I thought."

Evan shrugged and slumped lower in the water. "What does it matter? A man has duties to his family even when they're dead."

"How so?" Julian dipped his fingers in the water and swirled them across the surface, creating ripples that turned into little waves hitting the shores of Evan's chest and rousing the dark strands of hair. "Why should he answer to duty once he's free?"

"A gentleman is never free," Evan said grimly, and got up so abruptly, Julian felt wet heat soak through the silk breeches at his hip. He looked up, watching the towering presence of his host.

"Is that why you dislike your house? Why you sought out a cozier space by gathering all that's important to you here?"

Evan frowned at him as he left the bath. "I did no such thing," he grumbled.

Julian swallowed hard, trying not to notice the manhood that was obscenely close to his eyes. Instead, he let his gaze drift up the pronounced muscles, which had rivulets of fragrant water cascading down them. "Maybe you could show me the Isles before I leave for Italy."

Evan covered himself with a sheet, which quickly absorbed the water and only made the firm body underneath look more like an ancient sculpture. "Me? You met me yesterday," he said startled.

Julian chuckled, amused that he'd managed to wipe the stern look off Evan's face, even if just for a moment. The man was quite handsome when he smiled, too. He should be doing it more often if he ever wanted to fulfill the duty of siring an heir to the estate and title.

"And yet I never met anyone quite like you... Mr. Noir."

Evan burst out laughing, and it was so unexpected and so honest, Julian straightened to look into his face more directly.

"It's the name of my horse."

"The comparison between the two of you isn't that far-fetched."

Evan's expression flattened, but he walked off toward a screen, where he'd left his clothes earlier. "Are you saying I look like a horse?"

Julian exhaled, watching the white sheet cling to Evan's ass and thighs as he walked. The paler streaks of fabric that still contained some air between its surface and skin looked almost like fingers spreading over that tan flesh. Julian reckoned that in proportion, Evan was just as well endowed as the enormous stallion surely was.

"He has those burning eyes, same as you."

"Oh, Julian, you really are amusing. Maybe I should keep you," Evan said before disappearing behind the screen.

"Maybe it should be me who keeps you? I'd be much safer on the highways of the continent with a beast by my side."

"You can't afford to keep me."

Julian now regretted that the screen even existed. He pulled off the coat, then the waistcoat, all the time watching the Chinese pictures on the wooden panels. "How much do you charge? I might just scrape enough out of my budget. Safety is everything."

"Are you suggesting I be your henchman?" There was amusement to Evan's voice, and judging by the shadows on the wall behind the screen, he was in fact changing.

"I believe you would be a brilliant henchman. Most of the time, all you'd need to do is glare at them," said Julian, picking up a fresh shirt. He waited, watching the shadows as he slowly unwound the thread at his neck and pulled off the used shirt.

Evan peeked out from behind the screen with a frown that was slowly growing on Julian. "Are you saying I look scary?"

The dark gaze slid over Julian's bare skin like a hot poker. If Evan could parade around naked as he was born, so could Julian. "Maybe."

"You do know you're still my captive?" Moments later Evan walked out in a sombre, dark blue banyan and a long nightshirt worn underneath. The little smile on his pale lips was most confusing.

Julian put on a fresh shirt, suddenly feeling a chill to his skin. He once again donned the red banyan and closed it promptly, shielding his flesh with the expensive embroidered silk. "A willing captive."

Evan murmured and raised his eyebrows. "You have no clue just how pleased I am to hear that."

Julian leaned against the poster of the bed, his fingers itching for something to hold. "The Ghost of Tredele turned out to be a most intriguing man. I might be reluctant to go."

Evan licked his lips and put on a pair of slippers, as dark and ancient as most things he wore. "Come, I will show you something even more intriguing." He gestured with his fingers, and it was as if he pulled on a string tied to Julian's neck.

Julian was on Evan's heels, intoxicated by the fresh scent of the water that now clung to his skin and damp hair. Evan was nothing like his older brother had been, but that didn't make him any less fascinating. "Even more than what I've seen so far? Luck is on my side tonight."

They went all the way up a side staircase that creaked under their feet, and reached the mezzanine at one end of the room. The air up here smelled of dust and books. Evan glanced over his shoulder, as if to check if Julian was there, but carried on along the balustrade.

Julian leaned closer to one of the shelves, breathing in the dry scent of old paper. "Were those your father's?" he asked, tracing leather-bound tomes with his fingers. What he really wanted to say was, *Do you read as much as I do? Is there something you can recommend? That is quite a collection.*

Evan waved his hand dismissively, as if the library were a trifle. "My father's, and his father's, and his father's father's."

"What did you add?" asked Julian, walking so close behind Evan's mountainous form he'd walk into him, were Evan to suddenly stop. A part of him hoped Evan would suddenly stop.

"This." Evan reached a bookcase at the end of the narrow walkway, and when Julian was about to have a look at the books, Evan pushed the shelves forward. They were a door to a hidden passage.

Julian stepped back, stopping to breathe for a second. The wall opened into a black hole that called out to him like a trap to the rabbit. "*You* did this? Not some medieval forebear of yours?"

Julian could swear Evan straightened up a bit at the words. "Yes, I did. So that no one bothers me when I don't wish to be disturbed." And then there was that inviting gesture with just his fingers that Evan had made before, and he stepped into the darkness.

Julian took half a stride forward and stopped, paralyzed by the physical pull to follow Evan into the flytrap. If he disappeared here, no one would ever find him. And yet, wasn't it like something out of a forgotten tale? Hidden passages leading to different worlds, places where the supernatural mixed with the world of the living? What if Evan really was a ghost, leading him into the afterworld? Would Julian still follow if he knew he was being led to his demise?

"Don't be childish, I have candles farther inside." Evan reached out and grabbed Julian's clammy hand.

Julian gasped, and his voice echoed in the blackness that swallowed him once the bookshelf returned to its original place. Sweat was already cooling on his back underneath the shirt, but he still followed Evan like a puppy, all the way down the corridor that was becoming slightly brighter farther on.

Evan entered a circular room that made Julian think of a medieval tower, and in its middle, a wooden spiral staircase wound upward, through the hole in the ceiling. Only then did Evan let go of Julian's hand to light up a candle.

"Is this where you'll drain my blood and feed it to your hounds?" asked Julian, surprised when it came out as a whisper. His hair was bristling, but he didn't feel threatened.

"Maybe..." Evan said and began climbing up the stairs.

"You should at least attempt to soften that blow," said Julian, looking at the narrow stairs ahead of him. The light of the single candle was already fleeing from him up the spiral staircase, so he pulled up the long banyan and followed Evan.

"And how would I do that? My gaze alone could scare people off, remember?"

"It certainly has the power to tenderize the flesh of even the bravest man." Julian chuckled, holding on to the bannister.

"Which leaves me with no way to soften the blow."

Julian went up the spiral staircase with his mind slowly twirling as well by the time he reached the room where Evan was busy lighting more candles.

Julian stretched, watching the grim space of wood and stone come to life. It was as if Evan really had invited him into another world altogether, much more serene and ancient than the noise of the busy harbor town where Julian lived.

Even here tapestries adorned the walls, and one worn arm-chair stood next to a small table with three teacups piled up on it. Julian doubted Evan invited many guests here. Instead, it was a room where no servants dared to come, not even to take away the dishes. A few trinkets adorned a shelf, and there were islands of books laid open on the floor. Just by the window, a telescope stood proudly on a single leg, with its copper exterior reflecting light.

Julian glanced Evan's way and slowly walked across the creaking wooden floor, which seemed uneven in the sparse glow of the candles. The air smelled different than he was used to. It was cool and slightly damp, a bit like a cellar, but the many astronomical instruments standing on a table nearby caught his imagination. "Family heirlooms?"

"No," Evan said and lifted his chin slightly as he ran his fingers over the telescope. "They're mine."

Julian felt a stir in his chest, and his feet took him over to the window and the well-polished instrument waiting to be used. "Are you writing horoscopes? Predicting the weather?" he asked, not quite sure how this kind of business worked, but at this moment he wanted to know all about it.

Evan chuckled, and it wasn't like the dark laughter of when he'd tried to slight Julian. "No, I've spent some time at sea and learned a fair bit about navigation. Sometimes, I sit here and pretend I'm on a ship. Other times, I look for new stars, or wonder if there is life on the moon. Trifles, I know."

"They're not," breathed Julian, sliding his gaze up Evan's neck. Their eyes met, and the pull was more powerful than what he'd experienced even with the closest of his friends. Evan was wild, bearish, and interesting as the devil himself. "When I look toward the south of Europe for my future, you dream of the stars. There is nothing trivial about intellectual curiosity."

"Would you like to try and spot a creature on the moon? It's very bright tonight." Evan opened the window and came up to the telescope, still seeming slightly wary of Julian's reaction.

Julian trailed his tongue over his bottom lip and walked up to the looking glass of the instrument. He raised his hand but didn't dare touch it, unsure how to handle it. "Some people believe the stars are the home to the Kingdom of Heaven, but I never believed that. What do you think awaits us there?"

Evan stepped behind him, and reached to a screw to adjust something, enveloping Julian in his scent and presence. "When I see the stars and planets move, I wonder if the air turns back to liquid up there, and if the sky is yet another ocean. Have a look."

Julian looked back, first at Evan's throat, then to his handsome face and eyes that burned even darker than the first time he'd seen them. Only then he realized he'd stopped breathing and sucked in a gulp of air. "You are a romantic."

Evan shook his head, but his eyelids lowered slightly. "I am no such thing. Have you forgotten that I kidnapped you? Now look." He pointed to the telescope and moved its eye toward the moon.

Julian gasped when the reflective, polished surface of the celestial body he'd seen so many times emerged in all its porous glory. In disbelief, he looked at what appeared to be mountain ranges and valleys. The profound nature of the discovery sent a shudder down his spine.

Julian smiled, remembering just how ballads of rogues made everyone's blood run faster at his favorite tavern. Evan had no idea what he was talking about, but if they continued their acquaintance, maybe he could teach Evan a thing or two about people's sensibilities. "You dream of oceans in the sky. Would that make Venus an island?" he asked and slowly leaned forward, barely daring to touch the expensive instrument.

Evan was right behind him, his hot breath tickling Julian's ear. "Yes, and each of those islands is a whole new world to explore."

"Venus would have dragons," whispered Julian, curling his shoulders as heat spread all over him despite the chilly air in the tower. The dark sky was suddenly filled with shapes he'd never seen with the naked eye. New stars emerged from the shadows of the cosmos, beckoning him with their otherworldly glow. "They're so bright."

"And Mars?" Evan sounded amused as he gently guided Julian's fingers to the same screw he used earlier. "Adjust the focus if you need to."

Julian gasped, his hand twitching slightly against the warm touch. He both wanted to pull it away and just rest it between the cool metal and the heat of Evan's body. "Valhalla. A world of men who never die, even if speared by multiple swords. Men who drink every night and dance around huge burning pyres."

"Sounds outrageous. To think you can make Norse myth sound engrossing. Now I know where the story of the Ghost of Tredele came from."

Julian could swear Evan's chest almost touched his back.

"I have many more stories to tell if you're willing to listen. But you might be the greatest storyteller of all," said Julian, grinning at Evan as he once more thought of the ocean metaphor. Evan was so close that a lightning bolt yet again thundered between them soundlessly.

Evan pulled away.

"I highly doubt that," he said and looked to the floor with a thoughtful expression.

"Why? This is a beautiful thing. I've never been anywhere like this."

"They're just concepts I ponder on to amuse myself. There are much more pressing matters in the world than this. Let us go."

The hand sliding off Julian's left his skin cold, but he didn't say a word about it. "Such as?"

"Sweeping chimneys and sleeping." Evan snuffed out all but one candle and made his way to the staircase with it. Julian knew that was that for tonight, no matter how much he wanted to explore this room and all its secrets. There was no denying Evan when he wanted something.

They climbed down the stairs and back to Evan's kingdom, but Julian already missed the serene atmosphere of the tower. Maybe he could convince his host to take him there again tomorrow?

Evan took off the banyan once they reached the bed, and Julian glanced at Evan's calves and thighs, imagining they got so firm from endless horseriding along the cliffs and beaches.

"Shall I take the same side of the bed as last night?" asked Julian, laying out the red banyan across one of the chairs. Would Evan once again curl around him in his sleep?

Evan nodded and pulled out the rope without a word.

Julian froze, staring at it.

"Please don't make it tedious again." Evan sighed and looked up at him.

Julian clenched his teeth, and all the strange tingly sensations that had been crawling up his body that day were now completely gone. "Don't you dare."

"You are my captive, and until I get my ransom, I need to know you won't escape," Evan said as if Julian were a petulant child, fighting over a doll house.

"This is unforgivable. I will not stand for this," hissed Julian and made a point of sliding into bed as if he owned it along with the entire house. "You too should just go to sleep without making our lives miserable."

"This is the reality of our situation, Julian." As if Evan was in no position to change said situation!

"It is not. You treat me as a friend, invite me to your secret room, and then you dare to turn me into a dog you can leash? Despicable!" Julian pulled the covers all the way to his neck and stared at Evan, who stood between the two columns at the footboard. His heart was drumming as if the two of them were about to go to war.

Evan kneeled on the bed slowly, approaching Julian like a snake in the grass. It only reminded Julian of the indignity of last night, when Evan sat on top of him, and pushed Julian's face against the floor, pretending before a servant that Julian wasn't even present.

Julian took a deep breath, watching him in silence while his insides boiled with rage. But there was also a sharp pang of betrayal that he didn't dare specify. "Please, don't do this," he said, knowing he could not possibly overpower a man so strong and bull-like.

The frown was back on Evan's face, and no matter how calm he was trying to sound, all Julian could hear was a hot pounding of blood in his head. "I promise you will be released in the morning."

"I said *no.* You have no right to fasten me to your bed. I came here of my own will. I could have run when you rushed off to repair that damn chimney."

"Don't make it hard for me." Evan pulled on the covers, revealing Julian's chest.

Julian exhaled slowly, and then spat into Evan's face. It went slack, and Evan's eyes lost all their spark, turning into blackness when he descended on Julian and pulled his hands up with so much force it hurt.

"May the devil bugger your soul to hell," Evan growled.

Julian clenched his hands into fists and kicked, aiming for the groin, but Evan blocked him just in time.

"You should look at yourself in the mirror, you son of a whore!" yelled Julian.

"I think you do enough of that for us both," Evan said through clenched teeth. With his superior strength, he managed to hold down both Julian's wrists and tie them together all at once. Maybe he wasn't the Ghost of Tredele, Sir Evan Penhart? Maybe he was an impostor straight from the pits of hell?

The rope bit into Julian's wrists, and he growled through his teeth, pulling hard to free his hands. His gaze caught Evan's eyes. "Maybe you should. A man of your standing should not look like his own footman. But the dark suits you. You are just a shadow of your brother, buried in a fucking tower. You should have someone lock you in there forever, so you can dry out like a corpse, because that's the only thing that belongs in this house."

"I told you to stop talking about my brother! Isn't it enough that you parade around in his clothes?" Evan's face was becoming red, so Julian must have managed to rub some salt into the wound despite getting tied to the headboard as if *he* were the criminal.

Julian stirred, determined not to make the job easy for Evan. "Everyone loved your brother while you need to tie a stranger to your bed so that you have someone to talk to. You are a joke to all of Cornwall. You blacken your family name with your very existence, and you speak of duty, but I don't see your heirs anywhere around the house. I will *never* forgive you for this!"

"I do not care for your opinion, or for anyone's for that matter!" Evan yelled into his face as he tightened the knot with finality. "And I do not need anyone to talk to. I actually consider this evening wasted on you!"

The cold steel of Evan's words tore right through Julian's chest, but he wouldn't show any more weakness. "You should, because you will hang."

"How dare you threaten me when you're the one who wants to steal from your own father?" Evan glared at Julian, and it wasn't an amusing sight anymore.

"Yes. Yes, I do. You disgust me. You are not worthy of my friendship."

"Good riddance." Evan pulled away and slid under the covers as far away as possible. Once the candle was extinguished, Julian stared into the canopy above and listened to the uneven breathing close by, mirrored by his own, but he didn't allow the biting sensation around his eyes to overtake him and slowly exhaled.

He would have his vengeance one way or another.

Chapter 6

Julian

The next few days stretched into a never-ending silence that was almost like a physical presence always walking behind Julian's back. It kept clenching its hands on his shoulders when he sat in Evan's soft chair by the window or looked through the rich library of books that were his sole companions. Evan disappeared every morning and came back to the room only to sleep. For now, Julian sank deep into the literary world, helping himself to the collection of books put together by Evan's family over the years.

For someone so roguish and seemingly unrefined despite a genteel background, Evan's library was surprisingly diverse, ranging from contemporary philosophy to treatises on astronomy. It would have been easy to dismiss Evan's taste and assume the tomes had all been Sir Peter's once, but even Julian would not believe his late friend had been a man interested in science. The dates on notes inserted into some of the books proved that beyond doubt.

But despite there being many topics they could discuss they didn't share many words. Once the answer from Julian's father came, they would be both done with this charade and part ways with their pockets filled. In the letter, Julian had requested Father publish his response as a discreet advertisement in *The Western Flying Post*, but the delivery of the paper was running late, as per usual, and so Julian was stuck in the cluttered room that had become his permanent prison. He wondered if a stay in the

Bodmin gaol wouldn't have been easier to stand. At least he'd have someone to open his mouth to.

He wondered if Evan sometimes got so bored and starved for interaction that he spoke to the artworks gathered around his bedroom. With the servants in their cottage, Julian could imagine Evan walking the empty corridors in his dark banyan, open hair spilling down his shoulders, the candlelight tricking him into seeing movement in one of the paintings.

Julian's gaze strayed to a large frame hung across the room from the bed. The faint candlelight accentuated the contrast between shadows and highlights. With its dark hues and prominent spotlights, the picture was of a style that used to be popular some time ago, but the age of the painting did not take away from its beauty. Two men faced one another beneath a lone pine tree. Their naked bodies were visibly tense, with each muscle carefully depicted by the skillful hand of the artist. Their skin carried a glow that made the scene otherworldly despite the brutally honest portrayal of bulging veins and tendons so rigid they could snap at any moment.

One of the men had his arms up, tied to a branch so hard there was a sinewy shade to his fingers. He was backing away from his companion, but it was no use, as the pine was a healthy-looking tree, its cones so heavy with seeds they looked as if they were about to fall and spill their contents with the tiniest gust of wind.

Marsyas was usually depicted as a mature man, but the setting and the attributes of the two characters—a flute and a lyre—made the beautiful youth's identity clear as the air in winter.

His face was twisted into an odd expression indeed, one of both pain and pleasure, akin to the ecstatic portrayals of saints. His blue eyes were almost translucent when they focused on Apollo, who neared him with a cruel smirk, a curved knife in a hand used to pulling strings of the lyre. The scene caught the moment just before the climax of the myth, seconds prior to Apollo making Marsyas bleed and scream as punishment for his pride.

The painting, while never failing to make Julian somewhat uncomfortable, also fascinated him, kept inviting his gaze with its masterful depiction of the human body and intense emotion. He wondered what made Evan choose a scene so cruel as the one he set his eyes on first thing in the morning.

Each night, Evan fastened Julian's hands to the headboard, and Julian wasn't even fighting it anymore. He endured the humiliation with all the dignity he could retain. The camaraderie and banter of the first two days was long gone. Julian sometimes mused about the possibility of revenge, but he had been lying when he told Evan he'd expose him to the authorities. He despised the idea of pushing someone into the executioner's hands, but he loathed staying at Evan's dreadful house and being at his whim.

The sooner he'd get to leave for Italy the better. All he needed now was the ransom money. He would pack and leave this sad, cold island forever to be with people worthy of his interest.

Having noticed Evan's heavy steps before Julian even saw the door open in the far corner in the room, he posed himself to look like the picture of nonchalance with a cup of tea in one hand and a book of poetry in the other. He took a deep breath, steadying himself as the black and white blur that was his host stormed between the chests and furniture, all the way to the table where Julian sat.

The Western Flying Post slammed against the dark wood, and Julian couldn't breathe anymore, staring at the logo, the date, the articles on the front.

"So here it is," Julian whispered and opened the second page, looking for his father's answer. There was no reason to be polite anymore. He would be going home soon enough.

"Read it." Evan's voice was as cold as a rock on a rainy day, and he tapped the tabletop with his fingertips.

"I need to find it first," hissed Julian, slowly scanning the second and third page. Would the ad be even further into the paper?

"It's on the last page. Your father doesn't seem to hold you in the high esteem you had hoped for."

Julian smirked and turned the paper in his hands. "He probably doesn't want to draw much attention to it. He's always been too focused on how others perceive him," he said, finally finding the little bit of text among a chessboard of tiny advertisements. But as he read, blood started draining from his face and down his body, leaving his skin numb and cold.

"Mr. William Reece of Looe wants his son, Mr. Julian Reece, to know that he is not welcome at the Reece household. Mr. William Reece will not be held accountable for his son's debts, and disassociates himself from all and any wrongdoings Mr. Julian Reece might have committed. Any allowance Mr. Julian Reece has enjoyed will now be withheld, but in his generous nature, Mr. William Reece has one more piece of advice for his son. Mr. Julian Reece is encouraged to find an honest profession."

Julian stared at the print. He read it again and again as his heart thrashed like a trapped moth, about to be burned by fire.

"You are worthless," Evan said in that same stone–cold voice that resonated in the high–ceilinged room.

Julian's fingers clenched so hard he creased the paper before tossing it to the tabletop as the ink burned his fingers. He leaned back, unable to breathe with the black hole growing in his chest. Was his father washing his hands of him? Was *that* what this announcement meant?

He forced his mouth into a grin that was already pulled on by the gravity of what he'd just found out. "Nonsense. I don't believe that. It's got to be a trick."

Evan's gaze caught his, but there was no doubt to be found in those dark eyes. "Your father would rather see you put in a bag and thrown in the lake than pay a penny for you."

"That is utter nonsense," said Julian blankly, pulling the book to his chest, not even remembering what it was about anymore. His mind was in the throes of chaos that he couldn't yet rein in. Father couldn't have known it was all a stunt, could he?

"You lied to me to escape marriage, and now it turns out I'm not getting anything out of this?" Evan's voice rose, and Julian knew him enough by now to expect an eruption of the volcano within Evan very soon. It would destroy everything in its way and spit swearwords all around.

Julian stood up and put the book down. "Clearly, you were not convincing enough as a highwayman if he doesn't believe I'm in danger."

"Oh, so it is my fault? How should I convince him then?" Evan grabbed the front of Julian's cravat and pulled him closer, close enough for Julian to sense the heat of Evan's breath on his skin. "Should I send him your finger?"

Julian swallowed hard, assaulted by Evan's presence. "Your servant women would never forgive you if you did," he said, already knowing how oddly close Evan was with his help. He would take their condemnation with the same worry as any other man would that of his peers.

"And how would they know... if I cut out your tongue as well?" Evan whispered with a rasp to his voice that was far too much like a groan of pleasure. Had Julian misjudged Evan, and the man was prone to the kind of violence that no well-bred man should be capable of?

Unable to hold the hard gaze anymore, Julian looked down to the tousled front of Evan's shirt, to the dark hair peeking from between the folds of linen. "I'm certain there is something we can work out. I own... some things of worth," he said, glancing up again.

"Oh, you will pay me for all this trouble if you don't want to end up at the bottom of the sea. Or should I just throw you off a cliff and be done with it?" Evan hissed and squeezed the cravat tighter, robbing Julian of breath.

Julian clenched his fists as uncertainty clawed its fingers into his mind. Father was a tough negotiator, but not up to the point of bargaining with anyone's life. Had Julian's lie really been exposed, prompting Father to cut him off? Disinheriting a first-born son was one thing, a difficult legal process and often not successful, but as one of the younger children, Julian had no legal right to any of his father's possessions.

If Father chose to stop feeding and clothing him, there was nothing Julian could do but appeal to his good graces. Had he listened to Father's advice, he'd have become a lawyer, a doctor, a man of God, perhaps the message would not have come as such a shock but Julian's profession could not feed him yet, no matter how brilliant he was. What was he to do?

A deep shudder went through Julian's flesh, and he looked at Evan's forearm, suddenly feeling much more weight behind the threats.

He was ruined.

"If even your family refuses to ever see you again, what worth can you possibly have to me now?" Evan's nostrils flared as he watched Julian, still holding the cloth at Julian's neck as if it were a noose. Suddenly, the tiny unpleasantries Julian had showered on Evan in the last days felt like grave mistakes.

"I am not worthless," he managed, looking up into Evan's eyes. "I will repay you, but you need to let me go," he said as steadily as he could.

"Oh, do I? So you can run away without paying off this debt? Remember, you owe me half of the sum we demanded." Evan did let go of Julian though and took a step back, wrapping his arms around his chest. Julian didn't like the way Evan seemed to be assessing him now, like a cow he was not certain he wanted to purchase.

Julian touched his neck, only then realizing it showed his fear, but it was close to impossible not to be uncomfortable with Evan's gaze burning charred holes in Julian. How had he found himself in such an impossible situation? Surely, there was a way back into Father's heart. Julian needed to go back home and beg a little until that iron heart melted. Not all was lost, and Julian could still turn this dreary situation to his advantage. And if not, he owned some items he could sell and live off until someone purchased his manuscript.

"I will repay you. You have my word."

Evan's breath quickened, his gaze licking Julian from head to toes. "There's only one value you have for me."

Cold air wheezed at the back of Julian's throat, but he fought through the sudden fear and spoke, "And what value is that?"

"Strip, and bend over the bed."

Julian stared at him, completely thrown out of his thoughts. "I beg you pardon?"

Evan took a step closer, and was such a menacing presence Julian instantly took a step back despite willing himself not to. The massive room suddenly felt far too small, and the bed far too close. "I like the look of you, and I want to fuck you."

Julian's back hit the wall, and he clenched his hand on the backrest of the chair as the dark glare of Evan's eyes drew a vertical line all the way up his body. This couldn't be happening. Evan was likely jesting to humiliate Julian.

"No... I don't do that. I'm not a sodomite," he whispered.

"I saw your cock get hard in my bed on that first night." Evan approached closer, the dark eyelashes low over the eyes like curtains to hell.

Julian shook his head. "Lies. Stop making a fool of yourself. This is a hanging offense. Worse yet than highway robbery."

"You have nothing to offer but your body. I am a highwayman, so I may as well be a sodomite too. A man can only hang once."

Julian exhaled loudly, unable to hold in the air anymore. He shook his head and crossed his arms on his chest. He could try to run, but without a horse, it would be hours, possibly a whole day's way until he reached Looe. Even then, if Father would not give him permission to return home, all he owned were the suit he'd worn when he met Evan and the slim contents of his valise, while even the clothes on his back now belonged to a dead man.

"Aren't you ashamed of yourself?"

"You have already told me I disgust you." Evan came closer and pushed Julian toward the bed. "What do I have to lose? Bend over the bed. I will get what I want one way or another. Play nice, and you might even have a place to stay until you figure out what you want to do with your pitiful life."

"This isn't what's done..." whimpered Julian, stiff as a marionette without a puppeteer.

"I do it, so it is."

"You d—" Julian clutched at the front of his waistcoat, too choked up to continue. Had Evan been lusting after him all this time? Was this why he'd rubbed himself against him that first morning? Julian's skin itched all over when he realized Evan must have been looking at him the way men looked like women before trading comments unsuitable to female ears. "This is sickening," he said weakly. "You're better than that, sir."

"I'm afraid to disappoint you," Evan said, and his face could as well be a mask hiding all expression, because Julian could not fathom what Evan was thinking. "You on the other hand, are beautiful. But that's all you've got." Evan grabbed his arm and turned him around to face the bed.

Julian put his hands against his face, utterly confused by the praise interwoven with all the words and gestures of abuse. He shook his head. "There's other assets. I assure you—"

"I don't want any other assets."

Julian gasped when Evan slid his arms around him from behind and their bodies aligned. He stood still, paralyzed by a power within, and watched Evan's large, strong hands move over his chest.

When lips much hotter than any of Evan's heartless cold words pressed against Julian's neck, he couldn't stop a whimper leaving his mouth. The soft, warm touch was like a stranger to Julian's impenetrable exterior, and he shuddered, grabbing one of Evan's wrists but not holding it in place.

Evan's hot tongue trailed up all the way to Julian's ear. Something rolled inside Julian's stomach, giving him an odd sensation of weightlessness. No matter how much the rational part of his mind told him to be disgusted, he couldn't bring himself to feel that way. This was not disgust, even if it too made his skin feel odd.

Evan's arms tightened around him, like an anaconda hugging its prey in a deathly grip, yet Julian was already too hypnotized to try to pull away. He could be smothered tonight, and he wouldn't even see it coming.

Closing his eyes, he leaned back against Evan and let his hands fall to his sides, not even resisting anymore. What was the point? Evan had said it himself, he would take what he wanted, and Julian already knew how denying Evan worked out.

He didn't have anywhere to go.

Evan nipped on Julian's ear, and it was difficult to reconcile the position Julian was in with the image he had of himself. Was he someone to be lusted after by men? Evan ground his groin into the small of Julian's back, and at the same time, one of his hands slid down Julian's stomach, going straight for his cock.

Julian got to his toes, gasping at the caress that set his skin on fire despite his best judgment. He had nothing to say anymore, so he might as well get it over with and forget as soon as he left. He'd leave soon, but he needed to keep himself alive until then.

The way Evan clenched his hand on Julian's cock was nothing like the soft, feminine touch of a woman. Evan's hand was big, his touch confident and possessive, as if he had all the right in world to claim Julian. The gentle kiss behind Julian's ear didn't resonate with the way Evan held him tightly or the way his cock swelled against Julian's back.

And while the touch was a twisted compliment of sorts, the weight behind it made Julian cringe on the inside. Was this really all there was to him now? His supposed beauty? Had the conversations he'd shared with Evan at the beginning of his captivity meant nothing at all?

Evan reached up and pulled open the knot of Julian's cravat. His hot breath spoke of excitement, just as the kisses to Julian's neck did, yet Julian had no idea how that made him feel. Hot. Cold. Flushing all over.

As the neck cloth came off, Evan's fingers slipped to the buttons of Julian's waist coat, while his other hand still teased Julian's cock through his breeches.

Julian licked his lips, grinding against the warm palm, his skin already too hot underneath the linen as the waistcoat was all but torn off his back.

He was almost relieved when Evan roughly pulled it off him, as the heat was making him lightheaded. But as soon as he thought that, his shirt got taken away as well, and goose bumps prickled his skin all over, both from the cool air in the room and the heat of Evan's gaze. He never thought he'd be... evaluated this way.

Evan groaned and pulled close again, letting his hands roam free all over Julian's chest, even stopping at the nipples to rub them with his palms. It was a strange feeling that bordered between pain and a pleasure so unexpectedly it made his cock twitch.

Julian made a quiet peep, surprised by the tender sensation, and he curled his shoulders, unsure whether he hated or enjoyed it. The bed was in front of him, mocking his pride with its soft sheets and thick curtains. Would Evan keep him permanently chained to the headboard now that *this* was the only thing he wanted from Julian?

Evan's movements were becoming hastier, and he didn't take as much time with Julian's breeches as he had with the waistcoat. He pushed them down to Julian's knees, not even bothering to have Julian take them off completely. And despite the rising uncertainty, Julian still wondered if Evan would undress as well.

Evan unfastened Julian's drawers within two seconds, and then they too were sliding lower, leaving Julian's skin vulnerable to the cool air and the heat of Evan's body. He wanted to say something, but his voice died in his throat when Evan pushed him forward until Julian needed to rest his hands on the bed, obscenely bare in the most intimate places.

And he wouldn't just be looked at. Evan's hand was between Julian's legs before Julian could even ponder whether he agreed to this or not. The surprisingly gentle fingers closed over Julian's balls and toyed with them as the other warm hand trailed up Julian's spine.

A low moan escaped Evan's lips, and the sound was like warm rivulets of water trailing down Julian's back, down his cock, his balls. He bit back the sound that threatened to spill out of his mouth and clutched at the covers, leaning forward to bury his face in the fragrant folds of the bedding. The touch was like nothing Julian had ever felt. Possessive and steel hard yet oddly tender. No whore had pleasured Julian like that, then again, in this equation maybe it was him who was the whore? Selling his body to pay off a debt.

The room was as quiet as a crypt. The only sounds were their breaths. Evan backed off, leaving Julian by the bed with his backside exposed to view, his thighs spread slightly. All the hairs on Julian's arms bristled when he heard what had to be the unbuttoning of Evan's breeches.

He swallowed cotton-scented air and pressed his face harder into the top blanket. The fine wool caressed his face, so steady in contrast to the cool shivers running down his naked body. He hadn't even been undressed completely, as if he didn't deserve that much dignity. It would not happen in a bed. He'd be taken against the bed, with breeches and drawers pooling at his knees and keeping them close together. He didn't dare speak, but the rustle of clothing behind him brought his thighs to a tremble.

Like out of nowhere, Evan's hands were at the sides of his head, and what was unmistakably a stiff prick rubbed between Julian's buttocks. Hot and throbbing already, about to plow Julian as if he really were a whore to be taken in any way a gentleman pleased.

Julian was a caged animal, with no chance to escape now that it had been trapped by those strong arms that so easily overpowered him every night. A flash of fear was drilling its way through his head, but he refused to acknowledge that nothing would ever be the same after this. Nobody would know, and once he walked away from here, the humiliation of being sodomized would be buried at the very bottom of Julian's memory.

This would not define the rest of his life.

Evan took a shuddery breath once he lay on top of Julian with all the weight of his muscle. No man had ever treated Julian this way, and those treacherous hands once again slipped around Julian's body, groping pecs, stomach, and arms with no shame at all, as the thick cockhead pushed in and out from between the cleft of Julian's buttocks without haste.

Julian pulled the blanket closer, gathering it around his face and biting into the wool as he steadied his tense body. His thighs were cramped from the tension, and he shuddered, desperately trying to relax. He'd heard all about this. About the sickening way some men treated others, how they defiled their bodies with this ungodly act. Why was Evan making this so difficult? Why did his hands feel so warm when they were really just there to keep Julian still, were he to buck. The cock felt enormous, and it teased the sensitive flesh between Julian's buttocks, making him curl his toes with its sheer presence.

Evan was so heavy. His body smelled of hay and musk, as if he spent the morning in the field like a common peasant, and yet Julian didn't even attempt to push him off, remaining still, waiting.

Evan let out a pleased groan when he pushed his cock harder against Julian's hole. His hand traveled south of Julian's stomach, and when it found Julian's cock, it closed around it in that same confident manner as before. Just as Julian's mind tried to steady itself, Evan left a trail on soft kisses down the back of his head.

He couldn't stop a soft moan and curled his shoulders, arching underneath Evan's weight. He was so angry. He shouldn't be enjoying any of this, but Evan couldn't give it a rest, determined to turn him into the same kind of pervert he was.

For once, Julian wished his hands were tied to the headboard, so that there was a rational explanation as to why he was not clawing out Evan's eyes yet.

Evan closed his teeth over Julian's neck, as if he really were a monster out for Julian's blood, but that quickly changed into kisses again. Only now the raw truth hit Julian, and he was at loss.

A man. Was kissing him.

Not just pushing his cock in to take his pleasure but savoring Julian's skin as if it were the best thing he ever tasted. It didn't agree with the rowdy stories Julian had heard of sodomites, but he wasn't sure it should be of much comfort to him. Slowly, he rubbed his face against the blanket and turned his head to the side, gasping for fresh air. He opened his eyes and looked back.

Evan's black gaze was just inches away, and he started moving his cock up and down Julian's crack, in a deliberately slow motion. He didn't blink, didn't say a word, just breathed hard and watched Julian, his face flushed and hair out of order, falling on his forehead. Evan's hand on Julian's cock was also a constant presence, and as they watched each other, Evan took his time rubbing the fluid that escaped Julian's prick over the cockhead with his thumb.

Julian gasped, sucking in air as if he were about to drown. He couldn't stop looking back, thoroughly taken by the sight of the coal-like eyes that pinned him to the bed with more force than Evan's physical strength ever could. His heart rattled.

"Your cock is beautiful too," Evan whispered, never even blinking.

Julian's breath trembled, tension pulling on his vocal cords like a mad musician. Evan was beautiful too, even now, in his cruelty. "Will yours hurt me?" he whispered in the end.

Evan leaned closer and kissed Julian's chin. "No. It doesn't have to hurt." He stirred his hips again as if to prove that point.

Julian nodded, both relieved and ashamed at how disturbingly close he was to begging for mercy.

Evan must have sensed something now that they were so close, because he continued. "I've been in your position before, and all it takes is a skilled lover." He gave Julian's shoulder a kiss before pulling back to the side table by the bed.

A lover? Julian wanted to ask, but he bit back his words, breathing harder. His back was suddenly cold. As if all it needed for equilibrium was Evan's heat, no matter how perverse it was. Sodomites didn't take lovers. They fucked in alleyways and never even looked at one another in the day, for fear of discovery.

He hummed softly, not moving by an inch, still bent over like a cheap whore waiting for cock.

When Evan returned, Julian expected it to be the moment when that thick tool would push into him without mercy, but as Evan's cock pressed on Julian's buttock, it was something else that teased Julian's hole. Hard and slippery. Evan started twisting it in.

Julian yelped, backing away from the intrusion, and his ass closed tight around the slim bit that was already inside. "What in heaven's—"

"Calm down. I can't just ram into you," Evan said matter-of-factly, and just by saying that out loud, the fucking was becoming all too real.

The stiff, phallic object, not much thicker than a finger, kept pushing into Julian. Not on its own, of course, it was all Evan's doing, and when Julian glanced back, Evan's gaze was on Julian's ass, as if the attention he was giving it now needed careful supervision. His cock thick and hard out of the breeches, his chest rising and falling. Even without being undressed, Evan was a sight to behold. Pure power, lust, and determination.

Julian bit into his fist, trying to relax to the insistent invasion. He knew there was nothing he could do to stop it, not with Evan so set on this. The thing was cool, even if it absorbed Julian's body heat at a rapid pace, but hard and alien. It didn't belong inside him, and yet Julian's prick was still hard, dripping against the sheets. What was happening to him?

When Evan stopped pushing the thing in with surprising ease thanks to how slippery it was, the teasing was only starting. He pulled it out slightly, twisted it, pushed back in again, all the while pressing his cock against Julian's buttock from the side and watching him like a hawk.

That slippery wetness was at the tip of Evan's prick as well, and it reminded Julian of the way Evan rubbed against him that first morning. Had he wanted to do just this back then? Move away the covers and shamelessly insert his prick into Julian's ass while he was bound and defenseless?

Julian didn't even realize when he pushed back slightly, spreading his legs as wide as the tight breeches around his knees allowed him. He remembered Evan's cock in vivid detail, and it was much wider than the item that was now making Julian's insides tingle.

Evan groaned and pushed it in with a bit more force. It surprised Julian, but as promised, didn't actually hurt. When he was about to steal a glance up at Evan again, the weight of Evan's body was back on top of him, pinning him to the bed as his ass was being toyed with.

He moaned, rubbing one knee against the side of the bed as he lifted his foot off the floor. Sharp teeth grazed his nape, and he pushed against Evan's face without thinking, trapped underneath the hard body. Evan's hand slid into Julian's hair and held on to it gently, keeping his head down as the phallic item moved in and out faster.

And just like that, it was gone.

Evan pulled it out, dropped whatever it was to the floor, and for a moment Julian wasn't sure what was happening, but then it was Evan's cockhead—hot, throbbing, and slippery with some kind of oil—pushing at his sphincter and demanding entry. Evan was taking Julian's body as if it were his birthright to do as he pleased.

The tip pushed in, but its width was in such sharp contrast to the item, Julian's body clamped down on it involuntarily, as if seeking the previous girth. He arched his back, about to crawl away from the intrusion when sharp pain made him feel all the muscles around his anal passage. He pushed his face into the blanket and froze, biting on it as the heat of a man's cock burned his flesh.

"Shh... calm yourself." Evan blew some air on Julian's ear, but the exquisite mixture of pleasure and pain was getting the best of Julian. How was he to calm down when a man, and not any man at that— Sir Evan Penhart, a man as handsome as Hercules himself, and just as strong—was pushing his thick prick into Julian's body, intent on leaving his seed inside as if Julian were only a vessel for Evan's pleasure.

"I can't," moaned Julian, taking sharp breaths of air and begging for his body to yield to the huge cock. And it wasn't even halfway inside him yet. Julian wasn't sure whether he could even take all of it.

Sweat was a cooling presence on his skin, and as a drop slid down his nose, he wiped his face in the covers. His whole body was pulsing with heat that he couldn't even name.

"I'll go slow," Evan whispered, as if he were doing Julian a favor. With his hands free again and his cock lodged deep in the heat of Julian's body, Evan let his fingers find Julian's prick again, and despite the pain and embarrassment of it all, Julian was ashamed to admit his cock was still as hard as a rock.

He gave a shuddery whine and shifted his weight, relieved to feel the stiff pain in his ass disperse somewhat. Nodding to whatever Evan said, he accepted the hand around his prick without question. His mind was a tangle of colors, and when the cock started screwing itself into him again, it was difficult to say where pain ended and pleasure began.

Only now did it hit him that when Evan said he'd fuck him, the last thing Julian imagined was getting his cock milked by that big, confident hand. Was it something all sodomites did? He'd heard some men say that they could only be satisfied with a woman once they made sure she had her pleasure as well. Or was this more like men fondling women simply because they enjoyed the shape of their bodies?

It was hard to focus on such academic questions when Evan's hand moved back and forth, slippery, its fingers slightly rougher than Julian's. At the same time, Evan's hips touched Julian's ass, so that thick rod of flesh had to be all the way in.

Evan moaned deeply in delight and pressed his forehead against Julian's nape. The sensation of being split open and filled with that hard staff would be enough to make all of Julian's senses gallop. The weight on top of him knocked Julian's air out of his lungs, keeping him in the most confusing limbo where he shuddered with arousal despite this being so demeaning.

It was as if Julian's body wasn't his anymore but taken over by the dark beast mounting him like a submissive mare. He cried out when Evan rocked his hips slightly, teasing open something deep within Julian's bowels, a last barrier to complete surrender.

Evan's hand pinched the tip of Julian's cock, making him buck and drag his hands over the bed, completely mindless with the foreign sensations. Using this distraction Evan pulled his cock out slightly, only to push it in again. The friction made Julian lose all control over his lips, and he moaned loudly, spreading his thighs wider.

Julian couldn't believe just how overwhelming this unnatural act felt with its pace and sinful indulgence of the cruelest kind. No woman had ever bewitched Julian this way in bed. Evan's one hand was firmly planted on Julian's cock, giving it slow, deliberate strokes, but the other traveled all over his body. To Julian's thighs, hip, pressed on his ribs, slid under him and teased his navel, only to go higher and pull on his nipple, as if Julian were a pretty peacock to be poked and prodded.

Julian's thoughts wandered to the beautifully sculpted bodies of Apollo and Marsyas in the painting. In Julian's mind, they were as touchable as his own body, and in that brief moment, it was him and Evan depicted by the artist, not the creatures of myth.

But when Evan's fingers closed on Julian's throat, and the rhythm of Evan's hips changed from teasing to outright fucking, he couldn't even think anymore. His body didn't resist, soft and pliant to the brutal thrusts, as if it were the most natural thing in the world. The big hand clenched over his throat, but it didn't feel threatening, more like a collar that held a dog in place for its master.

Julian pushed back as much as he could, his mouth open and uttering little moans each time the cock pushed inside him. His prick was close to bursting, and his skin was so hot it could melt and let Julian absorb all of Evan.

"I want you to come on my cock," Evan all but growled into Julian's ear, stroking his dick faster, and plowing Julian's tight ass in the same merciless rhythm. "I want to feel those muscles milking me when I spill."

Julian pushed up against Evan's chest, rubbing against the rough fabric of the black waistcoat as his mind spiraled out of control and pushed Julian into the dark waters of the glittering ocean in the sky.

Evan let go of Julian's throat, and only now Julian truly realized what Evan meant, when his ass began clenching rhythmically over Evan's cock, as if Julian had no say over his body anymore.

Julian's muscles were liquid, and nothing hurt anymore, no matter how hard and brutish Evan was when slamming into Julian's ass those last few times. Evan's long moan sent shivers down Julian's back, and when his powerful thrusts slowed down, Julian knew his brutish lover was coming. He emptied himself into Julian's body, while still holding Julian's cock hostage in that hot, strong hand.

Evan stroked Julian's thigh with his other hand, as if he were petting a favorite horse after a race, but the sour impression was gone in an instant when Evan laid his weight on top of Julian and left lazy kisses in his hair.

Julian lay still, his skin still ablaze with all the sensations that he didn't understand. He'd never experienced anything quite like this, not the mind-melting heat of Evan's touch nor the power behind his thrusts.

He stared at the weaving of the blanket, painfully aware that a man had just buggered him. This shouldn't have ever happened, and yet here he was, still with a cock up his ass, and with the stud's weight carelessly resting on top of him.

And if the act of sodomy wasn't animalistic enough, Evan sniffed Julian's hair loudly, snuggling on top of him, as if they were now joined and he would never be parting.

Julian had no idea what to say, so he stayed silent, hoping Evan wouldn't say anything either. He couldn't bear another biting comment now, after he'd allowed this to happen.

Evan's hand left Julian's softened cock, but just as he thought Evan was about to pull out and get up, Evan just lazily smeared the seed over Julian's stomach with a happy grunt.

Julian shuddered, shifting his legs to relieve the cramps in his thighs. His whole body stilled the moment something dribbled down his balls, cooling the skin rapidly.

He'd never been so ashamed in his entire life.

Evan kissed Julian's ear before pulling up, but he wouldn't give any of it a rest, and stroked Julian's buttock before stepping away.

"I won't have to tie you up anymore, will I?" he asked, his words resonating over Julian with the power of an entity out of this world.

Julian clenched his buttocks and thighs when the thick cock slipped out of him, leaving him empty and drenched with a slippery mess of semen and oil. He should have asked Evan to close the curtains.

Wordlessly, he shook his head.

CHAPTER 7

JULIAN

It had been a candle. That bastard buggered him with a candle.

Julian was horrified when he spotted the slim stick of wax on the floor in the morning, and hastily kicked it under the wooden frame, not wanting it as a reminder of what happened last night. He'd hardly slept but was too frightened to rouse Evan with his tossing and turning to change position.

His ass was sore, a bit like a knee after falling down and scraping off some skin.

His muscles ached from the strain, and as heat rose in his body throughout the night, his mind started playing tricks on him. It was as if not one but two heartbeats echoed in his chest for once. After he eventually fell asleep, breathlessness woke him from the slumber in early morning hours, and he stayed motionless until dawn, listening to the calm breathing all too close.

What had happened to him? He could have screamed. He could have kicked at Evan or tried to claw out his eyes, yet something had paralyzed him. Something deep inside had made him submit to Evan's sick desires. And worse yet, a part of Julian had enjoyed the act despite his better judgment.

When he turned around slightly toward the first rays of sunshine peeking through the curtains drawn around the bed, there was no frown on Evan's face, and sadly, his looks were no less pleasing even though Julian now knew the man was a beast. As if to underline that he was in fact a barbarian, Evan's arms were bare, suggesting that he wore nothing underneath the covers.

No nightshirt. No drawers.

He was naked, only inches away from Julian.

They might have been separated by all the fabric, but Julian still felt the ghost of Evan's touch on him. The pale bruises on his hips, the invisible lines on Julian's sides where Evan had rubbed him, the firm touch around his neck…

Julian shuddered just thinking about it, his cock stirring at the memory of Evan's weight on top of him and the steady hand caressing his prick. The bastard had made him spend. He'd forced Julian to enjoy this, and there was no way Julian could ever wipe away the visceral memories of last night. The sight of the burning coals of Evan's eyes so close to his face, his smooth lips slightly spread and exhaling warm, sweet air on Julian's neck.

It shouldn't have happened.

It was an abomination.

Julian left the bed as quietly as he could, rolling off at a snail's pace, not to awaken the brute. It was a relief to step back into the light, but the shame of what had happened chased him away from the mirror and sent him behind the screen, to the wash stand.

He didn't want to be undressed and readily available once Evan awakened. If they were in bed together, all Evan would have to do, were he aroused in the morning, was roll on top of Julian and push up his nightshirt. Julian now knew he wouldn't be able to fight the man off with muscle or wit, and it scared him to the point where he feared taking off his linens to wash off the remaining traces of last night.

And yet the awareness of Evan's presence so close also made him peek through the curtains and re-evaluate Evan's powerful arms covered in a dusting of dark hair. His chest was so broad too. Filled with muscle tightly-packed under the tan skin.

He'd managed to have a quick wash last night before going to bed, but he still wiped his whole body with a soapy sponge, even though he knew he'd never be able to scrub off that touch. Worst of all, he wasn't sure if he wanted to.

Not all of it.

No woman had ever touched his cock the way Evan had. His palms had a different weight. They were warmer, rougher, and so perfectly right in size to knead Julian's flesh.

Julian shuddered just thinking about it.

He dressed in the plainest clothes he could find in Sir Peter's trunks. The beige suit was made of fine wool, but its late owner must have worn it at the dusk of his life, when he'd gained a substantial amount of weight, as it was too large on Julian and didn't show off his figure as much. It wasn't something a man wore when he wanted to be noticed.

In one of the chests he even found a gray wig and put it on too, hoping it would make him look older, a less attractive catch for the predator who still lay in his bed, as if sated after munching on a whole deer carcass.

Without the means to make fresh tea in the locked room, Julian sat by the table with a cup of yesterday's brew, which had gotten cold and bitter overnight, and waited, fighting against the prickling feeling in his buttocks. Was this how whores felt after a night of work? Was this how low he'd fallen? The comparison made him choke on air and made him long for absolution. If he could turn into a cypress tree, no one could ever harm him. No one would ever know of his shame

And there it was.

Evan stirred in bed.

Julian had purposefully left the curtain open so he could be aware of Evan's state.

He thought back to the night when Evan had taken him to his secret room, and he wondered if Evan had wanted to devour Julian back then already. What if he'd only given Julian those scraps of niceties to wrangle up his prey? Julian had heard stories from men trying to woo ladies they fancied, and those often involved deception and dishonest methods.

Evan rolled out of bed as naked as the day he was born. With his face obscured by the mess of dark hair, he walked over to the chamber pot, and relieved his bladder. He didn't even care where Julian was, or that he could be seen.

Julian stopped breathing, and his hair bristled, as if he were a rat that went into the way of a draft horse. The sound of urine drumming against copper roused memories of how long Evan's prick was, how thick it had felt inside Julian. So thick he could still sense the ghost of its girth every time he moved.

Evan was standing with his back to Julian, and despite his best intentions, Julian let his gaze wander up the muscular legs, over the buttocks, all the way to the landscape of Evan's broad shoulders. Would Evan welcome Julian's touch, or was his interest one-sided? No, he probably didn't want to be petted all over like a harlot.

Julian hoped he'd remain unseen. But when Evan turned around, he stalled with his eyes pointed straight at Julian and covered his prick. A silly expression appeared on his face soon after, and he uncovered his privates, stretching his body with a wide grin.

"Oh, it's just you."

Julian looked into the dark tea that he hadn't touched much so far and moved the cup, prompting the liquid to stir. *Just you.* What an appropriate thing to say to a man whom one considered worthy only of spending into.

Evan gave Julian a roguish smile and pushed away some of his hair, making Julian's heart skip a beat for no reason at all. "Where's the canary-colored jacket?"

Julian swallowed hard. He did not want to be noticed for his supposed beauty right now. Had wearing something plain been a misfire, or would the grayish garb chase Evan away? "I don't understand your meaning."

Evan shrugged, and his smile faded. "You seemed to have grown fond of it. If you'd rather wear this and a twenty-year-old wig, be my guest. Have you checked that thing for lice?" He turned around and walked over to the washstand.

Immediately, Julian's scalp started tingling, but he pushed revulsion away and drank the whole cup of bitter tea in one gulp. "If there had been any at the time of your brother's death, then it's a graveyard by now. I do not mind corpses."

Evan groaned, and Julian could imagine the sneer on his face without even seeing it as Evan quickly washed himself with the sponge. "If you don't mind corpses, I will show you something after breakfast."

Avoiding the topic of Sir Peter yet again. Maybe if Julian kept speaking of Evan's late brother, the bastard would become truly annoyed with him and never touch him again?

Julian squeezed one hand with the other as soon as he put down the cup, not even fighting the scowl from the bitter drink. "Disposing of me so soon?"

"Oh, you're not going anywhere, my pretty canary." Evan turned around and pulled his shirt on as soon as he was done with wiping off moisture.

Julian pushed himself deeper into the chair. The sense of entrapment manifested itself as a heaviness in his legs. He flattened a wrinkle on the dull brown waistcoat and glanced at Evan's bare feet on the floor. "Surely, you can see there is no gain in keeping me here. My father detests me," he said even though the words barely passed his mouth. It was still too fresh of a wound.

Evan pulled up his braces, and then buttoned the black waistcoat. "If what you've been telling me in the past few weeks is true, you're a gambler and a wastrel. Your father might be suspecting that the ransom is your ploy to pocket a handsome sum." Evan came closer and pushed his hair back. "I figured I need to keep you here for a week or two. See if the fellow changes his mind once his precious son really doesn't come back."

It was as if the air against Julian's skin originated from the midst of the frostiest winter in recent memory. He squeezed his hands into fists. There was a grain of truth in that logic, but surely Evan would expect something in return. And they both knew what it was. He gave a shuddery breath, flushing when he realized Evan probably heard it.

"I was wrong. You are not the *Ghost* of Tredele. You are a monster," he whispered, forcing himself to look up.

Evan's lips twisted into what was neither a smirk nor a scowl. "You didn't seem to think so last night."

Julian swallowed hard and pushed the chair away from the table until the backrest hit the wall. "You have not the slightest idea as to what I think. But you, sir, made your opinion of me abundantly clear."

Evan grumbled something and sat down in the other arm-chair with so much impact it creaked. "I complimented your beauty." He shrugged. "You will get your share of ransom money if your father comes up with it. Until then, you will stay here and pay for the privilege of my hospitality."

Julian was sweating under the wig. He blinked several times, unsure what he should do with his hands. Evan's words were a polite way of saying, *You will be my whore.* How could he protest without unleashing violence? "Your brother would have been ashamed of you. Sir Peter was a good man. Never hurt a soul. He'd never stand for this."

Evan's frown appeared at the sound of his brother's name like clockwork, and he slammed his hand against the little table in front of him so hard yesterday's plates rattled. "Your *Sir Peter* lost our family's tin mines in a game of cards, and died choking on his own vomit! *That's* your hero?"

Julian's mouth dropped open. He had not expected this. When he found out about Sir Peter's death, the man had been buried two weeks already after what had been reported as a brief but intense illness of the lungs. Could *this* really be the truth behind his demise?

As undignified as it sounded, Julian couldn't outright deny Evan's claims, because Sir Peter was well known for his fondness of wine. Julian pulled off the wig and dropped it on the floor, unable to stand the itching in his scalp anymore. "May he rest in peace."

"May he rot in hell," Evan grumbled, and he seemed almost at the point of spitting on the floor in his disgust.

Julian clenched his teeth and looked straight into Evan's eyes. "Good riddance, because if you're not lying, the two of you will spend an eternity together."

"I suppose even the truth of that rotting drunkard can't sway your opinion of him." Evan grabbed a scone off the table but put it away with a sneer after one bite. "After all, he was so charming and generous. He wore the finest outfits, and spent a whole year in Italy. And I suppose the Italian leatherwork he purchased there was worth every penny."

"At least he never lay his hands on me," said Julian sharply.

Evan raised his eyebrows. "Unlike on the poor maid who used to work at Tredele. Beat her black and blue when he found out she carried his child. That got rid of *the problem* that same night. Lovely man. Truly."

Julian gasped, staring at Evan, at a loss of words. "I did not know," he mumbled in the end. "But then what makes you two so different?"

Evan leaned back in the armchair, and finally seemed deflated. "I never said I'm perfect."

Julian crumpled the front of his waistcoat. He wanted to demand Evan let him leave, but where was he supposed to go? Tredele was remote, and he didn't believe he'd be lent a horse for the ride. And if Father really wanted to hear nothing from Julian, then he'd be in the streets, with no source of income. He had nowhere to go.

Evan sighed and rubbed his forehead. "Come, I'll show you someone purer than either of us can ever be."

Evan got up and grabbed his jacket.

CHAPTER 8

EVAN

Evan would have liked the luxury of waking up to breakfast ready on the table, but he cared for his privacy too much to allow servants in the house before he was ready for them. So it had become his routine to get dressed, and only stroll over to the servants' cottage when he was ready to have them come into the house. It was an eccentricity, but he was beyond caring at this point in his life.

With Julian quietly walking by his side, it was hard for Evan to keep being annoyed. Even the burlap sack of an outfit couldn't make Julian less attractive. And now that the ghastly wig was gone, all Evan wanted to do was sink his fingers in the reddish blond hair and hold it tight while fucking that gorgeous man again.

It had been so many years since he dared lay a finger on another man that his elation knew no bounds despite all the hurtful words Julian threw at him. A part of him knew he shouldn't have made the demands he had, but the temptation had been too much, and when the opportunity arose, Evan took it like the bastard Julian told him he was. It wasn't like Julian could possibly think less of him.

The problem was that yesterday Evan had considered stealing just that one night from Julian. All he wanted was to see that perfect body shiver, Julian's thighs open to him, to taste the sweat off his skin. Just once. To feel his muscles tense and relax under Evan. Just once. To hear the moans of Julian's climax and smell his seed. Once, and once only.

Today, Evan wanted to devour Julian for breakfast, tea, and dinner. He was certain there was at least a part of Julian that enjoyed last night, and if Evan could just unlock that part of him for the few weeks they might have together, they'd please each other immensely. No one would need to know, and they'd part ways once the ransom issue was resolved in one way or another.

In all honesty, Evan needed the money desperately if Tredele was to ever thrive again. He barely scraped by to pay his servants' wages as it was, but the need that Julian awoke in him made Evan want to forget all his responsibilities and spend his days under the covers with the beautiful, if black-hearted, creature.

The plain clothes Julian wore since morning seemed like a mockery of his bright personality, and while they did not subdue his beauty, his silence was like a void in Evan's chest.

The sun was bright and warm, but as soon as the two of them reached the shadow of the trees beyond the stone walls of the gardens that Evan's mother used to call 'representative', the wind brought upon a chill. It was that time of year when the grass was fresh, and the branches sprouted vividly green leaves, but with the somber mood upon Evan, he couldn't truly enjoy the spring aura. Far on the horizon, clouds formed a strange shape, bulbous, with a dark rim low above the ground. He hoped the wind would blow them away, as he wasn't ready for rain to further worsen his mood.

They climbed up the grassy slope Evan knew like the back of his hand, and the sharp silhouette of the old disused church already loomed ahead, as gray and unwelcoming as it was every single time Evan made his way there.

The wind tousled both their hair in every possible direction, but Evan went on until they reached the low fence of stone and lime. There used to be a gate here, but with no priest to take care of the site and Evan not caring for it, the damaged one hadn't been replaced for years now. The residents of the yard didn't care either way.

The gravestones were rough, some of them already crumbled by age. Evan's family lay elsewhere, a place much more dignified than this small plot on the hill. If the dead wandered the Earth, at least the ones buried here could enjoy a beautiful scenery for miles.

The particular gravestone Evan guided Julian to made his heart heavy every time he looked at it, but if he wanted to rattle Julian and get something more than insults out of him, he figured this could be a start.

Evan dared put his hand on the small of Julian's back, his heart beating like mad, even at the tiny gesture. How was he to even approach Julian about these matters? Evan hadn't taken a lover in years. He hadn't even had anyone to talk to, let alone fuck.

Julian stiffened and took a step forward, away from Evan's palm.

"Peran used to be my father's footman," Evan started, annoyed by how high-pitched his voice sounded. He cleared his throat to little effect. "He was a good man. Did his duties to the letter, always smiled, laughed like a horse. You know the kind? I mean..." Evan took a deep breath, surprised that bringing back those memories agitated him so much.

Julian stared at the simple gravestone for the longest time, not even trying to keep his long hair from being flung into his face with each gust of wind. "I think so," he said in the end.

Was this Evan's chance for a sliver of closeness? He pulled a piece of string out of his long leather jacket, and combed Julian's hair back with his fingers. Julian's shoulders stirred, but he didn't try to fight off Evan's hands, so Evan went ahead with tying his mane back.

Evan could recall Peran's dimples as well as the day Peran had been taken into gaol by the constable. His heart sank as he spoke, "But he committed the crime of sodomy, you see. It seemed luck was in his favor though. The jury decided there was not enough evidence the act itself had taken place, and since he was a man of such great reputation otherwise, the judge sentenced him to the pillory for an attempt at the disorderly act."

Julian gasped and turned his face toward Evan. He opened his mouth, not saying anything, but there was a sharp look in his eyes.

Evan stepped away and put his hands in the pockets of his coat, stinging from his own words. "He served his sentence in the worst of weathers, and even though the punishment only lasted two hours, people abused him so cruelly, and..." Evan took a deep breath, "so severely, that he died the next day. He was a good person."

Julian's Adam's apple moved up and down his throat, and his eyelashes fluttered. "People can be cruel."

"He didn't deserve to die or suffer." Evan stepped closer and ran his fingers over the warm stone. "Do you think what happened to him was just?" He looked at Julian, searching for reactions. Was there a part of Julian that he was simply afraid to express out of fear of punishment?

Julian stepped back and watched the gravestone for several minutes. "I think... the state should not concern itself with matters dealt with in private. People do worse things and don't have to die for it."

Evan stood shoulder to shoulder with Julian, watching him closely. "So you think it's not that bad of a crime to want another man? Yesterday, you said I should hang."

Julian's face stilled, as if it had turned into a mask, and then he rapidly turned around and shoved Evan at the grave. "Take your hands away from me!"

Evan exhaled and couldn't bear the cold knife twisting in his gut. The answer was on his tongue before he could truly think, as always biting back with a vengeance. "Is it because you have another lover? It didn't seem like your first time yesterday." In truth though, Evan couldn't tell. He had no idea if it was possible to discover such a thing without asking.

Julian stepped away from him, eyes wild and unfocused. His nostrils flared as he opened and closed his mouth several times. "I'm not like that," he said firmly in the end, then turned around and rushed through the opening in the fence.

Evan followed, already regretting his words. Not being around people really had taken a toll on his skill in saying the right things.

"Julian! Wait!"

But Julian ignored him and all but ran down the hill, toward the patch of tall trees between the church and the wall around Tredele.

Evan cursed beneath his breath and ran faster, until he managed to grab Julian's wrist. "Wait! ...Please."

Julian wobbled but didn't try to run and just looked at Evan's hand on his arm. His chest was working up and down as he took a few deep breaths before staring back at Evan.

"I just wanted to show you that it's not only... monsters like me who enjoy these things. Good people can too." Evan had to fight himself tooth and nail not to brush his thumb over Julian's hot, throbbing wrist.

"Since when do you care what I enjoy? You didn't last night," said Julian, hitting Evan with his words as if they were acid.

"I recall things differently," Evan hissed. "Did I not give you pleasure in return?"

"You need to keep a good opinion of yourself somehow," bit back Julian, this time not looking away. His eyes were bright again, but not with amusement of wit. They were hateful.

Evan let go of Julian's wrist, angry, confused, and hurt, all at the same time. How was he to navigate this? That night in his observatory, he'd been certain there was that glimmer of attraction. That tingling in his fingers and toes, so much like what he had felt around Peran. Maybe if he had acted back then, today wouldn't have been such a mess? Had he lost his only chance in years, or had he misjudged it terribly, and there had never been a chance to start with?

"We do not need to talk of this then," Evan said bitterly. He couldn't bear to look into Julian's face anymore.

"Let's not," agreed Julian, closing his eyes for a brief moment. He rubbed his face and pushed back loose strands of hair that had escaped the fastening at his nape. "I'm sorry about your servant."

Evan gave a nod, and they pushed on back to the house. He had a sudden urge to ride out with Noir and forget about all this Julian nonsense, but having him by his side, especially now that he knew the scent of Julian's skin so intimately, he found it difficult to leave him alone.

They walked through a narrow underground passage between a tapered valley leading the way to the river and the gardens, and despite the bitter taste in his mouth, Evan still wouldn't let his gaze stray away from Julian's elegant shoulders, which swayed in front of him like bait he knew he shouldn't reach for.

But as he thought of Noir, it occurred to him how enchanted Julian had been with Evan's horse, and so he walked past the main house and into the courtyard by the stables. He knew it was sneaky to try to gain sympathy through his mount, but at this point he didn't feel there were many cards left in his deck. For so many years, Evan had believed he'd never have a chance to approach a man again that he gave up on that dream. And now when there was the faintest glimmer of an opportunity, he wasn't in the least bit prepared.

Jory's tall form emerged from the open doors when they approached. He was arching his shoulders as he carried a large bag of feed, but as soon as he spotted Evan, he put it down and raised his hand in greeting. "Good morning... Sir. Mr. Berry," he said, taking off his hat to reveal the brilliant shade of red that he inherited from Mrs. Merryn. At least he didn't have his mother's sharp tongue. "Will you need of the horses, sir?" he asked, flashing them a bright grin.

At least Jory was happy to see him. "No, we won't be riding out today. But I will feed Noir myself."

Jory scratched the brown birthmark at the side of his cheek, but he seemed to have remembered his good manners and quickly stuffed his hand in his pocket. "Absolutely, sir. I groomed both of them earlier, but I still have to change their water. Should I do it now, or do you wish to have the stable to yourself?"

Evan stole a glance at Julian, his mind filled with images of his tight body in the hay, hands tied with the horse's reins, like he had so often done with Peran years ago. Since then he couldn't help but get excited at the image of a man tied up. Both shameful and arousing, giving him a sense of power and guilt over it all at once. If Julian knew that it was the main reason Evan had liked tying him up for the night, he'd most likely spit into Evan's face again.

"Mr. Berry and I will surely manage." Evan patted Jory's arm. "You can tell your mother we'll have dinner at dusk." Luncheon would be a less exciting affair, since the household was barely scraping by on rent, so he'd usually have a simple, cold meal of bread and cheese. "Unless..." He turned to Julian, desperate to please the man somehow. "You'd like to eat sooner?"

Julian's eyes darted from Jory to Evan, and he shifted his weight, finally in a mood that couldn't be described with a variation of the word *anger*. His pretty lips opened, and he shook his head gently. "No. dusk is... it is agreeable."

"Very well, sir," said Jory, picking up the huge sack. "I will just drop this where it belongs. There is an open one inside. You know where to find me," he said and winked, strolling toward the shed across the courtyard.

Julian looked after him, with his mouth still open.

Evan frowned. "Did you agree just for the sake of it? Would you prefer another time after all?"

Julian looked back at Evan. "Ex— no, no. I don't dine early. Not usually."

"Would you care to help me feed— bloody son of a crosseyed mongrel!" Evan bared his teeth at the sight of no one else but Mr. Thomas Blackwell, strolling their way on his black and white horse as if he had every right to be here. At least he didn't seem to have noticed them just yet. His mount looked like a cow, and it was strangely appropriate as the plump old man's ride. "Go inside, and don't you dare make a peep," he whispered, and urged Julian into the stable.

Quick footsteps died down behind him as he walked to meet his neighbor halfway, do his duty and greet the unwanted guest. There wasn't enough time to go back into the house and don a suit, so he raised his head and marched on in the same long coat he wore when working, although he tried to be as dignified as possible.

It was unnerving how well dressed old Blackwell always was. For a man of over fifty years of age, he was surprisingly up to date with current fashions, or so Evan had been told. What he could see with his own eyes was that Blackwell always wore expensive fabrics and bright colors, something his young wife was likely responsible for.

Blackwell's gelding stopped in the courtyard, and he raised his hand in greeting before getting off the horse with as much grace as a man of his age and stature could. "Ah, I'm happy to find you at home, Sir Evan," he said politely, even though they both knew Evan rarely left Tredele, sending his servants to deal with all kinds of business that did not require his immediate attention. He adjusted his tawny suit of the finest wool and pulled his thick hand over the white wig to put stray hair into place.

"Ah, yes, yes, I haven't had a chance to answer your letter, Mr. Blackwell, I'm very sorry about that. I've been so busy lately with all the repairs and adjustments needed in spring." Evan prayed to God that Julian stayed put and wouldn't decide on a sudden plea for help from Blackwell, but even though he believed his prisoner submissive for now, knowing he was hiding so close made Evan sweat. "What brings you all the way here?" They both knew. The loan Evan had already failed to pay back on time.

Blackwell patted the neck of his horse, only prolonging Evan's agony. "You couldn't call at Fairfield Park when I requested your presence last week," he said in the end, turning his watery gaze toward Evan. And that invitation had been surely about the debt as well.

Evan wondered how long they would both beat around the bush before the demands came flying into Evan's face. The stunt that resulted in Julian's presence at his home had been meant to secure the funds necessary to pay off Blackwell, but so far Evan had only lost money over the bargain he'd made. The wages of his servants came before his needs, so here he was, even further down the rabbit hole of impoverishment.

Evan nodded with a deep frown. "Two of my sheep fell ill, and I have too soft of a heart to just let the poor beasts die. I had to arrange some help for them, so my trip had to be postponed. I'm sure you understand. Doesn't Fairfield Park host a whole flock of sheep as well?" He tried to change the topic, even though he knew Blackwell wouldn't let it go. The man was infuriatingly kind, and too polite for his own good, but he was not stupid.

Blackwell sighed. "You have been missed. You remember my daughter, Elizabeth? She was asking for you," he said with a small smile.

Oh, yes. Elizabeth. The answer to all of Evan's troubles, yet the bane of his existence. If only Evan weren't more interested in lean male muscle and tight asses, she would do as a wife, but only because an arrangement with her would have solved Tredele's financial problems.

But no matter how much Evan was willing to sacrifice to pre-serve his heritage and make his ancestors proud, this was one step he wasn't willing to take. His life was miserable enough without a wife of just sixteen making a racket all around the house and changing everything he loved. Maybe him and Julian weren't all that different after all.

"Did she now? That's too sweet of her. I'm sorry to have been a disappointment."

Fortunately for Evan, Elizabeth spared him the ordeal of hav-ing to reject her and vacillating over the issue for months when she made it clear that Evan was much too old, and most of all, too boring for her taste. Evan was certain the girl got a good talking-to by her father after the incident, but the damage had been done. Blackwell had to be truly desperate to make the union with Cornwall's last surviving Penhart to pretend that catastrophic blunder had never happened. Then again, maybe not mentioning the debt in favor of talking about Elizabeth's supposed affections for Evan was a form of pressure that was acceptable in Blackwell's polite world of negotiation and not mentioning the unmentionable.

"As a matter of fact, she still feels terribly sorry for the way she acted during your last visit at Fairfield Park. The silly girl drank more wine than she could handle. I hope you can find it in your heart to forgive her the offense."

Evan smiled widely and shook his head. "I have already forgotten about it, and I look forward to making amends for the way I presented myself to her. I suppose a visit to the tailor will be a necessity before I visit at Fairfield again." Evan laughed, but his mind was calculating his options at a rapid pace. If Blackwell let him stall with the debt for a few more months, or at least weeks in hope of a union between Evan and his daughter, the ransom money was still a possible answer to his troubles.

Sometimes Tredele seemed like a noose around his neck instead of being a place to call home. But with all the expectations his ancestors put on him from beyond the grave, he couldn't bear letting the place go to waste.

Blackwell gave a curt nod. "Don't worry about our financial arrangement for now. I know I can trust you. I only hope my Elizabeth will see you again soon. Nothing too formal," he said and was already mounting his horse.

Evan nodded, hoping that his loose hair covered the sweat that had surely beaded on his forehead. Would he actually end up marrying Elizabeth one day and producing five or ten little Penharts to not let his family name be forgotten? The sole idea of this kind of domesticity made him want to go back to the stables, mount Noir, and just ride away from it all.

"That is most generous Mr. Blackwell. I'm sure an opportunity to call will arise soon."

Blackwell nodded, looking at Evan from the height of his gelding's back. "I believe that as well. For now, this whole matter stays between us."

They exchanged a few more polite sentences that left Evan's chest feeling raw with a growing sense of failure. He was glad to see Blackwell go.

His face quickly returned to its natural state from the fake smiles he was forced to produce. With his shoulders heavy with the burden of debt and responsibility, he made his way back to the stable, but he did stop for a moment, and took in the sight of Tredele. Built by his ancestors four centuries ago, the heavy stone walls of the great hall were as much of a fortress as they were a prison, just like all the rooms of the house.

"Julian?" he asked quietly when he walked into the stable. The last thing he needed now was loathing in those pretty eyes, and words that were worse than blades.

Something creaked, and Julian emerged from behind a wooden divider in his somber suit, with a halo of straw in his long hair.

Evan raised his eyebrows. "Do you like lying in the hay?" he tried, wondering if he could manage to turn this conversation into a fuck.

Julian frowned. "Does your stableboy like to lie in the hay?"

Evan was so thrown off guard by the question all he managed was a questioning grunt.

Julian sighed and picked some of the dried grass off his head, not looking Evan's way.

Evan swallowed and walked up to Noir's stall, petting the black head when it emerged over the gate. "Wait. Are you jealous already?" He gave Julian a quizzical glance.

Julian's mouth twisted, and he walked up to the second stall where the white mare the servants sometimes used was kept. "On the contrary. I feel sorry for the fellow. He is in no position to deny his master's advances."

Evan sneered. "Ah, right, because you assume he would surely want to refuse me." Since that's how loathsome Evan was to everyone. At least Noir didn't seem to think so, and nipped on Evan's hand with his soft lips.

Julian petted Snow's neck absentmindedly. "I can't imagine any man wanting to be put in that position."

Evan gritted his teeth at his advances being so despised. "You haven't seen enough of the world then. All some men crave is a prick poking them all night long."

"Maybe you should pick one from the madhouse then."

"You are being unnecessarily cruel." Evan looked away and focused on feeding Noir instead. The grain had been already prepared, so all he had to do was to toss it in the feeder. He should have never taken up Julian on the misguided ransom idea. He should have never revealed his proclivities.

Julian stayed silent for several moments until finally speaking again. "It is for me to decide whether it is cruel or not."

Evan scratched Noir behind the ear. "And no, I do not bed Jory. Even though I don't think it's any of your business."

"You're right. It's not. I don't want to hear anything about it," said Julian sharply.

Noir whinnied softly and moved his mouth over Evan's cheek, breathing hot air all over his hair, as if offering support. It was much needed, because Evan's heart was sinking into a dark hole. He couldn't afford to let Julian go no matter how much he wanted to get his life back to normal again. Blackwell was breathing down Evan's neck about the debt, and Tredele's roof was in dire need of renovation. Unless Evan succeeded at another robbery, the possible ransom for Julian wasn't something he could just let go of.

"Are you sure?" Evan tried and pushed the sack with feed Julian's way, suggesting he could feed Snow.

Julian glanced at the sack, as if contemplating whether it was worthy of his attention. In the end, he picked it up, clearly trying to not look as strained by its weight as he probably was. "I've never been so sure of anything in my entire life."

"What made you wonder about Jory then? Did you imagine me and him together?" Evan pushed on, watching Julian's every move.

Julian took a double handful of the grain sack and shoveled it into the feeder in the other stall, clearly not familiar with the process. He probably never groomed his own horse—if he even owned one. "Because I have firsthand knowledge of your predatory ways," he said tightly.

Evan rolled his eyes. "Predatory. Says the man trying to cheat his own family out of a substantial amount of money. You try to present yourself as much more proper than you actually are."

Julian shook his head without a word, moving more energetically until he decided he'd given the mare enough food. Evan knew he'd have to see to it that Jory fed her more later, just in case.

Evan took a step closer, hoping that tending to the mare could have had a calming effect on Julian. "Maybe secretly you really want to leave propriety behind…"

Julian glanced at him with a guarded expression. The silence stretched, and even the horses seemed to comply, too busy eating to disturb the tense atmosphere.

This was the moment for Evan to try his luck.

With his heart beating like mad, in one swift move Evan slid one hand to Julian's hip, and the other to the back of his head, leaning in to kiss those succulent lips that he hadn't yet had a chance to sample. How much he wanted to lie with this man in the hay, spend into him, and forget all about Blackwell, the debt, and Tredele, even if just for an hour or two.

But before their lips could meet, Julian slapped Evan so hard Evan saw stars and stepped back, still confused seconds later.

Julian was leaning forward, hands balled into fists, eyes steadily focused on Evan, as if he were preparing for violence. When he spoke, his voice was low and quiet, yet something about it tore right through Evan's chest.

"Don't *ever* try to kiss me again."

Evan clenched his teeth and took another step back, the bitterness of the rejection poisoning his blood. He couldn't believe it. Was he so out of touch with human interactions that he'd misread all the warning signs? Or was he so desperate for a warmth he hadn't received in years that he projected all his dreams onto the pretty face of a man he didn't truly know?

Either way, he now got the message loud and clear.

"Let's go back to the house. Luncheon will be served soon."

CHAPTER 9

JULIAN

Julian looked out the window. It was a warm day in April, and there was just enough sun to brighten the cold walls of Tredele, even at five in the afternoon. The clutter in the main room wouldn't let Julian focus on his writing, or even reading, and Evan had finally complied with his wishes and allowed him use the small study adjoining his bedroom.

It was very much like a prison cell, with just one window and walls crowded by tapestries that were far past their prime and cut to accommodate all fittings, with no regard to what they were depicting. The small space made Julian scowl, with its pale, earthy colors and the smell of dust, but it was Julian's own, at least for as long as Evan wanted him out of his hair.

Two weeks had passed since the incident in the stable, and Julian's actions then must have finally made his feelings clear, as Evan had completely withdrawn his attentions and hardly even spoke to him for the first few days thereafter. Julian had been satisfied with that turn of events at first, but as time went by, the constant silence was slowly creeping up his back and choking his throat. Being locked up most days, he hardly ever saw the servants either. He wasn't used to not having anyone to open his lips to, and once he was certain there would be no more foul play involved, he couldn't help but seek Evan's attention. Without people, even with the most interesting books lying on his desk, the days seemed to stretch into a never-ending string of nothingness.

Sometimes, just like today, Evan would disappear into his observatory for hours, and there had to be some secret way to opening the hidden passage, because when Julian followed him once, the bookshelves wouldn't budge no matter how hard he tried to solve the puzzle of the secret door. It felt like an appropriate metaphor for the wall that had grown between them, and the only positive change—not being tied to the bed each night, could not compensate for the lack of companionship.

Some nights, Julian lay in the dark, listening to Evan's breath just inches away and imagined the rope was tight around his wrists, secured above his head like Marsyas's on Evan's favorite painting. With Julian fastened tight to the wooden frame of the bed, Evan could have easily rolled on top of him and taken all the forbidden kisses he wanted. He could have drawn hot lines on Julian's thighs with his fingers and fuck him however he chose to. There would have been nothing Julian could do to stop him. And yet it wasn't happening, and the closeness in bed was a stark contrast to Evan's reserved behavior.

Now that Evan was speaking to him again and Julian allowed himself to wear bright colors once more, the two of them settled into a somber routine of spending time in one room without disturbing each other. They would share words about philosophy, horseflesh, or any other topic suitable in polite conversation, and Julian would sometimes read a few passages of the book he was working on, but their relationship remained distanced and tense. Julian was glad Evan provided him with a space of his own, where he could flee the constant reminder of that shameful night two weeks ago.

But that was not the end of Julian's troubles. Now that he had privacy, food and board, all the time in the world to write, his muse avoided him as if he were a plague-stricken beggar. With time, he became so starved for human interaction his soul felt as dry as his throat after a long walk in a desert, and it became painfully apparent inspiration came to him through human interaction.

He groaned and put his forehead against the huge mahogany desk which must have been over a century old. Was this supposed to be his life now? Lonely, miserable, and uneventful?

He scribbled a few more words, then covered them with yet another twist of ink. It was as if something had thrown a velvet curtain to block out the sun of his natural abilities. Even the spirit of the ancient gladiator, whom he had earlier seen in his mind with such clarity, now seemed like a shadow of the man Julian felt he was. If theories about characters being ghosts who wanted their stories told and whispered into the ears of men sensible enough to hear their voice to make that happen were true, then Julian's connection with Gaius the gladiator had been broken.

He put down the quill and stood up, stretching his muscles as he paced around the studio. Gaze cast to the floor, he entertained himself with carefully placing the tips of his shoes on the edge of one ply of wood and another. His mind wandered from the walls of the *Black Crab*, his favorite tavern in Looe, always bursting at the seams with sailors, free traders, and men from all walks of life, to the streets of London that never seemed empty, to comfortable discussions with his friends.

He remembered the evening when Evan took him to the observatory and told him about the sky ocean, which spurred to life all kinds of imaginary worlds in Julian's head. How splendid would it be to become a sky explorer and somehow reach the shores of those unknown lands as the first of his kind? What did the people of Venus really look like if they walked over ground that was as bright as the moon? If there were people in London with skin as brown as the mahogany desk, why wouldn't Venusians be green? It was entirely plausible.

Julian put his hand on the wall and continued his walk, brushing his fingertips over the old thread of the tapestry. His reason was preoccupied by the thought of the Chinese, with their exotic culture, originating in the skies when something budged slightly beneath his touch.

Julian stared into the face of Odysseus, depicted in the tapestry in a moment of triumph after tricking the Cyclops. His nose, sharp as a hawk's beak, protruded slightly under Julian's touch. He bent down and raised the thick fabric.

There was a door behind it. It had been there all along. And it was tiny, as if meant for a child, or... a fairy? He pushed on the handle with caution, wondering if Evan had known of it and let Julian find it as some kind of trap, or had Julian stumbled onto something Evan was ignorant of.

He took a deep breath and cringed when the door yielded to his force and opened with a loud, unforgiving screech. What he saw was nothing like he'd expected, and his mouth stretched into a smile. Inside the small cupboard-like room, wine rested on wooden shelves, waiting to be picked by a thirsty man like grapes off a vine.

And Julian was exceptionally thirsty.

He spent several minutes examining the bottles before finally picking up two and returning to the desk. His veins ached for the familiar warmth, and he uncorked the first bottle, smelling the sharp, fruity bite of the wine inside. If the rush of drink could guide his hand over paper, then all the better.

He took a swig straight from the bottle and melted into the chair, savoring the slight bitterness of it on his tongue. The sweet poison was exquisite, of a quality far superior to the offerings from Julian's favorite tavern. He was certain it must have been Sir Peter's collection, as Evan despised wine and didn't want Julian to have any, even at dinner.

Maybe it was the reason behind Evan's uptight attitude? Maybe if they shared a glass or two, some kind of understanding could pass between them again. With wine buzzing in their heads, they could simply forget that fateful night they'd shared, and move on.

Now that Julian had had two weeks to ponder said events, he reckoned that Evan must have somehow misjudged him. Because he now kept his hands away as if Julian's body were covered in pockmarks. Did it mean that Julian had given off signs he wasn't aware of? Or was it just Julian's handsome features that blinded Evan to the reality that his attention was unwanted? Julian liked to imagine it was the latter.

He drank, watching a seagull struggling against the wind outside. They were such fierce birds, so maybe they could be the key to reach the black waters of the night sky? Maybe they could transgress the thin fibre between the worlds and carry Julian high above? Could they carry two men at once, to face an adventure that would change his and Evan's lives?

Julian drank some more wine, again focused on the piece of paper in front of him. The clock in the room where he and Evan slept was ticking loudly on the other side of the wall, and by the time the sun was descending toward the horizon, Julian had two full pages covered with rows of ink. He had gotten sloppy at some point and stained the paper with imprints of his hand, but that was of no importance when Gaius the gladiator was speaking to him again.

Halfway through the second bottle, he wrote, And his face was just like my own, yet on the inside it held secrets no man could understand with a clear mind.

Julian's mind was no longer clear. It rocked him with the most pleasant kind of dizziness, the one that left one warm on the inside and utterly carefree. His fingertips tingled, and he rested his head atop one hand, breathing in the ink, which at this moment felt just as appetizing as wine. The main character of his book, Francis, saw something in Gaius, but even Gaius himself wouldn't yet tell Julian what it was. This unknown truth was burning a brand into the underside of Francis's skin, and by extension—also Julian's, his tar-black eyes speaking in a tongue Julian could not decipher. Something was missing still.

The loneliness of Julian's confinement made him all the more aware of voices in the courtyard, and he perked up when he realized they were approaching the wall of his study. The one window that provided him with light was small and nailed shut, but he could still hear the words well, as the wood was cracked in one place.

The world swayed around Julian when he stood up. Resting his hands on the desktop, he dragged himself all the way to the window and rested his flushed cheek on the cold stones just below the glass.

"I told you, girl. Julian Reece. He wore a green suit. Long hair, a reddish blond, doesn't wear his wigs too often," said an unknown voice outside, and the mention of Julian's name made him stiffen. Had Father not given up on him after all? Was he still being sought out?

His throat pulsed with unshed words, but he remained silent, listening on to the conversation.

"Maybe I will go ask my master," Esther uttered, and Julian could already hear that she was about to cry. The girl was far too sensitive for her own good. She now stood with her shoulders sagging and rubbed her forearm, as if she were freezing.

Even though the view outside was a bit of a blur, Julian still saw the man in black grab Esther's wrist. "No, stupid girl, I'm asking *you*. I have all the authority of the law to make you answer. You do *not* want to lie to me."

Julian took a sharp breath. A constable, or his deputy perhaps? Either way, he should not question Esther without her master's permission. Where was Evan when he was really needed?

"Mr. Pascoe, please. I know of no man of that name. I have me duties to attend to, and me master will be cross if I fail 'im."

"Are you saying that your master is a man prone to violence?" Pascoe asked, and when Julian squinted, he saw that he was still gripping Esther's arm. He now knew who it was. The grim constable, who'd sent a few of Julian's acquaintances to the gaol. A man universally disliked despite his skill as a doctor.

He wanted to start shouting himself, just to stop the bastard from shaking the poor girl, but then a tall, broad-shouldered silhouette emerged from the house, and Julian's heart pulsed with heat.

Pascoe let go of Esther immediately, and she stumbled a few steps back as a man Julian recognized as Evan even without seeing his face clearly, stormed through the courtyard.

"You will let go of my maid at once!" Evan raised his voice before he reached them. "Shouldn't you announce yourself if you wish to see me, or talk to my servants?"

Pascoe set his shoulders straight, like a bird trying to appear bigger by spreading its wings. "Sir Evan. I'm glad to see you. The girl failed to tell me where you were," he said, and Julian wanted to climb on the windowsill and call out to Evan that the bastard was lying.

"No, she did not fail at all, Mr. Pascoe. She was instructed to tell you I am away if she sees you."

Julian's eyes went wide at both the rudeness and the audacity of those words. Those things were done, not said out loud.

Pascoe shook his head. "Your arrogance will one day be your downfall, sir. I am merely doing the job I've been entrusted with by this parish. Or don't you want the villain who'd taken poor young Mr. Reece persecuted and the victim found?"

Julian's breath stilled as he watched Evan. This was about the two of them. His back instantly dampened with sweat as he watched Evan in search of a crack that would somehow betray the truth.

"We have never been on good terms, Mr. Pascoe, and everyone knows I rarely have any guests. You are wasting your time here out of spite, because you know damn well that If I knew of that poor man's fate, I would have sent word to his father," said Evan, and even Julian was in awe of the excellent quality of his lies. "If there is nothing else I can help you with, I advise you should leave, Mr. Pascoe."

"I merely believed yourself or your servants could have heard of the incident and shed a new light on the events. It's been a fortnight since Mr. William Reece received the letter of ransom, and the man taken seems to have vanished. He could be dead for all we know, and even his own family washed their hands of him."

"Mr. William Reece's announcement in the Western Flying Post led me to believe he reckons his son was complicit in his own disappearance," Evan said to Pascoe's silence.

Julian stepped away from the wall, his mind muddled from the wine. He didn't want to listen to any of this anymore. He'd been avoiding the papers since he'd read the response, but the truth had been pushed into his face yet again.

The tense voices outside became a blur, as the conversation continued for a while, but Pascoe finally left, not knowing that his hunch to search for truth in Tredele was on point.

Julian grabbed the bottle from the desk and swirled the red liquid before taking two gulps so large they made his throat ache from the sheer volume of liquid passing through at once. If his father did not want to see him anymore and would not pay the ransom, then why was Julian still here? Evan should have understood by now that there was no chance in hell for compensation.

Julian heard the quick steps outside his study as if through cotton, so when the door swung open and Evan barged in, he startled Julian so much the bottle almost slipped through his fingers.

He pushed back against the wall, blinking to focus on the tall form of his host. Even when Julian was in his best disposition, Evan was a threatening presence, but now that everything seemed blurry at the edges, the man was like the Cyclops, ready to consume Julian in some kind of bloody feast. His eyes burned as powerfully as Gaius the gladiator's.

"I—" Evan looked around with his mouth still open. "What in all hells is this? Who brought you wine?" He walked up to Julian and... smelled him loudly.

Julian curled his shoulders, but even the icy touch of the wall couldn't make him sober now. "No one. Only you have the key," he said, annoyed when pronouncing the words turned out to be a struggle.

"I can't believe this," Evan hissed and grabbed his arm. "Are you completely drunk?" He looked back to the desk, where another bottle stood proudly, as if announcing to the world that Julian had in fact emptied two bottles of wine.

Julian groaned and pushed away from Evan, but the moment he moved from the wall, the uneven floor proved too much for him, and he tripped over a crack, falling on the desk with a loud rattle. Cold wetness stained his fingers, and when he opened his eyes, he noticed a dark spot of ink spreading over the wood like the cloud that had overcome his mind.

"Christ! Are you all right?" Evan pulled him up and held him steady with ridiculous ease. "Do you feel sick? Look at me," he demanded, but his piercing gaze was trying to meet Julian's, and when it did, all Julian saw in Evan's eyes was care. Not even a trace of anger was left in their black irises.

He stared back, pinned in place by the pure darkness in that gaze. "I found your wine storage," he mumbled in the end. "It made me so, so warm."

Evan glanced to the door that was once more obscured by the tapestry, and sighed. "And I'm the villain here," he grumbled, "yet you steal from me at leisure. Let's go, you need some air, you drunk."

"You locked me in your castle, all alone," whimpered Julian and slapped Evan's arm without much enthusiasm.

"You said you needed peace for your writing." Evan shook his head, and wrapped his arm around Julian's waist, leading him forward, but the moment Evan pushed him, Julian flew forward again, falling to his knees with a loud crack. He scowled and rolled to his side, patting down the aching joints. This happened every single time he drank too much—one of the reasons to stay in the tavern until morning.

"But I'm lonely here."

"Oh, God... You're embarrassing yourself." Evan leaned down and helped him get back to his feet. Julian wanted to protest, say that he was better off staying on the floor for now, but then the world around him spun much more rapidly than expected, and he didn't have to walk anymore. Evan picked him up in his arms, and held him in a tight grip.

Julian's head rolled over Evan's shoulder, and he looked up at him, too stunned to say anything at first. He could feel the floor calling out to his body, dragging his weight down, but Evan seemed to carry it with such ease, as if Julian weighed nothing at all. He touched one of Evan's arms through the sleeve, assessing its thickness, and the muscle beneath the linen was steady despite bulging from the effort.

"You're like a giant."

Evan groaned. "I can always count on a compliment from you. What next? A morgawr?"

Julian frowned and finally hooked his arms around Evan's neck to secure himself. He looked up at him from the safe cradle of Evan's arms. "Why? You look nothing like one."

Evan rolled his eyes and readjusted the way he held Julian with a grunt of strain. "You told me I'm a monster, and a ghost. Now a giant. Why not a morgawr?"

The side of Julian's forearm brushed against Evan's unshaven jaw, and it made his heart rattle. Julian swallowed, suddenly aware that they weren't moving. "Morgawrs are ugly," he said in the end. Evan was a most handsome man by anyone's standards.

Evan continued the march toward the bed through stacks of books and trinkets. "And I am not?"

Julian let his head fall on Evan's shoulder and turned his nose closer to the fabric that had soaked in Evan's natural scent all day. He must have spent a great deal of time in the sun, or at least that was how the garment smelled to Julian. "No, you're not."

Evan sighed. "You really *are* drunk. I hope you get better soon. I'm much more used to you hating me."

Julian snorted, pulling harder at Evan's neck, afraid the man would drop him after all. "It's you who hates me."

"I only hate you because I cannot have you." The words struck Julian with their raw honesty, leaving him at a loss. The dizziness in his head wasn't helping in coming up with an answer, but then Evan carefully put Julian down on the bed.

The mattress was a welcome embrace, albeit a cold one when compared to the closeness of Evan's chest. Julian reached out to Evan, pulling his fingers over his arm, but was frustrated when his hand fell to the covers under its own weight. A heavy feeling he didn't expect sat on his chest like a bad dream.

"You only care for my body," he whispered.

"Not only, but I do care for your body, so do tell me: will you be sick? Should I bring a bucket?" Evan stroked Julian's hair.

Julian tossed his head over the pillow, then leaned into the touch, surprised by how soft it was. "Liar. Everyone only cares about my body. You. My father who wanted me to breed some woman from London. The people who drink on my money at the tavern," mumbled Julian, closing his eyes to memorize the gentle trail of fingers over his scalp.

Evan sighed loudly, but his hand stayed in Julian's hair. "Why do you care what I think?"

Julian shuddered and opened his eyes to meet the burning embers of Evan's gaze. He reached out to them and rested his fingertips just below, on Evan's cheek. It scorched his skin the way a blazing fireplace would in the middle of winter. How could he answer such a multilayered question?

"I liked talking to you."

Evan pulled his hand away, his gaze no less intense than before. "You need to focus on something. I'll bring the writing you did today, and we can talk about that."

Julian moaned and tried to grab Evan, but he was already gone. He tried to follow, but the air was like a deep river, pulling him down again as effortlessly as a whirl would. "Don't leave me again. I'm going crazy."

It seemed like forever until Evan approached Julian as sound-lessly as a cat, and pulled off his shoes.

"How are you feeling *now*?" Evan asked and climbed on the bed, pulling Julian farther toward its center.

"Like a sheep for tomorrow's dinner dragged into the cave by the wolf?" whispered Julian, looking up to the handsome face so close by. His whole body was burning with the wine, and so any kind of touch felt more intense than usual.

Evan groaned and pulled away, focusing on the pages instead of on Julian. "You're not a fair maiden."

"No, I'm a whore," muttered Julian, watching his feet, which seemed endlessly far away. His mouth was dry, and he longed for more wine to drown all his sorrows.

"Oh, so we're back to that one again?" Evan rolled his eyes and looked over the paper. "How much do you charge, whore?"

"Not sure. You bent me over before I could think of a price."

"You better think of a price then, because I've heard men like me are much more open about their cravings where you dream of going. Where was it? Rome? Venice? Naples?"

Julian's mouth dropped, and his eyes started stinging, as if Evan kicked sand into them. "I'm not going anywhere. My father won't pay the ransom, so you'll have me rotting at your mercy."

Evan went silent for a while. "He will pay up, I am sure of it." He put away Julian's writing and leaned over him, to untangle Julian's messy cravat. A thoughtful gesture, as it helped Julian take a larger gasp of air.

He swallowed hard, sensing the warm fingers that were still resting against his throat. "How about your father. Did he love you?"

Evan stilled, watching him with surprise written all over his face. "I... I was only ever meant to be my brother's shadow."

Julian put his hand over Evan's and squeezed it. "You're not a shadow," he said with an undignified slur at the end. "You're too intense to be a shadow."

Evan lay down next to Julian, his thumb slowly trailing over Julian's palm. "You're the one who said I was the Ghost of Tredele."

Julian watched him with his throat tightening. The touch was so soft, so considerate. Like that time their hands met on the telescope in the observatory. "I did not call you that. It's stories of people who never met you. You're more like a storm that comes without warning, and one cannot know what it will leave in its wake."

Evan sighed loudly, tickling Julian's ear with his breath. "Do you like it when it rains?"

Julian gasped at the warm sensation against his skin and slowly rolled to his side, now bringing their faces so close Evan could surely smell the wine on him just as well as Julian sensed Evan's scent. It was all hay, sun, and stone after a storm. Masculine and intoxicating in its own way.

"When I was a boy, I used to walk in the rain. I would go barefoot and collect frogs. Rain has its own music, you know it too?" he asked, seeking answers in Evan's eyes.

Evan pressed on the middle of Julian's palm with his thumb. "I do. I like to sit in my observatory when it rains and listen to the tapping against the glass. I'm sorry if a storm was too much for you to bear."

Julian sighed, watching Evan's long fingers slide against his skin, as if the conflict between them had never started. He liked that alternative world. "I would welcome a storm with open arms as long as it doesn't leave me a charred shell."

Evan moved his fingers to Julian's waistcoat and swirled them in between the buttons. "A storm doesn't always have to bring lightning..."

Julian took a deep breath, squeezing Evan's hand before he even thought about relaxing his muscles. And once it happened, he just held on, taking deep gulps of air. "But it did. You don't think much of me. You told me so. You told me you have no other use for me. You burned me."

Evan looked away. "You told me I disgust you, and yet you hold my hand," he whispered.

Julian clenched his teeth when his muddled thoughts returned to that moment when Evan had rolled him around and leaned over him. A warm shudder trailed down his spine. "I'm disgusted with myself."

"Is it because you drank so much wine?" It seemed to be an attempt at a joke, but it didn't make Julian feel any better.

"No. It's because I let you bend me over when I knew how little I mean to you," whispered Julian, curling his knees toward his chest.

Evan mirrored Julian's movement, and their knees touched, stirring embers somewhere between their bodies. "I guess I am a monster after all."

Julian shook his head. "I don't know anymore. I look out the window of the study all day in hope something happens. It did today. Esther is lucky to have a master like you," he said, avoiding Evan's eyes, but it beckoned him to focus on the warm lips in front of him instead. Julian still remembered their whisper against his skin. So soft and warm, like summer rainfall arousing goose bumps all over his back.

Evan bared his teeth. "That scoundrel Pascoe shouldn't have come here."

"You dealt with him." Julian pulled on Evan's forefinger, playing with the warm flesh, just for the pleasure of it. "The moment I saw you emerge from the house, I knew you would," he said with a small smile. No matter how furious at Evan he sometimes was, the man still seemed capable of almost anything. There was something unnaturally firm about his presence, a pull Julian couldn't deny.

"How did you know?" Evan reciprocated the touch, looking straight into Julian's eyes.

Julian exhaled. "You moved with this... aggressive vigor. I know you enough to be aware of what that means. You can hardly be stopped when you're passionate like that."

"I lose my temper all too often. It is for the better that I don't go out that much. I'm afraid gentlemen and ladies consider me a bull when I should be a peacock."

Julian chuckled and brushed the back of his other hand down Evan's chest. "I'd much rather watch a bull than a peacock. A peacock might be pretty, but it so often lacks substance. It cannot stand against anyone charging at it. A bull on the other hand..." He chewed on his lip and raised his gaze at Evan, searching his face to know whether he had been understood.

"A bull will trample what's in his way, even when he does not wish to. It's in his nature." Evan twirled his finger over the lowest button of Julian's waistcoat, and it was almost as if the touch was already charring the expensive silk.

Julian gasped and opened the upmost button, unable to look away from Evan's face. "A bull has the power to bend the world to his will. I don't want you to think I'm a worthless peacock."

Evan's gaze became tender, and he flattened his hand against Julian's side. "I don't think that way. As mad as it was, I admire your audacity. You let yourself be kidnapped by a highwayman to get your way. I have many advantages over you in my own home, yet you dared strike me several times." A flash of amusement went across Evan's face. "Trying to get ransom money out of your own father? Is it moral? Not in the slightest, but it makes me think we are more alike than you might think. You reach out for whatever you want, no matter what stands in your way. I think you are much more than a pretty face," he finished in a whisper.

Heat spilled all over Julian's chest, like hot custard. He smiled and caressed Evan's hand with his fingers. His heart drummed in his ribcage as he looked into the coal-black eyes, seeking an understanding he'd never before shared with anyone. "Since I remember, I always felt there was a side of me no one knew of. Even I. It's always there, but it escapes my grasp. Like a separate presence somewhere in my mind. Like I don't truly know myself. And yet you are here, and you seem so certain of your thoughts. I find it admirable."

"Believe me when I say that I too am often caught between impossible choices. Only when I set my mind to something, I follow through. Sometimes with disastrous consequences. But I do believe it is better to fail at times than to never take a leap of faith." His knee nudged Julian's gently. "If you feel your writing, your dream of travelling to Italy, are worth pursuing, then I don't judge you for it. I know how it feels to ache for things that seem too damn slippery to grasp."

Julian opened the second button of his waistcoat and hesitated, still holding on to Evan's hand, as if it were the only thing separating him from a tragic fate. "Earlier, you told me I am to meet men like you in Italy, but I think you're wrong. There cannot be anyone else like you."

Evan bit his pale lip, and his touch on Julian's side became more noticeable. "No one else can be the Monster of Tredele after all." He watched Julian as if there was no one else more important in the world, and the half-drawn curtains around the bed only intensified that feeling.

Julian's chest compressed, and he inched closer, hoping to relieve the tightness that he somehow both appreciated and hated. Moving his hand from the buttons of his waistcoat to the front of Evan's chest required a single gesture, and then he could feel it. The powerful heartbeat beneath Evan's ribcage. "No one but you would take me to the sky ocean."

Evan's fingers inched all the way to Julian's hip, and he moved closer, making Julian dizzy when the scent of wine mixed with Evan's own. "I am not a monster. Nor am I a ghost. I am made of flesh and bone." He moved his other hand over Julian's, and pressed it harder to his own chest. "Can you feel that? I'd build you a castle in that sky if you could only want me the same way I want you."

Julian opened his mouth and pulled on Evan's shirt. Then pulled harder, rolling to his back, his mind clouded by emotions that were hazy from the wine yet somehow sharp and intense.

Like pain. So very much like pain.

"I do. I can feel it."

Evan rolled on top of Julian with a gasp, and Julian could sense what lay behind it when Evan's cock pressed against his stomach. He was getting hard already.

"Do you want to feel it closer?" Evan whispered.

Julian could neither breathe nor talk, but he nodded fervently and rubbed Evan's shoulders, opening his legs to accommodate Evan's hips. Little shivers trailed up and down his body, only fueling the heat inside him. The same heat that was now filling his prick.

Evan raised himself slightly on his elbows yet was still pleasantly heavy. As if the weight grounded Julian instead of trapping him. Memories of being under Evan flashed through Julian's mind. That time when Evan's cock was buried deep inside of him and spurted hot seed while Evan had a firm grasp on Julian's neck.

"How close?" Evan asked in that deep voice of his, now seeped in lust. He ground against Julian at an agonizing pace.

Julian opened his mouth, swallowing the sweet, heavy air Evan had just exhaled. His hand moved lower, toward the bone-melting heat between those firm legs. A small moan escaped Julian when his palm rubbed against the hard flesh straining the fabric of Evan's breeches. He couldn't believe he was doing this, and yet his instincts were pushing him deeper into unknown territory, Evan's cock was now not intimidating, but a thing of beauty to explore. After all, didn't men visit museums and study the art of human flesh for hours? How was this different if Evan was such a fine specimen of the male sex?

Evan groaned and lifted his hips to accommodate Julian's hand, and even arched against it slightly, like a stallion ready to rut with a mare. The thought sent a shiver down Julian's spine, all the way to his ass.

Still holding on to Evan's hand like a child in need of guidance, he squeezed his fingers over the bulge, only to seek the buttons at the front of Evan's breeches. He didn't know when it happened, but suddenly he ached to sense that hard flesh against bare skin, to touch and explore it for as long as Evan allowed him to.

Evan's eyes were pinning Julian to the mattress, as if Julian's touch was the only intoxication Evan needed. Once Julian opened Evan's breeches, Evan guided Julian's hand all the way inside his drawers, to the throbbing heat that was his cock. With a flush on his face, and a little moan escaping his lips, Evan was a thing of beauty.

"You truly are a force of nature," whispered Julian, shuddering when the wet tip of Evan's cock grazed up the middle of his palm, all the way to his sensitive wrist. Evan was now pinning Julian's other hand to the bed, and Julian turned his face to nuzzle at his tense forearm, brushing his nose against the fine hair dusting the skin there.

Evan lowered his face to Julian's ear, and whispered against it, "I can be your storm. All you need to do is ask." As if to emphasize his point, he slowly pushed his cock against Julian's hand.

Julian choked out a moan, arching his chest up until it touched Evan's. His senses weren't even his anymore. Evan took over all of them, and in the haze of powerful arousal, Julian tugged on another man's cock for the first time. It was so different from touching his own, so undeniably alive when it pulsed with vigor, hot and smooth in Julian's grasp. It was the fruit that he'd never been meant to pick.

Evan's grip on Julian's hand became even stronger, yet it only had Julian craving more, even when it bordered on pain. When Evan pushed against him, laying more of his weight on top, Julian whimpered, feeling the tremble in his body go all the way down to his thighs, now settled against Evan's hips. His mind might have been clearing up before, but he was now drunk on Evan's touch, and he didn't want to sober up from that any time soon.

Without thinking of the implications of what they were do-ing, he settled on stroking Evan's cock despite his own fingers trembling as he did so. When Evan had descended on Julian last time, he'd touched him all over, had him strip, and indulged in touching. It seemed that he didn't mind offering up his body for exploration either, and the thought that this exquisite man was available to Julian without consequences made it impossible to resist the temptation of it.

No one would ever know that he'd done this.

Yet he would remember this night forever. He rolled his head until the side of his neck filled the slot between Evan's shoulder and jaw, and gently twisted his hand over the thick, throbbing prick, something he very much enjoyed himself. The way Evan's body arched over him was answer enough to the question as to whether the sentiment was shared.

"Your shirt—" Julian grazed his lips against the dark stubble that had grown since Evan's last shave a few days ago, and the scratching sensation made him curl his toes in the bedding.

Evan pulled back, and his nostrils flared when their eyes met. Despite his cock still being in Julian's grasp, he kneeled between Julian's legs and unbuttoned his waistcoat so fast the last button on it snapped off. Evan paid it no mind, and once he threw it to the side, ripped his shirt off, pushing the dark hair onto his face.

Watching his haste made Julian only squeeze Evan's cock with more boldness. It was for him that a man like Evan was so aroused that he stripped at command. The power of that knowledge made Julian tremble with excitement.

He pressed his hand to the hard abdomen, which flexed beneath his touch, rubbing against him like a cat. Julian moaned, too excited to hold in his arousal as the boldest man he knew shed his clothes for him and glanced into Julian's eyes, seeking approval.

Julian pulled him closer with his thighs while swirling his thumb over the slick cockhead that was so readily available all of a sudden. Was this why priests warned about sodomy? Because it was so easy to just fall into?

"No one has touched me this way in far too long," Evan whispered, his cheeks flushed, his nostrils flaring, eyes hardly visible from under his hair. The words only made Julian want to touch

more of that bulky body and lick every hair on Evan's skin—
Lick? No. He would most certainly not wish to lick a man.
How would a thought like that even appear in his head?

Julian pushed his palm up Evan's chest and squeezed one of
the pectoral muscles, uttering a moan he simply couldn't stop.
It was so meaty and firm, like the juiciest of beef, nothing like
the softness of a breast. In fact, there was absolutely nothing
about Evan with even the remotest resemblance to a sensual
female body. But no matter what Julian knew of desire, it was
the musk of Evan's arousal, and the harsh landscape of his
body that turned Julian's loins into a burning furnace. With
his eyes firmly trained on the lips he now so longed to touch,
Julian found himself giddy that Evan was indeed not bedding
the handsome stableboy.

"I've never touched a man like this before," he uttered.

"Feel free to explore all you like." Evan's voice was even
deeper than before, reminding Julian of how it sounded when
he'd told Julian his cock was beautiful and that he'd make him
come to feel his ass clenching. Raw, dirty, so ungentlemanly yet
so unbearably irresistible. Evan seemed to just take whatever
he pleased, and Julian found himself at Evan's mercy even
now, with Evan's throbbing hot cock in his hand.

Julian's gaze strayed to the dark, hardened nipples, and lower, over the planes of short coarse hairs, down to Evan's open
breeches. All this masculine beauty within reach, available for
Julian to gorge on.

"You are so heavy," whispered Julian, even though he knew
the servants slept in a cottage in the gardens and couldn't
possibly overhear any of their words. His lips tingled with
need, and he leaned up, burying his face in the valley in the
middle of Evan's chest, immediately swept off his feet by the
scent of fresh sweat clinging to skin and dark, curly hair that
now tickled his cheek.

Evan let out a chuckle, and Julian moaned when the thick
fingers pushed into his hair. Pressing Julian's face harder against

his own skin, Evan rocked his hips back and forth slowly, working it through Julian's hand as if it were a cunt.

Julian groaned, his cock straining against his breeches just from thinking about such an indecent comparison. He opened his mouth and licked sweat off Evan's skin, shuddering violently at its taste. It was all salt and the bare essence of arousal, distilled just for his pleasure. He closed his eyes and rubbed himself against the hard, pulsing chest, leaving messy, wet kisses all over the pliant skin. He tightened his thighs around Evan's hips and rocked his own back and forth, his prick rubbing against the stiff fabric at the front of his breeches while Evan's fucked the warm hole of Julian's hand with growing enthusiasm.

"Yes, pretty boy," Evan whispered, as if to himself, not to Julian. "You're all mine," he rasped, and sped up the pace at which he pushed his cock into Julian's hand, while still holding Julian's head tight against the meat of his own chest and all but smothering him in arousal.

Julian squeezed his hand tighter around the pulsing length of Evan's cock, delighting in the slippery friction. He was already imagining Evan's seed coating his forearm and then soaking into his skin, as if Evan's body in his arms was exactly where it belonged.

"Oh, God," he whimpered and put his free arm around Evan's neck, pulling him as close as possible. In his wild imagination, Evan already pulled Julian's hand behind his back and held it there to restrain him from touching at will.

Julian moaned when his cock twitched in his pants.

"Hold still for me." It was more of an order than a request, and what followed made Julian fervently grind into Evan.

Evan grabbed Julian's wrist, and pinned it to the covers and pushed down on him with all his weight. The animalistic way he started stabbing Julian's fist made Julian clench his ass at the memory of being a vessel to such vicious rutting.

Even the intense emotion expressed on Evan's handsome face became a blur as fantasy and reality intermingled, milking Julian's prick into his tight breeches. His hands trembled, and he arched under Evan's weight, shaken by tremors of pleasure vastly more powerful than the ones he achieved by his own hand. He held on to Evan's cock so tightly he almost managed to halt its slick glide through his palm.

"Squeeze it like you would your arse." Evan demanded in a raspy tone, panting, sweaty, and so deliciously debauched Julian could hardly think about denying his request. Despite having just come, it still made Julian think of that thick prick pushing into him instead of a fist. Would it still hurt at first, or would the pressure be as elating as it became by the end of that night?

He fulfilled his orders as well as he could, despite his fingers cramping from the effort. He drunkenly looked up at Evan's face over him, and there was nothing in the world he cared for more than this moment. This pure, animalistic bliss.

"Yes..."

Julian's eyes went wider when Evan's lips spread into an honest, satisfied smile, and he made his last harsh thrusts, coming all over Julian's hand, spreading his seed in Julian's palm, and letting it drip down Julian's wrist.

Julian melted into the covers, wishing for nothing more than to have Evan's lips seal this moment against his. But he didn't ask for it, too groggy to attempt it himself, so he lay back, accepting Evan's weight on top of him with a lazy smile. He could sense the other man's rapid heartbeat against his flesh when Evan dropped on him, as if Julian was there to serve as his mattress for the night. His breathing was rapid, blowing a *staccato* into Julian's ear as they lay wordlessly, still caught up in the illusion that the world beyond Evan's bed ceased to exist.

"I told you I admire you reaching for whatever you want. I'm happy you chose to reach for me," Evan whispered into Julian's ear, and licked along its shell, barely catching a breath.

Julian's heart stopped.

Oh, God, he had indeed reached for another man and invited him to perform this kind of act.

The ground crumbled beneath Julian's toes, but it could have been just the prelude to an avalanche.

CHAPTER 10

JULIAN

The excitement that had buzzed in Julian's veins not that long ago slowly morphed into nausea and a headache that made him feel as if it wasn't the wine that caused it but a rattle of boulders inside his skull. Evan lay so close—too close—and his body radiated heat that felt like the touch of the sun on Julian's skin.

But as hours passed and the clouds dispersed from Julian's mind, the earlier enthusiasm was slowly replaced by growing distress. There was a crust of dried seed on Julian's hand, but he couldn't bring himself to wipe it off yet. He listened to Evan, watched the gentle glide of his chest underneath the covers. In the many nights before this one, Evan had been restless, often waking up or turning underneath the covers deep in the night, yet now he seemed as peaceful as a babe.

But no matter how handsome he was, or how excitingly bestial he'd acted when he fucked Julian's hand, there was a rotten core within him that was already affecting Julian's flesh. Before he came here, touching another man's prick would have never even occurred to Julian. He had never been one to freely engage in touch, neither with men nor women, and yet last night, he'd reached out for it with open arms.

Evan's prick had been such a pronounced weight in his palm, and no matter how much Julian thought about it, stripping the matter of all its layers, he couldn't deny having enjoyed it. All his life, he'd considered coupling a somewhat dirty deed. He'd never shared those thoughts with friends, but he couldn't un-

133

derstand their affinity for breasts, which—while aesthetically pleasing—were just lumps of flesh. He'd always much rather toss off himself than let a harlot lure him into her slick honeypot. It all seemed unnecessary and tedious. But there was something about Evan that called out to Julian on a plane that he'd never walked before.

Evan was all hard muscle and rough skin that smelled of leather, hay, and all things masculine. It wasn't perfumed by costly elixirs but herbs and things that brushed against that herculean body throughout the day. His eyes burned with a passion previously unknown to Julian. His lips smiled so cruelly, but even those grimaces were sensuous to Julian's hungry gaze. All night, he reminisced about Evan's weight on him, the firm touch of his hands, the breath ghosting against skin.

And somewhere around three in the morning, when the moon was still high in the sky, in a moment of absolute clarity, Julian realized that had Evan not been so condescending on the night when he forced himself on Julian, Julian would have yielded willingly.

He would have done so in the observatory when the cold air seemed hot and Evan's fingertips met his on the telescope. Evan's words had been poetry back then, and Julian wanted to be a willing victim to the trap of his masculine charm. It had been coming since the day the two of them met, and the seduction had been completed not the time Evan first took Julian's body, but in the moment Julian reached out for Evan's touch and all but begged for it.

The seed he'd spilled into his drawers had since been wiped off, but as all the puzzle pieces were slotting together in Julian's mind, it became increasingly clear to him what it was that he hadn't known about himself all along.

He would have been willing to a man's advances were he approached in the right way.

Women left him cold, but Evan's sheer presence made Julian's whole body tingle.

He couldn't stay here.

He couldn't end up like the poor servant who had previously been in the care of Evan's family. Now that Julian had been fucked, a doctor's examination of his backside could prove deadly. He'd heard of this in form of rowdy stories from the courtrooms, and he'd laughed at the perverts like everyone else, but now that it could potentially affect him, cold sweat was beading all over his body.

He was certain Father would not bribe anyone to save Julian's hide were this to ever surface. He'd be all alone with his humiliation, and he'd be hanged like a common criminal for an act he had not invited.

He couldn't stay here.

Julian's head rolled over the pillow, and he looked at Evan's face, so completely relaxed in his sleep. Would it hurt Evan to not find Julian by his side in the morning? Did Julian care? Would parting from Evan and the influence of his charm get Julian back on the right path?

Even now, as Julian was about to leave the bed as quietly as he was able to, his fingers longed to touch the stubble on Evan's jaw, and he imagined having his skin scratched by it.

But if he touched Evan, he wouldn't be able to leave. His lips itched for Evan's mouth, which would be just as decisive in its caresses as the rest of him, but Julian secretly knew giving in to those desires would only make things worse. It was still dark, and even the servants would be in their beds, so if he wanted to run, now was the time.

He slid from beneath the covers, wary of any sounds he made, but once his naked body was out in the big room and kissed by its icy air, it became a struggle to keep his teeth from clattering.

His original clothes, the precious green suit, were easy enough to find. He dressed himself carelessly and pushed toward the door with an urgency that both choked him and made his muscles move faster.

Julian had close to nothing, and his father would not support him anymore. He was pretty sure he could find shelter with one of his friends for at least a while, but having some money would be essential. He swallowed, looking around the room in desperation, and when he saw a small but intricate clock lying undignified, under maps and books, he figured Evan wouldn't miss it. He'd probably not even realize it was gone with all the clutter and trinkets in this strange room.

Julian quickly put it into a pocket in his coat, scowling when the gold and silver burned him. He couldn't believe he was stealing from a man whom he made love to just this night. It didn't help one bit that it was Evan who stole *Julian* first.

A few hours ago, Evan had been so honest with Julian, so upfront about his needs and cravings. He'd showed Julian a gaping wound that Julian was now about to sprinkle with salt.

His hands itched for ink and paper, but what words of comfort could he possibly leave behind? A formal letter of apology, a single sentence to express his dismay, a short poem that only the two of them could fully understand? Any of those options seemed too dramatic or too cheap to pursue, so he slid out the door without leaving behind anything except for his pride.

Tredele was deathly silent at night, so he pulled off his boots and rushed through the cold medieval corridors in just his stockings, feeling as if the cold floors were pushing him away from their master. Julian would leave Evan to drown in the loneliness of Tredele's walls, and Evan would once more become Sir Recluse, the Ghost of Tredele.

Outside, he was met by an unpleasant drizzle and the bleating of sheep in the far off distance. He could barely see in the darkness, but he knew Tredele well enough by now to find his way to the stables.

He walked forward, with no light to guide him, ready to trip at any moment, but he reached the stables without ever falling into the mud, breathless and desperately ashamed of what he was doing. He'd never even dream of taking away Noir, so he quickly saddled Snow and left, leading her down the hill that housed Tredele.

Julian had the moonlight as his guide, but as the horse gingerly cantered along the road, he realized he wasn't certain where to go next. There was a village somewhere nearby, but where exactly—East? West? North? South?—he did not know.

It was dusk when he noticed a road sign on a rock, and his heart soared with relief at the sight of the word 'Looe'. He wasn't sure just how far away it was exactly, but it couldn't be more than an hour or two if he calculated the road to Tredele right.

But as he rode, never meeting a soul, as the sun rose up the sky, his mind began filling with doubt. Shame rose in his chest in burning hot waves, and in addition, without another sign in sight, he was starting to doubt his way. He did not recognize the road, but just as he was starting to get more anxious, seagulls screamed close by, and he reached the top of a hill, from which he spotted the familiar seaside town with its bridge at the mouth of the river. The streets were already bustling with life.

Julian gave a shuddery breath and went on, trying not to think too much of the man he left behind. The clock in his pocket was like a stain on Julian's best waistcoat, never to be removed completely. But if he gave away his pride and let a man have his way with him, he might as well become a thief.

Julian let the mare slow down when it carried him across the bridge between the two parts of town, and he hung his head, not wanting to look at the small chapel in the middle. He felt like the worst scoundrel of all. And yet even a scoundrel needed to eat, drink and wrap himself in warm clothes. Julian needed to find shelter.

Only now, when he was approaching his favorite tavern on a stolen horse (would Evan have him hung for that?) did he realize that the cravat around his throat was Evan's not his. He instinctively pulled a part of it up to smell it and imagined that it now held his neck the way Evan had during that first brutal time together.

He closed his eyes briefly and nudged the side of the mare, prompting her to hurry between the stalls with food that were already being set up for the day.

He could not go home. He dared not look in the eyes of his social equals and see their pity. His first thought led him to the home of Martin, one of his closest friends, of the unsavory sort his father detested. He had money from sources that weren't entirely clear, as he did not discuss his trade with Julian, despite being able to provide him with many items at prices that did not empty Julian's purse too much. But no matter how long he knocked at the door of Martin's cottage, no one answered, and there didn't seem to be a fire burning inside either.

So Julian went to the next best place, the lodgings of Simon, one of his most frequent companions on the informal evenings Julian drew so much inspiration from. Standing close to the shore, the narrow white cottage already had smoke coming out of its chimney, and Julian smiled, jumping off the horse and hitting the door three times.

It took a while, and Julian imagined Simon rolling out of bed, his head ringing after all the ale he'd drunk the night before. At last, the door opened.

"J–Julian," Simon uttered, his beady eyes going wider, as if he'd seen a ghost. "I thought I'd never see yew again!"

Simon's sister peeked out from behind his shoulder, nodded, then returned to her tasks, and to the meal that smelled of butter and eggs. Julian's stomach grumbled, reminding him how long it had been since the last time he ate.

Julian smiled, glad to have been missed by someone at least. He put his hand on Simon's shoulder and squeezed it. "It's been a difficult few weeks, my friend. Do you know where Martin has gone?"

Simon nodded. "Gone to sea. Is it true yew've been taken by a land pyrate? The constable has been out looking for yew, but... Teresa's master gave 'er the last paper, and she read it to me..."

Julian's heart sank, and he looked away, embarrassment hitting him in the face like the smelliest of fish during a brawl at the market. "Did she now? Well, at least you know why I'm in need of some assistance," said Julian, forcing himself to look up and smile.

"Yew know, Julian, I get work at the docks from yewr faathur. I dun't want to be on 'is bad side." Simon pushed back his greasy hair.

Julian swallowed, gripping the side of the door. "I know, Simon... I would have never bothered you if my situation weren't so dire. My pockets have been cleaned."

The silence between them stretched before Simon finally spoke. "I'd pay a 'undred shillings to hear the story of wat 'appened to yew, but I drank away my purse last night. Not even gettin' paid 'til next week, I'm on my sister's mercy."

Julian swallowed hard, looking toward the warm flames of the stove inside. "I know how you feel. Until I build back a relationship with my father and make him see his mistake, I can't even afford horsebread," he said with a small smile, even though there was nothing to be happy about. Would the potential of Julian and his father reconciling carry enough weight for Simon to offer Julian a bed and a warm meal?

Simon sighed and shifted his weight from one foot to the other. "Wait 'ere," he said and went into the house. "Is that Mr. Julian Reece?" he could hear Simon's sister say, but he didn't hear the answer. Soon enough Simon was back with a big pasty that must have been reheated for the morning. "All I got, Julian. And dun't tell your faathur I fed yew."

Julian's fingers trembled when he accepted the food. He spoke to Simon briefly, then left him to prepare for the day's work, shaken as he walked away, tugging on Snow's reins. His knees refused to work properly, and he walked at a snail's pace between the horse and the houses, more than aware that everyone in this town knew his face. They thought him a wastrel, he knew this much, but the weight of their gazes, ranging from pitiful to outright spiteful, made him want to melt into the mud beneath his feet. He hid away close to the docks when he ate his food, but the warmth in his stomach didn't lessen the humiliation of overheard conversations about him. He couldn't believe he'd thought it a good idea to return here of all places, when Looe was where he was so unwanted.

Soon enough, gossip of him coming back would fly like the seagulls watching his food. His need to hide from prying eyes was becoming overwhelming, so Madame Canard's brothel seemed like the obvious choice of a temporary hideout. Maybe he'd manage to sell the pretty clock to one of the girls and get enough funds to leave for Plymouth.

Julian shivered. Was this his life now? Selling stolen goods to whores?

Stiff with shame, he approached the large house close to the seaside. It never really slept, but as he walked closer to its doors, the sight of his father's associates discussing something in the street kept him from stepping any closer. He could not stand the humiliation of being ridiculed by people of his own class. Not right now.

He pulled on Snow's reins and walked all the way to the back door, like a beggar asking the kitchen maids for scraps. He tied the horse in the backyard and approached the small wooden door.

With his heart in his throat, he knocked.

A small boy opened and swiped the gaze of his childish eyes over Julian, mouth set in a scowl. "Wat can I do for yew, mister?"

Julian stretched, knowing his suit would make him look presentable despite the sleepless night. The fact that an urchin like this one did not recognize his authority was a bad sign indeed, and matters needed to be amended at once. He cleared his throat.

"Is the madam asleep?"

The boy raised his eyebrows, as if he understood something. "Iz this a secret meetin'?" he asked, and held out his palm.

Julian frowned. "I frequent this bordello, and I request being let in, or none of the wenches will ever see me again."

That seemed to do the trick, as the boy let him pass. "Sorry, mister," he mumbled and locked the door once Julian entered.

He looked down. He'd never been in this part of the building before, and he supposed it was not very dignified to arrive at the backdoor uninvited, but he tried to act with as much dignity as possible. "If the madam is awake, I would request her presence. If not, well, any of the wenches will do for now."

"Iss, mister, right away. Wait in the parlor, mister. I will fetch the Madam, or any of the other wenches," he repeated word for word and disappeared.

Julian exhaled, shutting his eyes when he walked through a curtain and into the public area of the bawdy house. The air was stale, heavy with sweet perfume and the stench of last night's wine, nauseating after hours of inhaling the fresh breeze.

The house was quiet, just as it was every morning, with just a distinct sound of creaking wood above, and a distant snoring coming from behind a screen in the corner to disturb the peace. Fanny, one of the younger girls employed in the establishment dozed in one of the settees in the parlor decorated with thick fabrics and elaborate-looking trinkets that might as well be worth nothing at all.

Julian watched her in silence, clutching his gloves as he sat in a chair across from her. The furnishing looked comfortable, but it lacked substance within the seat and all but swallowed Julian whole. Somehow, he'd never noticed when he was merry and drunk—now, even the tiniest of inconveniences seemed disturbing beyond belief.

Julian had been at Madame Canard's many times. He became a man here, but in daylight it looked like a different place entirely. The curtains were worn and cheap, thinned from washing and constant handling. The fabrics thrown over the furniture were meant for easy cleanup, and after a whole night they were stained by coupling and drinking that had taken place here. There were crumbles and broken glass on the floor. Someone's shoes lay in the middle of the parlor, and Julian wouldn't be surprised if the man who left them here walked home barefoot, too intoxicated to notice the mud cooling his feet.

He reached into his pocket and traced the tiny clock with his fingers. He shouldn't have taken it. What if it was some kind of keepsake that Evan would miss after all? With Julian having left his house in secret, the theft would be yet another blow.

Julian licked his lips, still sensing the saltiness of Evan's sweat on his tongue, only sharper with the memory of dark curls tickling his face.

"Julian? Is that you?"

Finally, a friendly face. Barnaby Rowland ran down the stairs, rousing Fanny from her slumber with the racket he made. "We all thought you've been murdered in cold blood by that bastard highwayman," Barnaby said, approaching Julian in quick strides. He sat in a chair next to Julian and slapped him on the shoulder. "What happened, dear fellow? You don't look so well."

"If I lost everythin' I'd be pale as the snow as well:'" said Fanny, yawning as she pulled up her blouse, which had uncovered one of her nipples while she slept.

Julian felt his jaw clench, but he forced a smile. "My father is misinformed. Now that I'm back, all I need is to speak with him about the ordeal I've been through."

Barnaby nodded eagerly, and poured Julian a glass of water from a jug on the table. "What have you been through? The speculations about your whereabouts have spurred so much gossip. Martin Even organized a search party, but we found nothing."

"Was he 'andsome?" Fanny asked with her eyes shining bright.

Julian gulped down the cold wine from an almost empty bottle someone had left behind, in an attempt to give himself time to think, but nothing of substance came to mind.

"How would I know?" he asked the girl. His mouth dry despite the drink he'd just had. "He was quite old already. Maybe a desperate footman expelled from service?"

"Your brother said the man was dressed all in black. James Hunt said that too. That he was tall, and strong like two men."

Barnaby nodded quickly, wiping some crust off his lips with his neckcloth. Well-born, yet with no affinity for manners.

Julian took a deep breath and clenched his hand on the nearest solid object, which happened to be Fanny's knee. She laughed and slapped his arm, but he held on. He could not bring any suspicion to Evan's doors. "As all footmen are. They are trained for protecting their masters, aren't they?"

He cleared his throat and glanced at Fanny, who stared at him with curiosity in her big eyes. "He was a brutal, rough fellow. You might have liked him, silly girl."

"Let go of me, wench!" yelled a man fast approaching from the entry corridor. "I am not here for a taste of your rotten fruit. I am looking for Julian Reece, and I've been told he used to frequent this... establishment."

Julian stiffened, and all at once, it hit him that he knew that voice. It was the same man who'd scolded Esther the day before at Tredele. A well known man, feared by many. His heart thumped, but Barnaby, bless his cursed heart, stood up and called out toward the entrance.

"He is here. Alive and in good health!"

Fanny looked down to her breasts and pulled the blouse up even higher.

Pascoe walked in with his back straight as an arrow, and his face stern. Dressed in black and white, he could have been a priest on a moral crusade.

"Julian Reece. Alive. And well," Pascoe said it in a way suggesting he wasn't happy with that outcome.

Julian grinned, even though it hurt the muscles around his lips. "Constable. I see you've been looking for me. I already feel much safer."

"You have been abducted over a fortnight ago. Where is the highwayman?" Pascoe stepped closer, lowering his gaze to Julian and pointing his nose down, as if he intended to pin him down to the chair with it.

A racket at the back of the house, where Julian had come through earlier, turned all heads. "Where is he?" hissed someone, thumping his boots against the wooden floor. "I know he's here, his horse is outside!"

Julian's muscles turned into dry wood, and even his heart stopped.

Barnaby grinned and turned around to look at *Evan*. "And you might be...? I can't remember this place ever being so amusing in the morning."

Evan stopped mid-stride at the sight of Julian next to the constable. Tall, dressed in black from head to toe, and with eyes that could burn a man alive, he looked significantly more threatening than in the shirt and waistcoat he wore around the house. The black riding boots reached all the way over his knees, the long coat clung to his form and made him seem even taller, as did the tricorn hat. Evan was catching his breath, face still of a reddish hue after having galloped all the way to Looe.

Julian couldn't breathe. His gaze met Evan's, and the burn of it made him slide his palm off Fanny's thigh. The sight of the work coat flowing around Evan's strong form gave him a shudder.

"He's—" started Julian, and at once everyone's eyes were on him. There was a crack in Evan's confident exterior, a glimmer of ice in that fiery gaze, but as the silence stretched longer, Pascoe squeezed Julian's shoulder and shook him.

"What is it about Sir Evan Penhart that frightens you so?"

Barnaby's eyes went wide. "The Ghost of Tredele himself? I mean... forgive me, Sir Evan," he mumbled, trying to stand straight.

Evan groaned, but his eyes never left Julian's face. "I must agree. What is that you fear, Mr. Reece?" His voice was stone-cold, nothing like the excited rasp in which he spoke to Julian in bed just hours ago.

Julian steadied himself, took a deep breath, and shot to his feet. "My friend, I was merely surprised to see you here," he said, walking past Pascoe, straight toward Evan.

Evan shut his lips so hard they went white, and his frown deepened by the second. Julian needed to salvage this situation before it could all end in a disaster for both of them.

"You see, Sir Evan, Mr. Reece was just telling us about the highwayman who abducted him." Pascoe lifted his chin with a self-righteous sneer.

Evan stiffened, giving Julian yet another clue to believe that there was history between those two men. He brushed imaginary dust off Evan's shoulder but avoided looking into his eyes, consumed by flames that had ignited in his chest the moment Evan came in.

Julian laughed. "He knows all about the highwayman. The bastard kept me for ransom until the hope of it dispersed, then wanted to dispose of me," Julian said, looking back at Pascoe and the others.

Fanny's eyes glistened with joy at the story of danger and excitement, but she wasn't Julian's intended audience. Pascoe was.

Julian stepped away from Evan and gestured up. "Built like a bear that man was. He kept me tied to a chair for days, but I had not been idle. Any chance I got, I worked on that rope, scraping it against the wood. It was slightly uneven, you see, and it was slowly starting to give," he said, clutching his wrists together and rubbing them against the nearest chair.

Pascoe's eyebrows lowered above his eyes, but he listened, at least.

"One night, the villain came in. He punched me so hard I fell over, along with the chair," Julian said, to Fanny's squeak, which could be both an expression of fear and glee. He didn't have the slightest idea which with that girl. "He saw that my father would not pay, and he decided to get rid of me. For the first time, I saw his face then," he said in a heavy tone, meaning to be profound.

"Did he 'ave a scar?" Fanny wondered out loud, her eyes as wide as saucers.

"What did he look like, Mr. Reece?" asked Pascoe through clenched teeth.

"He did have a scar," said Julian, gesturing at Fanny with a broad smile. "A big, nasty gash across his lips. He could've been considered a monster from the woods, so ugly he was. His hair was so fair it must had whitened with age, and his eyes were a watery blue. Strong as an ox, but definitely a man prematurely aged." He glanced at Pascoe, spurred on by the gaze that Evan was scorching his back with. "A cruel man he was, too. He beat me savagely—mind it, still tied down like a hog—but I finally snapped my hands free and threw a candle in his face.

"He roared like a wounded animal and stumbled back, so I ran." said Julian, moving back and forth, hunching his shoulders to imitate the way the imaginary him was skimming through the woods, tripping over undergrowth. "I ran blindly through the night until I had no strength left in me. But there was a road, so I thought—better risk being apprehended than die and let the wolves tear my flesh," he added, much to Fanny's amusement. "It was only getting gray then, and the air was milky from the fog, and I shuddered with the cold. The next thing I remember was the thumping of hooves on the road.

"The stallion that emerged from the fog was like a beast from hell, but it was not carrying a demon. It was this man who rode on its back," Julian said, making a broad gesture toward Evan, his heart hurrying at the mere thought of him. "He took me to his home and nursed me to health as if I were no stranger but a friend of many years. I would not be here if it weren't for him," he added with such conviction he almost believed it himself.

Pascoe mulled over Julian's story. "And yet, when I visited Tredele just yesterday, I was told you were not there..."

Evan stepped forward, standing now so close to Julian, goose bumps erupted all over Julian's arms. "Mr. Reece introduced himself with a different name and told me he'd been attacked by a group of men on that same night I found him. Perhaps he was afraid that villain would somehow find him and finish what he started. But as you can see, he's ridden for Looe first thing on the morning after I told him of your visit."

Julian took a shuddery breath, forcing his constricted lungs to expand. "That is correct. I came to Looe today to inform you that I am alive and well, Mr. Pascoe. I doubt you will see that highwayman again soon. He spoke of London a few times, and that must be where he headed after our fight."

There it was, Julian had chosen to protect a criminal with his word. A highwayman and a sodomite. His shoulders slumped as he leaned against the door, rubbing his eyes. "Forgive me. I must have overestimated my strength. It seems I am still affected by what that bastard put me through."

"Oh, Mr. Reece, yew poor soul," said Fanny, walking over and pulling his head against her voluptuous bosom. He gasped, choked by her sweet perfume, nothing like Evan's earthy scent. "Yew need a bed. How 'bout yew sleep, and I entertain your friend? He deserves an 'ero's welcome. If I went agist hospitality, the madam would be cross with me."

Julian's eyes snapped open, and he straightened, enraged at the thought of Evan being molested by a creature who, while lovely, wasn't of the kind Evan desired. "That will not be necessary, but I appreciate your concern."

Barnaby got up from his seat, and extended his hand to Evan, no doubt now wishing to befriend a baronet, even though he was committing a dreadful *faux pas*. "I am Barnaby Rowland. Mr. Reece is a dear friend, and I am most grateful for your kindness to him. Would you do me the honor and drink with us, sir?"

For the first time, Julian dared to look at Evan, his heart already in his throat. A silent understanding passed between them, but Julian didn't know what it really meant. Evan's lips did not curve into a smile though, even as he reluctantly took off his glove and shook Barnaby's hand.

"No, Mr. Rowland. Thank you, but I will be on my way," Evan's voice became fainter.

Barnaby wouldn't give it a rest. "But any time you woul—"

Pascoe butted in with a hiss. "If at any point you would like to share more details about the criminal, I assume you know where to find me, Mr. Reece?"

Julian gave a curt nod, leaning against the wall. "Of course, Mr. Pascoe. But there is not much to tell. I've been a hopeless captive."

Pascoe didn't even spare them all another glance and stomped out of what he surely considered a den of sin. His distaste of Evan remained a mystery.

Barnaby grinned, oblivious to the tense atmosphere between Evan and Julian.

"Are you sure I cannot tempt you for a drink, sir?"

Julian slowly raised his eyes to Evan, unsure what he wanted him to say. Deep down, he knew he didn't want to part without so much as saying good-bye.

Evan spoke to Barnaby, but his gaze settled on Julian. "No, thank you for your consideration, Mr. Rowland, but I must decline. I am not much of a drinker, and I have duties to attend to. Good day," he said and walked off toward the back corridor, his gait much less energized than when he entered.

Julian watched him go, and his hand ducked into the pocket of his coat again, tracing the watch gently. He stiffened when Barnaby patted his shoulder.

"How you could stand being around such a recluse, I don't know."

Julian scowled, offended as if the insult has been directed at him. "Not everyone is entertained by the same things."

When the last glimpse of the black coat disappeared in the far off corridor, a void opened in Julian's chest. Would that be the end of it?

He grinned at Barnaby and squeezed his shoulder. "I hope Fanny takes good care of you. I need to still return to Tredele. If you meet my father, do mention we spoke in person. But don't let him know where," he said, already backing away. His muscles ached with the need to run.

Barnaby sighed. "I'm sure he will be happy to hear you are alive and well. And making valuable acquaintances."

Fanny laughed. "I used to jest Zur Recluse just needed some muff to be done with his 'ermit ways, but now I actually wish he'd come more often."

Julian laughed without humor. He was hot and cold at the same time when he sped up, finally bursting into the yard at the back of Madame Canard's. The bright sun was a shock to his eyes, so he shielded them with his hand and sought Evan with his gaze.

There was no sight of him, yet he'd left Snow with Julian. What a gift it was for a traitorous swine who stole from Evan and deserted him after a night of passion.

"Wait," whimpered Julian, at loss already. He knew what way Evan would have gone at least, but he still mounted the mare as quickly as he could, nudging her to move.

He sped up as soon as he was out of the narrow street where he needed to lower his head under a line of laundry. People made way for him, and a few heartbeats later Julian spotted the dark silhouette of Evan and Noir combined moving along the road he'd used himself a few hours prior. His chest swelled with relief, and he urged Snow to run to catch up. Evan let out a long sigh to acknowledge Julian, but didn't say a word, nor did he as much as look Julian's way.

Julian glanced between Snow's ears, unsure what he should say. Why wouldn't Evan speak? Surely, there were bitter words for Julian somewhere in that powerful chest?

It felt like forever before they reached the hill beyond town and Evan opened his mouth.

"Is there a reason you are following me?" he asked in that voice devoid of emotion.

Julian clenched his teeth and quickly pulled out the clock, showing it to Evan.

Evan grabbed it with a scowl. "So you not only steal my horse and betray my trust? Does your greed know no end?"

Julian didn't have the will to fight him and hung his head in shame. "I'm sorry. I wasn't thinking."

"Is there anything else you stole, that you are still following me?"

"No."

"Why are you here then? Clearly, all you wanted to do is *escape my clutches.*"

Julian exhaled, closing his eyes to regain his composure. "Where do you think I should go? The most valuable thing I have now is your horse," he said, not even looking back toward Looe, where his father lived. Now at least he'd know where to seek Julian, were he to ever change his mind.

"It's not through my actions that you are in this position."

"I know. You've been kind to me, for the most part," said Julian, glancing at Evan's stern profile.

Evan bared his teeth. "If you wish to stay at my home any longer, you will need to accept punishment for your betrayal and theft."

Julian's body hair bristled when he remembered the harsh pain that seared his body when Evan first entered him with his prick. Was that the punishment he meant?

He clutched at the reins but slowly nodded his head in the end. There was nowhere he could go, and the guilt over being responsible for yesterday's seductive smiles being replaced by scowls on Evan's face made him more miserable than he'd care to admit.

Evan answered with a nod.

It was going to be a long way to Tredele.

CHAPTER 11

EVAN

The long ride to Tredele was torture with the silence between Evan and Julian. When Evan had found Julian
gone, at first he thought the man went off to ease his bladder,
but when time passed and there was no sight of him, Evan left
the bed. There was no sight of Julian in the kitchen, in the front
yard, or really, anywhere else, and when Jory informed Evan
that Snow was gone, the bitter truth seeped into the very base
of Evan's skin.

Had last night's closeness only been a ploy to make Evan less
attentive in guarding his prisoner? The thought stung more
than he'd like to admit.

Just when Evan convinced himself there was a glimmer
of hope that he and Julian could share a bed and a growing
friendship—If not a friendship then at least an understanding
of sorts—it turned out all Julian really wanted was to run away
from him. It made Evan despise both Julian and himself. Had
his cock a mind of its own that it would rule over his head? How
could he have not noticed the loathing in those pretty blue eyes?

But he didn't really ask himself that. He'd been blindsided
by the ache for companionship and pure, unadulterated lust
for Julian. All he could think of whenever his mind drifted off
was fucking him again. Anything would do, really. Whether
he'd be allowed to rub himself off against Julian's buttocks
or something as simple as touching his beautiful fair skin.
He'd take any scrap of affection Julian was willing to give, yet
nothing but contempt was coming Evan's way.

The punishment he intended to administer would be his last indulgence, so he had to make it count, because he promised himself enough was enough. His pride would not allow him to chase after a man who detested his affections, and so Julian would be out of his grasp even if living at Tredele. Because Evan would let him stay indefinitely.

As much as the betrayal of trust stabbed Evan through the heart, he could not deny shelter to a man who lied for him when faced with Pascoe. Even with all the bad blood between them, Julian wouldn't endanger Evan or disclose him as the highwayman. The two of them had worked in a perfect tandem of lies.

Noir seemed to be sensing the tension in Evan, because the beast got anxious himself. At least controlling the horse was something Evan could focus on. He stroked Noir's mane, already planning to groom him later. Every time life threw dirt into his eyes, Noir was there to soothe him.

Julian kept silent, like a ghost at Evan's side when they crossed the stone gates of Tredele and approached the house through the front yard that used to be representative and now remained a sad expanse of patchy grass. His lack of responsiveness tugged at something in Evan's chest, and it was almost like guilt, even though there wasn't much Evan should be feeling guilty about at this point. It was Julian who helped himself to things that didn't belong to him and fled, only to crawl back to ask for forgiveness. He would get that much.

Jory awaited them by the stables and accepted the horses into his care without comment. It was he who'd notified Evan of Snow's disappearance, so he likely knew his own mind about Julian's disappearance, even if he wouldn't say anything out loud. Evan could only hope he did not share the news with the other servants, though that could be just wishful thinking.

Once Evan got off horseback, he decided on his choice of indulgence, and detached the reins from Noir's bridle. The leather was worn and soft, pleasant to the touch, and he rubbed it between his fingers, watching Julian slide to the ground. Without a word,

Evan led the way back to the house, but Julian did not try to catch up with him and walked a step behind Evan, as if he were his valet.

Julian's elegant gait fueled the sense of anticipation that made Evan twist the reins in his hands, but Evan couldn't fully enjoy it with bitterness coursing through his veins. His touch was not wanted. His attentions were uninvited. His affection was undesired.

Julian found them all repulsive.

Just thinking of it made his cheek ache where Julian had slapped him for the attempted kiss all those weeks ago. Evan should have known not to approach the man again. He should have settled on friendship and enjoyed Julian's company like a decent man would have done. But it was too late for that now.

Julian's boots tapped against the stone floor of the majestic old hall, the oldest surviving part of the house. Evan didn't particularly like spending time here, but whenever he entered, a sense of melancholy overcame him so strongly he felt watched by all the ancestors who walked the halls of Tredele. The tall whitened walls were still decorated the way they had been a hundred years ago, with old pieces of weaponry on the walls surrounding the few portraits delegated here by Evan's late mother.

She used to hold banquets here many years ago, but Peter had the long benches removed as soon as their father died. The hall since stood empty for the most part, and only one thing stood on the stones unmoved, in the same place Evan remembered it from his childhood years. The suit of armor that used to belong to one of Evan's ancestors stared after him with its empty, black eyes. It almost felt like an accusation, as if the eyes knew what Evan intended with Julian.

The house was a relic of the past, no matter how crucial it had been to the history of Evan's family and to his name. It saddened Evan that with time, even the most cherished memories became corrupted by loneliness and watching the deterioration of his childhood home. Julian would never understand or respect such a past, but no matter how desperately Evan longed to dismiss his mocking, Tredele was not what it used to be. It was Evan's sense of duty that kept him here like it had kept him by the bedside of a father he'd detested.

The house was a relic of the past, no matter how many memories it carried for Evan's family, and Julian would neither know of it nor respect it, still jailed here because of the stupid stunt he pulled by allying himself with a criminal. He was now surely regretting his rash decisions when he could be fucking a younger woman and enjoying any luxuries her dowry could afford him, without a worry in the world.

When they entered Evan's room, he assessed it quickly and went over to the large desk that used to belong to his father. There was no reason against making it the stage for Julian's punishment and Evan's enjoyment. He would preserve the damn piece of expensive old wood for posterity, but he would do with it as he pleased, because it was his now, regardless of his father's wishes.

For several years now Evan had used it as a huge shelf of sorts, to keep books and porcelain figures, but for its new purpose, all those needed to go.

"Put your hands on the desk," he said to Julian as soon as he made enough room for what he intended. He did not look Julian's way, taking off his coat as heat climbed up his legs and twisted in his stomach.

When Evan finally took a peek at his now-willing guest, Julian's eyes were wide, his face covered in spots of pale and red, but he approached the desk and stared out the large window in front of it. He was nervous. Evan could see it in the tense set of his shoulders and the arch to his back. The hair that escaped the bundle on the back of his head was trembling on the pale background. Was he afraid of Evan, or merely disgusted by being subjected to another man's touch?

"Shall I undress?" whispered Julian so quietly Evan could barely hear him.

Evan regarded Julian's backside, and weighed the reins in his hand. This was another thing he hadn't done in years. The last time he wielded leather against a man's skin, it was for the pleasure of them both. This time, it would be for the last glimpse of Julian's ass he'd ever get to see. And even though he knew he could get much more than that from Julian right now, he couldn't bear the thought that he was unwanted.

"Pull your breeches and drawers down only," he said in a voice that didn't feel like his own. It was the voice of Sir Evan Penhart of Tredele administering just punishment. He would not get to be himself around Julian ever again. He'd been so foolish to think Julian wanted to get to know the real him.

A shudder went through Julian's body, so sudden and forceful, the tremors were obvious without even having to touch him. He nodded and slowly worked on the buttons at the front of his breeches.

The room suddenly felt small, with two breaths echoing off the walls in a silence that could only be described as deathly. Julian pushed down the clothes stiffly as an automaton, and once the breeches were gathered at his knees, the shirt tails slid lower, obscuring the fine backside.

"Pull it up," Evan said as he rolled up his sleeves, fighting the growing need to curse everything to hell and mold his body to Julian's. "Tuck it under your waistcoat." Even watching the pretty peacock follow orders was filling Evan with illicit heat.

Julian did as he was told, and the pristine linen trailed up his buttocks, uncovering their sensuous curve. He spread his thighs as far as he could with his bottom clothes still on, and braced himself against the desk, hanging his head low. It was a perfect picture of submission.

If Julian considered him a monster, a man to run away from, Evan could keep him frightened just that while longer. Julian might have been unreachable, but in this moment, when he was so open, so available to satisfy any of Evan's desires for one last time, it was impossible for Evan's mind not to wander.

Evan took a step closer, contemplating the pale, clear skin of Julian's ass and seeking for just the spot he wanted to see darken. The leather reins burned his palm as he stood there, silent and rigid, before smacking them against the bare skin. The sound clanged in Evan's ears and trailed down his neck like a warm drizzle, to roll down his cock.

"That's for stealing my mother's clock."

Julian's whole body arched, but he said nothing, clenching his ass under the red trace that remained after the hit and was now only slowly melting into the creamy skin of Julian's perfect backside. He pushed his hips forward, as if trying to escape the next stroke, but Evan waited until those to globes of flesh pushed back toward him again, so vulnerable below the folds of the shirt.

He took a deep breath, raised his hand and sent the reins down on Julian's ass from a different angle. His heart thudded at the sight of Julian's whole body stirring forward, as if pushed by Evan's own hips during a rough coupling. The smack was even louder this time, and Julian whimpered.

"That's for stealing my horse," Evan said with a rasp to his voice. A warmth was gathering in his chest and slowly spreading throughout his veins as he watched Julian flex his buttocks and withdraw his hips once more, as if he hoped to escape the rest of the punishment this way. That wouldn't be the case.

But then Julian lowered the front of his body to the desk and rested his cheek on the cold wood, glancing back, much like he had that time Evan fucked him. The healthy flush on his face was so ripe Evan could only imagine how sweet it would be to taste that juicy fruit, to push his prick between the plump lips and feel Julian's tongue roll over the head.

Evan made sure Julian saw him weigh the reins in his hand before smacking his ass with them, putting in much more force than before. "I opened up to you." *Smack.* "And you betrayed my trust." *Smack.*

The swish of the reins was just the prelude to Julian's moan, but Evan's prisoner didn't argue and just clenched his teeth, bear–

ing whatever was coming his way. His hands curled on the other edge of the desk, squeezing it so hard his knuckles went white.

"Don't you dare do that again." Evan licked the leather of the reins and made the last time they slapped against Julian's ass count. The smack resounded through the walls along with Julian's hiss. Julian's whole body stirred with frenzy, shaking and dancing away from the pain.

Evan stared at the red welts on Julian's skin, tense and panting, his hand still firmly squeezed on the leather. He both loved and detested all that supple flesh that was teasing him. Julian had allowed him a taste, only to take it away once *he* got what he wanted.

He'd promised himself to be done at this point. He tried to make himself put down the reins and end this, but with Julian looking back so pleadingly, the monster inside Evan took over. It was as if his arm acted on its own when it served five more lashes to Julian's backside. Each breath Evan took burned his lungs, but whenever he put his hand down, sending the leather strap to caress the supple flesh, the relief was so immense he could hardly think.

Evan threw the reins to the floor to stop himself, knowing this would not end for as long as the instrument was in his hand. He adjusted the hardening cock in his breeches. It was high time to finish this.

"Pull up your breeches," he ordered, hating the way his words shook with effort.

Julian rolled his face over the desktop, hiding its chiselled edges from Evan's view. His ass and thighs were shaking, criss-crossed by beautiful red lines that beckoned Evan closer. He could open his breeches and push in. Julian would allow it this one last time, and his behavior made this much abundantly clear, but Evan knew putting his prick where it wasn't wanted wouldn't satisfy him no matter how pliant Julian was.

He stepped back and wrapped his arms around his chest, watching Julian blindly reach down to pull up his clothes. He was slow, and if Evan didn't know better, he'd think Julian was trying to tempt him into more as he slowly rolled his bare hips, squeezing his thighs together.

"Face me, Julian."

Julian pulled his drawers over his ass, careful of the tender skin. He then put on his breeches but didn't button them up, leaving the shirt tail to cover his groin as he slowly turned around, watching Evan with a haunted look on his flushed face.

Evan watched the spectacle with both shame and delight, and he cursed himself for feeling this way. But men like him needed to suffer permanent regret and dissatisfaction if they did not want to turn into real predators, it seemed. "That settles the matters of which we have spoken. I apologize that I did not see my advances were truly not welcome," he found those words hard to bear, yet they still passed his lips with ease. Self-control was something he'd learned at a very early age, and even if he sometimes let his instinct get the best of him, he would not have that happening now. "I have misjudged you, and after your rejection in the past, still took advantage of your state yesterday. That will not happen again.

"I also want to thank you for lying for my sake. Pascoe would have me hang for what we both know is true." Evan took a deep breath. "If you do not despise me to the bone, we can move on from this, and as a token of my gratitude, I want to offer you a place to stay here at Tredele for as long as you wish. We now both know no ransom money will be coming, so this humble offer will give you time to arrange necessary matters at your leisure."

Julian blinked, watching Evan as if he'd just seen him for the first time. Clearly, he'd expected an offer far less gentlemanly. Then again, Evan had not shown himself from his best side.

"Thank you," said Julian in the end, looking up shyly, hands clutching the front of his clothes. "That is a very generous offer indeed."

"You are not a prisoner here anymore, so next time you wish to leave, tell me and we will make the necessary arrangements."

Evan could no longer bear looking into those big bright eyes, and at the lips that begged to be kissed. He was a vile criminal, and a sodomite who'd allowed himself to believe anything good could ever happen in his life again.

Nothing ever had since his hopes and dreams had been trampled.

Julian nodded, relaxing against the desk, only to rapidly get to his feet, flushing dark red within a split second. Evan must have made his backside sorer than intended.

"You can stay here tonight, and I will arrange for a room to be prepared for you tomorrow." Evan clenched his lips, knowing there was nothing left to say.

Julian didn't want him.

There would be no ransom and no way to pay for repairs or cancel debts. Instead, he would have a new mouth to feed, and another room to be kept warm.

"Are you certain that is what you want?" asked Julian, slowly pulling back his tousled hair. "The sleeping arrangements, I mean."

"Nothing is ever the way I want it to be," Evan said bitterly, before walking away without waiting for an answer. He was too choked up with anger and shame to risk having to speak now. Maybe his brother had had better ideas about life after all. At least he'd lived it to the fullest and did not care whether he ruined everyone else in the process.

Relief washed over him when he closed the door behind him and stormed to the room Frederick, his butler, used as an office during daylight hours. It was still early in the year, and being outside the one heated room in the house gave Evan a much needed chill. The last thing he wanted to deal with right now was the hard cock pushing at the front of his drawers. It had been difficult enough to stop at the whipping when Julian practically offered himself on a plate and even asked if he should undress without being prompted. Julian would not be able to ride a horse for a few days, and each time sitting would be a reminder of what Evan did to him.

And then the welts would subside, gone like the fleeting touch Julian had offered Evan.

The day was coming to an end, and Frederick would be back in the garden cottage when the servants lived now. It was an unorthodox arrangement but suited Evan's need for privacy just fine. He grabbed a blanket from the butler's pantry and made his way through the well-known maze of corridors, all the way out of the house. He could not bear even being in the same building as the man with that playful smile and eyes full of longing that would never be directed at him.

He rattled the door of the cottage. A large family used to live here in the day of Evan's grandfather, but with just four servants to house, the little cottage surely offered some spare beds that were warmer than any of the abandoned rooms in Tredele.

The door opened, and Mrs. Merryn looked out, a pleasant smile painted over her face. "Sir? Do you wish I fix you a plate already? You didn't want dinner tonight…"

"No, thank you, but you can prepare one for Mr. Reece, as I have found out today that is his actual surname. I wish to stay here tonight. And tomorrow, first thing in the morning, I would like you and Esther to prepare a room for Mr. Reece. He will be staying longer after all, so it is a necessity."

"Here? Master, you can't. You should be in your own bed," Mrs. Merryn said with a slight frown, lowering her voice, possibly not to alarm her husband. "Is this because you and Mr.… Reece had an argument?"

Evan groaned. Jory must have talked about Snow's disappearance after all. "Sometimes tensions run high between friends, I am sure it will settle once he has his own space."

Mrs. Merryn chewed on her lip. "Master, I do not think this is proper. You should not have to give up on your own bedroom for the sake of your guest."

Evan squeezed his fists. He would do as he pleased, even if it meant he'd be sleeping in the stable tonight. "Fine. I'll deal with it. Prepare whatever is necessary for Mr. Reece's room."

He could read Mrs. Merryn's disapproval as if she were an open book, but faced with the decisive tone, she nodded and gave him a short curtsey. "Very well, sir. I will attend to it at once. Which room would suit him best?"

"The green room, two doors down from mine. It is big enough for his needs yet small enough not to require so much firewood. The nights still get very cold between stone walls." Evan wished it was night already, so he could excuse himself and hide away in the darkness somewhere instead of having to deal with this mess.

Mrs. Merryn closed the door behind her and rushed toward Evan's family home, her long skirts and apron floating in the sharp wind. Evan shuddered. He hoped she would not approach Julian to give him a piece of her mind. For a woman in service, Mrs. Merryn was unusually outspoken, a trait he enjoyed most days, but most definitely not tonight.

He took a minute to follow, as he didn't want to talk to her or anyone. Tredele now felt like an ice-cold dragon, made out of stone, a monster to devour every last bit of Evan's life. At times like this he really did wish to fail his ancestors and sell the grounds to the highest bidder.

Or burn it down to the ground.

Chapter 12

Julian

He'd been spanked like a little child.

Julian's feet felt as if they were screwed to the floor. It was over a minute since the sound of Evan's footsteps dispersed somewhere down the corridor, and Julian's gaze still lingered on the door in expectation of seeing his host return for yet another round of lashes. That wouldn't have been the first time Evan's temper got the best of him. He could still come back, pin Julian with his dark gaze, and bend him over the desk.

Julian shuddered and took a few tentative steps, brushing his fingertips up and down the door before opening it as quietly as he could. The linen of his drawers scraped against the tender flesh on his ass when he looked out into the corridor, finding it as empty as expected. Yet another reminder of what just happened.

He pulled the drawers all the way up, until the fabric scraped against his skin, and he shivered, remembering the unexpected strikes at the end. When Evan started his perverse attempt at disciplining Julian, it had seemed like the blows would be easy to take, but each subsequent one was yet another layer of discomfort. And yet, the burning heat of them was so delicious. It triggered something unknown within Julian's loins and made his prick stand harder than ever, drizzling clear liquid into the tail of his shirt while Evan struck him over and over with a fury that should have caused a completely different reaction. It was as if at that moment Julian's whole life was in Evan's hands, and instead of giving him a fright, it had sent a thrill down Julian's body.

He gently brushed his fingertips up and down his aching buttocks, gasping at the strange mixture of pain and pleasure it gave him. He paced back to the desk, just in time to see Evan storm through the courtyard, away from the house. He chewed on his lips and rocked against the stern mahogany desktop absent-mindedly.

His cock was still achingly hard, trapped in his pants like it had been for the first few nights in Evan's bed. This was something he couldn't quite understand. If Evan wanted his body so much, why hadn't he taken him when Julian was so completely at his mercy? Being an expert in knots, Evan could have easily tied Julian's hands in a way that didn't make them numb while securing him very effectively.

Even on that first night they'd spent together, he could have pulled up Julian's shirt and touched him for as long as he wanted and however he wanted. He could have handled Julian's prick and slid warm, oiled-up fingers into Julian's resisting body. He could have flipped Julian over, kicked his legs open, and forced his thick rod inside him. And if that hadn't been enough for him, he could have taken his pleasure in the morning as well, forcing Julian to spend with those rough yet skillful hands.

He slowly traced his lips with his tongue, brushing his groin over the side of the desktop again and again. A moan left his lips when he grabbed one of his aching buttocks and squeezed it harshly. His other palm brushed over the smooth old wood, and in his mind, Evan's voice blew heat all over his nape, firm and commanding.

Bend over.

Julian's breath rasped. He slid one hand into the back of his drawers, which in turn tightened the fabric over his cock and balls. The imaginary Evan was already pushing Julian's shirt up, exposing the flesh he'd himself marked with a pair of reins of all things.

Spread your legs.

Push down your breeches.

And Julian obeyed without question. His gaze trailed over the floor, all the way to a large mirror. It was standing at an angle, but he could see the outline of his ass as the fabric slid lower, uncovering the angry welts on pale skin.

It seemed Evan had uncovered yet another thing Julian had never known about himself.

He lay with his chest on the desk, cuddling up his cheek to the wood, and the warm fingers, rough from honest work, trailed up and down his sides, kneaded his ass, making him mewl with discomfort despite his cock already twitching for relief.

Julian squeezed his standing cock and scratched his teeth against the wood, watching his ass rock back and forth in the mirror. Evan could find him like this, half-naked and wanton, practically begging for being defiled again. He'd fasten both Julian's arms and legs to the desk, and he'd make Julian's buttocks even redder, with his hand this time, pinching and squeezing the flesh after each blow.

He'd deliver the strokes until Julian screamed for mercy, ready to beg that he would do anything for the lashes to stop. He'd wiggle his ass, making Evan all the more excited. But Evan wouldn't just take him then and there. He'd slide a slick finger over the outside of Julian's hole, and tease it until Julian begged to be filled. Only then would Evan pick up a candle—oh, that shameful candle— and slowly tease it into Julian to prepare him for an invasion much thicker.

Julian howled silently, imagining Evan's cock against his tender hole. As ecstatic as he'd felt by the end of that one time Evan had taken him, the initial pain had left him feeling violated and looking for blood afterward. There had been none, but he couldn't deny being afraid of submitting to something like it ever again, no matter how exciting of a concept it was to be taken advantage of this way. It was only in his mind that Julian was free to wonder if it was merely the loathing in Evan's eyes that had made the act so excruciating.

But now, all that mattered was the dull throbbing in Julian's groin that needed to be taken care of. He swirled his thumb around his slick cockhead and peeked at the mirror again.

And went completely still.

There, in the corner of the mirror, behind the partially open door, stood Evan and watched him.

Julian's throat clenched so hard he was afraid he'd choke to death, but his cock could not have been any harder, so after the initial shock wore off, he resumed the slide of his palm against his prick.

Evan's lips were parted, his face without much expression, but his eyes burned. If only he'd come in, tempted by the sight of Julian, and... they didn't need to actually fuck. Evan could embrace Julian from behind, rub against him, toss him off. That would have been more than enough to take the edge off Julian's arousal.

Julian moaned louder and twisted his ass gently, never looking away from Evan's reflection in the mirror. He moved his hand over his prick faster, opening his mouth to call out to Evan, invite him in for some play. But he couldn't. Nothing came out, and he just watched the body that somehow managed to fill the whole doorframe.

At this angle, Evan might not even have seen his own reflection in the mirror and believed himself invisible to Julian, whose backside was wantonly turned toward the door.

Julian couldn't possibly invite him. He wasn't a sodomite. He was just confused, influenced by Evan's presence and charm. He had to keep his fantasies to himself and settle for the Evan of his imagination instead of the real thing.

And yet, he spread his legs and whimpered, clenching and relaxing his buttocks, just to see how Evan would react to such relentless teasing. Could he possibly open his own breeches and take out his cock? Would Julian see God's most magnificent work being pumped in Evan's hand until it left seed dripping down Evan's fingers?

Julian imagined himself turning around, and with Evan too shocked to move, crawling across the room to have a taste of the warm seed. *Oh, he'd lick it—no, he would not.*

This was all much too confusing yet made the cock in Julian's hand harder by the second, even though all Evan did was suck his bottom lip into his mouth, never even blinking.

Julian's mind was frying over the heat within, and he pulled back his hand, keeping it above his ass, with Evan's imaginary hand holding on to it, making it impossible for Julian to fight off his advances.

In that moment, a phantom cock entered Julian, and he bucked, moaning while his hand worked his prick at a rapid pace, completion already within his grasp. In his fantasy, taking a cock didn't hurt. It was all about animalistic pleasure, being overpowered, pinned to the desk and pounded until the beast had his fill, leaving Julian open and dripping with seed.

He came, squeezing his left hand into a fist, and milked his prick until it hurt so much he needed to let go of it. He half expected another cock to replace it, a real one this time, but nothing came. No sound. No touch.

He glanced into the mirror, still gasping for air.

He looked just in time to see Evan move away from the door as quietly as a cat.

Only now reality started seeping back into Julian's mind, providing him with an explanation for his loneliness in this act. Evan had actually apologized for the two times they'd been intimate. Called that time when Julian broke into his wine storage and reached for Evan's cock himself once he was besotted 'taking advantage of his state'.

Julian slid to his knees, still holding on to that damn desk, and rested his forehead against the wood. That encounter the night before had been Julian's fault. He'd been the one to make the first move, and yet somehow Evan believed it had been the other way around. But maybe it was better this way, since Julian did not want to disclose the truth. Not now, and not ever.

He didn't want to be pilloried and humiliated.

He didn't want to die.

Yet he still trembled at the memory of Evan's words. *I could be your storm. All you need is ask.*

Julian was restless after Evan's departure. He washed himself and applied some oil to his aching behind, but in the end, he decided some air was needed. No, that wasn't right—he needed to clear the air with Evan. As comfortable as Julian used to feel at Tredele, without its master around the medieval walls seemed cold and unwelcoming, so Julian wore the tightest breeches and the greenest suit, and walked into the dying sun outside, trying not to wince at the scraping of linen against his bruised flesh.

Evan was nowhere to be seen, so when Julian spotted Jory herding sheep to a fenced-off part of land, he sped up to ask the man about Evan's whereabouts. When he approached, Jory tousled his ginger hair, as if trying to hide his eyes behind it.

"Wait! I need to speak to you," called out Julian, wincing when the linen pressed against his ass, feeling as if the contents of a whole needle box were scraping against his skin.

"Um... yes, Mr. Reece?" Jory mumbled, patting the last sheep on the back before closing the fence behind it. Evan must have revealed Julian's real name to the servants.

He turned around, and Julian was once again faced with Jory's pleasant face. It was more than pleasant in fact—if Julian were even the right person to judge those things. Evan swore that he'd never approached his servant in an ungodly manner, but what if he started considering it following Julian's suggestion? Those things were not unheard of.

Julian smiled the sweetest smile he could muster while his chest was burning with the need to see Evan and talk to him, not just listen as he had back at the house. "Have you seen your master anywhere?"

"Mr. Reece, it's not my fault. I said I would do it, that I would cut more wood if necessary, but Master seemed so angry, I couldn't refuse his request. I'm not lazy. All he needs to do is ask, and I'd get to it." Jory became so agitated his face flushed.

Julian frowned. "What are you saying?"

"Master is cutting wood for your new lodgings, sir. Behind the barn."

"My new lodg—" Julian's heart beat faster and he turned on his heel, rushing across the vast glade by Tredele. So now he'd be expelled from Evan's room. He thought Evan enjoyed their late-night conversations as much as he did, so why change a good thing?

He ran through the stables to reach the barn quicker, but once he saw Evan's silhouette from far away, his gait slowed down so much he almost stopped.

Evan wasn't wearing either a waistcoat or a shirt, and his breeches were held up with suspenders. The orange-tinted sunlight was free to roam all over his skin while Evan drove his ax into a piece of wood with a loud crack.

Julian slowed down, first because of stiffness in his muscles, then because he wanted to look sufficiently dignified upon his approach. He chose elegant clothes for a reason. He wanted to show himself from the best side and make Evan take him seriously, not like a man whose breeches he'd lowered less than an hour ago.

But the closer he got, the harder to ignore it was that Evan wore no shirt, exposing his muscular chest and arms to the whole world. Maybe this wasn't the best time to talk after all? How was Julian not to be distracted by the sight of Evan's dark nipples and chest hair, just out there, for anyone to see.

Evan looked up at him, breathing hard after he'd swung the ax yet again. Julian stopped for a moment, only to resume his walk, determined to face his fears and the person who'd somehow managed to alter his perception of men. He stood far enough not to enter Evan's personal space, but even a few steps away from Evan's herculean form, he felt as if he could smell the sun and fresh sweat on the man's skin.

Evan couldn't ignore him anymore and let the ax rest on his shoulder as he sighed deeply. "Anything I can help you with?"

His skin glistened, and Julian found it excruciatingly difficult to keep his eyes on Evan's face. Did he like the suit Julian was wearing? "I— we didn't have the opportunity to talk. At least I didn't—"

Evan raised his eyebrows. "Do go on..."

Julian opened his mouth, but his mind went blank, and he had no idea what to say without making a fool of himself. Where was his usual suave charm when it was truly needed? He used to be able to talk his way out of the direst situations, but faced with the man who fucked him in his dreams—and had actually fucked him twice in reality—he was losing the plot. "This is difficult," he said in the end.

Evan let out a long breath and ran his fingers through his hair. "You want to leave after all."

"No," said Julian, stepping closer, but he stopped when Evan moved back, clearly trying to keep the original distance. "I'm sorry. I shouldn't have left without a word. It was not like me at all," he said, desperate to not have Evan think of him as not dependable. He *was* dependable when he wanted to be.

"But you did." Evan must have realized this would be a longer conversation because he dropped the ax to the ground and put his hands on his hips.

Julian winced. "I panicked. I can't explain why I did it, but I want you to know I regretted it as soon as I reached town."

"I'm sorry I made you feel as if leaving was your only choice."

Julian swallowed hard, feeling an unpleasant fullness in his throat. Evan was so close Julian could touch him if he only walked a few steps closer, a bull watching his opponent. "I wasn't myself."

Evan scowled at those words. "What are you trying to say?"

Julian exhaled as evenly as he could, pushing his hands into the pockets of his coat. "I suppose I—I provoked you."

"Anything else?" Evan grabbed the ax and turned away from Julian, putting a new piece of wood on the block.

"I value your friendship," said Julian quickly. "I know I have angered you, and I have no assets that might be of worth to you, but maybe I could provide the companionship you need. I don't think there's reason for us to separate. The bed is big enough for two men," he said in one breath, then stared at Evan in complete silence.

Evan swung the ax, and his powerful form stretched for a second before he chopped the wood in two. He stood there for a moment, contemplating his answer, and the wait made Julian's palms sweat. "My instinct is to push you away, to tell you I do not need companionship, and that I am more than fine with the company of servants and sheep, but that would not be true." Evan looked at Julian with less of a frown than before. "I've grown fond of you, and I would wish for you to stay here for as long as you like. But I won't share my bed with you. I am not made out of stone."

A deep shudder trailed down Julian's back, and he rubbed his hands over his flushing face when he pondered the message behind Evan's words. He was still very much wanted, even though he'd hurt Evan's pride today. He understood why Evan didn't want to sleep next to him anymore, but at the same time, his mind was serving him offerings of invisible fingers trailing over his body already. There would be more of a chance for that if they remained physically close.

"I will not break your trust again."

Evan gave him a nod. "I am happy to hear that, and I promise not to behave inappropriately toward you."

Julian cursed himself silently. Now that he was so free, he yearned for the rope around his wrists. It made perfect sense without making any sense at all.

Julian nodded and glanced at the tips of his shoes. "Do you need my assistance?" he asked in the end, unable to find a simple excuse to stay with Evan.

"No, you are my guest now. I am... not in the best of moods, and I'd rather do this on my own. I assure you, I will be much better at dinner. I will see you then."

That was Julian's cue to go. He pressed his lips into a tight line and nodded at Evan before turning on his heel and making his way back to the house. He could sense the burning weight of Evan's stare on him, and it made his heart beat so fast he needed to slow down.

He appreciated the honesty of Evan's words yet couldn't help feeling choked up.

Evan would not tie him up again.

He wouldn't reach out to grab Julian's arm and turn him around.

He wouldn't let Julian explore his body, nor would he touch Julian's.

Julian deeply regretted slapping Evan for trying to kiss him that one time, because he would now never get a taste of him.

CHAPTER 13

JULIAN

Evan's ass was a piece of art in its own right. Clad in a pair of buckskin breeches held up with suspenders that pulled the fabric tight against the firm flesh, it was an exquisite sight.

Julian followed Evan's lead up the ladder and into the cramped space just below the roof. It was leaking again, and with Jory having no experience in matters of construction and Frederick not being young enough to push through on his hands and knees, Evan decided to deal with the damage himself.

Julian volunteered to help and was now crawling between beams so dry the whole construction creaked when he moved. The dust was so thick he could sense it melting into his hands, but he swallowed his disgust and went on, listening to the distinct sounds of little rodents running around them as if it was their birthright to live here.

"You really don't need to be here. You will get dirty," Evan said. "I'll deal with this and return to you shortly."

Julian stopped moving, thinking of the grime underneath his palms, which might as well contain mice droppings. "Why can you get dirty and I cannot?" he asked in the end, after taking a deep breath of the dusty air. He moved forward, hoping to brush against Evan by chance. He did not want to be useless to the household, and no matter how much he disliked having to overexert himself, the need to change Evan's opinion of him was too great to stay idle.

Evan groaned, and he must have gotten to the right spot under the roof, because he got up and pushed up a plank, flooding the area with sunshine. "Because you're so... oh, you know."

Julian frowned. "I'm what?"

"Pretty," Evan said flatly. "And you don't like to get dirty," he followed up quickly. Before Julian could get a glance of his face, Evan peeked through the trapdoor, looking over the roof.

Julian stared at Evan's chest, now clearly visible with the bright sun shining through the linen fabric. He and Evan had settled into a comfortable routine in the last few weeks. It was now May, and just as the weather became warmer, so did Julian's relationship with Evan. They spent a lot of time in each other's company, even reading in the same room and discussing philosophy until late in the evening, before they retired to separate rooms. But throughout their time together, Evan never really mentioned anything related to Julian's appearance, almost as if he'd forgotten about the infatuation already.

Julian swallowed hard and moved closer, taken by the scent of fresh air and Evan's body. "You allowed me into your home. I want to repay your kindness."

"Kindness would not be what I'd call it, but I agree that you're free to get your hands dirty, if you wish. I need to move a bit lower on the roof to see what the issue is. If you really want to help, you may hold the rope I tie around myself." Evan climbed through the trapdoor and squatted on a ledge outside, holding on to a beam right next to the opening. Wind pulled on Evan's hair and shirtsleeves, creating a picture so becoming that for a moment Julian wished he had the talent to immortalize it on canvas.

Julian licked his lips and moved closer until he kneeled underneath the open trapdoor and stood up, immediately hit by a sharp gust of wind. With his fair mane blown into his eyes in the way, Evan was just a shadow, but Julian reached out and grabbed his arm. "Shouldn't you tie the rope first? I can't have you falling off and breaking your back. What would happen to Tredele with you gone?" he asked, attempting a joke.

Evan frowned deeply, but held on to Julian with his other hand. "I have some distant cousins to take care of the house when I'm gone."

Julian pushed back his hair and looked into Evan's handsome face, already scorching hot where he was being touched. There was rarely an opportunity for any physical contact between then, but despite the initial belief that once Evan stopped pursuing Julian, the unfamiliar feelings would go away, Julian had only become more attached to his host. None of them ever mentioned the two times they fucked anymore, but Evan slowly crawled beneath Julian's skin, like a layer of warmth and longing that wouldn't let Julian fall asleep without thinking of the darkest eyes he knew.

It was almost as if being around a man with Evan's proclivities was enough to pull Julian to sin. Each time their gazes met and struggled to part, the presence under Julian's skin turned into an itch that begged to be scratched. It would have been wise to leave temptation behind, but the thought of never seeing Evan again was like a needle pinned in Julian's eye. So he stayed, and they both pretended that they'd only ever been friends.

"Don't be an imbecile then. You don't even know who is your heir? Come back here at once!"

Evan crawled closer, with a worried look on his face that Julian hated to see. It never brought anything good. "Move out of the way. I need to get the rope from down there."

Julian sighed and kneeled down, finally letting go of him. He watched both of Evan's legs dive inside, focusing on his crotch a tad too long. Would being around Evan drive him mad eventually? Maybe this inexplicable affection was already the symptom of impending doom?

For now, it seemed he would stay for a while in Evan's care. With his family unwilling to break their silence and associate with him again, it cost Julian a lot of injury to his pride to ask his father for his belongings to be returned to him. There was no answer at first, but then one afternoon a fortnight ago, Hunt had arrived with a carriage filled with trunks containing everything Julian ever acquired, from the new shoes he'd not yet worn to the old toothbrush that missed almost all its bristles. It was humiliating to have a servant shy away from him, as if he believed Julian to be poxed, but he gritted his teeth and endured.

When Esther unpacked Julian's belongings in the green bedroom, and with his books added to Evan's vast library, for the first time Julian felt at home in Tredele. On that same evening, Julian read Evan from a book of his favorite poems, and with the fire burning between their chairs, Julian realized he did not long to leave just yet.

With the prospect of Evan's company, even the trip to Italy didn't seem an attractive enough perspective to break the invisible chain that constantly drew him to his host. So he settled in his poverty, telling himself he didn't have enough money for the trip anyway.

'All you have to do is ask,' Evan had said, and Julian struggled to keep his lips from forming the request on their own accord.

Evan moved past Julian to a wooden chest, which fit just barely underneath the slope of the roof.

"How bad is the damage? It is such a big house. Maybe it would be wise to hire a man with experience in such repairs?" asked Julian, watching the buckskin mold to Evan's ass and thighs when he bent over toward the trunk. Evan's face seemed more handsome with each passing day now that they were not constantly arguing, and many times Julian found himself facing temptation but did nothing to express those feelings. Because, well, he did not want to follow through, but what about Evan, who did not have such qualms? Was he merely hiding his resentment, or was a chaste companion enough for him? Julian didn't dare ask for fear of damaging the delicate balance they had created.

He assumed Evan wasn't meeting any other men for intimate companionship, because they spent so much time together that Julian would have noticed. The two times they'd been together, Evan had seemed extremely... virile, so would a man like that be able to contain his masculine energy without releasing it every once in a while? Who did Evan think about when he was alone in his room at night? Evan had said something about being a 'skillful lover'. Did that mean he had a lot of experience? With numerous men?

Julian bit his lip when Evan pulled his shirt off, and with the suspenders down, even his breeches slid a bit lower. The sight of all that tan skin on show instantly grabbed Julian's attention, and he discreetly looked to the trail of dark hair under Evan's navel, but Evan was already pulling the suspenders back up.

When Evan answered Julian's question, Julian was so distracted he forgot what he'd asked about. "I'm sure it's fine, I can manage it on my own," Evan said, and started tying the rope around himself, only reminding Julian just how skilled he was with knots.

Julian swallowed, watching him handle the thick bundle of thread just as proficiently as he had the cord around Julian's wrists. "Will you have an heir eventually?" asked Julian in the end, his mind constantly repeating the moment Evan called him *pretty* for no good reason. Could someone like Evan even have a family and father children?

Evan sighed, and wouldn't look into Julian's eyes as he approached the trapdoor. "This is not the right time."

Julian cleared his throat and rubbed his hands over his thighs when he noticed how clammy they were. His chest swelled with uncertainty. "I merely— I've been thinking, and we are friends now, are we not?" he asked softly.

Evan needed to get back to his knees to move back to the opening in the roof, so he crawled under the low-hanging beams, all the way to Julian. When he stretched, glancing at Julian with a question in his eyes, only an inch or two would be necessary to cross if Julian wanted to kiss him. But, kiss a man? What kind of preposterous idea was that?

Evan's eyes softened, now uncommonly tender. In the bright light shining through his iris, it did not look that dark at all. "Yes, we are friends."

Julian smiled, choked up. In that moment, he wanted to lean forward and press his mouth against Evan's. It tingled with anticipation, and he soothed the tension within by biting into his own flesh. "I want to understand you better. I never knew a man... so different from other men."

"Oh, is that so?" Evan gave him a half smile and carefully moved through the opening in the roof, his abdominal muscles stretching and beckoning Julian's face closer. In the bright sunlight, the sheen of sweat winked at him from beneath the dark hair. "Haven't you met many different gentlemen at your favorite place, Madam Canard's? Or perhaps in Plymouth?"

Julian scowled. He wasn't certain whether it was a slight or not. "I meant... men who do not desire women."

The silence was only helped by the loud singing of birds outside, followed by a sudden cawing. The sunshine couldn't make the chill in Julian's stomach any better either.

"What is there to know?" Evan grumbled in the end, pulling himself out of the attic, squatting on the ledge outside once more.

Julian sighed and looked out, standing by the open trapdoor, his eyes trained on Evan's muscular thighs tensing as he moved down the slope of the roof. "How did you know?" he asked in the end, gently stroking the rope. That was the one thing he needed to know the most. How would a man know he had such proclivities in the first place? How could he be certain? Those were questions Julian kept asking himself each night while he played with his prick thinking of Evan. Each night he told himself it would be the last time, and each night he failed.

Evan stopped once he reached one of the dormers close to the trapdoor. It physically hurt Julian's stomach to watch Evan balance on the old slate covering of the roof, even if he did seem to be managing just fine. "I guess I have always felt there was something wrong with me. When I was at the age my brother talked about the bosom of the dairy maid, I was more interested in our footman."

Julian brushed his hand over the moss-covered slate just below the opening. His mind suggested a connection, one he didn't like. "The footman who lies buried on the hill?"

Evan ran his fingers through his hair, pushing it off his face. "He was a beautiful man."

Julian clutched the edge of the opening. Watching pain trail over Evan's face made him feel so very small and inept. Were he close enough, he'd squeeze his hand. "And were the feelings mutual?" he asked, worried he might hear a story that was not as romantic as the information Evan had given him earlier.

Evan shrugged and looked down the slope below. He didn't seem eager to examine the roof anymore. "What does it matter?"

"I want to know those things about you. How does one start a relationship with another man when it's something so forbidden?"

Evan looked up at Julian, his expression blank, yet his eyes were filled with emotion. "One needs to decide that the other man is worth dying for. And then you take a leap of faith." It sounded grim with Evan standing so close to the edge of the roof.

Julian stared at him, his feet growing roots and clutching at the floor. His heart seemed to have grown so large it was close to bursting through his ribs. "So you knew because you wanted to kiss him, and hold him? And you were ready to die to get that?"

"Nothing seemed more important at that time. The first time we kissed, I knew I was where I belonged."

Julian massaged his throat, swallowing. He knew all too well that his betrayal had been yet another addition to Evan's pain. "You must miss him terribly."

"I get to visit his grave. It's been a long time. I... haven't met a man I would die for since then." Evan ruffled his hair, obscuring his face.

Julian exhaled, petting the rope, as if somehow Evan could feel his touch on its other end. Julian should have let Evan kiss him in the stables. Maybe then he'd know the truth about himself. None of the women he'd fucked had ever made him feel the way Evan did. There had been physical pleasure to the acts, but no girl left him remembering touch, and heat, and scent for days on end.

Maybe he was as cursed as Evan was.

Only unlike Evan, Julian never even considered an attraction to men a possibility. He hadn't given it any thought, and so he'd never reached out for the sinful pleasures that no one discussed openly. Until that one night with Evan. "I doubt most men would readily die for their lovers," he said quietly.

"Have you never been in love?" Evan moved over the dormer and rested his feet on the edge of the roof, making Julian's heart gallop in panic.

"Don't fall down, I beg you," he said, leaning out of the trapdoor. The question sent a quivering sensation all over his chest. He didn't know. He had no idea.

"I'll be fine! I think the bloody crows are making nests somewhere and damaging the slates. Squeezing through a hole and making it all worse. I will roast these damn beasts for dinner!"

Julian grabbed the rope and pulled it tight to his chest. "That's the first time I heard of a gentleman hunting on his own roof."

"It's my house, and I will eat a crow if I choose to!"

"Sir?" Frederick yelled from the ground, and for a blood–curdling moment Evan leaned back to see the man below. "There is a letter for you from Fairfield Park. It's supposedly of utmost urgency!"

Julian pulled on the rope, forcing Evan to straighten his back and stop leaning down over the abyss. "You heard him. Maybe forsake this idea for now and write the man back."

Evan punched the roof with a groan. "How important can it be?"

"Very, sir! I was informed that I should present it to you at once!"

Evan looked up at Julian. "Would you go down and get it for me?"

Julian glanced at Evan. Then at the roof. "I am not leaving you here."

"Don't be silly, just tie the rope to a beam in the attic. Frederick? Mr. Reece will come down to the second floor and get it!"

Julian still hesitated, but the weight of Evan's gaze made him comply. He tied the rope to two subsequent posts before crawling back to the ladder, and then to the second floor, where Frederick was already waiting, the letter on a silver platter, as if Tredele functioned like any other great house. At least now that the charades were over, he was known under his own name, though he did not want to know what the servants thought of his actions.

"Thank you," he said and hurried back with the letter, which was sealed with red wax.

Fortunately, by the time Julian returned to his place at the open trapdoor, Evan hadn't yet fallen to his death. "What's the writing? Is the 'P' big and round?"

Julian looked at Evan, carefully assessing his position on the roof before glancing at the script. "Yes. It looks very stylish."

Evan shook his head and carried on with inspecting the roof. "It's from Blackwell's wife. Can't imagine what urgent business she might have with me."

Julian cracked the seal and unfolded the letter to find rows of neat writing. Each subsequent word made his throat flush with greater heat. It was an invitation to a masquerade at Fairfield Park, and he was expected along with Evan!

He exhaled, reading through the letter over and over. *People.* Maybe they could see some people!

"We are invited to a masquerade in two weeks. How wonderful! What will be your costume?" he asked, imagining Evan in the mask he wore on Julian's first evening at Tredele, in a tricorn hat and a black cape, like a Venetian gentleman at the annual carnival.

Evan didn't look up. "I told you it's nothing urgent. There will be no costume, as I won't be attending. And don't open my letters, or I'll have you sent to the gaol."

Julian frowned at him. "Why not? I know you have not been attending any functions in recent years. Don't you want to dance? Find out what other people think about current literature?"

"I can't dance. These bloody birds think my roof is a joke!" Evan was getting more agitated by the minute, and he actually ripped out a loose slate and tossed it away.

Julian squeezed the letter in his hands, shocked by the outburst. "But I would really want to go. Wouldn't it be a pleasure to mingle? If no one taught you to dance, or if you don't know what dances are popular right now, it is not an issue. We have two weeks—more than enough for me to teach you all the fashionable steps." It was on the tip of Julian's tongue that dance was a human mating ritual. They'd be touching for hours, swaying to imaginary music, and at some point, maybe their senses would become cloudy enough to allow a kiss.

"*You* want to go?" Evan looked up with a deep frown, as if it hadn't occurred to him that Julian might have the same needs as most people. "Why?"

Julian gave him a small smile. "With my father out of the picture, I need to establish new connections," he said innocently. Evan didn't need to know Julian was secretly hoping to give him dance lessons and walk into the ballroom alongside a baronet.

"What kind of connections? Is it necessary? You are to leave for Italy. Or is it a wealthy lady you are looking to woo?" Evan eyed him from below.

Italy. In the recent weeks Julian had hardly ever thought of the trip he'd planned for so long. "You are well aware I do not wish to marry yet. I am merely devoid of society. I miss being around people, and I believe it would do you some good to meet someone else but me for a change."

"You used to want to stay a bachelor, but that was before you lost your father's favor. I supposed something might have changed." Evan shrugged and slowly made his way higher, poking at the slates with a small hammer. "And I do not see why you believe being around people would do me any good? I am perfectly content with your company."

Julian scowled. "I am very content with your company as well, but surely you see I cannot spend my whole life here, at your charity. You treated me with such contempt when we first met, and I forgave you. Can't you do this much for me?"

Evan stilled, but then pulled out another slate with an angry hiss. "Fine. But I will not dance. Or enjoy myself for that matter."

Julian exhaled with relief, surprised he managed to pressure his stern baronet into anything. Clearly, the man still thought Julian was pretty enough to keep around. "Fantastic. You will not regret this. I heard Fairfield Park is a delightful house. The family only moved in three years ago. I'm so curious how it turned out."

"Oh, It's just *lovely*," Evan said in a voice oozing with contempt. Two crows cawed all of a sudden and flew out from under the roof so quickly, Evan wobbled, his eyes opening wide as his whole body tilted back.

Julian gave a wordless cry and clutched the rope, tugging Evan back with all the strength he had.

Evan grabbed the dormer, and swore horribly. "Are you done talking about bloody Fairfield? That place does not have a soul."

Julian hugged the rope and watched Evan's bare chest shimmer in the sun. "But the *crème de la crème* of society will be there. Can you imagine the costumes, the quality of entertainment? It will be magical."

"Fine, fine. I already said I'll take you with me." He didn't even look at Julian, grabbing something under the tiles.

And then it came. The moment when Julian realized he couldn't attend a masquerade, as he had gotten rid of his costumes just last year. He took a deep breath, staring at Evan's back, which arched from the strain so beautifully it could be the perfect allegory of strength.

"Will you... would you lend me some money?"

Chapter 14

Evan

Evan sold his telescope.

There was no way around it, as it wouldn't have felt right to sell his family heirlooms to satisfy Julian's fancy. Or to please himself for that matter, because seeing Julian smile was like having sunshine reach every part of his old and dusty house.

Maybe it was for the better? The time had come to stop looking toward the stars and face the reality that he was barely scraping by. Tredele needed investment if it was to survive, and if he truly wanted his family name to live on, it was time to settle and produce an heir.

Evan had always despised the idea of marrying some girl out of necessity and making them both miserable in the process, but it seemed that everyone needed to play their part in the end. No one could escape the clutches of their position or their means. So even though he'd evaded Blackwell's daughter so far, he now needed to make a good impression and find a way to charm her.

The idea of marrying a girl he had nothing in common with still didn't sit well with him, but if the alternative was to sell his family seat, a lucrative marriage was the better option. What he most feared about all the changes that would be coming his way was that his quiet harmony of living with Julian would have to be over. Then again, it would have been over at some point anyway. Julian wanted to leave Cornwall, and as soon as he could convince a patron to sponsor the trip to Italy, or even better—go with him, he'd leave Tredele without thinking much about Evan being left behind.

It hadn't rained for a while now, and the streets of Looe were pleasantly dusty. Julian had been chirping all the way from Tredele, which was so incredibly fitting, since he wore the canary yellow suit that Evan used to hate on Peter but absolutely loved on his new friend. It went so well with the reddish hue of his sandy hair, and made Julian look like a golden god who had come down from the heavens to grace the world with the joy that came so naturally to him.

While unhappy about being emotionally blackmailed into agreeing to attend the masquerade, Evan was too smitten by Julian's enthusiasm to stay angry for long. But no matter how much he enjoyed listening to Julian's hopes for the costume party, the fact that he was enthusiastic about visiting Fairfield Park—a great house supposedly modern and tailored to contemporary taste, so unlike Tredele—was a thorn in Evan's side.

He was proud of his heritage, but it was impossible to ignore that the man Evan wanted to please most did not truly appreciate the dusty, cold rooms and furnishings gathered throughout the last three hundred years. Maybe at least he would enjoy having the costume for the ball made for him at the tailor's. As much as Evan cringed at the costs the whole endeavour would incur, seeing Julian sparkling like freshly opened champagne was all the could have wished for.

He was so lost in his thoughts that it took him longer than usual to notice a shift in Julian's mood. He'd been unusually quiet since they reached town, and even pulled his hat lower on his forehead while he rode alongside Evan.

"I've come to think you like attention. Is that not so?" Evan asked.

Julian blinked and looked up at him, only to straighten up and push the tricorn hat higher so they could look at each other more comfortably. "So many of those people know me. And worse yet, they also know Father and I are not on speaking terms anymore. I was left with close to nothing. They surely pity me now."

"I'm sure they do. Once the most appreciated guest of Madam Canard's, now only a friend of Sir Recluse." Evan hated the nickname with all his heart, but wanted to cheer up Julian. And it worked, with the flicker of amusement back in Julian's eyes.

"Sir Recluse and Mr. Penniless. What a pair we are."

"Will that be your costume? Shall I get you a beggar's bowl?"

"No," said Julian and slapped Evan's thigh. "Silly man. My costume will be as exquisite as my taste."

"Should mine be as unrefined as mine then?" Evan lifted an eyebrow in amusement, trying not to think that he'd rather have Julian's touch on his thigh last much longer.

Julian narrowed his eyes, but the smile never disappeared from his face. "No. You need something bold. Something that sets you apart from the crowd. You're like a big, powerful bull, and I think you would look quite magnificent with a pair of horns."

Evan licked his lips, trying not to show how much Julian's vulgar language affected him. The word 'bull' was never used in polite conversation. It evoked images of a carnal connection of the most brutish kind, and now Julian wanted to dress Evan up as one? Evan winced, even though he knew he'd go with almost anything Julian came up with. "I'd rather not draw too much attention to myself. I take up too much space as it is."

"Don't be so modest. Aren't you a baronet? The one heir to an ancient name at that? You deserve all the space you might wish for," Julian said, and while he seemed amused by the conversation, his words didn't feel like empty flattery.

Evan's mind drifted off to the only space he wished for. The one beside Julian in his bed. Evan could play the bull for him there, but that would never happen, and yet Julian teased him so with the deliciously improper language. "If you are to help me choose, I would like to make a good impression on our hosts," he said, thinking of Elizabeth and how she'd always seemed to consider him grumpy. Evan needed all the help he could get to change her perception of him, or she'd never accept her father's plans. Blackwell was not the type of man who'd force his daughter into a union she absolutely refused.

Julian's smile became even brighter. "I am thinking solid black and dark red. Like bull's blood on the sands of a tauromachy," said Julian in a dark voice as they rode through town toward the centre close to the sea.

"Is that... something that could be considered attractive?" Evan tried, trying not to think of the way Julian's mouth curved when he named the animal again. "Would it not be seen as intimidating?"

Julian shook his head. "You are a bold man, and your costume should reflect that. Please, forgive me, but you would not be an attractive Harlequin."

Evan frowned. "Why is that?"

Julian sighed and looked into the sky briefly. "Because a man can only be dressed up to a certain level. The wrong costume will look alien on him, like teeth on a goose."

"Ah, so what will your costume be? You hadn't seemed to have made up your mind before yesterday."

They were already approaching the tailor's shop, its signboard rattling softly against the iron support in the wind.

"How about a guess? What would suit me best, Sir Evan?" asked Julian before sliding off Snow's back.

Evan couldn't help a little smile as he watched him, and it only made him realize how little he used to smile before he met Julian. "A canary? I think it would suit you well." He got down to the ground as well, and patted Noir's neck.

Julian glanced at the bright yellow of his jacket and fastened the mare to the fence. "Always mocked for my choice of suit."

"No, I believe..." Evan looked away, both embarrassed and to make sure no one overheard him. "I believe it's very pleasing on you. Goes with your hair."

Julian's gaze remained on Evan's face for longer than usual, but he smiled even when he averted Evan's eyes. "Ah. I shall wear it more frequently then."

"I'd rather you didn't. It makes my mind wander." Was that too inappropriate? Should Evan have kept his thoughts to himself?

Julian stroked Snow's thigh, looking oddly contemplative for a few moments. "In our mind is where we are free," he said in the end and held Evan's gaze.

Evan gave a curt nod. His nightly fantasies of debauching Julian were definitely where he was free, but it still made him happy to hear Julian acknowledging that he did not consider them intrusive. "Isn't that a glorious thought." He dared to wink at Julian before going into the tailor's shop.

The apprentice looked up from above a table piled with bales of fabric. "May I help you—?" he started, but when Julian pushed in after Evan, there was recognition in his gaze. "Gentlemen."

Julian's warm, long-fingered hand slid over Evan's shoulder like the most charming of snakes. Evan knew it would be almost as deadly if teased the wrong way.

"Good day. Me and my friend, Sir Evan Penhart, of Tredele, wish to commission costumes for a masquerade."

Evan nodded, and the apprentice just stared at him for a moment as if he'd seen a... *ghost*. Very fitting. Evan cleared his throat.

"Oh, yes, right away, please come this way," the apprentice said and guided them farther inside, through a long corridor with a low ceiling and through one of the doors there.

The airy room they entered was the same Julian no doubt used to visit often when he had his father pay his bills. With comfortable chairs for the gentlemen to sit in while their friends were measured, and portraits of hounds and horseflesh adorning the pale gray walls. More bales of fabric, tailored to a contemporary gentleman's needs, were housed in open cupboards made of whitened wood.

"Splendid," said Julian, glancing around the numerous shelves, his eyes glistening as if he'd never seen anything more profound than expensive fabrics. "Can Mr. Shackleton see us now?"

The apprentice bowed his head. "I'm afraid he's with another customer at the moment, but I will pass him the information that you are already waiting, Mr. Reece. Sir Evan."

"Very well," said Julian and gave a regal nod. "We will take our time browsing."

Evan couldn't help but think that Julian would have made a much more respectable baronet than he did. After all, his vices were shared by many otherwise respectable men. He spoke once the apprentice left after a few more pleasantries.

"What will your outfit be then if not a canary?"

Julian grinned and put his hat on a small table. "A peacock."

Evan smirked and took off his coat and hat. "How appropriate."

Julian followed his example and carefully put the yellow coat over the backrest of a chair. "The colors will look dazzling during the dances."

Evan's mood instantly soured. The dances. He had a vague memory of a few that he had been taught by traveling dance masters when he was much younger, but he was sure *society* had come up with new, ridiculous figures since he'd last attended a ball "Considering I'm to wear black and red, it is a good thing I will not be dancing."

"What do you mean?" Julian frowned and stepped closer, with all his enthusiasm and loud, melodic voice. "You can't refuse to dance all evening. Think of all the ladies who will miss out on a partner because of you."

"I'm sure they are better off in want of a partner than having their toes crushed."

Julian pulled his teeth over his plump lower lip, as if stifling a laugh. "I do not want to brag, but I am known as an accomplished dancer. I can show you all the steps you might want to learn."

Evan groaned. "I don't think it's a good idea. I hardly think that I could master such an intricate art within a fortnight."

He was still pronouncing the last syllable when Julian stepped forward and took hold of Evan's left hand. With his feet forming a graceful wedge, he bowed so perfectly Evan longed to reciprocate the same way.

Evan lost the ability to speak, mesmerized by the smile on Julian's face, and all at once overwhelmed by the way their hands touched. He'd been going out of his way to not make Julian uncomfortable in the past weeks, and so he'd avoided any physical contact. The sudden touch was like thunder preceding a lightning bolt.

Julian's gaze pinned Evan in place. "The Cotillion. Very modern and light. I'm certain it will be in the set at Fairfield Park. Start with a bow."

Evan thought the idea ridiculous, but he still bowed slightly, unsure if he would be instructed about women's steps, or the one performed by men, or if there was even a difference in case of this particular dance. All he knew was that Julian was holding his hand, and the warmth streaming from that graceful limb made Evan want to grab Julian's wrist, and his arm, and any other part of Julian that he'd be allowed to touch.

"Good. Now we'll align in one step," Julian said, demonstrating the move for Evan to follow. He made it look so effortless, and even though the step did not require God-like physical prowess, taking it still made Evan feel like a bear performing ballet.

Evan fought the urge of pulling Julian his way, and let Julian lead him instead. A flush was surely spreading all over his face, and up to his ears as he poorly imitated the smooth glide of Julian's body when they did tiny steps to the sides, only to repeat the movements with more vigor. Julian sang a joyful melody and squeezed Evan's hand tighter, pushing and pulling to direct Evan's ungraceful limbs.

"Are you teaching me the steps for the lady?" Evan asked in the end, doing his best to follow anyway. He didn't want Julian to consider him a brute.

The grin that showed all of Julian's teeth was enough of an answer, but the rascal shrugged. "There is not much of a difference at this point. The man uses his right hand to hold the lady's hand," he said and made a low jump to end the sequence of figures.

Evan stood next to him, squeezing Julian's hand harder, as if somehow the touch would wordlessly communicate the depth of his affection. It was all in vain. No matter how many times he'd look into Julian's eyes, he would never see the fire reflected back at him.

"You will walk in a circle with other people near you after this part has been completed. Maybe let's try to memorize the beginning first as we w—"

Evan let go of Julian's hand when the door opened, and a tall figure clad in black and white stormed in, pinning him with hawk-like eyes.

"Sir, I have not seen you all the way here in years. What are the odds of us both meeting at the tailor's?" asked Constable Pascoe without even a hint of surprise in his voice.

The apprentice walked in behind him, his whole posture speaking volumes of just how guilty he felt about allowing this to happen.

Evan took an excessively long step away from both Julian and Pascoe.

"Close to none," Evan said, a chill instantly freezing up his body. Of course the bastard would come sniffing around as soon as he heard of Evan's visit in town.

Julian didn't appear even the slightest bit concerned and walked up to Pascoe with a curt bow. "Constable! What brings you here? Since Mr. Shackleton is still assisting another customer, maybe you require some advice? Solid black is a safe choice, but isn't it also a sign of perpetual mourning? As a doctor by profession, you ought to be wearing soft browns, I think."

Evan sneered. "Unless your patients die often enough for you to wear mourning garb indefinitely."

Pascoe's wrinkly face tensed, and he looked at Evan from head to toe. "I suppose you would know much about that, sir. I have not seen you out of mourning for years…"

Julian frowned. "That is most insensitive, Mr. Pascoe. Sir Evan had lost his entire family within a short period of time."

Evan could bathe in that moment of confusion on Pascoe's face. The man's intention was to suggest Evan was mourning a past lover, yet he'd forgotten all the other tragedy in Evan's life in the process. Evan gave Pascoe an icy glare and waited to see what the man would do.

Pascoe cleared his throat. "Yes, I apologize, sir. But I can see you've become fond of a new friend lately. That is a step forward out of mourning, I hope?"

Julian smiled at Evan. "I would like to believe someone as genteel as Sir Evan considers me his friend. He saved my life, and he should be celebrated for it."

Pascoe nodded. "A fine man indeed. He must be a true friend to be providing for all your needs after the unfortunate issue with your father, Mr. Reece."

Evan's blood boiled, and he stepped closer. "I spend my money wherever I choose to, and as a matter of fact, I enjoy spoiling my friend." He wouldn't even blink, too riled up already.

Julian went quiet for several seconds, and in the end just waved his hand. "Oh, the stories old wives tell. I am not nearly as penniless as my father made it seem in his anger. But those are no one's matters but my own."

Pascoe exhaled and turned to look at a wall of black fabrics. "Indeed. Though I am disappointed with the quality of your memory, Mr. Reece. This highwayman could still be around, but without your guidance I can do nothing to apprehend him. Forgive me, but the inability to put a guilty man in the hands of the law makes me beyond frustrated."

Evan stepped away, because all his instincts told him to hurl fists at the bastard. "I thought Mr. Reece's description of the villain was very detailed."

Pascoe's cool gaze trailed over Evan. "He is merely one of many criminals who ought to hang but remain free to do as they please."

Evan walked off to look at some red brocade, because even his nape was throbbing with heat at the proximity of the human turd. "Oh, is that so? Who else would you hang, Mr. Pascoe?"

"Ah, I would start with the fellows who allegedly came here to commission ladies' dresses for the masquerade at Fairfield Park. Yet another way for sodomites to spread their disease to good Christian men," hissed Pascoe, getting louder with each subsequent word.

Evan curled his fingers over the brocade. "Ah, yes. Sodomites. Your favorite topic for some reason, Mr. Pascoe."

Julian's laugh was as brilliant as it always was, but to Evan's ears it sounded forced. "Mr. Pascoe. It's a *masquerade*. It is the whole point to look like someone a man is not. Hardly a reason to throw accusations at men who were simply born with no good taste."

All hairs bristled on Evan's forearms when Pascoe turned to look at Julian. "These kinds of games are exactly what leads to debauchery, loose morals, and eventually, the crime of sodomy."

Julian smirked. "Frills and skirts cannot possibly turn a man who worships the female form into a different kind of sinner. As a doctor, surely you must see that."

"As a doctor, I know what is unnatural, and what has been intended by God. The things I have seen in my profe—"

Evan grabbed Julian's arm and led him toward the door. "We have no time for this nonsense, Mr. Pascoe. Good day."

Julian grabbed his hat and coat on the way and followed Evan's lead after a brief nod to the constable. "Good day, Mr. Pascoe."

Evan didn't even listen to hear whether Pascoe answered or not, but his agitation rose when they met the tailor on the way. In the end, they arranged that they would come back in two hours for a scheduled fitting. They would have enough time to share a meal and regain their composure after meeting the pitiful scoundrel yet again.

Once outside, Julian donned his hat and gave Evan a tight smile. "I don't have faith in a doctor who puts all his trust in the divine. I am no atheist, but there are limits."

"He is not a man of God, he is the spawn of the devil," Evan hissed.

Julian followed him in hurried, energetic steps. "You certainly hold no love for him. And neither he for you. Why else did he look for me at your house in the first place? It did not make sense, if he didn't know the truth. Who would have mistrusted a gentleman like you?"

"He seeks all and any wrongdoings at my house. It was by sheer accident that he stood correct that one time." Evan mounted Noir and urged him forward, knowing that Julian would follow without prompting.

Julian caught up with him soon enough and looked up at Evan from Snow's much lower back. "I don't understand. Is there history between the two of you?"

Evan took a deep breath, suddenly overwhelmed by the possibility of revealing this deeply rooted thorn in his side, the story that he never told anyone. But what did he have to lose now? Julian already knew all there was to know about Evan's proclivities.

Instead of stopping by one of the many taverns, Evan rushed the horse up the hill and along the river, as far away from the coast and people's prying eyes as possible. It was only when no one was around to hear their conversation that he slowed down, letting Julian catch up with him. "He knows about... what I am. But I evaded him years ago, and now he is simmering with anger that he will likely never prove it to the jury."

Julian looked ahead, silent as a mouse when their horses trailed along the trees and the cliff on the other side of the road. "A doctor could deliver the proof, could he not?" he asked eventually.

Evan looked at him with a deep frown. "What on earth are you talking about? No doctor can taste the kisses on my skin, or smell a man's hands on me. But if I understand correctly what you are implying, I have not been with a man for fifteen years—" he stalled, watching Julian's bright eyes and slightly flushed cheeks. Fifteen years of loneliness before Julian, and yet, could he even count the stolen intimacy as truly being with him? It would have been better if they both forgot about it. "For fifteen years, and even back then, I doubt an intimate examination could be considered proof. Not to mention that no one in their right mind would dare impose something so shameful on a gentleman."

"Fifteen years? Truly?" asked Julian, pulling on the reins to slow down Snow's gait. His gaze trailed up and down Evan's face with such pity it was difficult to stand. The long-fingered hand rested on the saddle so close to Evan's thigh he could sense the heat radiating off the pale flesh.

Evan pulled on the reins, making Noir stop. "Why does that come as such a surprise?"

Julian trailed his tongue over his lips, eyes straying from Evan's face. "I merely—you are a handsome man. I wouldn't have guessed."

"A handsome man who likes his neck without a noose around it. I didn't know how to look for a man like Peran. Nor did I want to for years after what Pascoe did to him." Evan licked his lips. "You see, most everyone was at church that day, so he and I fucked in the stable, without a care in the world. Pascoe had just become a constable then, eager to report that he had caught a poacher on our land and convince Father to pursue the case with the magistrate. Instead, what he found was two men who had completely forgotten the world existed around them. My father did not even try to hide his disgust. He could not have our family name tainted, so he protected me, but Peran didn't have such luck.

Father was furious, reckoned it was he who pulled me off the right path. He wanted Peran to pay."

Julian's lips trembled, and he shook his head. "That is dreadful. Could neither of them be persuaded to turn a blind eye this one time?"

Evan gave a bitter laugh and looked at the river, flowing by without care, even though its waters were about to merge with the ocean soon. "Oh, no. Father was adamant I was the young victim of a pervert, even though it was me who had Peran fastened against the door to an empty stall. He threatened to ruin Pascoe if he as much as laid a hint of accusation on me, and at that time, a Penhart's word meant infinitely more than Pascoe's."

"You tied him down?" Julian swallowed, and his nostrils flared as he took a loud inhale of air.

Evan groaned, already knowing what scenes were playing out in Julian's mind. "No, I did not overpower a man twice my size. He asked me to. After the first few times he had me, he asked if I wanted to fuck him instead. I'd never heard anything more arousing. Even though he was both older and bigger, he loved me on top, he loved me tying him down, licking his arse with leather. Sometimes we'd be at it twice a day. He was everything I needed. Like a revelation. His body under mine—excuse me. I'm sure you do not want to hear any details," Evan said quickly when he noticed Julian's eyes widen. "I had declined testifying against him so fiercely that my father beat me bloody. On the day of his trial, Father locked me in a chest, so that I couldn't leave Tredele and testify in regards to Peran's good character. No matter how hard I punched, the lock wouldn't give.

"You can only imagine the torment. I thought he'd be hanged, so when I found out the next day that he would merely be pilloried and fined, it was the greatest relief." Evan took a deep breath, his gut twisting deep in his body at the memories. "Oh, how wrong I was. Death at a hangman's hand would have been far more merciful. My father took me to Bodmin and made me watch

Peran's ordeal," he finished as his voice broke. It had been so many years, yet the pain of that day would never go away.

Julian raised his hand, hesitating, but then pushed his palm against Evan's arm and squeezed it firmly. "I'm so sorry. I can't imagine going through something like this. How did you remain sane?"

"Maybe I didn't?" Evan glanced at the pretty fingers. He'd suck on every one of them with pleasure. "Didn't you say some people call me the mad baronet?"

Julian didn't look away this time, his blue eyes tender and intense as he rubbed Evan's arm and shoulder. "You're not mad. At least not when you're at my side."

"Pascoe most definitely thinks I'm sane, and that makes my crimes and desires all the worse, as I chose to commit those sins with full knowledge of what they were. He told me all those years ago that I was filthy, and would not get away with what I've done. That one day my feet would slip and he would be there to bring the law upon me. He can't bear that I am walking free, and for years he's tried to investigate me for any crime he could think of. Apparently being a sodomite makes me capable of the worst atrocities. Let's just say I was not eager to look for a man like Peran under such scrutiny, no matter how many times my body whispered to me about it."

Julian shook his head, his face twisting in disgust. "That man is a monster. He is harassing you and your servants. I knew him as an unpleasant man before, but I've heard nothing of that side of him."

"He is a nuisance, but I don't think he'll ever have a chance to catch me on the deed again," Evan said bitterly, looking into the pristine river, so unlike the murky waters in his heart.

Julian was still touching him, and while it was yet another temptation, Evan welcomed even that scrap of affection.

"If Peran wasn't the only one to enjoy… being taken, then maybe not all is lost for you," said Julian in subdued manner, with wind drowning his voice for any undesired ears.

Evan couldn't help his lips twisting into a smirk. "Why would you care if a vile sodomite has anywhere to take his pleasure?"

Julian's hand slid off his arm. "There's no reason to be cruel to yourself and the one friend you have these days," he said tightly.

The truth behind Julian's words made Evan bite his lips in shame. "I apologize. Sometimes, I feel like this issue is a wound that never sealed. Touching it makes it bleed, and I am not the kindest of men when wounded."

Julian smirked and shrugged his shoulders like the commonest of men. "I know. But you can also be kind."

Evan made Noir turn around, and started a slow ride back to Looe. He'd never thought he would tell the story of Peran to anyone, yet sharing it made his heart lighter. "Oh, can I now?"

Julian urged Snow to quicken her pace and took the lead, beaming at Evan as if the sour mood dispersed along with the morning fog. "Maybe you will be kind enough to tell me how to make sure men don't take advantage of me in Italy."

Evan frowned, once again reminded that as soon as Julian secured the funds to do so, he would be off to Italy, forgetting about the bad dream of Evan's touch.

"Nothing can save you with a pretty face like that, canary," he said, watching Julian's every move with the attention of a hunting wolf. And was it ever true. Julian's smile seemed to sparkle like sunshine on the waves. Evan would sell his soul to kiss his lips.

Julian's neck flexed, his gaze never flinching away from Evan's as he led Snow back. The mare walked close to Noir, close enough for Julian's knee to open a burning hot gash in Evan's thigh with its accidental touch. Was it accidental though? He could swear it was Noir who pulled him closer to Julian. Always trying to be the helpful friend. At least the beast wasn't jealous of Evan's affection.

"Truly? What is it that's so difficult to resist about me?"

Evan watched the conceited pretty thing circle him, and couldn't believe the audacity of his behavior, yet still was left unable to be angry with Julian. Now that Julian felt safe, he'd even milk Evan for compliments, and no matter how doomed Evan's infatuation with Julian was, he would still give in to the teasing. He wouldn't make it easy on Julian though. If he opened the floodgates by asking such questions, he would listen to the answer.

"Your tight breeches." Evan snorted.

A pink flush climbed up Julian's neck and stayed on his face, but the blue eyes did not look away. "At least now I will remain alert at all times. Next time a man lowers my drawers, I will know how to handle him."

Evan felt a shiver of arousal at the sole memory of that encounter. "Oh? How would you deal with him then?" Evan would very much like to see Julian 'deal' with a cock again.

Julian sucked his bottom lip into his mouth, staring at Evan, as if bewitched. "He'd need to tie me up next time."

"Or maybe he'd just need to pour enough wine down your throat for you to show your true colors?" Evan raised his eyebrows, searching Julian's handsome face for reactions.

Julian blinked and led his horse back on the way to Looe. "Drink does not show a man's true colors. In fact, it shows his worst colors. I spent too many nights and days of my life intoxicated on wine not to know this."

Evan slouched. And just like that, the spark was gone. "Don't drink in Italy then."

Chapter 15

Julian

Magnificent.

That was the only word that could possibly describe the graceful pearl of modern style that was Fairfield Park. Julian fell in love with the house from the moment he walked through an entrance of Roman-inspired columns into the hall that was all mauve and white walls, tasteful furniture, and marble tabletops. Numerous candles had been lit, letting the interiors bask in their soft glow. It was a sharp contrast to the cold walls of Tredele and their dusty air. With lively music played in the largest room, Julian trailed behind Evan, intoxicated by this assault on his senses.

The costumes he could see around him were of superb quality—all finest fabrics, even those that consisted only of a Venetian mask and a hat and spoke of the wearer's lack of imagination. After all, not everyone could be him and Evan.

Their outfits had turned out beautifully, and Julian truly felt like the prettiest peacock in his majesty's own garden. His jacket was of the most exquisite sapphire silk, embroidered with gold thread, and his waistcoat—a brilliant emerald. A simple black mask that covered only the area around his eyes and a hat with peacock feathers completed the costume that was among the most flamboyant at the masquerade. No one needed to know it had been bought with borrowed money.

Evan on the other hand, was a work of art. Despite his outfit not being eye-catching in the sense in which Julian's was, it still set itself apart from the crowd with its quality, color, and well, Evan's form. All black except for the red damask waistcoat, Evan looked awe-worthy, and slightly threatening with the big black horns attached, and the Venetian mask that only reminded Julian of that first night when Evan stripped him after the kidnapping. Shamefully, the thought of being tied to the bed by Evan now only gave Julian a shiver of excitement, the threats of revenge long forgotten.

Julian enjoyed staying half a step behind Evan, just to watch his figure in the black jacket with large epaulettes and tight in the waist. The black breeches Julian insisted Evan had made for him were as awe-worthy as they were distracting. They made Julian wish the jacket of Evan's costume didn't have a tail.

Another thing Julian enjoyed was watching how other guests eyed Evan. It made Julian proud to be around a man of such prominence, to be considered his friend. The other gentlemen present might all have more class or sophistication than Julian's eccentric friend, yet Evan was a force of nature, a man who caught the eyes of women as he passed, and whom no one would dare brawl with.

"How are you holding up?" whispered Julian into Evan's ear, knowing how dubious his friend had been about attending in the first place. Now that Evan agreed, it was Julian's responsibility to keep him from committing any social *faux pas* that would make him uninvitable in the future.

"It is what it is," Evan muttered, looking around, as if searching for prey, not inviting conversation.

Julian sighed, watching the flared bottom of Evan's mask, where he knew Evan's lips hid from his gaze. "I promise I'll make the evening entertaining for you. You are a decent dancer after the last two weeks of training. Perhaps the best pupil I've had so far," he said, even though Evan was the first person Julian had ever taught anything. A detail that did not need to be spoken of.

"I find that hard to believe." Evan nodded at Blackwell who was approaching them with a wide smile.

Julian put his hand on Evan's shoulder and gently pulled him back, gasping when the muscle shifted beneath his touch. "I am not a liar, my friend. You have excellent posture."

The dancing lessons had been a most entertaining time, but also torture. The two of them had been physically close each day, even if touch rarely went beyond the necessary hand-holding and brief moments that Julian stole to improve Evan's posture. Tension and the odd heat between them rose without words, and Julian could swear Evan had been on the verge of capturing his lips more than once.

But nothing happened.

No matter how much Julian teased Evan with his words and innocent touch, Evan would not take the bait after that one time in Looe when Julian got a fright when Evan said the unspoken and suggested Julian's drunken behavior revealed the truth about him. It was now too late. The chance was gone, and Julian did not know how to approach the topic again without daring to make the first move.

"Sir Evan! How happy I am to see you here at last," Mr. Blackwell said with his cheeks red from the wine he must have drunk. He was wearing a simple white mask, and the golden outfit he wore was as flattering as it could be on a man as round as him. His wig was decorated with golden flowers to match his beautiful wife's ensemble. Julian had long wished to be acquainted with such a fine new neighbor, but his father refused to introduce them. Now Father was not present, and Julian did not need him to do his bidding anymore.

"No, it's me who is flattered by the invitation," Evan said.

Blackwell's gaze strayed to Julian. "And you are—"

"Mr. Julian Reece," Evan said, and even though he barely touched Julian's back as he did so, it felt as if the feathers on Julian's hat were about to rise from excitement. "A dear friend of mine. I can imagine you have heard rumors about me taking care of him after the highwayman attacked him. We've grown fond of one another, and he's remained at Tredele as my guest since."

Julian's mouth spread into a triumphant smile. It was a joy to listen to Evan talking about him with such affection. As if Julian's refusal to yield to Evan's advances did not matter at all as long as they shared the platonic companionship.

"It is a pleasure to make your acquaintance, Mr. Blackwell," said Julian with his most polite bow.

Blackwell nodded with a frown that grazed his forehead only for a brief moment. He must have heard of the rift in Julian's family, and for a horrifying moment, Julian was afraid Blackwell would mention Father or Horace. Fortunately, Backwell was too polite of a man to make a guest uncomfortable, whether he approved of his wife inviting Julian or not. "The pleasure is all mine, Mr. Reece. I am happy to see you well after that dreadful incident."

Julian glanced at Evan. "Sir Evan is the one responsible. I might not have been here if it were not for him. Any man should feel privileged to have him as a friend."

The skin around Evan's eyes wrinkled slightly when he smiled, and once Julian spotted the creases, he found it difficult to look away. They were not alone anymore, and Julian needed to work on holding in his frantic feelings before they spilled out at the worst possible moment. Or at any moment for that matter.

Blackwell stepped a bit closer. "You must tell this to my daughter, Elizabeth. She is incredibly fond of such ghastly stories. I personally blame it on her reading too many novels, but she is my only daughter, and I find it hard to refuse her anything." He laughed and led them through the magnificent ballroom with wallpapers the color of Julian's eyes.

The musicians played a piece that reportedly had been brought from France just a few months ago, and the guests created a whole palette of colors and styles, dressed as everything from shepherdesses to Harlequins. It was like a breath of a big city in the quiet corners of Cornwall, and Julian snatched a glass of wine from one of the servants before following Evan and Blackwell through the ballroom.

He arrived just as they stopped in front of a fashionable sofa occupied by two women, who seemed only barely apart in age. The older one wore a Greek-inspired outfit that accentuated her voluptuous bosom, and the lunar jewelry she accessorized it with suggested she could be impersonating Artemis. The younger woman, just as attractive as her companion, was dressed as a pirate queen, or something of the sort, with strips of expensive fabrics sewn to her gown, and one of her eyes covered by a heart-shaped patch.

A servant appeared, carrying an armchair closer, so they could all sit together. But Julian didn't miss the way the younger girl pouted when they came over. All became clear when the introductions began and it turned out the ladies were Mr. Blackwell's second wife, Constance, and daughter, Elizabeth.

"It is such a rare pleasure to have you here, Sir Evan," Constance chirped with a smile so wide it revealed a slightly crooked fang, possibly the only flaw to her beauty.

Evan gallantly kissed the air above her hand, only to bow to Elizabeth, who hesitantly presented her hand for similar treatment after a discreet nudge from her stepmother. After all the necessary formalities were done with, the five of them sat down, with Julian eager to possibly gain the sympathy of the ladies, who had most likely also heard of his ordeal. He could not be borrowing Evan's money forever, and this was just the event he needed to establish and re-establish connections. And rich ladies had powerful husbands.

"I must say this, Mrs. Blackwell, this might as well be the most exquisite masquerade I have ever attended. One might think we are in London."

At those words even Elizabeth perked up a little. "I do so wish to go to London for the season. There is so much to do out there."

Mrs. Blackwell nodded. "Have you been, Sir Evan? One can never know what a man as mysterious as you is up to."

Evan straightened up slightly. "I— No, I'm afraid London is not to my taste."

Elizabeth was quick to pout again. "How can you know this if you have not been?"

Julian smiled at her, even though her attitude was quite shocking in a girl her age. "London is magnificent but busy and loud. Not everyone prefers that to the clean air and peace of the countryside."

"Precisely," Blackwell said and patted Julian's back with approval. "Elizabeth, you need to stop this nonsense. There is nothing even remotely pleasant about that gargantuan city. Besides, I do not want you too far away from us when you marry." He wanted to say something more, but a servant in blue livery approached him from behind and whispered into his ear.

Blackwell frowned, but then nodded and stood up, adjusting his clothes. "My apologies, there is something I need to attend to."

As soon as her husband left, Mrs. Blackwell leaned forward a bit, exposing more of her bosom. "Mr. Reece, you must tell us more about the highwayman. My husband does not understand, but Elizabeth and I find it so terribly exciting."

Evan slouched. "A common rogue, nothing to speak of."

Elizabeth frowned, as if those words personally offended her. "You do not know him, sir. He could be anyone. And he might strike again, kidnap a lady this time and do—"

"Elizabeth!" her stepmother hissed.

Julian hardly kept his mouth from crooking into too wide of a smile. He wanted to make a good impression on their hostess. If he played his cards right, she was the kind of woman who could be the key to his future. Were she a lover of literature, then maybe she'd be inclined to patron Julian. But it appeared that there was another kindred spirit within their small gathering. Elizabeth shared Julian's own fantasies of the dark-eyed highwayman, who'd carry him away on the back of a black stallion, for no purpose other than tying him down and molesting his defenseless body.

Julian cleared his throat. "It's quite possible, Mrs. Blackwell. I advise you against traveling on Sundays. The roads are empty, leaving the traveller even more exposed."

Mrs. Blackwell nodded. "I can imagine. How could a lady protect herself from such a brute?"

"I am certain that vile man is long gone," Evan said.

Elizabeth shook her head. "I reckon he is merely waiting for the right time to strike."

"Perhaps he is," said Julian, smiling at Evan before focusing on the ladies again.

He didn't fail to notice that the room was being prepared for dances, with the carpet rolled-up and taken out by a group of servants. "He is a dangerous man. Strong as an ox yet graceful. He would make a fine footman, were he not on the path of crime."

Evan leaned forward and gestured at Elizabeth's gloved hand, taking a better look at the large rings on her fingers. Both the ladies stilled, and Julian felt his face flush at such boldness. He had no idea why Evan would do such a thing.

"You should be careful on your trip to London, Miss Blackwell. Such beautiful jewelry would make perfect bait for a highwayman," Evan said, glancing into her eyes.

Julian drew in a sharp breath, staring at Elizabeth's small hand. Evan's voice was soft, very much like during the quiet evenings he shared with Julian, when he read out loud and his words curled up around Julian's ears like soft balls of cotton.

Julian looked up, meeting a sly gaze from Mrs. Blackwell and gave her a polite nod, pretending to share whatever opinion she had of all this.

"Those are just trinkets for my pirate costume. I would not dream of wearing so many rings outside of a masquerade. That would be vulgar." Elizabeth slowly pulled her hand closer to her stomach, but she watched Evan as if he'd changed from an ox into a wolf.

Mrs. Blackwell stroked her stepdaughter's arm with a smile. "Elizabeth is modest and unconcerned with such trivialities. It's only on rare occasions such as these that she indulges in extravagance."

Elizabeth looked away with that childish pout that seemed almost permanently at home on her pretty face. "I would indulge every day if I could have my way."

Evan nodded with a smile that was barely visible under his mask. "It's perfectly understandable. A creature as beautiful as you, Miss Blackwell, should only be surrounded by finery. Fairfield Park seems to only exist to express your good taste. I can imagine you and Mrs. Blackwell influenced the design tremendously."

Julian barely registered their hostess's answer, too shocked by the sudden change in Evan's behavior. Was this the same man who complained about having to be here just ten minutes back? Who insulted Fairfield Park despite it being such a fine estate, and who always spoke his mind, no matter how uncivilized that made him sound?

He was charming, but in a very different way than when it was only him and Julian. This was a deliberate performance for the eyes and ears of the ladies, and Julian wasn't sure he liked what he was witnessing.

The music stopped playing, and the dancing was about to start, distracting Julian further. He'd stopped listening to the conversation a minute ago, and he couldn't follow it anymore, with Evan engaged in some kind of word charade with Black-well's wife.

Worst of all, Elizabeth seemed to be watching Evan with an interest that made Julian's skin crawl. Did Evan not see what he'd just done? In his striving for politeness, he could get the girl infatuated with him in no time. This wouldn't do at all. Julian needed to help Evan untangle this growing mess.

Julian cursed himself in his mind when he heard only half of Evan's sentence.

"—it would be better to wear all the jewels, otherwise, a highwayman might insist on searching for them..."

Mrs. Blackwell laughed and swatted Evan with her fan. "Sir Evan! You cannot be serious."

Evan nodded, his eyes on Elizabeth, Julian forgotten as if he were an empty armchair. "No, it's true, I wouldn't overestimate the honor of a robber."

Elizabeth laughed as well. "What about the honor of a gentleman cow?" she asked, using the polite term for a bull, as was suitable for a lady.

Julian laughed out loud and looked into Elizabeth's eyes, eager to help his friend out of a situation that might come with dreadful consequences. "A gentleman cow is a farm animal. It's constant in its ways and would rather calmly stay in the fields than stray to the highways. You are safe."

Evan gave Julian a puzzling glance, but quickly looked back to the ladies. "I am sure a matador would not call such a beast *safe*."

Mrs. Blackwell's eyes opened wider. "The matadors seem so exciting! Have you been to Spain yourself, Sir Evan?"

Evan hesitated. "No, I've merely read about the matadors and the animals they fight, but it is a dream of mine to see this magnificent spectacle. I cannot leave Tredele for long at this time, but it should be a possibility in the future." At least he wasn't lying to please the ladies this time.

Elizabeth sighed and leaned back on the sofa. "Gentlemen cows are also too big to dance gracefully. Unlike peacocks. Am I right, Mr. Reece?"

Mrs. Blackwell sent her stepdaughter an icy glare, but it was too late, the damage was done. Evan sighed and let his gaze drift to the tall mirrors.

Julian hesitated, his gaze trailing over Evan's mask. The indignity of Elizabeth's rudeness felt like a blow to not only Evan but also Julian. He couldn't believe a girl brought up in such a lovely home would behave like this. And yet, he could not afford to be rude in return.

"Miss Blackwell, I'm sure all animals are adequately graceful with the right partner," he said nevertheless. His gaze strayed to the floor, which was slowly filling with couples, and when he noticed a flicker of interest in Elizabeth's eyes, he rose to his feet and bowed. "Might I have this dance, or has it been already promised?"

"Not at all, Mr. Reece, I'd love to. There is so little happening around here that I've been dreaming of this ball for weeks," she said and quickly got up.

By the time the dance started, Elizabeth managed to tear more lies about the highwayman out of Julian. If she believed the countryside boring, no wonder she strived to know more about things that were considered far too exciting for a lady. Blackwell really should reconsider his decision to keep her away from the kind of leisure she wanted. If she could not live in the way a young lady should, she would eventually get in trouble. But it was not Julian's place to lecture her father.

Still, despite the thread of sympathy for her rebellious streak, he could not bring himself to forgive her for the way she treated Evan. Julian was nevertheless happy to see that Evan did not give up on this masquerade and in the absence of Mr. Blackwell chose to apply his newfound dancing skills with their hostess. He stood straight, taller than most men in the ballroom and broader in the shoulders, something even more apparent next to the dainty frame of Mrs. Blackwell.

Julian tried to catch Evan's gaze, but it was a futile attempt with him engaged in conversation.

"Is it not boring to live with Sir Evan?" Elizabeth asked as soon as they came closer for the first figure of the dance.

Julian pressed his mouth shut, only to force a smile and gracefully lead her across the next few steps, his gaze briefly straying to Evan, who did not move like an ox anymore. He had the grace of a magnificent stallion. "Not at all, Miss. Blackwell. He is a most interesting man. What affected your opinion of him, if I may ask?"

"Oh, I do not wish to be rude, Mr. Reece, but I'm convinced a man such as yourself would understand my meaning. Sir Evan lives in that dreary house, and rarely calls on anyone. Isn't there more to life than whatever it is he is spending his days on?" She looked into his eyes with a flush coloring her cheeks.

Julian gave a mental sigh. She was trying to charm *him* now? What were the odds? "I do not wear petticoats, yet that does not mean I cannot appreciate them. He is a good friend, even if his tastes don't align with mine in everything."

She laughed, and squeezed Julian's hand a bit more boldly. Yes, she would most definitely get in trouble if not married off soon. "I knew you would understand, Mr. Reece. You do not seem like a man who would be happy spending his whole life in Cornwall, whereas Sir Evan is set on doing nothing but reading books and walking around Tredele. I even heard someone saw him herding his own sheep. But that can't be true, can it, Mr. Reece? It must have been one of his manservants."

Julian's heart sank a little bit. As much as he'd detested Tredele at first, with time, he'd discovered its unique charm, although Julian's opinion might have been affected by Evan's attachment to his family seat. Still, those were only words, and Julian needed this young lady's help in getting to her fabulously wealthy father. "A gentleman is allowed some eccentricities. Sir Evan enjoys the life he leads, but I do strive for something more. I have my eyes on the Mediterranean. God willing, my plans will take me to Rome, then Venice, then to Naples. I wish to set my new book there, and I could not possibly do Italy justice without seeing it with my own eyes, smelling it, and tasting it with all my senses."

Elizabeth gasped and actually missed a step. "Oh, Mr. Reece. That is most exciting. I knew right away there was something special about you, and only now you say you are a writer? That is too modest of you. I can imagine someone creative can find something interesting even in a man as ordinary as Sir Evan."

Julian felt his face flush with anger, but he doubted expressing it in Evan's name would win either of them any favors. "I assure you, he is not," he said in the end, suddenly at odds with his usually golden tongue. Even Miss Blackwell's perfume started to smell like rotting fruit, and he was relieved to hear the music end.

Elizabeth was smiling from ear to ear and took her time letting go of Julian's hand, only to join the clapping. "Mr. Reece, what a glorious piece of music that was, don't you think? Or perhaps it was merely the peacock leading me that made it feel so smooth." She fanned her flushed face.

Julian exhaled but bowed to thank her for the dance. He was about to compliment her in return when a heavy palm descended on his arm.

"Is that not Mr. Julian Reece?" asked a voice Julian had known well for years.

He spun around and stepped back not to push the lady away and smiled at Miles Hughes, a man of some wealth, who frequented Madame Canard's nearly as often as Julian used to when he could afford it. His heart thudded at the sight of the familiar narrow face.

Julian gave him his wide smile, eager to greet all the other men, whose features he could identify despite masks and costumes. He was acquainted with them all and called them his friends. They were the ones his father approved of—well bred and equally well associated.

He made sure to introduce Miss Blackwell first before looking into Hughes's eyes with hope rising in his throat. After so many bottles emptied together and numerous discussions on politics and philosophy, Hughes would surely be sympathetic to Julian's cause.

"It is delightful to see you all. I needed a few weeks of peace after the ordeal that villain put me through," he said, making sure to remind everyone he survived something none of them ever had to endure.

Hughes looked back at the other men before settling his eyes on Julian. "I am surprised to meet you here in all honesty. And in such a fine suit as well. Where in God's name did you scrape the money for it after the misfortune with your family?"

The several pairs of prying eyes, including Elizabeth's, burned through Julian's fine silks. His throat ached with the humiliation, but he managed a smirk, looking straight into Hughes's eyes. This wasn't like the man he knew. True, Hughes had a mean streak, but he'd never acted so standoffish toward friends.

"Maybe a blind editor bought a manuscript of his and paid him an advance," suggested one of the men in Hughes's ensemble, whose voice Julian did not recognize. How did a stranger know of Julian's affinity for crafting words?

Hughes picked up on that. "Is that so? Did you finally manage to finish one of the novels you've always been talking of? I always believed that your father would eventually pay a publisher to accept something of yours, since you have no profession. But maybe poverty worked wonders and gave you the motivation you've been lacking all along."

Elizabeth looked up at Julian with her pretty, yet cow-like eyes. "Didn't you say you were a writer, Mr. Reece?"

Hughes gave Julian an expectant look, and Julian could hardly grab at words drifting in the foggy space inside his skull. He was being deliberately humiliated. He couldn't believe it. "I am, Miss Blackwell. I have not yet sought being published, as I strive for perfection," he said in the end, barely keeping his voice level.

Hughes snorted and looked back at his friends. "Considering how much time you've always spent in the company of men who can't even read, it must be hard for you to better yourself. Maybe you should keep to Tredele? Don't you think a reclusive life is one that would suit a writer, Miss Blackwell?"

Elizabeth clutched her fan. "If it's a necessary course of action... At least reading is one thing Sir Evan is fond of."

"We've heard you live at Sir Evan's expense now, Reece? You must terribly miss the company of sailors. Perhaps you should employ yourself at the Western Flying Post?" Hughes laughed and patted Julian's shoulder, as if it were a good-natured joke, not a needle pushed under his nail.

Julian laughed, but even to his own ears it sounded bland. He needed to leave this company fast. Suddenly, even the fine costume felt like dead weight on his shoulders. Eyes that he believed to be appreciative now seemed to mock him. Would the ladies laugh at him behind their fans, were he to look closely enough? The sense of entrapment settled on his chest and curled around his throat, fueling the sense of betrayal and alienation.

"Not in the slightest. It seems we are both up for surprises tonight, because I did not expect to see you here either. You barely leave your favorite establishment in Looe," he said, not mentioning the name only because of a lady being present.

Despite the other gentlemen still standing behind Hughes, Julian did manage to squeeze a few smirks out of them.

Hughes waved his hand dismissively. "Oh, I merely decided for this one last outing before I leave for London on Tuesday. I have been away from our house there long enough. I'd invite you to join me, but I wouldn't want to thin your savings too much at such a trying time."

Julian clenched his jaw and glanced at Miss Blackwell, with his head spinning as if he were heavily drunk. Or poisoned by the venom a man he believed was his friend had just poured into his veins. "You must be tired, Miss Blackwell. Shall I escort you to your mother before the next dance?" he asked, wordlessly begging for her to say yes.

Her earlier liveliness was now subdued, and she nodded quickly. "Yes, please do, I feel a little flushed."

Julian gave her his arm, nodded at his former companions and wordlessly led Miss Blackwell through the room, trying not to look around as shame boiled inside his chest, burning his lungs and heart as it rose, ready to spill and force him to make an even bigger fool of himself.

He had nothing but Evan's hospitality. Even the clothes on his back were not truly his. Grateful that Miss Blackwell didn't speak to him anymore, he approached the corner where the Blackwells chatted to Evan with smiles on their faces. But the moment Elizabeth let go of Julian's arm, he needed to lean against the wall to keep himself up. All he wanted was to simply leave, but he could not ask this of Evan when he seemed to enjoy himself so much. Maybe Julian could ride home on his own, or perhaps wait for Evan in the gardens where he wouldn't have to face hurtful words or mocking stares?

Mrs. Blackwell looked his way, bringing Julian straight into the center of attention, so far away from where he wanted to be at the moment. "I was just telling my husband what a great dancer Sir Evan is."

It was a slight overstatement on her part, with the slim amount of time Evan had for practice, but he had been an eager student and was at least decent at the most popular dances. Julian could imagine that simply being close to Evan made a woman consider the experience immensely pleasurable.

"And his costume," said Mr. Blackwell. "Don't you think it is very daring, Elizabeth?"

Julian's mouth dried, and he glanced at Evan, whose face was so handsome without the mask he must have removed after the dance. Snippets of the earlier conversation rolled into place. Were the Blackwells trying to make a match between Elizabeth and Evan? What a ridiculous notion that was!

Elizabeth smiled slightly, looking up at Evan. "Yes, very much so. You look... different than last time somehow."

Evan gave her a nod. "I owe much to Mr. Reece's taste. He made me understand a man needs to strive for improvement in all matters."

Being acknowledged was exactly what Julian needed at that moment, and yet, with even Miss Blackwell turning away from him now that she knew he had nothing and Evan pushing himself into a disastrous predicament, he could not appreciate it as much as he should.

Mrs. Blackwell fanned herself and rested her head on her husband's arm. "If there was a woman present in your life, you would have known it long ago, Sir Evan," she said playfully.

Evan smiled at Elizabeth, and she reciprocated shyly. "I think it was the idea of marriage that spurred the need for introspection. I wish to be the best man I can, not only for myself and for Tredele, but most of all for the woman I one day marry."

Julian's head drummed with a cacophony of sounds as he looked up, staring at Evan for so long his eyes started itching with dryness.

Marriage? Evan could not marry. He did not want a woman in his life, and Julian knew this for a fact. He knew it because he'd experienced his touch, his hunger for male flesh.

How could Julian stand knowing that Evan was in his bed with a lawfully wedded wife, while he remained a few rooms down the hall, agonizing about someone else's hands trailing up and down Evan's powerful chest?

He could not stand that, and finally admitting this in his own mind made him breathe again. He should not have pushed Evan away. But despite jealousy burning deep in Julian's chest, he knew this was not merely about the things he wanted. Evan would never be happy with a woman, and Julian would be there to protect him from making the biggest mistake of his life, even if it meant offending the wealthy people he sought to befriend. That was what friends did for one another.

Julian smiled. "If only Sir Evan hadn't told me the other day that he does not wish to marry a woman half his age, I'd have said he and Miss Blackwell would have been a match made in heaven. Then again, there is no rush, is there? Haven't you only married your lovely new wife at forty-five, Mr. Blackwell?"

Evan frowned, still as a statue, but before he could get a word in, Elizabeth spoke. "Is that so, Sir Evan? Do your interests lie in widows? An experienced woman able to deal with a house as grand as Tredele?"

Mr. Blackwell's dark gaze settled on Julian without a word.

"I will have to give it some thought," Evan mumbled, pulling back into his shell so rapidly even his voice lost its clang.

Julian exhaled and kept his face neutral, hoping he'd somehow merge with the wall despite the flamboyant suit that now felt like a foreign presence on his back, ready to choke him when he least expected it.

Mrs. Blackwell hid her face behind the fan and cleared her throat. "Elizabeth, you look flushed. Let's walk for a few minutes," she said and pulled on her stepdaughter's hand.

"I need some wine, please excuse me, gentlemen," said Evan, and he was off without another word. A blatant lie, since his lips never touched intoxicating drinks.

Julian bowed to Blackwell, excusing himself before the man could strike him, and followed the beacon that was the horns on Evan's head. He needed to know what happened between their last conversation about marriage and this abominable situation.

As expected, Evan wasn't looking for a drink but slipped behind the thick curtains, into the darkness of the night on the terrace.

"I can sense you, Julian," Evan said without turning around, already making his way down a flight of stone steps, and into the garden. "Leave me be."

Julian broke into a run, breathing in the cool air that smelled of newly cut grass and was so much lighter than the smoke and perfume-heavy air inside the house. No one could see him now. And for the first time, Evan had addressed him informally, with his Christian name. The rush of it made Julian's heart soar. Was this the depth of their friendship now? He would dip his toe in there as well. "Evan, wait!"

In the darkness, the black clothes melted into the scenery, making it difficult to follow Evan the moment he stepped away from the glow coming through the windows.

"No! I am not yours to command. Leave me," Evan growled, but as bad as that was to hear, at least it gave Julian a better sense of where Evan had gone.

He stormed down the trail toward the living walls of a maze that was the pride of Fairfield Park. Every step was like a leap into the unknown, but if he wanted to catch up with someone as stubborn as Evan, there was no time to waste on treading carefully. The cold air made Julian's lungs ache, but he ignored it and followed the sounds of rustling ahead. He fell face-first into the wall of tall bushes and closed his eyes to protect them from the little branchlets, but the entrance was close enough for him to find by touch.

"Evan!"

A hand came out of nowhere and grabbed his throat, pushing him farther into the bushes. "Do you want to ruin me?" Evan grunted, his face suddenly only inches away.

Julian grabbed the thick wrist, curling his shoulders and instinctively turning his face away. The horns stood out on the background of the night sky, and for a brief moment, it was not Evan but the Minotaur holding Julian in his clutches, ready to devour his flesh in every way.

"Why didn't you tell me?" The words exploded out of Julian's mouth unexpectedly, but it was exactly what he wanted to know. A shiver ran down his spine when the grip around his throat tightened, but he didn't try to run or otherwise free himself. Evan's hand was hot against his skin, so very like that one time when Evan had speared Julian with his thick prick.

"Tell you what exactly? Do you need to know each thought and dream I have?" Evan pushed Julian even farther but let go of him. In the quiet garden, his ragged breathing was coming loud and clear.

Julian touched his neck, hoping to keep at least some of the heat that had been brushing against it just moments ago. "You do not wish to marry. I know that better than anyone."

"I have no other choice, you little rat! And you go stabbing me in the back after begging me to attend?" Evan began pacing in the narrow corridor between the bushes. His head cast a shadow on one of the walls, yet again creating the illusion of a mythological monster having come to life in front of Julian.

Julian watched his tall form move while his eyes gradually became used to the darkness. His heart skipped a beat. "What do you mean?"

Evan stopped and spread his arms, nostrils flared as if he really were a bull. "I'm broke, Julian. And in debt with Blackwell. All I have left is Tredele and my title. I'm trying to make the best of it."

Julian's feet were screwed to the ground. "I—but the costumes," he uttered, touching the expensive silk that encased his whole body, all bought with money from Evan's purse.

Evan let his arms fall. "I sold my telescope and a few other things. What use is it to look at the sky, when the ground is crumbling under my feet?"

Julian's fingers tightened on the brocade at the front of his jacket, and his stomach turned, making him nauseated. "Y–you sold your telescope to buy me a suit?" he whispered, staring at the pale oval that was Evan's face.

"I wanted to make you happy. A foolish attempt at trying to keep you with me a while longer. Why would you stay, if I had nothing to offer?"

Julian rubbed his face, shivering, as if the chill in the air only got to him now. His heart was twisting inside his chest, about to burst from the dull pain of it. "Is this how little you think our friendship means to me?" whispered Julian. "Just now, a man I knew most of my life humiliated me in front of everyone, but you accept me into your home and feed me. This is... invaluable. Not the money. This," he said, shaking his head.

Evan didn't meet his gaze. "I thought you accepted this state of affairs because you had nowhere left to go. I can never repay you for what I've done to you." He moved a step farther into the darkness, but Julian was right behind him, holding on to Evan's arm. Remorse. That was what it was. Julian swallowed hard, remembering the harsh words Evan had said to him that horrible night, and he couldn't help but relive the humiliation of them again.

"I... I've grown fond of you despite the... things that happened. I cannot explain it."

Evan's dark eyes glistened when he looked up to meet Julian's gaze. "If I want to keep Tredele, if I want to help you, I can't see any other way than marriage. My brother lost our mines, gambled away most of our fortune. Tredele is a well into which I throw everything I have, yet never see it fill. Its state is a shame I carry with me every day. I wish I could give you more. A better room, a roof that doesn't leak... "

Julian stepped closer and rubbed Evan's shoulders, looking up at him in the narrow corridor of the maze that kept them both safe from prying eyes. And when Julian thought of the despair hiding somewhere in Evan's voice, he almost rose to his toes to kiss him. They were so close he could have done it. Still, he was too scared to take that step and gently shook Evan instead.

"I believed they were all your eccentricities. But there's nothing? Nothing at all?" he whispered, seeking truth in Evan's dark gaze. It was a frightening thought to have Evan faced with such impossible choices, but just thinking about him getting married for income was sickening.

Evan shook his head. "The land brings in some rent, but everything sinks into my servants' wages, minor repairs... There's nothing left after that. I am not who you thought I was."

Julian swallowed hard, faced with the fact that he was keeping Evan in the dark as well. "I know who you are. You scare me sometimes, but I enjoy your company. We will think of an answer. Surely, there must be another way than marriage." Julian clutched Evan's arms harder. "I do not want you to spend the rest of your life in misery."

Evan took a shuddery breath, and Julian felt its heat on his skin. So close, yet he still wasn't able to push himself forward those few inches.

"What do you suggest I do? Become a highwayman again?"

Julian stepped back, his face lax as his mind finally came back to life. Seconds stretched, and he looked up at Evan with something solid building within him. "Actually... I know of a wealthy yet cruel man who plans to travel to London this Tuesday."

Evan frowned. "You cannot be serious..."

Julian laughed, feeling so much lighter already. "I am very serious. This time, you shall have a companion."

"*You* want to become a highwayman?" Evan's eyebrows rose, and he cocked his head to the side, watching Julian with renewed interest.

Julian grinned and stepped close enough for their toes to touch. The cool air felt so fresh in his lungs it made him lightheaded to breathe. "You don't think I have what it takes? Think again."

Evan smirked, and it was an expression so becoming on him Julian's heart raced. "I suppose you did try to extort money from your father and had no qualms about hitting and kicking..."

Julian reached up to grab one of the horns on Evan's head. "And I will be with a bull. This plan cannot fail."

CHAPTER 16

JULIAN

Droplets of rain fell off the rim of Julian's tricorn hat. It had been four days since the masquerade, and during that time, Julian managed to establish the route Hughes would be taking, as well as the time it should take the bastard to reach the spot Julian and Evan chose for their ambush.

He hadn't gotten much peace last night after retiring to his room, with plans still very much alive in his mind. Hours passed while he listened to the clock ticking nearby, and for a moment, a creak outside his room gave him a flicker of hope that maybe Evan was as restless as he was. But no one had come through the door or knocked, leaving Julian to his own thoughts.

Deep in the night, his mind had become even more troubled, forcing him out of bed and to the desk where he filled pages with lines of text, some of it crossed out, some underlined and moved about on the paper. Those pages he could not read to Evan. They were too raw, too personal in the way they unraveled that hidden corner of Julian's soul that he himself was only beginning to discover.

He glanced at Evan's towering presence on the other side of the road. On Noir's back, he looked like a giant in the solid black outfit, even more so with the rain making the leather of his coat shine in the sparse light of the grayest day in recent months.

To make Snow more difficult to recognize, they'd colored her with coal to make it appear as if she had spots, but if the carriage didn't arrive soon, their efforts would go to waste in this rain.

When Julian offered to be a part of the stunt, he didn't think all that much of it, but as reality dawned on him with every drop of rain hitting his oversized coat, he was coming to terms with the fact that he was about to commit a crime punishable by law with hanging.

Nothing could go wrong. Or so he told himself.

They chose the spot perfectly, at the incline of a hill to prevent the carriage from speeding up, especially with the ground so muddy from the rain. There were trees entangled with ivy on both sides of the road, and with the clouds layered thick as clotted cream on a scone, not much light was coming through, making the day seem as if it were already dusk.

Julian squeezed the pistol underneath his coat. Evan had showed him how to use it, and assured him it would likely be just an accessory of intimidation, but Julian was still scared of the fiery power the weapon could spur.

He closed his eyes and listened to the creaking of wood and the constant tapping of the water against the leaves and his own shoulders. The scarf he used for obscuring his identity was now cold and wet, and it clung to his neck and face, but he didn't dare lower it, to not tempt fate.

And then he heard a new sound, like numerous maids churning butter at once, followed by the familiar clatter of wheels. Evan gave Julian a short nod, and disappeared between the trees. Despite Evan being more imposing, and having more experience, they decided that Julian would do the talking and stop the carriage. So far, there had been gossip of one highwayman, so if things went awry, Evan could intervene with the advantage of surprise.

If everything went according to plan, they would acquire an immense sum, as Hughes was bound to be travelling with money and chests filled to the brim with finery and trinkets. The future of Tredele would be secure for the time being, and Evan could possibly pay off his debts. Julian made Snow walk deeper into the bushes, to avoid the coachman spotting him. It was not very likely in this kind of drizzle, but he could not afford alerting the man if he wanted to leave their victims alive. Hughes was a cruel, mean man who turned his back on a friend as soon as he ceased being useful, but Julian was not a murderer, and neither was Evan. At least that was what Julian hoped.

His heart raced as the horses passed him behind the trees, laboriously plunging their hooves into the mud as they led the way for the shiny black carriage. The coachman was buried in a coat with a collar so high he was not likely to spot a highwayman, even if he appeared in front of him, but Julian still hesitated, squeezing his hand around the weapon. Some of the trunks were stored at the uncovered back of the carriage, piled up under a water-resistant sheet and fastened with rope. Julian licked his lips, already sensing the taste of the bounty on his tongue.

He had rehearsed this in his head a hundred times, but would he actually be able to go through with the stunt? What if Hughes travelled with other people Julian didn't know of? There was no time to think once the horses passed the point he and Evan had agreed on.

It was as if a different person altogether stepped into Julian's boots, and he rode into the muddy ground of the highway. The moment he was on the tail of the carriage, his lungs filled with a fire that made him urge Snow to go faster. At the back of his mind, Evan was a constant presence, watching him, evaluating Julian's character and willpower. Julian could not disappoint him.

With the pistol firmly in his grasp, he aligned himself with the door and pulled it wide open, blinking when the rapid movement sent water into his face. With all the power he had in him, he called out, "Stop!"

The coachman tried to urge on the horses, but it was no use in this mud, and on an uphill road at that.

"What on earth—!" Hughes pulled away the window curtain, revealing another person inside. A woman in a blue dress.

"I said stop the damn carriage," roared Julian in the lowest tone he could muster. He pulled out his small sword and pointed it at Hughes's chest, which escaped him narrowly as the bastard backed away against the woman. With his left hand, Julian pointed the gun toward the coachman, who was now barely visible on top of the carriage. "Get up and show yourself. Arms up!"

This time the coachman listened. He must have realized trying to run in this weather was futile. "I got nothin'!" he yelled back, his voice followed by thunder far away on the horizon.

Julian's left hand shook slightly, but he kept his right one steady, so close to Hughes's treacherous flesh he could gore all the rotting insides, leaving a shell dressed in silk and fine wool. He looked at the man's wide eyes, then at the woman curling up on the other side of the carriage, her left breast partially exposed. Julian exhaled, composing himself despite the cold water spilling down his back.

"What a beautiful creature you travel with," he said, evoking the persona he knew from pamphlets about the most famous highwaymen. He would be pleasant as long as his victims cooperated but ruthless if they would not. That was the plan. "I am sure you would not want her to be harmed."

Hughes had his hands raised slightly, but sneered at Julian. "Take her if that's what you want. She's paid for."

The woman's eyes went wide and she slapped Hughes right on the face. "You bastard!"

Julian would have laughed if he weren't in the rain with two deadly weapons ready to be used. Hughes was even more of a scoundrel than he'd thought. "I can buy enough women with what you have on you," he said, nodding at the chain sticking out of Hughes's pocket. It was attached to a very expensive watch.

"This?" Hughes waved his hand. "Worthless trinkets. Wouldn't you really rather have a taste of this fine flesh first?" He reached for the woman's breast and teased her nipple.

Julian lowered the gun to grab the leather bag he'd prepared, and tossed it into the carriage. His blood ran faster with every second, and as high as he was on the power he held over his newly found enemy, he did not wish to stay here any longer than necessary. It was a sorry spectacle.

"I like them with less meat on their bones than this one," he said quickly. "I want the watch and your purse in this bag, along with your buttons, and the buckles of your shoes."

Hughes sneered at him, and before Julian knew what was coming, Hughes pulled out a pistol with his other hand, and looked straight into Julian's eyes. "My powder is dry. What about yours?"

Julian's lungs emptied, and in a split second, the world slowed down, the muzzle of the pistol becoming the sole focus of Julian's life. He raised his gun, and the door on the other side of the carriage opened with a bang when it slammed against the wall of the carriage. Evan's gloved hand grabbed Hughes's collar, and he pulled the scoundrel back.

A deafening shot resounded through the air.

The bullet went right through the roof of the carriage.

The harlot screamed.

Snow backed away, whinnying in panic and almost knocking Julian off her back.

Evan dragged a swearing, squealing Hughes out of the carriage, and by the splash on the other side, Julian figured Evan must have dropped the scoundrel into the mud.

The pieces of wood and the water spilling inside the carriage were like a token of the damage the pistol could have done to Julian's flesh. Julian touched his chest and slid off the back of his horse, dropping the reins as he rushed toward the front of the carriage, to the coachman, who at this point had left his seat and was hurrying between the trees.

"Run! Good riddance!" he called out, as the pulsing in his head made the edges of his vision white.

He could have died just now.

He could lie bleeding in the mud, and there would have been nothing anyone could have done about it. He'd be gone. Without finishing a single book. Gone from Tredele and away from Evan without ever disclosing the truth about what he kept hidden within his heart.

He circled the carriage with soft knees and was right on time to see Hughes yelling with his face halfway pushed into the slush.

"Take everything! Just go!"

Evan snarled at him, and kicked his face so hard Julian would swear he'd heard the rattling of teeth. "You fucking shit-licker! I'm sure as hell taking this away before you hurt yourself, worthless cunt!" He leaned down and grabbed Hughes's pistol out of the muddy water.

Julian walked up to Evan, going breathless when his eyes met the stern black gaze. He exhaled, and then looked down at the expensive silks on Hughes's back that were now soaking up the dirt, and he brought down his foot, pushing the man's face straight back into the mud. "Cockroach... the world would be a better place without you," he grunted, resting one hand against the side of the carriage. The mocking laughter from a few days back rained down his shoulders, and he swallowed hard, barely keeping himself in check. The sword burned his hand through the glove, itching for Hughes's blood. "You're traveling far. Will you tell us where to look, or shall we cut you open and search for gold in the smelly sack of your gut?"

Evan raised his eyebrows, and gently put his hand on the one Julian was holding his sword with, but other than that, he didn't interfere. Like a demonic black presence, there to allow Julian's darkest needs to spill. Julian wanted to turn and press into Evan's arms right there, over Hughes's shivering body, with the woman watching.

"Please! No!" Hughes whined like a pig begging not to be slaughtered, the comparison only emphasized by the way he rolled in the mud. With his mouth partially submerged in murky water, each word came out accompanied by gurgling. "It's all in the luggage!" he said with blood spilling down his lips, his fingers trembling so hard he could barely take his watch out fast enough.

It was a lie. No one in their right mind left their most valuable things out of sight, and in heavy rain on top of that. Not that the contents of the trunks were not of value, but what Evan and Julian needed were not fine clothes.

Julian exhaled and met Evan's eyes again, so bold and dark without sun to reflect in them. This man had just saved Julian's life, and he was there to save Julian from his own wrath as well, to stop him from crossing lines he hadn't meant to cross.

Slowly, Julian scooted down and dragged a golden ring off Hughes's slippery finger, uncaring whether he'd break it in the process. He kicked the bastard's side next, just hard enough to make him roll over. With the blade of his sword against Hughes's lower stomach, he smiled at the wealthy Mr. Miles Hughes curling up his shoulders, very much like a frightened maiden.

"I will not take your family jewels if you do as I say," hissed Julian, drinking up the fright in Hughes's brown eyes. The sword cut through the leather as if it were butter.

"Whatever it is, it's yours." It was hard to tell whether he was crying or not with the mud and rain sticking to his face, but Julian liked to think he was.

Evan handed Julian a key taken off Hughes, so he walked up to the open door of the carriage and looked at the harlot. She didn't try to run, curled up in the seat and with hair sticking to one side of her face. Julian raised his hat slightly and gave her a curt not.

"I apologize for the inconvenience, Miss. I promise you will not be harmed if you show me the place where this man locks the items he needs kept safe."

She took a deep breath, staring into Julian's eyes as if she tried to memorize them even in this light, but in the end, she pointed her finger at the seat across from her. Julian stepped into the carriage, keeping his distance in the cramped space, to not unnecessarily frighten the poor girl. With one glove off, he slid his fingers underneath the soft covering of the seat and poked at the wood until an opening was revealed.

The key fit it perfectly, and the hidden compartment opened, revealing two valises, which turned out quite heavy when he picked them up. His heart soared without him even looking inside. He knew the contents would be of enough value to save Evan from having to enter a union he'd regret. With heat dancing in his chest, he half-heartedly looked underneath the other seat as well, but since it merely stored provisions for the trip, he said his good-byes to the woman and left the carriage with his hands full.

His face was relaxed into a wide smile as he jumped off, and the contents of the valises made metallic clangs. The rain was still cold, the sky still gray, but with the funds Hughes had meant to finance his London endeavours with, he and Evan would be having many sunny days. He showed both the leather bags to Evan and secured them to Noir's saddle. His head was spinning with a sense of triumph, so much so that when he glanced inside the carriage again, he delved one hand into the purse Evan held in his hand to count the coins Hughes carried on him, and pulled out a shilling.

"For your trouble," he said, offering it to the woman.

She smirked and declined. "No, thank you, kind sirs, I am enjoying the view," she whispered, pointing to Hughes helplessly rolling in the mud as Evan tied him up like a hog for slaughter.

The sheer proficiency with which Evan worked the rope sent a shiver down Julian's spine. It made Julian wonder if that first time Evan had tied him up had been exciting for Evan. Whether that had been the reason for the stiff cock Julian had felt the next morning against his flesh. He'd like to think it was.

"Suit yourself," he told the woman and stepped away from her to cut through the crucial straps in the harnesses of the horses, to prevent the travelers from easily making their way to the nearest town. He almost enjoyed the snapping sound of leather breaking. "Make sure that bastard does not choke on the horse droppings and dirt."

Evan gave the scene one more quick look, and as he passed Julian, approaching Noir, he stroked Julian's back, as if it were the most natural thing in the world.

"We're done, let's go," Evan said, his voice muted by the wet scarf covering his face.

"Yes," said Julian, at first following Evan like a pup, only to realize Snow stood on the other side of the carriage. Flushing all the way underneath the coat, he rushed to his horse and mounted her damp back. The cold made him shiver, but the heat of Evan's caress was like a permanent marking on his back.

He spurred on Snow and followed Evan, who already moved toward a small road that would ultimately lead them home.

Julian had never felt this alive, and the man who orchestrated it all was right in front of him.

CHAPTER 17

JULIAN

They went off the beaten track in the end and rode down a barely-visible trail between the trees. Branchlets caressed Julian's arms while he followed Evan without a word, watching his firm shoulders sway along with Noir, as if the master and his horse were one body. The roof of leaves protected them from the worst of the downpour, but with the rush of excitement from the robbery slowly evaporating, a dull sensation swelled inside Julian. Had Evan not intervened, Julian would likely not been here.

He'd have bled into the mud, staring at the cloudy sky one last time. When put in this kind of perspective, death did not seem like a crossing of the souls from one realm to the next. Maybe it was the murkiness of Julian's heart that prevented him from feeling God's touch, but all he sensed was emptiness that would take him away in death.

The undergrowth was somehow more fragrant, as was the bark of the trees. The steady drum of the rain was music that rose to a *staccato*, prompting Julian to speak. But he could not. They were not safe yet, and even though the downpour would wash away their tracks, he waited for Evan's cue despite the pressure inside him. His throat was swelling with words of gratitude, Evan's touch still somehow present on his back, and it was the need to feel its heat again that kept Julian steady after the very real danger to his life.

They eventually reached a muddy road leading toward a creek at the bottom of the hill. The lush green colors became steadily muddled as the rain became thicker, slipping underneath Julian's collar and making him shudder from the cold.

There wasn't much light left when Evan stopped Noir under an old stone bridge, just tall enough to provide them with shelter, and slid off to the ground. "I'm soaked, and the weather is only getting worse. We've got over an hour's ride to Tredele. Let's wait it out a bit, because I can barely see."

Julian dismounted Snow and led her into the shadow of the bridge, assaulted by the fresh yet muddy scent of the water. He licked rain off his lips and quickly fastened the reins to a young tree that grew past the shadow of the bridge. As soon as he could, he slid into the relative dryness and took off his hat. At least the hair it had covered was dry, but water snuck underneath his coat, leaving patches of damp fabric all over Julian. His body felt so cold it was almost as if it was completely drenched underneath the coat. He took it off and spread the garment over a mossy rock, leaving it there along with the tricorn hat.

The sacks attached to Noir's saddle clanged with precious metals again, and Julian gently squeezed one with his hand, sensing the hard edges beneath leather. Silver spoons perhaps? They would only find out once they were back in the safety of their home.

"How far from the carriage are we now?" he asked, standing straight under the arc of the bridge above. It was indeed rather gray from the thick clouds and rain taking away daylight, but the water beyond the bridge still glistened, alive with the constant downpour.

It struck him that this image reflected the turmoil he'd grown inside over the past few weeks.

Evan approached him and looked at the murky sky, but shook his head. "This bridge is about an hour's ride away from Tredele on a good day. So we must be at least two hours away from the carriage. In this weather it will take longer." He pulled his hat off and shook his head, sending droplets of water Julian's way. "I'm impressed with you."

A string of tension snapped inside Julian, and he laughed, rubbing the wet glove over his face before dropping it on top of the hat and coat he'd left to dry. "I almost died back there. I would have if you hadn't been there," he said, swallowing the rock that formed in his throat.

Evan opened his coat, his face as serious as ever in the faint gray light coming through the thick pane of water. "But I was."

Julian stared at him, unable to tear his gaze away from the handsome face, the hard eyes that could be so soft and tender in moments when Evan forgot to keep his guard up. He took a step closer, and his body, even though mostly dry where it had been covered, shuddered. "Yes. Of course you were. You're like a rock that keeps me from drowning in the waves."

The corner of Evan's lips lifted slightly. "Or rather a rock tied to your ankle when all you wish to do is sail away to Italy."

Julian's chest clenched, squashing his heart until it beat as fast as the wings of a dragonfly. "I could not sleep last night," he said slowly, approaching Evan step by step. "I took my quill and wrote for hours. And now when we were riding, I thought of you finding those pages, had Hughes shot me. I wondered if you'd understand any of the gibberish I produced."

Evan frowned. "And what would I have found?"

The rain beat against the ground around them relentlessly, yet the space under the bridge was a cozy hideaway for just the two of them.

Julian laughed and pushed back his hair, moving step by step, still hesitating how much he should reveal. "I understood what my writing was lacking. Why I could never finish a single book." He swallowed, silenced by the power behind Evan's gaze. Its sharp blade pierced Julian's breastbone, opening up the Pandora's box he'd kept hidden away all this time. "I now realize that I've misunderstood my own characters, because I have misunderstood myself as well. I was unable to be true, but now, even if certain things cannot be written about plainly, I can finally express them. So I had a storm pour its rage over Rome, and I described the power of it in such intricate detail. And the gladiator, Gaius, his ghost really, told Francis all about it. But that scene is actually about this," he whispered, touching his chest.

Evan leaned a little closer, and even that was enough to send Julian's heart into a gallop. "What do you want to say?"

Julian lowered his gaze to Evan's chest and touched it with his palms in hope he could somehow soak up the cold dampness out of Evan's clothes and make him warm. He slowly moved his hands up to Evan's face. Touching the wet skin gave him such a rush he could barely hear anything but his own breath and heartbeat anymore. "There is a storm inside me as well," he said in the end, and as he leaned forward and stood on his toes, the kiss somehow happened. Just a brush of soft, warm skin against his lips, and yet it sent a jolt of sensation all the way to his knees, to his neck, to his chest. Cradling Evan's face in his hands, Julian opened his mouth and gasped, shivering when his tongue tasted the seam of Evan's mouth.

Evan's hot mouth opened to him without question, and the kiss that Julian had once declined so fiercely now pulled him in, making him close his eyes and experience it through every inch of his skin. Evan's hands were on his waist, his hips, and then on his buttocks, the kiss becoming only more fervent. The stubble under Julian's fingertips reminded him exactly whom he was kissing. There was nothing soft or gentle about this moment, and Julian wouldn't have it any other way.

Evan's tongue explored every last bit of Julian's mouth with such hunger it was threatening to consume them both. Julian shivered all over, but it had nothing to do with the cold. He was feverish, and his mind whispered to him verses he'd written the night before, until the two characters from Julian's novel became him and Evan, embracing in the drizzle.

Evan led Julian deeper into the shadow of the bridge, pulling his pliant body step by step until Julian's back hit the stone wall. Not once did their lips part, as if Evan were afraid he wouldn't be allowed to kiss him again if he stopped for even a moment.

Julian arched against the frosty surface, but didn't dare move an inch farther. Evan leaned over him like an impenetrable barrier, and with the heat of his body steaming from underneath the open coat, Julian trailed his hands lower, to the firm sides of Evan's body, to his waist and narrow hips. He gasped for air, for a short while forgetting how to breathe, too intoxicated by the sultriness of Evan's lips.

So this was what the world had been withholding from him all along due to his undiscovered inclinations. A raw, unstoppable need that could no longer be tamed.

Evan pressed his scorching forehead against Julian's, his eyes wide and attentive. "You don't get to take this kiss back. It's mine."

Julian whined, already seeking Evan's lips again, and placing soft kiss after soft kiss around that warm mouth as he spoke. "It is only yours. I was not prepared for the thunder when it first came over me. It scared me, and lightning burned my hands, but I still chased you. Now my eyes are clear, and I finally see that my place is in the eye of the storm," he whispered, glancing into Evan's eyes, and a shiver trailed down his spine when his tongue teased the rim of Evan's mouth. "Right here."

Evan exhaled, teasing Julian's lips with his warm breath. "I'm not a poet, I don't have such fine words," he rasped, watching Julian, as if he saw him for the first time. "But you will not regret this. I will keep you safe. I will make you happy." He leaned in for another kiss, which once more made Julian realize that every kiss he'd ever received had been only a shadow of this one.

Julian smiled, elated and warm inside as Evan's hands caressed him both gently and with a passion that seemed difficult to contain. "I will read you all of it once we're home," he teased, pulling Evan closer and rubbing his chest against Evan's. It was a simple touch, and yet the lightning bolt of sensation made him rock his hips against Evan's thigh. "You make me happy every day I'm allowed to be at your side."

"I can't wait until we're home," Evan said and gave him one more kiss before sliding to his knees in the mud, his movements frantic as he instantly reached to the front of Julian's breeches.

Julian's head spun, and he held on to Evan's shoulders, shocked to see him in such a vulnerable position. On his knees, as if he was ready to worship every bit of skin on Julian's body. "Good heavens," he whispered breathlessly, struggling to keep still when Evan's rough hands rubbed against his manhood through the fabric.

Evan looked up at him with a wicked smile that rarely appeared on his lips. "It will be heavenly. You have my promise." He leaned forward and kissed Julian's cock through the white linen of his drawers, which was peeking through the open front of the breeches.

Julian pushed his fingers through Evan's unruly hair and reached down, already frantic to release the tension building up within him. In his most secret thoughts, it has always been him serving Evan, not the other way around, as Evan had never expressed the need to forfeit his dominance the two times they'd been intimate, but seeing him like this, flushed with need to take care of Julian's cock before his own, made Julian breathe freely again. "I did not expect this," he whispered in the end, whimpering when rough hands pulled out his prick.

Evan looked up at him as he licked the upper side of Julian's cock, all the way to the thatch of hair growing around the base. "I did not expect this either." He stroked Julian's stomach, sliding his hot hands under the wet shirt.

A tremor shook Julian's body from the heat contrasting so sharply with his own damp skin, but he could not look away from Evan's masculine face, his open mouth so close to Julian's cock. It was the most obscene and beautiful thing he'd ever witnessed.

Whores had done this to him, and it had been pleasant, but nothing like this. Nothing like the searing heat that was Evan's tongue and the cool sensation that remained once it was gone. There had been no broad arms or leather. No burning eyes or stubble scratching against Evan's thigh. He stifled a howl of pleasure when the short bristle on Evan's chin trailed over Julian's balls.

"You serving me... I did not think you could ever want that," he uttered, caressing Evan's face with his thumbs.

"What I want is to touch you all over." He kissed the base of Julian's cock. "I want to mark you as mine. I want to suck your cock and swallow your seed. I'm serving myself." Evan smirked before taking all of Julian's prick into his mouth, all the way down his throat.

Julian opened his lips, catching cool air as he relaxed against the cold stone wall, weightless with the pleasure of the tight, slippery channel that accepted him so eagerly. He closed his fist over Evan's hair, breathlessly crying out as red hot pleasure filled his veins. For once, there was nothing scary about Evan's intimate touch.

"Yes..."

A deep groan trembled all along the length of Julian's cock, making him moan and curl his toes in his boots. Could this be the kind of life that awaited Julian in Evan's company? An endless well of pleasure?

Evan sucked on Julian's prick as if there were nothing more delicious in the world than Julian, and his hands drifted back to Julian's ass, squeezing and kneading the sensitive flesh without asking for permission.

Julian hoped Evan would never again ask for permission to touch him. His mind was clouded by a warm fog, and as Evan went on, caressing Julian with his tongue, sucking on the loose skin around Julian's cockhead, squeezing the tip between his tongue and the roof of his mouth, Julian did not even realize when his whole body started tingling. The sensation went from his toes and rushed all the way to the top of his head. His muscles flexed and relaxed in tandem with Evan's caresses, his cock swelling as if it were about to burst.

"I'm… I'm close," Julian whispered, petting the tousled dark hair and clutching it to his stomach, eager to sense all there was to Evan's touch.

Their eyes met, and the fierce emotion of the contact was choking in its power. Evan wouldn't stop bobbing his head over Julian's cock, taking it deep into the tight heat of his lips, but it was the fingers shamelessly pushing between Julian's buttocks that had him lose all self-control and come right into the waiting mouth.

Pleasure washed over him wave after wave until he could hardly stand on his own and rested his weight on Evan's shoulders and the wall. He closed his eyes, suddenly so pumped out he could crawl into Evan's arms, into the bed where they would sleep together, and fall asleep like a babe.

"It *was* heavenly," he whispered, blinking his eyes open to take in the dark flush on Evan's face.

Only now did Evan slowly pull away from Julian's still throbbing cock, and rested his face against Julian's pubes, breathing in his scent, and leaving little kisses down his cock as he slid his hand into his own breeches, tossing off rapidly.

"*You* are heavenly," he murmured, and Julian couldn't stop himself anymore. He slid down the wall so rapidly Evan lost balance, but Julian pulled him close, reaching for the heat between Evan's thighs. The thick prick twitched in his hand, so very warm and alive, and yet alien to the touch. The last time Julian did this, he'd been too drunk to memorize the sensation very well, but Evan's cock was exquisite and fit into his fist so well, as if it had been meant for it.

Julian leaned in and opened Evan's mouth with his, startled by the bitter aftertaste on his lover's warm tongue. It took him two heartbeats to realize that it must have come from his own essence that Evan had just swallowed with such greed. Just thinking about it made Julian push harder against the hard body in front of him.

Evan pulled him close, the strength in his arms the only thing Julian could think of. Nothing else mattered. Not the rain, not the mud, not even that he almost died today.

"Yes. That's it," Evan groaned, holding on to Julian as he came all over Julian's fingers, thrusting into the tight fist with that thick shaft.

Julian rubbed his face against Evan's cheek and pulled on it with his teeth, eager to taste the skin he'd admired for so many weeks. "It throbs in my hand. I don't want to let go of you, my tender, powerful bull," he whispered, trailing a line of kisses to Evan's ear and burying his nose in the damp hair. Only now was he sensing the cool touch of the mud on his knees. He did not care at all.

Evan took a shuddery breath. "You don't have to let go. I'm all yours." He gently bit on Julian's ear from the other side, still slowly pumping his cock into Julian's palm as if to tease him, remind him of what he also wanted to do.

Julian swallowed hard, trying not to think about that too much yet and turned his head, rubbing his nose against Evan's. There was a sense of peace inside him that he'd never experienced before. As if he'd truly come home. "I wanted it to happen sooner. I was burning when we danced together." He took a deep breath, leaning farther into Evan's arms and closing his eyes in shame. "I do not wish for you to marry, Evan. I am not willing to share you."

Evan sighed and wrapped his arms under Julian's, pulling him into the tight embrace Julian had dreamed of for so many weeks now. "It was a leap, not a step, to admit that, wasn't it?"

Julian licked his lips, resting with his breeches and drawers still lowered. "What I just did is irreversible. I cannot blame anyone else for how I feel about you. It might be forbidden, or even sinful, but I've never known passion like this before. If that makes me a bad seed, so be it."

"Of course you are bad. You're a highwayman now." Evan kissed Julian's neck, and one of his hands slid to Julian's buttock again, squeezing it as if Evan simply couldn't get enough of being able to touch it.

Julian laughed and rubbed his nose over Evan's cheekbone, filled with a sense of completion, despite the insecurity still biting him whenever the hand on his ass traced his skin in a way that made him shiver with undeniable pleasure.

He was ruined. And he did not care.

Chapter 18

Evan

Evan could still taste Julian's kisses and seed on his lips when they arrived at Tredele. It was late, and Evan had told his servants that they shouldn't wait up for him and Julian, so they quickly removed the tack off their mounts and left the horses in their stalls with the food and water Jory had left for them. Still drunk on the success of the ambush and on Julian's sweet words, Evan grabbed Julian's gloved hand and pulled him across the yard, each step spraying their legs with water. It was a relief to leave behind the constant drizzle and lock the doors behind them at last.

Esther had left the fire burning in Evan's bedroom, and the contrast between its heat and the icy cold clothes sticking to their bodies was most welcome. But what truly kept Evan warm was the certainty that he didn't even need to ask Julian whether he wanted to stay with him tonight. He knew it would be so.

Julian tossed the stolen valises to the floor as soon as they entered, and pulled Evan down for a kiss as intense as if he'd been thirsting for it since they left the cozy den underneath the bridge. He was flushed and cool to the touch from being so damp, but as soon as Julian's back hit the wall, he started unbuttoning his waistcoat, without ever breaking the connection between their lips.

Evan could hardly believe this unexpected luck, but here he was, with the man whose touch he craved so much, given a kiss that had been earlier denied as if he were repulsive. Each meeting of their lips was both the sweetest surprise and a dark fantasy come true. He now wished there was an easier way to take off clothes, so that they wouldn't have to part. Julian wanting to touch him was a revelation Evan could bask in forever. And to know that Julian's desires did not waver once he found out Evan's income was measly, that he had debts, and his one valuable possession—Tredele—was in dire need of expensive renovation, was the sweetest thing of all.

"We need to tear all this off, or we will be too ill to move," rasped Julian with a wicked smile on his face. His waistcoat was already on the floor when he started working on the buttons of Evan's clothes, and this time it seemed like it was only an excuse to rub Evan's chest.

Evan spread his arms to the sides, happy to be served this way by his flustered companion. "We can't allow that now, can we? I can think of many things I'd like to do to you. All night and all day."

Julian grinned, and with the light from the fire dancing on the side of his face, he looked like a little demon who'd somehow entered into the human world to seduce Evan.

With the waistcoat taken off, Julian pushed his hands under Evan's shirt and trailed his fingertips over his stomach, then up his chest, swirling them through the short body hair that stuck to the damp linen. "What kind of things?"

Evan flexed his muscles and straightened up as Julian peeled the soaked shirt off him. "Deliciously dirty things. Whatever you wish, and whatever you allow."

Julian's gaze caressed Evan's chest with such intensity it almost felt like physical touch. His handsome face relaxed, and he smiled softly, finally raising his eyes to look at Evan. "I had dreams about us being together," he said and took hold of Evan's hand, pulling it to the loose tail of his own shirt.

Evan was more than happy to oblige and revealed the flesh he wanted to kiss all over. "Oh, did you now?" He stole another kiss once the shirt was off Julian. "And what did we do in those dreams?" He looked around for candles, desperate to get more light in the room so he could see all of Julian and explore every inch of his skin. He wanted to see the fire in the blue eyes reflected back at him, to have Julian smile at him as they rolled in the covers, without a care in the world.

Julian's bare skin touched his, and he could not stop a moan escaping his lips as they embraced, still in their wet breeches. Julian opened his mouth and suckled on the skin just above Evan's nipple, teasing it with the scorching hot touch of his tongue. "I was tied down, and it was so dark. A moonless night. I heard you move, and then your hands were on my thighs. You were lifting my nightshirt, and you lay on top of me. You touched me *everywhere*, and I could do nothing to stop you," whispered Julian, without looking up. It was almost as if making that last step into the unknown had prompted Julian to lose all his other inhibitions.

Evan was instantly attentive. "And you enjoyed that?" He slid his fingers to Julian's wrists and held them tight. "Hadn't you promised me a slow and painful death for tying you down?"

Julian let out a growl that sounded as if it had been made by a bear, not the most beautiful man Evan knew. "If a stranger touched me like you are right now, I would not appreciate it either. Being tied down like a hog, even after I told you not to go through with it... that was not pleasant. I did not trust you then, and I did not wish to be so helpless in your hands."

"Now that you are a highwayman yourself, I imagine you un-derstand it was a necessity?" He leaned down to Julian's ear and whispered. "But I don't deny it. I am a scoundrel. It gave me a thrill to have you tied up in my bed. Even if I wouldn't have done anything about it, it excited me that I could have."

Julian shuddered against Evan, finally looking up. He made a movement with one of his hands, but Evan held it where it was, challenging Julian with his eyes.

Julian exhaled loudly and licked his lips, arching between the wall and Evan's body. "I was afraid you would keep me like that. Naked and tied up, ready to uncover at any time," he said slowly, his voice low, with a dark quality Evan had not heard from him before.

Evan forced Julian's wrists against the wall, enjoying the struggle against his superior strength. "Were you afraid, or did you wish for it in secret? That you would never do anything again other than take my cock each day..." Talking such filth excited him to no end, but he watched Julian for signs of displeasure. It was like walking over thin ice, but he was a bold man, and he would push on until the pristine surface gave a creak.

Julian blinked and lowered his gaze, his breath trembling loudly in the quiet room. "I am... I believe both are true. Nobody taught me how to be this way."

"There is no way to learn it." Evan slid his knee between Julian's thighs and rubbed it against Julian's balls, which were still encased in the damp fabric. "You have to surrender yourself to it, open up to liking things you would have never thought you would, but also try those you end up not enjoying. All you need to do is tell me your thoughts. Though I assure you, I don't just live to please. My desires are very firm in the shape they have taken over the years." He squeezed Julian's wrists harder, pushing against him, and enjoying the fact that he was taller and able to cage Julian with his bulk.

Julian smiled. He suddenly yanked his hands up, as if wanting to break Evan's grip on them, but his eyes became cloudier when Evan held them in place. "I knew you were watching me that night when we came back from Looe."

Evan stilled, his mind going blank. "You did?" he asked, but then answered his own question. "You liked being watched..." The revelation tugged on his cock, as if Julian had taken hold of it already, so he pushed his hips against his... lover. Already on the day Julian had hurt him so deeply by running from Tredele, Julian had been secretly eager for his touch.

Julian closed his eyes, gasping and rolling his hips toward Evan. "I saw you in the mirror. And I—" He chewed on his lip, breathing harder. "I hoped you would come back into the room and touch me. I had those red welts for so many days, and I kept finding excuses to touch them," Julian said softly, looking toward the desk where it had all happened. It had gotten covered with trinkets since, but Evan already knew he would gladly make it a scene for a repetition of that past act.

Evan leaned down to nip on Julian's lip, barely able to contain his excitement. "I couldn't fuck you anymore, but at least I could see you squirm, see your arse bounce every time I hit it with the reins. I figured it was the last pleasure I could take from you, but, oh, have I ever dreamed of stepping between your legs afterward and pushing my cock between those flaming cheeks."

Julian shivered all over, curling his shoulders and burying his face against Evan's arm.

Evan smiled and kissed the top of his head. "Go to the bed, and we'll take time figuring out what else you enjoy."

Julian left an imprint of his teeth on Evan's arm and stepped away, with a red flush spread out over his pale chest like marks left behind by Evan's palms. He opened his breeches and quickly pulled them off along with his drawers. Only when he pushed off his stockings and shoes as well, Evan realized it was the first time he saw Julian truly naked. There was definition to his muscles, even though his body was not as robust as Evan's own. His skin had a beautiful creamy complexion, his ass was pleasantly rounded.

And all of this male flesh was Evan's to touch and caress.

Evan went over to a side table and grabbed a candle. He wanted to make sure he would see all of his pretty canary tonight.

"No. Not that," said Julian behind him, and when Evan glanced his way, Julian's gaze was swaying between Evan's face and the candle as he sank down to the mattress.

Evan cocked his head to the side. "Why not?"

Julian looked away, curling up his knees and hiding the lower part of his face behind them. "It's... demeaning," he muttered in the end.

Evan frowned, unsure what to answer to such a strange accusation. "Excuse me? I don't follow... I want to see more of you tonight, and I don't care how many candles go to waste in the process. But I don't think it's what you're talking about."

Julian rubbed his face with both hands, yet Evan suspected it was merely an attempt to hide behind them. "It's merely... you used one of them in an... intimate way with me."

The answer finally sank in, and Evan lit the candle quickly to stop holding it. "Oh. I..." He stepped closer to the bed, unbuttoning his breeches as soon as he deposited the candle on a holder by the bed. "It's just a trick Peran showed me." Now even he was becoming uncomfortable when the reality of Julian's accusation penetrated his mind. "To... prepare a man for the deed."

Julian bit on his thumb, still looking away and hiding his lovely body from Evan's view, as if he'd become frightful again. Everything about his position spoke of discomfort. "*The deed.*"

Evan pulled down his breeches and sat on the bed next to Julian in the damp drawers. He pulled him close for a hug. "It was something we both enjoyed," he muttered softly. "Though I suppose he enjoyed it more. It made the whole experience less painful, or rather... not painful at all if the body was ready for it."

Julian didn't shy away from the touch and slowly moved his fingertips over Evan's forearm. "It is painful."

Evan held in the helpless moan that wanted to escape his lips. He didn't know what to say at first, since spearing Julian with his prick had been on his mind from the moment they first met. There hadn't been a day when he hadn't thought of spreading Julian's thighs and fucking his tight ass as if they were both in heat.

"I'm sorry..." he mumbled in the end. "Peran loved it. It hadn't occurred to me that you wouldn't. But that's fine," he forced himself to say, because how else could he have answered? He wouldn't force Julian into something that didn't give them both pleasure.

Julian wasn't the nasty, conceited wastrel who offended Evan at every turn anymore.

Julian was now... his.

Julian relaxed underneath Evan's arm and slowly moved his hands around Evan's midsection, pressing against him tightly. "I want to make you happy, but this frightens me. When you did that the first time... never before had I felt such contempt toward myself," he said in a quiet voice but pushed even closer to Evan.

Evan spread his legs to pull Julian against him, and kissed his cheek, frantic with despair pooling in the pit of his stomach. "Lust got the best of me back then. I hadn't had an opportunity to be with a man all those years, and you were there, so beautiful, so available... I lost my mind. No wonder you hated me." He sighed and rubbed his forehead. "We will find things we both like, things you don't feel bad about." Guilt was bitter on Evan's tongue, but Julian was still in his bed. He was not running away, so there were pieces to put back together.

"I stopped hating you long ago," said Julian, slowly looking up.

Evan sighed, gently stroking Julian's arm. "I would hope so... I thought I felt interest from you. I don't know how to navigate these waters either."

Julian touched Evan's cheek gently. "There was interest on my part, but at that time I hadn't realized yet what kind of interest it was. I was... smitten with you since that night in the observatory. I am not exaggerating when I say that I never before... considered being with a man intimately. It was only after you... touched me for the first time that those thoughts started growing in me," said Julian, avoiding putting a name to what exactly had happened.

Evan looked away but pulled Julian's hand to his lips to kiss his fingertips. "Was there *anything* you liked about that night? Or is the way I... express my affection too rough altogether?"

"Oh no, I like you being rough," said Julian, with something akin to panic burning in his blue eyes. He petted Evan's arm and pushed back his reddish blond hair. Its color was so perfect, especially now, when the strands glistened in the warm light of the candle. "This is difficult to talk about. I... there was pleasure in it too," he said in the end, picking on the hairs on Evan's forearm, as if to distract himself. "I loved your hands. They squeezed me so ruthlessly, as if you could not stop yourself from touching me."

Evan's heart skipped a beat. "At that moment it felt like I couldn't. You yielded so perfectly I was unable to resist. A gentleman is taught some rules when it comes to courting a lady, or marriage, but no one ever showed me how I should go about being with a man. Even what I had with Peran was so different from *this* it would be difficult to compare. So I acted on instinct, and my instinct was to devour you."

Julian shuddered but pushed into Evan's arms nevertheless. "I didn't know how to say no to your hands, even though I knew you despised me and wouldn't even try to hide it. I still do not know what that says about me. In my heart, I've never felt as ill as that night. First, my father rejected me, and then you just helped yourself to my body. And yet, I know I could have fought you more fiercely. Do you understand my meaning?" he asked, staring at Evan's hand and softly brushing his fingers over it.

"I do. I was angry. You knew exactly how to stab me with your words. Yet it's no excuse. I'm sorry, I cannot take back time." Evan looked to the flame of the candle, at loss over what to do. How were they supposed to move forward from this tainting memory? Maybe Evan really was a monster who couldn't escape his own nature?

Julian exhaled and entwined his fingers with Evan's, squeezing his hand tightly. "I know you are a good man, Evan. I trust you. I merely needed to hear your present feelings about this. The truth of the matter is that I do think about those deeds sometimes, and maybe we could make an attempt in the future. But not yet." He pulled Evan's hand to his lips and brushed his soft mouth over its back.

Evan sighed and pulled away, trying to untangle himself from Julian's arms as his new lover struck his most vulnerable side with a whip of softly-spoken words. "My cock's not covered in thorns. If what I want is unpleasant to you, we can settle for other things. I'm sorry I caused you such grief."

Julian's fingers grabbed Evan's jaw with surprising strength, and he was pulled back to face those bright eyes. "It's not. In fact, I think it looks quite delicious."

Evan pursed his lips. "You do not need to force yourself into things you don't want. No matter what happens, you will always have my affection."

Julian sighed and caressed Evan's face with his thumbs. His gaze was intense as he leaned over and kissed Evan's lips. "And you have mine. Do not pull away from it. Or are you not willing to let me have a taste of you?"

The sole thought of having his cock in Julian's succulent lips had everything else around them blurring. "No, that does sound... agreeable." Evan chuckled and slid his fingers into Julian's hair. Even if he never got everything he wanted, he would still die a happy man if Julian was by his side.

Julian answered him with a smile that only broadened when their faces came closer. "Agreeable? Is that how low you believe my skill at it to be?" he asked, and Evan sensed Julian's hand moving up his thigh, touching him through the wet linens.

"My hopes are not high," Evan mocked. "I believe you will require plenty of practice. Daily."

Julian chewed on his lip and rubbed their noses, slowly pushing Evan to his back. "Is that so? You merely intend to make me dependant on it, as if your seed contained opium."

Evan enjoyed the fantasy of having Julian addicted to his flesh and coming back for more each day. "That is my intention. Have you ever dreamed of another man's prick in your mouth?"

Julian's breath was warm on Evan's lips when he answered, pulling his palm over the front of Evan's drawers and teasing his cock back to life. "Yes... I've had whores do that to me, so I knew of it, and once you became such a presence in my life, I did think of that too."

Evan could get drunk on those words. "Your dream is about to come true then." He reached down and pulled his half-hard cock out of his drawers, more than ready to watch it disappear in Julian's mouth.

Julian's eyes became foggy, and there was no way in hell he could be faking this kind of interest. It made Evan's blood run faster.

Julian stuck his fingers under the fabric of Evan's linens and roughly pulled them lower, getting off the bed to undress Evan completely. "I want to see all of you."

"All yours."

Julian's eyes flickered with emotion, and he leaned in to meet Evan's lips while pulling off Evan's remaining clothes. "Any suggestions?" he asked in the end, blushing furiously.

Evan bit his lip, indulging in this display of shyness. "Your head between my legs."

Julian laughed, visibly relaxing, but when he moved to kneel down, and Evan's blood simmered in his veins, the sound of thunder resonated throughout the whole house. Only it was not thunder, and it carried on with loud metallic clangs while the walls around them shook.

Julian stepped away, glancing toward the door. "What was that?" he asked, already grabbing one of Evan's shirts, which were piled on one of the chairs.

Evan pulled on his nightshirt and jumped off the bed, heading for the door. The sound had come from somewhere outside. "Stay here," he said, worried that something might be collapsing in one of the farther parts of the house.

Why now? Why now out of all the times if this bloody house deteriorated every day? Did a beam crack in the kitchen? He'd noticed it was somewhat unsteady the other day.

"You cannot be serious," hissed Julian, already pulling his boots on over bare feet. He rushed to the door and opened it before Evan reached it with the candle in hand.

"I don't want something falling on you, and I know Tredele better." Evan pushed him into the room, but he already knew it was a lost cause. Julian rarely listened to anyone.

Just as predicted, he followed Evan into the corridor, but as soon as they left the warmth of the bedroom, Evan's heart sank when a cold draft chilled his bare legs. Breathless, he ran down the stairs, into the oldest area of the house, which still had the original stone floor.

His heartbeat slowed down, and so did everything else. The grand hall where Evan's ancestors had celebrated the most fantastic banquets during the height of Tredele's existence was too bright, and when he came even closer, it was impossible not to notice the rubble—wood and stone—piled up everywhere like rocks emerging from the ocean of the floor. He rushed inside like a maniac, stepping into the wet slush of plaster and dead leaves.

He couldn't breathe. The suit of armor proudly worn by one of Evan's ancestors on battlefields three hundred years back was nowhere to be seen. The walls that housed a collection of old and new weaponry, one of the prides of Tredele, had turned into waterfalls. And when Evan looked up, into the angry mouth of the collapsed roof, heavy droplets fell on his face, trickling from the teeth of broken beams and the monstrously thick clouds above.

The carnage was so severe the furnishings and decorations might have never existed. The glass in some of the tall, narrow windows had broken, leaving gashes that only let in more rain and cold wind.

The past that had always been the pride of the Penharts lay in ruin, and there was nothing Evan could do about it.

He grabbed the arm of a broken statue only to throw it at what remained of the ceiling in helpless anger. "Will this ever end?" he screamed into the night, heaving from exasperation. He couldn't repair Tredele fast enough. It was like a hungry toddler, always screaming for more attention that he could not provide.

He shuddered when gentle hands pushed the wet shirt tighter against his body.

"Oh, God," Julian whispered, staring at the ruin that was like an accurate representation of Evan's own life. "Is— is there anything we can salvage before it dawns?"

"It's all soaked or crushed. This house is set on humiliating me. Is that it, Father?" he yelled into the clouds, ignoring the raindrops falling on his face. "Is your ghost back to haunt me? Wishing I wasn't desecrating your house with my perversion?" He grabbed Father's favorite crossbow off the wet wall, kicked one of the doors open, and tossed it out into the storm. "Fuck you, and fuck all your things!"

He took a step forward and curled up, grabbing the swinging door as sharp pain seared through his foot.

"Evan, don't move," yelled Julian. "I'll bring your shoes before you lose all your toes."

Evan couldn't stop gasping as he looked around the wreckage. For the first time in his life he truly wished he'd sold the house to Blackwell long ago. At least he'd be free of the weight of responsibility. Anger had him so heated even the rain couldn't cool down his skin.

He looked up to the portrait of his parents, meeting the two pairs of eyes watching him with contempt as rivulets of water raced down the pale faces sculpted with oil.

"I hate you, and your goddamn house," he whispered, letting his head hang low and the rain drizzle down his hair.

Leaning against the wet wall, he felt hope finally leave his heart. Why was his every success followed by failure and catastrophe? Did he not deserve some peace? Responsibility was a dead weight on his shoulders. It grew each day and would pull him down until he grew a hunched back.

Completely drained, he couldn't even bring himself to care about the trinkets and heirlooms that were now buried under the piles and piles of rubble.

He didn't even notice at first when Julian rushed in with a pair of simple boots Evan used when working outside. With a look of determination on his face, he kneeled down and pulled up Evan's injured leg, crooking his head to have a look at the wound.

Evan tried to pull away, not even caring to see what exactly had happened. It was yet another cut, nothing like the open gash right above him. Tredele was indeed an open wound in his heart, one that wouldn't heal. Those old walls would never let him forget how despicable he was and what a poor master he made. "It's fine," he muttered but hissed with pain when Julian probed the broken flesh.

"It's not fine," said Julian and started quickly wrapping a clean white stocking around Evan's foot. The rain drizzled on Julian's back from one of the tattered edges of the roof, completely soaking his shirt. Julian didn't seem to care.

"This house is purgatory for my sins… It's my cross to bear. You should go back to bed and stay warm." Yet Evan didn't have the power in him to push Julian away when his care provided such relief.

Julian looked up and his shoulders slumped when he exhaled, heating Evan's icy cold foot with his own breath. "Don't be ridiculous. You did nothing wrong. It's not your fault your father and brother left you a property in ruins," he said and pulled the boot on Evan's foot, as skillfully as if he'd been a valet his whole life.

Strangely, now that they'd kissed, that the intimacy between them had reached a new level, Evan was ready to tell Julian things he'd be ashamed to tell even the closest of friends. "Peter gambled away our mines, and the rents are barely enough to keep up with the demands of this house. I declined selling to Blackwell, that's why he's so eager to marry off his daughter to me. So he can get his hands on Tredele."

Julian put on Evan's other shoe and slowly rose to his feet, pushing close to escape the rain, but in consequence, he pressed their bodies tightly together, until they were divided only by the two wet linen shirts. "Why? Why does he want Tredele?"

"He wants to raze it to the ground and build something new, perhaps? You'd think a man his age, a man like him would enjoy these old walls." Evan shook his head and pulled Julian close. "Right now I wish I'd sold it and been done with it, but I don't want to betray my ancestors. If my grandmother knew what has become of Tredele, she'd have wept."

Julian pulled Evan out of the room and into the corridor where he sat on the first step of the stairs, still holding Evan's hand. The sound of the rain pouring into the old hall was deafening. The chill of air and the howling wind above muted all of Evan's senses, but he could still hear Julian.

"If you married his daughter, Tredele would still be yours to with do as you pleased. You reckon he believes Elizabeth would convince you to follow his guidance? Or is there something else?"

"I have... a large debt with him. It wouldn't go away with the marriage. I'd be on his leash." Evan was ashamed to say all this out loud, in front of a man whom he wanted to charm, and yet it was Julian's right to know everything he was getting into. He squeezed Julian's hand, trying not to think of the repairs that would be necessary to salvage all that remained of the entrance hall.

Julian brushed his lips over Evan's knuckles, as if he'd been doing that for years and hadn't just kissed Evan for the first time a few hours ago. "Can we make do with what we took from Hughes tonight? For the roof, I mean."

Evan licked his lips, shivering at the easy way the word *we* passed through Julian's lips'. As if the house were Julian's responsibility in any way. "We'd have to count it up but there is a chance, depending on how well we can sell the trinkets in Plymouth. You will also need to find out... how much you need for your travel expenses." Evan looked down to his wet boots, struck by the thought of Julian leaving now, after he'd only just begun revealing his true colors. It had been difficult enough to think about before but was unbearable now. *Stay*, his heart whispered.

Julian's fingers tightened on his. "You mean, how much we need to buy back your telescope."

Evan swallowed and looked at Julian's face. "What good is that?"

Julian sighed, and his mouth curved into a pale smile. "Without it, we cannot look for signs of life on the flying islands, can we?"

Evan ran his fingers through his hair, unable to express all the ways in which he cared for Julian. "We cannot. I suppose it is of utmost importance then."

Julian got up and stepped closer to Evan when a male voice made him frantically pull away. "Sir, are you there? I can hear voices," called out Frederick from somewhere beyond the collapsed hall.

"We are inside," yelled Julian, and moments later, the door leading into the courtyard unlocked and Frederick entered in his nightclothes. His eyes were widening by the second, and in the end he pulled his fingers down his wrinkled face, shaking his head over and over.

"Oh, dear God."

Evan groaned and approached him, resigned to his fate. "I was just dealing with this madness, but there's nothing I can do while it's rain—"

"Sir, some of the pieces can still be salvaged. The old master would haunt us all in our dreams if we left all those heirlooms to rot," said Frederick, and Evan knew there was some truth in Frederick's words. Every item that had been gathered here had value, some merely sentimental, but some could help Tredele get back on its feet.

With Frederick gone to fetch the other servants, Evan fought a sense of revulsion rising within his chest. He did not want to deal with this ruin.

Someone rapped at the door, as if the hall were still standing whole. Evan rubbed his face, wondering how everyone managed to get here so quickly from the cottage, but what he saw in the open doorway made clouds descend from above and fill his ribcage with thunder.

"Mr. Pascoe," Evan said, not even attempting to hide his contempt for the uninvited guest, who dared to come over so late in the night. But then his mind returned to the earlier hours of this day, and he struggled not to let the pang of uncertainty be known to the constable.

He and Julian should have hidden their loot instead of dashing to the bedroom like two adolescent sweethearts. They should have put the tack back in its place instead of tossing it to the floor. They should have cleaned the horses and wiped off all traces of coal from Snow's white coat.

Evan's feet felt like they were made of lead, keeping him in place while his head became so empty it could fly up like a soap bubble. And Pascoe was not alone either. Two men in dark coats stood on either side of him. One Evan vaguely knew from his past, of a severe-looking face with a characteristically crooked nose. The other, a slim and tall fellow of about thirty had a face with no features that would have made it memorable.

"And your companions are?" asked Evan dryly, unwilling to humiliate Pascoe and his men by not requesting their names. Not when there were two stolen valises filled with money and trinkets lying on the floor of his bedroom.

"My deputies. Mr. Mark Davies," said Pascoe, gesturing at the tall man before turning to the one whose face Evan found somewhat familiar. "Mr. George Atkins."

Ah, a boy Evan used to meet at church when the one on his land was still functional. Nevertheless, he was not happy to see this familiar face. Pascoe could not request to search Evan's home without any evidence against him, but this was the first time he'd come to harass Evan with men to back him up.

It chilled Evan to the bone that Pascoe might have obtained some kind of proof of Evan's guilt. A witness perhaps? His thoughts ran wild, and he could only hope it did not show in the movements of his body.

Pascoe's face twisted, but he swept his eyes over Evan, before taking in the flooded hall. "I see we've come at a bad time."

Evan glared at Pascoe and spread his arms when he remembered that there was nothing indecent about his incomplete and wet outfit. It was well past midnight. No reason for both him and Julian to not be wearing nightshirts. "What could have possibly brought the three of you here at this time of night? Have you heard the roof fall down, and came over to give us a hand? Any and all assistance would be invaluable," he said, physically unable to keep his tongue devoid of spite.

"Has help arrived so fast?" asked Julian, appearing at Evan's side, as if he had every reason to worry about the state of Tredele. With his hair completely drenched, the thick curls sticking to his neck and face the same way his thin shirt clung to his chest, he stepped closer to Pascoe and made a curt bow. "Gentlemen, I am happy to report that no person was hurt by this disaster."

"That's most fortunate," said Pascoe dryly, watching them both with a cool, level gaze, but nothing about his tone suggested he was concerned with the safety of any of the people living at Tredele. Evan could not mistake the bitter repulsion coloring Pascoe's face for anything else than the loathing he'd held for Evan the last fifteen years.

"I can see the two of you are becoming better acquainted every night," Pascoe said in the end.

The two deputies frowned and glanced at one another, seemingly unfamiliar with Evan's history with Pascoe. *Thank God.*

Evan glared at the constable and took a step forward to obscure Julian at least partially. "Forgive me, gentlemen, but I cannot imagine what you could want from me at this ungodly hour."

Pascoe straightened up even more and raised his eyebrows. "I have come to inspect your horses."

Evan's heart sank. "W–why is that?"

Oh, this was bad. His voice had betrayed him, and it was impossible to cover for that tremor now.

Chapter 19

Evan

Pascoe's mouth twitched. "There was another highway robbery earlier today. The victim, Mr. Miles Hughes, described two men on horseback. He could not give many details about the robbers themselves, but he did remember one of the horses very well. White with very odd spots of irregular color. The other was a raven-black giant. It so happens that I have a very good memory for horseflesh, and it is my duty to make sure I do not overlook anything."

Julian stepped forward, tapping his tongue against his palate, as if he were calling over his horse, not engaged in a battle of wills. "Mr. Pascoe, can you not see this is the worst possible time to approach Sir Evan about something as trivial as a hunch about horses? What you just described, you would surely find in most stables around the county. Why is it that you're pursuing my friend with such vile determination?"

"If you think it is me who is vile, you either don't know your friend very well, or know him well enough not to care. Are you refusing to show me your horses, sir? Shall I remind you I am a representative of the law?" Pascoe looked at Evan in a way that made him want to punch Pascoe's teeth in.

"You are obsessed, Mr. Pascoe. What is it that you are accusing him off? Robbery? The word of a gentleman should be sufficient to put your suspicions to rest and let all of us rescue what remains intact from this poor hall," Julian said.

But Evan knew there was no way out of this. He had neither the money nor powerful friends to deflect Pascoe's accusations, and with two witnesses of fine character, Evan's word against theirs would have stood weak indeed. He licked his lips and pointed Pascoe across the yard where the stables emerged from behind the house. "Let us go," he said.

Would this be it? Would this be the night when Pascoe crossed the line and Evan had no other choice but to tear his ribcage open with a sword? He considered taking a broken one from the rubble but ended up deciding against such a suspicious move. Could he do it? Could he kill a man without remorse the way Pascoe had Peran die from horrific injuries? Correction, could he kill *three* men to save his skin?

Julian walked with them. Back in the servants' house, the light was on, with shadows moving about in one of the windows. They knew nothing of that was going on, thank God. If worse came to worst, Evan would deal with his troubles himself. His temples throbbed with heat at the thought of Julian being dragged off to the gaol.

"Your friend is a gentleman only by name," said Pascoe, clearly not worried for his life with two men in their prime to aid him in case of violence.

"What a charming story, Mr. Pascoe," said Julian without a trace of fear to his voice. "Next you will tell us that all the whores working at Madame Canard's moved to a convent on the continent while the town was asleep."

Evan smirked, his eyes focused on the small sword hidden away between the folds of Pascoe's coat. If he acted quickly enough to surprise the deputies, then this would be the night of payback for all of Pascoe's wrongdoings. Evan wasn't cold from the rain anymore, or crushed by the renovation costs that were to come. He itched for blood, and Pascoe only needed to provide him with a good enough reason to shed it.

Pascoe rushed forward as they approached the entrance of the stable and pushed inside with a frantic gasp of someone on the cusp of a major discovery. Evan's hands tingled. He stood close to Pascoe, measuring how easy it would be to pull out Pascoe's sword while the bastard was busy looking for candles. He could push Pascoe in and deal with the two unsuspecting deputies first before descending on the gray vulture like an angel of justice.

His breath caught, and all plans clouded when Julian stepped closer, catching Evan's gaze in the sparse light coming from outside. His eyes were wide, but he pointed his chin to a corner where a pitchfork waited like a soldier ready for orders.

Evan should have known there were few things more valuable to Julian than his own skin, but instead of triggering distaste, Julian's determination to remain free added fuel to the fire within Evan's chest. They might be outnumbered, but they had far more at stake. Pascoe lit two candles, and the sight revealed by their glow had all of them silent for a moment.

The mare was as white as the snow she was named after.

Evan pursed his lips and the tension that had been gathering in his muscles suddenly dispersed, making him wobble ever-so-slightly.

Pascoe approached the animals, rushing between the two stalls, as if he could not accept what he was seeing.

Julian's hand briefly brushed over Evan's arm, and he snorted loudly. "Mr. Pascoe, in how much detail do you wish to examine the horses? I always believed your expertise in orifices is limited to humans."

Evan bit the inside of his lip to not laugh out loud. Jory must have taken care of the horses unprompted. That golden boy deserved a good few shillings for both his effort and his silence.

"Would you like to *examine* my sheep as well, Mr. Pascoe?" Evan asked with a straight face.

It was impossible to miss the stifled sound coming from the two deputies.

Eventually, Davies cleared his throat. "Mr. Pascoe, must have been a false lead."

Atkins groaned in agreement.

Pascoe looked around, frantic, but then pushed the candle into the holder on the wall and walked off to the stable door. "To hell with you!" he exclaimed on his way out.

The two deputies followed him without much hurry, clearly considering their journey to Tredele a waste of time. With a short, somewhat apologetic good-bye, they were out of sight at last.

Julian let out a long breath and rested his hand against the wall, pulling the front of the wet shirt away from his body. "That... was so close. I hope they came here on foot and will die of the cold," he whispered.

"No, he's got a horse, unfortunately. They must have left their mounts at the gate," Evan whispered back with a smile. "Jory?" he called out, and just as he expected, the boy peeked out from behind one of the pens.

"Sir," he said, emerging with his hands behind his back. "I know you told me not to wait up, but I was not asleep yet when you came back, so I did my job."

"You've done well. Never speak of this to anyone, understood?" When Jory nodded, Evan went on. "Come by the house tomorrow at noon, I will have something special for you."

Jory bit back a silly smile and nodded again. "I will, sir."

While Evan dismissed Jory, asking him not to be disturbed and to tell the others to leave any further actions in the ruined hall for the morning, Julian walked up to Snow and petted the smooth wood of the gate to her stall, as if it were her neck. "Your servants are extraordinarily loyal."

"They know who pays their wages... and they're almost like extended family." Evan's gaze slid to the wet linen sticking to Julian's back, just above his buttocks, and he had to remind himself that he wasn't allowed to have this. But still, with the danger gone, his body was heating up once more in need of consolation.

"What will we do about the hall? Do you wish to repair it or perhaps make it into something else altogether?" Julian asked.

Evan approached him from the back and grabbed him under the arms and knees, quickly tipping Julian over and picking him up. "Let it all rot," he said and carried Julian over to the pile of soft hay at the back of the stable, where the fresh scent of the drying grass was the strongest.

Julian put his arms around Evan's neck. He gasped and looked down, as if he couldn't believe he was being carried with such ease. But the truth was that Evan had a couple of inches on him, both in height and in the shoulders, and even so, Julian was no maiden. He felt solid in Evan's arms, and carrying him more than those few paces would have been a challenge.

Julian's gaze was intense when he rested his cheek on Evan's wet shoulder. "You surprise me every day."

"Oh, no, it's you who has been the biggest surprise of my life. And now you will surprise me with your skills in what I am owed." Evan leaned forward and dropped Julian into the hay, following with haste. He climbed on top of Julian like a bloodthirsty beast, straddling his chest.

Julian gasped and pushed his hands up Evan's thighs, under the wet linen. His touch was fire to warm Evan's bitterly cold skin. His hair entangled with the dry hay, his mouth opened a bit wider, already hungry for Evan's prick.

"What would Mr. Pascoe have to say about this?" Julian asked, eyebrows twitching with amusement.

"He'd surely say we're both *vile*." Evan was drunk on the triumph against Pascoe. The broken roof was a trifle in comparison to the risk of imprisonment, death, and letting that scoundrel win. But enough with Pascoe. Evan would let nothing spoil his time with Julian.

He rose slightly for his cock to be closer to Julian's face and slipped his fingers into that golden-red hair. "Since I can't fuck your arse, how about I fuck your mouth. Would *that* be agreeable?"

Julian exhaled, his chest moving rapidly between Evan's thighs. It was regretful that the candles were so far away, but there was no way Evan would leave Julian's warmth to fetch one.

He'd have enough time for the most detailed examinations of his sweet bird's body another time.

"Show me how it's done," Julian whispered, pushing his fingers even farther up Evan's body. His tongue caressed the small dip in the middle of his lip, and this time it was not just sensuous. With Julian's gaze caressing Evan's face, it was a provocation. An invitation to proceed with the dirty deeds Evan dreamed of.

His skin was still chilly, yet his cock was already filling again, eager to push into the succulent insides of Julian's mouth. He pulled Julian's head closer by the hair. "Lift my shirt."

Julian's eyes fogged up, and he shivered hard enough for Evan to sense it on him. He grabbed the loose fabric and pushed it up, hips already arching behind Evan. "Take it all off, please."

Evan smiled, zeroing his eyes on Julian's face. "Good. I like you begging. Will you beg for my cock, too?" He slowly pulled off his shirt, making sure to flex his muscles for Julian to see.

Julian's blue gaze moved between Evan's chest and the manhood in front of his face. The prick was still only partially stiff, but it wouldn't stay so for long with those delicious, warm lips so close, so available.

"Oh, no, don't make me," whimpered Julian, but it sounded more like a veiled suggestion than a protest. His chest kept moving, nipples hard as little pebbles underneath the damp shirt as he squeezed Evan's pectoral muscles with a soft sigh.

"I might not make you beg, but I will make you suck. You've dreamed about this, dirty bird? About kneeling between my legs and servicing me with your mouth?" Evan's chest rose and fell with heavy breaths, and he started stroking his cock right in front of Julian's plump lips, watching the dark head emerge from his fist over and over.

In the sparse light, Evan couldn't see Julian's expressions in all detail, but the burning touch of his breath was making Evan frantic with lust. His cock stiffened, now completely attentive to Julian's pretty mouth, which opened and closed in the shadows of Evan's form.

"I have. I have dreamt about you taking me," uttered Julian softly, kneading Evan's thighs again.

"Because you want to be mine?" Evan suggested in a hoarse whisper and leaned forward to rub the tip of his prick over Julian's lip.

That soft, warm mouth opened up slightly, rubbing against the tip of his manhood. "I am already yours," whispered Julian, and Evan moaned, grasping the hay next to Julian's face as the sweet words vibrated through the very core of Evan's prick and caressed his balls.

"Take me then, all of it." Evan slid his fingers into Julian's hair and got a good grip on it before pushing his cock into the slippery heat. He flinched when Julian didn't open his mouth quick enough and his teeth rubbed against the underside of Evan's cock, but it was such a fine contrast with the soft, wonderful tongue that trailed over the spot immediately after that Evan couldn't stop himself from groaning.

Julian shivered, and his knees brushed against Evan's back as he curled up, raising his head too and slowly accepting inch after inch.

"I will fuck you slow at first..." Evan watched Julian's eyes glisten with arousal while he made the first shallow thrusts. He wanted Julian to get accustomed to the new sensations first, not frighten him with unhinged lust yet again.

And yet despite it being so expressly forbidden, Evan's mind wandered to a hypothetical future in which he had Julian pinned down in the hay with Julian's long legs resting on Evan's shoulders. In Evan's fantasy, Julian welcomed the invasion of Evan's cock and guided him into that snug hole between his buttocks with his own hand.

This time, Evan would be patient. He would be patient and gentle, at the very least until Julian was comfortable enough to take a plowing.

Julian moaned around his cock, holding on to Evan's hips and flexing his tongue against it. His eyes were deeply focused on

Evan, awaiting approval, so full of adoration and a need Evan had not seen for so long. Too long. For this kind of ardor, he was ready to make sacrifices. He wanted to appear taller and stronger so that Julian knew his lover was worthy of admiration.

He pulled Julian's head closer, carefully watching the flushed cheeks, the clouded eyes, the nostrils that flared when Evan's cock was in. Each time he withdrew, the ridge under his cockhead pulled on Julian's lips while Evan's balls rubbed over damp skin. Julian flickered his tongue over the smooth, sensitive flesh and dipped the tip into the small hole at the cockhead, as if he intended to somehow screw it inside.

Evan couldn't bear the teasing anymore. He shifted his knees to trap Julian's arms underneath, and dipped his cock straight into that wanton mouth. His breath was in tatters, brain boiling inside his skull. He knew he wouldn't last long, so he started making quicker thrusts, ravaging those hot eager lips like it was the last time he'd ever get a chance to.

He instinctively pushed deeper, his cockhead knocking at the back of Julian's throat, but Julian didn't know how to open up to him and coughed, shivering under Evan's weight. Evan groaned when Julian's muscles convulsed around his shaft, but he pushed on, hot and sweaty despite the chill in the stables. The scent of hay was intoxicating, and he couldn't get enough of the sight below him, drunk on the blue, watering eyes.

Julian's face was dark with a hot flush, lips wet with saliva, cheeks hollowing as he tried to suck on Evan's length the way Evan had done to him under the bridge. Yet despite the frantic coughing and moments when Evan withdrew to let Julian breathe, Julian never once made an attempt to push Evan away. Every single time, even with tears streaming down his cheeks, he opened his mouth wide and provoked Evan with intense stares. Julian was ripe and ready to take Evan's seed.

Julian's eyelids flickered, and he closed his eyes, fighting for breath when Evan thrust in harder again, but his hips bucked behind Evan, stabbing the air even as his throat closed around

Evan's prick, massaging the head. Julian suckled around the girth, moaning softly and clutching at the hay. He was so beautiful it made Evan's cock twitch and grow as he alternated between deep thrusts and shallow strokes over the softest of tongues.

"Will you swallow it all?" Evan could barely find enough breath to speak. He never thought he'd find a man to share his dark passions with ever again, but there Julian was, so pliant in the way he accepted the rough treatment, and flushed with excitement as if it were his cock being sucked.

Julian moaned around the tip of Evan's prick when he pulled it out just enough to let Julian speak. His eyes opened, and with his gaze never leaving Evan's face, he pressed a wet kiss to the slippery cock. "Please, let me," he begged.

"All for you, my pretty canary. Go on, suck." Evan thrust his cock right back between Julian's lips, and a shiver went down his spine, all the way to his throbbing prick. He forced his cock in farther, just a few more times, rough and quick, his prick slippery from the saliva.

He grabbed Julian's hair hard, and kept his head in place when he came into that waiting mouth, filling it with his sperm. He'd make sure Julian drank every last drop.

Julian blinked, breathing loudly through his nose, but he obeyed, trembling each time he swallowed, teasing Evan's prick with the insides of his wet, wonderful mouth. A trickle of seed escaped his lips, but he didn't seem to care, hollowing his cheeks around the thick girth and teasing Evan until the sensation bordered on pain and he needed to pull away.

Evan released Julian's arms and slid lower, straddling his stomach. "That was... so good... for a first time." He loved seeing his cock still stiff against Julian's chest. He didn't care what people like Pascoe thought of him. He'd have his Julian however he pleased, and it was no one else's business but theirs.

Julian whimpered and licked the corner of his mouth, gathering some of the seed that spilled out his mouth earlier. He cuddled up into the hay, breathing hard as if he'd run all the way from

Looe. "More practice?" he asked in a voice raw from the harsh trusts. It was one of the most delightful sounds Evan knew.

Evan grinned at him and cupped Julian's cheeks. "I will feed your hungry mouth every day."

Julian laughed and rubbed his fingers over Evan's wrists, arching toward him and opening his swollen lips for a kiss that Evan was more than happy to give.

All of Tredele could rot and crumble as long as it meant he could have this.

CHAPTER 20

JULIAN

The sun was low over the horizon when Evan and Julian approached Looe. It was getting warmer each day, and the scents of nature mingled with the salty breeze from the sea, creating a most intoxicating combination. They didn't hurry, knowing that Julian's favorite tavern would only be filling up now, and because they both enjoyed their conversation and moments of comfortable silence too much to give up on opportunities for it.

The collapsed roof at Tredele was more work than any of them expected, even with the hired help, but despite having to work harder than ever before, the last month had been bliss. The secret door in Julian's mind was now wide open, and all the thoughts that had previously been banished into the vast forbidden library behind it were flowing freely. And Evan was there to greet them all with open arms.

To say their relationship had changed since that first kiss would have been an understatement. Evan was not a man of many smiles, but he always had them for Julian. He was not shy to touch without prompting anymore, his lips ready to trail kisses all over Julian's body.

At first Julian had been afraid he'd be just a toy, a consolation for Evan's affection-starved body, but as the days passed, he noticed their conversations becoming more relaxed and frank, as if Evan wanted to bare his very soul to Julian. He could be so deliciously rough sometimes, but then came the most tender kisses, the glances of worship. And when they lay close in bed, hands folded together, Julian couldn't imagine their relationship going sour.

There was so much joy in him even his skin peeling after too much time spent in the sun couldn't have made him unhappy. He did complain, but Evan was there to make him feel better with his dreamy hands and lips, and a dollop of sour cream massaged straight into Julian's aching skin. It was a bizarre thought that all the affection, the appreciation for the male form had been lying dormant in Julian for so long, remaining unnoticed until Evan unlocked it with the subtlety of a hungering bear.

Julian was drunk on the newfound pleasures, and Evan happy to provide him with opportunities to indulge. Sometimes Julian would wake up at night to a stiff prick poking against his ass. It did not frighten him anymore. Overwhelm?—yes, but with Evan's eyes so tender whenever he looked at Julian, there was no reason to not put trust in him.

That did not mean Evan hesitated to leave Julian aching sometimes. His prick was thick enough to make Julian's voice rasp after firm use of his throat, and his hands left bruises on Julian's arms when he held him down, but those discomforts Julian welcomed with open arms. He begged for them sometimes, slowly losing the sense of what was right or wrong.

Sometimes when Evan rubbed his hips against him, he was on the verge of asking for something more, for the most intimate touch possible, but he still wasn't certain whether he could take Evan's prick inside him again. Now that he'd become comfortable with Evan touching him, he was starting to think that maybe the pain he experienced on that first night had merely been rooted in the fear and humiliation, but he could not be certain. He'd hurt Evan with rejection once already, and having to do so again, after giving him another taste, would have been cruel.

So Julian waited, swimming in the warm waves of Evan's lust, drinking his seed and accepting the delicious punishments Evan chose to give him. Even now, he could sense the spots where Evan's palm had left its shape in pink, and he closed his eyes, flexing his buttocks against the saddle. There would be a time when he would let Evan between his legs again, but until then, they had many other pleasures to explore that served them both.

All the temptations of the flesh that he secretly mocked his friends for, hurried marriages that had made some of his acquaintances miserable, broken vows of holy matrimony, or forsaking other business just to stay that day longer with a mistress—he understood them now. If men wanted women as much as Julian wanted Evan, it explained the endless coins tossed into the laps of whores and the rushed vows.

He had not been dedicated to matters of the mind only, as he'd fancied himself to be. He'd simply never tasted the flesh he wanted to savor. Evan's cock, so warm and fragrant in Julian's mouth, on his face, in his hand. Evan's hands, strong enough to lift him up. Evan's chest, bulky and heavy enough to make Julian feel trapped and protected at the same time.

Evan was on his mind day and night.

"How long has it been since you amused yourself with friends?" asked Julian, approaching the houses on the edge of town.

Evan furrowed his brows. "Years ago, I enjoyed sailing, but the men I traveled with never considered me a friend, so I can't say there was ever a time in my life when I experienced anything akin to long-lasting friendship. I have Noir." He patted the horse's neck.

Julian frowned. "Not at school even? Why would you be so lonely?"

"I can't pinpoint it. I suppose none of the connections I ever made was strong enough to last. I always felt... different. I could never be honest about my thoughts the way my friends were."

Julian sighed and discretely brushed his hand over Evan's arm. He would be the first one to admit that Evan was not an easy person to befriend, but the man was also fiercely loyal and intelligent, so Evan's loneliness must had been due to the choices he himself made by rejecting other boys his age.

"You have me," he said softly.

And there it was. The type of tender smile that only Julian got to see. "And that is all the friends I need. Though I would dare to say you are much more than a friend."

A warmth pooled in Julian's chest, and he winked at Evan, petting Snow because he could not risk public affection once they entered town. "That I am. I simply wish you were appreciated more."

Evan shook his head. "What if I stole some of your sunshine in the process? We couldn't have that, now could we?"

Julian laughed. "You couldn't possibly do that. I have enough for both of us."

"I think I learned how to be alone."

"You are unlearning it quite rapidly. I can't imagine you throwing me out of your room any time soon."

Evan gave him a pleased smile. "It would have been like throwing out a cat. You'd come back through the window anyway."

Julian gently urged Snow to walk faster and looked at Evan from over his shoulder. "I wouldn't be able to resist begging for more cream."

"I pamper my kitty."

"Twice a day," said Julian and pulled his foot out of the stirrup to playfully poke Evan's calf.

"It will get fat soon."

Julian snorted, but the truth was that some of the food on their table was more than Evan's household could possibly afford. He couldn't bring himself to mention it though, knowing Evan was already feeling humiliated enough by the desolated state of Tredele. "That is why it needs to leave the house from time to time."

It was now getting dark quickly, and the streets filled with people in need of leisure. The town itself was small, as was its population, but a thriving port always brought about men in need of drink and women. Julian enjoyed it here, even if the prolonged trips to Plymouth he used to make several times a year had given him a sense that his desire for the new and unusual would never be fully satisfied in this small corner of the world.

Evan stopped Julian by pulling on Snow's reins and pointed somewhere farther down the street where a puppet show delighted the crowd of men, women, and children. Julian shrugged, as he did not fancy that kind of entertainment, but Evan led Noir closer, so Julian figured he could indulge his lover if it was something Evan enjoyed.

The booth was painted with bright colors, and the puppeteer changed his voice to enact a conversation between a man and a woman. It soon became clear that the traditional characters had been given new roles for this particular act.

A puppet in a colorful dress hit the other one over the head. "You scoundrel! My virginity? Instead of a chest full of embroidered waistcoats? How many does a man need for the season? I reckon a man needs only one for every season."

The crowd around the booth with puppets roared with laughter.

"Virginity?" came a male voice from the other puppet, in the accent of the higher classes, exaggerated to an absurd degree. "I've had you just yesterday!"

She hit him again. "The 'ighwayman doesn't need to know that!"

Julian snorted, rubbing his face to hide the grin he could not stop.

Evan pulled the tricorn hat farther over his forehead and leaned over as their horses stood so close the two of them could almost touch. "She reckons the highwayman must be handsome. I can't imagine why. Apparently, he had piercing blue eyes, more beautiful than the sea in the summer."

Julian glanced at him, his heart already racing at the compliment. "Or maybe he was tall and graceful like a stallion of Arabian blood."

Evan lowered his eyelids slightly, like a purring cat.

The puppet of Mr. Punch, dressed in a black coat and a tiny tricorn hat dashed between them, and hit the one which was undoubtedly a caricature of Miles Hughes. "Give us all yew have or yew'll be the wan spreadin' yewr legs. For my horse!"

The crowd gasped, laughed, one old woman screeching so loud she scared away a seagull.

"That is quite accurate," said Julian with a loud snort. "Though I believe Noir would have deserved a mare of superior qualities."

Evan nodded, barely stifling a laugh when Hughes started begging for mercy.

"Please, sir! Have all yew want! I'm a virgin!"

The roar of cackles was loud enough to drown Julian's thoughts but did not stop him from sensing a pang of uncertainty deep in his gut. In the eyes of all those people, would it make him laughable that he'd given himself to Evan willingly? He'd heard such things said in jest many times, but now that they were part of his experience, he couldn't bring himself to laugh. Was his kind worthy of nothing but jokes and contempt?

"None of that," said the puppet of the highwayman, hiding his face in a gesture of revulsion, "unless yew hide all yewr gold in yewr ugly arse!"

"Actually," said the female puppet, moving toward the other to in a seductive way. "This so-called-gentleman was so scared of losin' his gold he had it melted and fashioned into a staff. A very thick wan," she said, opening her arms.

"Is that so?" the highwayman roared, and made the Hughes's puppet bend over, only to pull out a string of colorful cloths, to the crowd's delight.

"My riches!" moaned Hughes.

The female doll trailed through the miniature stage and gave the highwayman a loud kiss. "So charmin'. A man who can deal with... any situation," she squealed as the fabric piled up around them. The puppet-Hughes shuddered in supposed agony and fell back, disappearing from sight, and Julian felt at odds with the very thing he'd laughed at just months ago. He glanced at Evan to see the familiar scowl.

"Madam, 'ow much would I owe for the pleasure of yewr company?" asked the highwayman puppet and bowed.

The woman giggled. "The pleasure is all mine." She picked up a red cloth and handed it to him.

The highwayman pulled her closer, and then gave her a slap on the buttocks. "I like yew. Yew deserve a pair of breeches more than that sad fop. Maybe yew oughtta mount the horse with me."

The female doll looked at the crowd and put one of her hands against her lips. "Mr. Sonora will have somethin' to fear when he drives by next week."

"A goldsmith? We aar in luck!" laughed the highwayman, and they rode off the stage to a round of applause and the sound of coins being thrown into a pot.

Julian leaned back in the saddle. The Italian goldsmith, whose work was beloved by his mother and sisters for his fresh and unique designs, had not been in the area for some time now. How much jewelry could be carried by a man who traveled far in order to sell it in all corners of the country? The quantity of jewels and precious items Mr. Sonora should have with him could be incomparable with what he and Evan obtained from Miles Hughes. His gaze trailed to Evan, and his partner in crime nodded at him with a smug smile.

So that matter was settled. They now understood one another without words.

Julian nudged the horse and led the way to the tavern.

Entering The Black Crab was like coming home. Unlike Madame Canard's, here Julian met the men his father called 'unsavory', and the men who, unlike Miles Hughes, spoke plainly and to the point. If they didn't like someone, they made sure it was clear, and if they considered someone a friend, one could drink with them 'til morning and lose not a penny from their pocket when falling asleep at the table.

The scent of ale and sweat could choke a sailor, but the constant breeze between the front door and the back brought in fresh air from the sea to make being in the The Black Crab bearable. Julian considered the place cozy, and he couldn't wait to see what Evan thought of it, since trying to make Evan more sociable was a secret personal project of his. He wanted the whole world to see the clever and sharp-witted Evan he knew, not 'Sir Recluse' or 'Ghost of Tredele'.

The tavern had a ceiling so low they both had to bow their heads at the entrance and could only straighten up once they reached the large room where food was being served. The scent of fresh fish soup brought a smile to Julian's face, but the sight of familiar faces in the far corner made it widen.

Evan was right behind him, like a shadow in his black clothes. He was swiping the people and interior with that analytical blank look Julian couldn't figure out and always needed to ask about.

Julian was about to do so again when someone walked into him, and then smothered him in a short hug. It was Simon, the one man who didn't spare Julian food despite being often employed by Julian's father and having reason to worry about repercussions. What a contrast to Miles Hughes he was.

"Julian! Thought I wouldn't see yew 'ere again. Now that yew live with a lord in a big 'ouse." Simon laughed and patted Julian's back again. His eyes were red and hazy from the drink he must have had so far. His speech was so slurred Julian needed to listen carefully in order to understand him. "But a seagull likes the stinkiest fesh best, am I right?"

"I am not a lord," Evan said as he removed his leather gloves.

Simon waved his hand in dismissal and whispered to Julian, "They aar all the same, that lot. Matters not to me what his title is if he's got a fat purse and watches the world from a clean carriage while others make do day by day."

As if that description did not include Julian himself. It was not something pleasant to hear when not in the context of a joke.

Julian's mind raced when he noticed a vein bulging on Evan's throat at the rudeness of the encounter, but then a large form grew at his side, and he was pulled into a harsh embrace that smelled of ale and sea. "Julian Reece! We all thought ya were dead," hissed Martin. He was one of the men Julian trusted the most in his life, despite having the face of a villain and an accent that, while not refined, was not local. They never talked about Martin's earlier life either.

Martin pulled back, lowering his head to stare Julian in the eyes with an ever-present frown. Julian always thought Martin looked like one of the pirates of the Caribbean sees, with harsh eyes and an unfashionably long beard under a nose that must have been broken numerous times. "Lad, ya should 'ave visited us all much sooner. Have ya forgotten all about us?"

Julian took a deep breath but was unable to keep a grin at bay and squeezed Martin's shoulders. "A lot has happened, my friend." He looked back and touched Evan's arm, wordlessly asking him to be understanding to the slush that had come out of Simon's mouth. The man must have already drunk through the day's wages, so some leeway needed to be given. "I want to introduce you all to Sir Evan Penhart, baronet and my host at Tredele. Be kind to him, as I owe him my life."

Evan straightened his back, so imposing in his black suit, but gave them all a nod, even though his frown could equal Martin's. "Julian insists this tavern is the best in all of Looe."

Simon's lips parted, but then he laughed out loud, elbowing Martin and almost falling into his arms in the process. "A *Sir*, in the Crab? The end of the world is near."

Martin sighed, regarding Evan with a cool stare. "If it's good enough for Julian, it's good enough for everyone else."

Julian gave Evan a tight smile, unsure where the sudden tension had come from. "They have the finest watered gin in all of Looe."

"I don't drink," Evan said sternly, and it made the men seated by the table go quiet with befuddlement.

"No wonder they call yew Sir Recluse then." Simon laughed and patted Evan's arm, but Evan was increasingly looking like a bear prodded with sticks.

"I am no longer a *recluse*. Julian lives with me."

Julian put his hand on Evan's arm and pushed him toward a spare place on one of the benches by the long table. There should be soup or milk that Evan could have? He'd forgotten that his lover never touched anything that could intoxicate him, too afraid he'd be as susceptible to it as his older brother. And Sir Peter had been *very* susceptible to drink.

A bit later, they all sat down with their cups, and Julian was intent on making his friends appreciate Evan. He would not have it any other way. As ale steadily filled his stomach with warmth, his tongue untangled even further than usual.

It was a pleasure to know he did not have to invent things to make Evan seem interesting. Astronomy might not be to the taste of any other man in the Black Crab, but sailing was, so Julian spun the story Evan had told him one night when they lay down on the floor of the observatory with their breeches at their knees.

When Evan had been on his way to the Isles of Scilly, the ship was caught in a storm that tossed the vessel left and right until one of the passengers fell overboard, into the unforgiving waves. Evan rescued him then, jumping into the water with just a rope to keep him afloat. Without Evan, the man would have been food for the fish, and hearing about such a heroic act had made Julian's skin throb despite having just come.

The men, especially those who'd spent years of their lives at sea, tried to challenge the truth behind the story, asked Evan tricky questions, and Julian's heart soared when Evan answered each and every one correctly, giving credibility to Julian's words.

It made the men look at Evan differently and the tone of the conversation changed.

Evan was a man of sparse words, but every now and then, he would say something so to the point it made the others pause, or made a joke so dark even Simon couldn't believe it could have passed a baronet's lips.

It made Julian so proud to be Evan's, even though none of their companions knew or even suspected their relationship to be anything other than friendship. He pushed his leg closer to Evan's and laughed at yet another witty comment he made. When he looked up, his gaze met Martin's, who sat with his back against the wall, watching Julian for a moment before sparing him a smile and raising his cup. It did not take long for the simple conversation to move into being one over a game of cards, with rounds of ale at stake.

Julian's fingers tingled with anticipation as he browsed through his hand. He had not played for weeks now, and following a long, dry spell, the drink got to his head very fast, prompting him to laugh louder and talk boldly.

He missed this, even though while at Tredele, he felt like he lacked nothing.

Despite Evan not participating in emptying the barrels of ale at the Crab, he sat next to Julian and watched. His sole presence was enough for Julian to feel giddy about the secret they shared. Yet nature won, and Julian stuffed the cards into Evan's hand when he needed to go relieve himself.

With the gamble being just a few cups of ale, he didn't care much if he lost, so he took his time navigating the narrow rooms of the tavern and kept himself upright by leaning on the wall with one hand. He always found it distasteful that there were traces of brown and black at this height along all the walls, from men touching the white surface with their dirty hands. But Julian's besotted mind was beyond caring. He stumbled into the urine-smelling alley through the back door and did the same thing every other man did here before returning into the stale heat of the Crab.

A man stood so close to him he could feel an arm brushing against him, and when the stranger pulled out his cock, for a moment Julian was so stunned he didn't even register that it was no one else's but Martin's. It was a lovely cock, of a good girth from what Julian could see in light so bad.

He felt his chest flush and quickly pulled his prick back into his drawers, adjusting it without a word. He took a deep breath and closed his eyes. It was dangerous to have his attention slip this way. A thing as mundane as another man's cock was now something to stir an unhealthy excitement inside Julian, and with his mind soaked with warm ale, staring too long was a real possibility.

"Ye dizzy, lad?" Martin's hand landed on Julian's shoulder, the other undoubtedly still holding that thick prick, because Julian could hear the stream hitting the wall.

"Barely," said Julian, unsure how to step back and excuse himself when Martin was holding him in such an obscene situation. He looked up into his friend's harsh face and smiled, trying not to think about a naked manhood so close. "I've not drunk a long time, that's all."

"Yer well-bred friend keeps ye thirsty?" Martin laughed and tucked his cock back in. "He could spare some wine, I'm sure. Why don't I buy ye another one, eh?"

Julian kept staring. He wanted to protest, but it occurred to him that unlike many of his other friends, who depended on Julian's purse when it came to good times at the Crab, Martin never failed to offer buying a round for Julian as well. "Ah... there is wine. I don't think he wishes for me to drink it. His brother drank himself to death, apparently." The moment he said this, the bubbles from all the ale he'd drunk came out of his mouth in a loud gurgle. "Oh, God... I shouldn't have said that. Please forget about it," he muttered, grabbing Martin's bicep through his old woolen coat.

Martin quickly held him up, because Julian didn't even notice he'd stumbled. The strong hand burned him through the waistcoat, and it felt different despite the many times Martin had helped Julian home when he was drunk.

"Since when do you care what others say? Is it some sort of deal ye have with 'im now that ye father... ye know."

"Deal?" asked Julian, blinking in surprise. There was something incredibly intense about the sharp edges of Martin's face. "What do you mean? I merely... I don't want to betray his trust."

"Did he really save ye from an 'ighwayman?" Martin's fingers trailed up and down Julian's side ever so slightly, brushing his ribs as if they were the strings of a harp, about to sing. Julian gasped, not wanting to reject his friend by backing away and yet so utterly confused by the touch. Had Martin done that before? Possibly. It never occurred to Julian to think twice about it, but now that he searched his mind—yes, Martin did that sometimes. Once, Julian could hardly walk so Martin took him to his lodgings instead of home, and in the light coming through the window, Martin had watched him, laid out on his side next to Julian on the uncomfortable bed. He'd touched him like this then as well.

"W-what makes you doubt that?" uttered Julian.

"Nah, I don't doubt." Martin gave him a cocky grin that made the pale scars on his lips stretch. "I just wish I'd been there. If I saved ye, ye wouldn't live that far from the Crab now."

Julian gave a breathless laugh, watching Martin's arms until their eyes met in the cool light of the moon above. "Hardly. My father does not want to see me anymore. I'm utterly ruined," said Julian, smiling despite the shame that settled in his heart.

Martin wouldn't even blink, leaning closer. "Ye know I'm a free-trader, right? I'd have kept yer head above water until ye worked somethin' out," he whispered.

Julian took a deep breath, startled when he sensed Martin's breath on his lips. Frozen in place, he watched the man as everything he knew about him slowly collapsed. "And what would I have done for you in return?"

Martin laughed and leaned back, never stopping to look into Julian's eyes. "Yer a resourceful lad, we'd find a use for ye. And until then ye'd entertain me with yer fancy conversation. I missed it, ye know? No one else speaks like ye."

Julian smiled, both excited and warm inside at the compliment. "Conversation? Is that what they call it now?" he asked, taking in a gulp of air and watching Martin through this new set of eyes Evan had given him. He'd always noticed how strong and steady Martin was, but his crooked smile, lined with scars, was not only roguish. It was attractive in the same way a dangerous animal could be, and in the same way Evan's smug smiles attracted him. Martin wasn't fashionable in any way, with his long beard, even though it was always combed and shiny, and in the faded colors he wore, but his green eyes could pierce a man's soul if Martin stared long enough.

Martin raised his eyebrows slightly, and his smile widened. "What would ye call it then? So smart with all ye pretty words."

"Perhaps a meeting? That would encompass much more than words," said Julian, blinking away the haze of ale to meet Martin's gaze. This man had been teasing him like this for ages. How could Julian have not noticed?

Martin nodded. "Aye. A meeting. What would we do if we met? Would ye cut me hair into fancy locks? That wouldn't do. Mine's a mess like wet seaweed." He grabbed Julian's hand and guided it to his hair.

Julian gasped but didn't resist, mesmerized by his discovery. "It is good as it is, Martin. Soft and clean." His eyes darted to Martin's face again, and he breathed in the man's salty scent. If he knew... if he noticed before, he'd have understood himself fully that much earlier. "How long have you wanted to *meet* me?"

Martin's gaze became sharper all of a sudden, as if the meaning of Julian's words was now passing between them without words, yet with perfect clarity. "Since we met," he said slowly. "Remember? Ye were puking all over, a vile lad stole yer purse.

Ye thought ye found it later, but I got it back for ye. Couldn't have ye discouraged from coming to the Crab."

Julian gave a shuddery breath, hot and cold at the same time. He could not believe how blind he'd been all that time. "Yes. You saved my skin many times. Why haven't you told me?"

"Tell ye what?" Martin gave him that cocky grin again and tousled Julian's hair.

Julian exhaled. "You are doing it again. Waiting for me to speak first, but things have changed now for me."

Martin chewed on his lip for a while, and his touch on Julian's side became firmer. "Ye got yerself a gentleman now, eh?"

Julian's lips trembled, and he looked to their feet, suddenly shy. Even if Martin understood, Julian couldn't be frank about his relationship with Evan. Everything that left his lips needed to stay ambiguous. "It's rather that he's got me. Taught me things I'd been blind to."

Martin sighed deeply, and his hand wandered to Julian's hip. "I could 'ave taught ye a thing or two..."

Arousal pulled on Julian's testicles, and he frantically stepped back. He knew all about the things he could do with Martin now, but it wasn't Martin who'd held him last night, whispering sweet words into Julian's ear. "Not anymore."

Martin leaned the empty hand against the wall. "It ain't fair," he groaned. "How was I supposed to... when yer Reece's son. One misstep, and I'd have me neck in the noose."

Julian folded his arms on his chest. He couldn't help but wonder how Martin's beard would feel against his thighs, but he chased those thoughts away. "Many things ain't fair. I did not know what you wanted with me, and now... I..."

Martin waved his hand dismissively, but his frown was deeper than usual. "Ah, leave it, lad. It is what it is," he said bitterly, and turned around, not waiting for an answer.

Julian watched the door shut behind Martin, and the stench of urine and mud became so thick all of a sudden his stomach protested, pushing him toward the entrance to the Crab.

Had he just lost a friend?

CHAPTER 21

JULIAN

J ulian stumbled through the rooms of the Black Crab, bare-ly missing a wooden beam that hung too low over one of the doorways. The conversation with Martin left his mind in disarray and yet sharp as a razor, as if shock had purged his blood of the ale. He was about to enter the room where they all drank when his face met a broad chest, and he fell back, hitting his head against the wall.

His blood was not purged enough yet after all.

Evan grabbed the sides of Julian's shoulders and looked into his eyes, breathing hard. "Julian. I was worried you got sick."

Julian rubbed the sore spot on his skull and relaxed against the wall, thinking clearly again. Evan's eyes narrowed with worry, his thick eyebrows low over eyes that were as dark as the deepest mines of Cornwall. "No, but I could use some air," he said in the end, barely keeping his hand from wandering to Evan's chest. Another man's touch was still ghosting over him, and it felt unfamiliar. No matter how much Julian had always liked Martin, he was not Evan, and perhaps the frank conversation broke Julian and Martin apart forever. Then again, since when did Julian owe anyone his body? It was his to do with as he pleased.

"Certainly, but... please lead, I don't know this building well, and it seems to be a labyrinth."

Julian nodded, watching Evan's handsome face with a small smile. As tempting as it had been to feel another man's touch, he did not regret rejecting it in the end. "You should feel at home then. So is Tredele," he said and directed his steps to the main entrance.

It was dark outside, and with just some of the windows lending the glow of candles, Julian would have to find his way. He put his hand on Evan's forearm and pulled him along the wall of the Black Crab while the shouts and bawdy songs followed them through the open windows and echoed in his skull.

"Amusing and charming as always," Evan said, but squeezed his hand over Julian's ass in the darkness. "Were you drinking even more where I could not see you? I'm sure you've had enough for one night."

Julian moaned and pulled him into a narrow alley two houses farther down the street. Here, not many people passed at night. All light came from one's own lantern and the stars, so darkness would offer the privacy they needed. "Possibly. I might have over-estimated my capabilities after so many weeks of being chaste with beer and wine."

Evan forced Julian's chin up, to look into his eyes despite the darkness enveloping them further. "I knew it. I knew I should have stopped you sooner. Are you dizzy? Is your heart racing?"

Julian groaned and opened his lips, lazily caressing Evan's salty fingers with his tongue. "I am quite all right. It will pass."

Evan stilled, and then slowly ran his thumb over Julian's lips. "Are you enjoying yourself?"

"Very much so. What about you?" asked Julian raising his gaze, but in the murky air of the alley, only the shape of Evan's face could be discerned.

"I'm doing my best. For your sake." He leaned in and kissed Julian on the lips. "But in all honesty, the experience is not com-pletely horrible."

Julian laughed, opening his lips for the caress. Evan's scent cuddled him like the softest of blankets. "They are good fellows, aren't they?" he asked and touched the wall, leading Evan farther into the dark labyrinth of back streets. Two more turns and they entered a narrow passage between two rows of houses. Julian pulled on Evan's hand and took him under a wooden staircase that would offer protection, were someone to walk by with a lantern.

"If by good you mean joyful, yet utterly despicable." Evan laughed and kissed Julian again in their tiny nest away from prying eyes. Between a tower of wooden boxes and the staircase, in the shadow of the overhang, they were safe enough to forget everything but their mutual company.

Julian's drunken heart raced, and he slid his arms around Evan's neck, arching against him like a cat. A few stolen kisses would not hurt anyone. "I made the most incredible discovery just before you found me."

"Was it that gin should not be mixed with ale, even if it's watered down?" Despite the darkness, Julian heard the smile in that handsome voice as Evan pushed his whole body against him.

Julian stifled a moan and pushed his fingers underneath Evan's neckcloth, loosening it slightly against his Adam's apple. "No... there are more men like us... I had no idea."

Evan backed away ever so slightly. "I beg your pardon?"

Julian groaned and pulled him close, rubbing their cheeks together. At this moment, he wished he could just chew on Evan's flesh, and it would taste like honey and cream. "Martin. He is like us. I've known him for years and never noticed."

"And how exactly have you noticed it now?" Evan trailed his fingers up Julian's chest, pressing him against the cold stone wall.

Julian sighed and grasped the burning hot hand, leaning into Evan as his world spun again. "He looks at me this way... now I know what it means. And he always touched me in such an odd manner. And he teased me... I have been so, so blind. How many of us is there really?" he asked against Evan's neck.

"I don't know. I've only ever met three. Julian. How did he tease you? Did he touch you?" Evan's grip on Julian's hand tightened.

Julian sighed and rubbed Evan's chest, kneading the thick muscles. "Helped me stand upright. He is a good man, Martin. Just not happy that I like you better."

"You told him about us?" Evan hissed, pushing Julian back at the wall and cupping his cheeks. "He better keep his hands off you."

Julian clutched at Evan's arms. "I did not tell. He guessed and still tried to steal me. Can you imagine? He liked me this way for so long... Maybe we could invite him to Tredele, and he could tell us what he knows about all this," he said quickly. Martin might be angry with him now, but an invitation would be a decent peace offering, surely.

Evan grabbed Julian's jaw and held it so tight Julian stirred from the discomfort of it. "Invite him to Tredele? So he can fuck you? Do you even hear yourself? I don't want that scum to *teach* me anything."

Julian stiffened. Evan's words were like a slap to the face. "Did you just call my friend scum?"

"You said he knew about us, and still tried to steal you. How would *you* call such a man? How would it make you feel if Jory climbed into my bed and offered up his body? How would you have called him then?" Evan's sweet breath danced over Julian's face his eyes dark like two back holes in his face. They drowned Julian in their intensity.

He gave a shuddery breath, sensing the burning hot anger radiating off Evan. "It's not like that. Some people... they have many lovers. How could he know I do not wish for such a thing? An honest mistake."

"The mistake of a bastard!"

Julian watched him in the dark, his heart beating fast and drumming in his ears. "Please, I want to know more people like us. Men who do not hate us and don't fancy the things I feel for you a joke. Don't you?"

Evan spun Julian around, flattening him against the wall, his strong body melting into Julian's from behind. "Only if you always remember who you belong with," he whispered into Julian's ear, the short stubble on his chin scratching against it as he pushed his hips against Julian's ass.

Julian shivered, motionless as his muscles turned into soft dough, ready to be kneaded into any shape Evan wished for. The cold stones were rough against his skin, and he was grateful for it, because at last he could think more clearly. "I have a mind of my own. Men cannot pass me around at their will. Why do you think I would let anyone touch me the way I allow you? It was frightening enough… to open myself to you this way. I merely want companionship and friendship from others."

"Men are scoundrels, and I bet you've been to Madame Canard's often enough to notice that when it comes to someone they desire, rules do not apply anymore. You might want to let someone touch you simply because you decide it feels good in the heat of the moment." Evan slid his hand to the front of Julian's breeches and slowly ground his hips against Julian's buttocks shamelessly.

Julian stiffened, pushing closer to the cold wall. The rough surface rubbed against his fingers as he clenched them hard. "You insult me."

"No, I crave you so deeply even the slightest possibility of losing you makes me want to crush someone's teeth." Evan kissed the side of Julian's neck and squeezed his cock.

Julian bit into his lip to keep a moan in and pushed his groin against the warm, skilled hand of the man who already knew him so well. Evan was hot against his back, and the sharp contrast between him and the stone façade of the building had Julian shivering. "You will not lose me. I want no other man," whispered Julian, turning his face toward Evan. "You are mine."

"I will show you how badly I want you. I promise it won't hurt." Evan's breath was becoming ragged over Julian's skin, giving him goose bumps. "And I am already yours a hundred times over."

Julian opened his lips and blindly sought out Evan's, but his teeth met the stubbly chin, which did not ease Julian's excitement. "I know. You can trust me as well."

"Pull down your breeches," Evan whispered, letting his hands slide up Julian's waistcoat. "You have no idea what a honeypot you are to men."

Julian's mind dazzled him with white emptiness, and he shuddered, cock stiffening under the skillful touch. Evan's weight against him was a promise of safety, even though they were out in the open, and someone, just maybe, could walk by. Julian's teeth clattered. Would he say yes? Yes he would. His body was tingling with arousal, and he hadn't even undressed yet. Since that fateful night when the roof collapsed at Tredele, Evan hadn't mentioned his darkest intentions even once. Was this the night when his patience evaporated? "Evan… here? I–I will be… how will we return to the tavern?" whimpered Julian.

"We will be fine…" Evan nipped on Julian's ear and pulled it with his teeth. "Not dirtier than the other men there. I have this… need for you. I can't bear that he touched you and that you let him."

Julian clutched at the protruding stones. He knew they should not be making another attempt at something so intimate here, not where he could not clean himself, but with Evan touching him with so much passion, kissing him so fervently, he couldn't push the word *no* through his lips. He rolled his shoulders, pressing his cheek against the rough stone and quickly unbuttoned the front of his breeches. "I wouldn't let him do that…"

Evan backed away just enough to undo his breeches as well. Julian didn't even need to see him to feel his powerful form and sense the arousal in the air. He could have Evan's big hands trail over his skin all day, grabbing him possessively and showing him dozens of new ways in which they could give each other pleasure.

"Why not?" Evan asked, following the question with his tongue trailing up behind Julian's ear. As soon as Julian pushed his breeches and drawers lower, Evan's cock was there, stiff and hot, pushing against his back.

He stiffened, his whole body throbbing with a frantic mixture of lust and fear so visceral he could sense Evan's prick splitting him open already. "Because I love you," he whispered, gasping for air as his throat constricted. He felt utterly vulnerable next to Evan, and he both longed for it and felt intimidated by it.

"Oh, sweetheart..." Evan kissed his cheek gently, but his thick cock was sliding in between Julian's buttocks and nestling there as Evan hugged him closer. "I love you more than you will ever know," he whispered. "I thought my life would never be whole again, but you made it so."

Julian sought out Evan's hand, so hot on the inside he could barely think straight. His heart was bursting with the heavy, wonderful feeling that he didn't even know how to describe. He was a writer, but now words were failing him. The prick between his buttocks was hard and throbbing, and so warm it was making his insides melt a little, ready to yield.

"Do it... I want it. It's all right," he whispered breathlessly, clutching Evan's hand.

Evan held him tight, his arms so strong they almost lifted Julian off his feet, but the pain Julian expected never came. Evan pushed his cock in right beneath Julian's buttocks and between his thighs. When Julian initially tensed up, he could only sense the thick prick better. Hot. Throbbing. Already being pulled out and pushed back in between his legs.

Evan grunted and nuzzled Julian's nape.

Julian stood there, shocked by what had just happened, but the moment the puzzle pieces fell into place, he tightened his thighs over the thick, wonderfully hot shaft. Of course Evan would not break Julian's trust and make an attempt without being given proper permission. Julian was ashamed of thinking he would have. Evan might be a brute, but he was a brute who kept his promises.

"Oh, dear God," whimpered Julian, already pushing back against Evan's hips until only the tails of their shirts separated them.

"Yes," Evan hissed, and the heavenly friction would surely make him come soon. He didn't have to be gentle either, so the thrusts quickly became frantic. "Oh, yes... let me in like that," he muttered into Julian's nape as his hips slapped against Julian's buttocks time and time again.

Julian reached back, holding on to Evan's coat and melting against him as the harsh prodding pushed him back and forth. He sucked in his lips, desperate not to alarm the owners of the house above with the moans threatening to spill from his lips. Evan's hand was snug around his cock. It worked him hard and fast, in the same rhythm Evan's hips slammed against Julian's ass, making the most delicious of sounds.

Evan's cock dove between Julian's thighs, poking his balls and rubbing the heated skin over and over. He pushed harder against Julian, flattening him against the wall and thrusting harder. Faster. The friction of the constant motion set Julian's body aflame, and for once he wished to feel that thick girth do the same inside of him. Even if it hurt him again, he wished to sense Evan inside his body, above him, touching him. His skin itched with need, and his blood flowed faster than any river Julian knew of. All he desired was to be even closer to the man he loved. And wasn't this the reason why anyone else would choose to give up the reins to their own body into the hands of another? To agree to such deeply physical invasion into their very being?

Evan groaned and bit on the side of Julian's jaw when he came, right between Julian's throbbing thighs. He never stopped working Julian's cock, and his other hand wandered to Julian's ass, squeezing it and kneading without inhibitions.

"So bloody pretty," he murmured.

His voice vibrated over Julian's ear, down his neck, and when Evan's rough fingertip caressed the head of Julian's cock again, pleasure exploded inside Julian like a volley from hundreds cannons. He shook all the way to his feet, slumping against Evan as the slick spend cooled between his thighs.

Evan chuckled quietly and held him tight. "I've got you." He kissed the back of Julian's head and rubbed his face against it.

Julian slowly let his head roll back and looked at Evan in the darkness. The sounds of the town were just a backdrop for the ragged breaths and quick heartbeats. In that moment, he felt a connection he'd never experienced before, something that transcended the feelings of love that he could name. It escaped his grasp before he could unwrap it with his mind, but when Evan's lips met his, everything else ceased to matter. "There is no one else I would trust with my body the way I trust you," he whispered with a small smile.

"I might be stubborn and prone to anger, but I would never betray you where it matters," Evan promised and kissed Julian once more.

Julian moaned into his lips and squeezed his burning thighs, spreading the cooling seed as he rubbed them together. "I know," he said, untying his cravat. He pulled it off and opened his legs slightly to wipe off the wet stains without looking away from Evan. "Still, you're a puzzle for me to solve."

"I know you like your mind occupied, so I won't make it too easy on you." Evan kept caressing Julian with his lips while they put their clothes in order.

"You know me so well." Julian spun around and tightened the knot at Evan's neck with his own breeches still down. He couldn't stop himself from making his man regain the stoic façade he maintained in public. Evan's true face was only his to admire.

At first Evan reached toward Julian's hands, but then straightened up and let Julian help him with a self-satisfied hum. "I am growing fond of this trip after all."

Julian stifled a laugh and quickly pulled up his breeches, snug against him and with the remaining seed no doubt soaking into Julian's drawers. "Maybe you could be persuaded to make this a regular occurrence."

"Only if I have something tempt me into it." Evan ran his fingers through Julian's hair. "Let's go before your dear friend Martin misses you too much," he said without a trace of anger.

Julian leaned in and pressed a wet kiss to Evan's mouth. "He can miss me all he wants. It's not him who has me."

Julian's emotions had never before flowed so freely, and once unleashed, it was impossible to curb them. Stolen kisses and rough touches where no one could see went on until he and Evan left the dark alley and needed to present themselves respectably once more. At least, as respectable as one ought to be at the Black Crab.

Julian's head was buzzing with brilliantly colorful thoughts, and he struggled not to put his hands on Evan as they entered the tavern. Something was telling him there would be another highway robbery around Looe soon. One that could possibly allow Evan to pay his remaining debts and maybe even fund a voyage to the continent? With Evan by his side, anything seemed possible.

Martin looked up at them from a dark corner where he sat surrounded by his friends and other smugglers. Julian had heard gossip of Martin's and his crew's dealings, but he'd never heard it from the man himself before tonight. In truth, Julian never wanted to know too much about the business his so-called unsavory friends conducted behind the back of the law. He drank too much, and sometimes he let things slip, like when he revealed the truth about Sir Peter to Martin in a pissing alley. All he could hope for was that Martin would not make a peep about it.

In the far-off corner of the tavern, men cheered loudly, drumming on tables and shouting encouragements as two of them wrestled their fists amidst empty bottles. Julian's gaze passed over naked muscle that shone in the candlelight, but he then looked to the men he himself was approaching.

"Yew disappeared for so long we 'elped ourselves to yewr drinks. Thought yew left with no good-bye again," said Simon, grinning from above a hand of cards.

"Must 'ave been pressin' matters," Martin said. He drank his beer and watched them both as if he could see the imprints of hands on their bodies and the seed on their breeches.

"Julian's head was still light from all the ale he'd had earlier. He needed some air, and I didn't want to see him fall off the pier in the state he's in," Evan said.

Simon laughed so hard there were tears in his eyes. He pointed at Julian, barely keeping himself upright in the bench. "It's true! It's 'appened before. Yew told 'im, Julian?"

Evan raised his eyebrows and shot Julian a sharp glance.

Martin snorted. "Fished 'im out meself."

Julian opened his mouth, wanting to laugh it off, but one look into his lover's face was enough for a stab of shame to push between his ribs. He smiled nevertheless. "I remember flying, but maybe it really was water, considering I woke up wrapped in someone else's clothes."

The heavy groan from Evan at his side was deflected by all the other men roaring in amusement.

Martin called a barmaid over for more ale. "It was me Sunday clothes, you wretch. Had to go to church in me work rags!"

Julian could feel Evan's skin simmer next to him. Knowing him, there was much more vice going through his imagination than there had in reality.

"Don't we all make sacrifices for our friends?" he asked and squeezed Evan's knee underneath the table.

"Especially those whose stomach's are empty and ringin'," said Simon, grinning at Julian, as if him appearing at Simon's doorstep and all but begging for food had been in jest.

"I would have done the same for you," said Julian.

"We should visit 'im sometime. Try meats from a fine gentleman's table," said Daniel, a man Julian knew as one of Martin's closest associates. He could be one nasty fellow when angered, and he had the face to prove that, but was also very dependable. Julian had always been fascinated by the gray tattoos on his arms and chest. They were small designs, much like the cartoons

Julian sometimes drew on the sides of his manuscripts, mostly dates, names of ships he used to serve on, and most prominently—the depiction of a mermaid. No wonder he was acting so boldly if he could survive the pain of having the pictures permanently drawn on his flesh with needles.

Julian's heart sank when Evan opened his mouth, and he was ready to hear his lover damage the newly forged acquaintance with Julian's friends.

"Julian likes company much more than me, but since I have grown fond of indulging my friend, I can already invite all of you for a feast at the end of the summer. I have been planning to make Tredele less of a ghost from the past and more of a living, breathing estate. Isn't that right, Julian?"

Julian watched Evan, clutching his knee even harder as a soft heat enveloped his chest. It was a compromise. Evan could not possibly invite any of Julian's friends to call at Tredele, but a feast for the local residents was an acceptable way to treat them. Maybe they could have sweet bread with fruit? With more people around, Tredele surely would be more like a home than the ghost it was. "That is more than agreeable," he said and grinned at the other men, who didn't seem as enthusiastic as before now that the possibility became real for them. He wondered how much it took to reach Tredele on foot. Surely, it could take all morning on a Sunday. Did they have enough time to spare?

Martin sipped more ale with his gaze darkening by the minute. "True. Most 'agreeable' to *indulge* a friend."

Just like that, the atmosphere became far too heavy for Julian's liking. He cleared his throat and sipped from his new cup. "I've been wondering as I was outside, do any of you know of a man who fits the description I gave? The highwayman who almost took my life?" he asked, knowing it would surely lighten everyone's mood.

Daniel leaned closer with a grin so wide one might think they were talking about women. "Are yew seekin' revenge?"

Martin nodded. "I'd hang the man meself for what he's done to you. Not for Hughes though. The man can have 'im." He chuckled.

Hughes's pistol exploded in Julian's mind, the bullet breaking through the ceiling of the carriage. The image was quickly replaced by Hughes's lanky body tossing about under Evan's boot like a fish thrown to the shore. He smirked. "He sure can. But if I can trace that villainous bastard, he will not come out of it unscathed."

Simon snorted, his nose leaking foam it gathered from the top layer of his ale. "Ah, Julian. When have yew become such a rogue?"

Evan's lips curved into a small smile. "We have been practicing fencing, and Julian seems to fancy himself good at it, because he's looking for a living target."

"He should walk the roads between Looe and Liskeard. I bet the highwaymen will be hunting for gold there on Tuesday," said Daniel, pulling on his badly crooked nose.

Simon snorted and patted his arm. "Yew spent too much time dillydallying by that puppeteer's booth today."

"Anyone's good with a sharp piece of metal. How are you with your fists, *sir?*" Martin asked, trailing his gaze up Evan's face.

There was a brief silence at the table. Julian's stomach twisted as he looked into Martin's tense features. He could not be serious.

Eventually, Simon broke the silence and pushed on Martin's arm with a somewhat nervous chuckle. They were in a public place after all, and if Evan came out of here in a condition that was anything but perfect, there could be hell to pay. "Never knew yew so eager to fight after drink. Maybe yew should 'ave some milk, with the babes?"

The men laughed, relaxing again, but Julian's gaze wandered to the table in the other corner of the room, which was still bursting with voices cheering on their favorite arm wrestler.

Evan stared at Martin without a hint of amusement on his face. "If you would like to try me, we would need to leave the Black Crab, as I should hate to make trouble for the innkeeper."

Julian gasped, clutching Evan's thigh. But he could not tell him to laugh it all off and shake hands with Martin. Not in public. He frantically grasped at the only loose thread there was. "Friends, if you're so eager to measure yourself, there is no reason to leave the Crab. Look at those fellows. They found a way," he said and nodded toward the table, where two fists trembled over the wood, one man in the lead, his teeth bared, the other almost aligned with the tabletop for balance. Then he screamed, and something snapped, but Julian could not see, as a crowd pushed tightly around the wrestlers, eager to peck on some meat.

Martin pursed his lips. "The man who loses buys a round of drink for all."

Evan was already getting up. "Agreed."

Julian's hand slid off Evan's leg. He glanced at Simon, hoping he of all people could stop this ridiculousness, but all he got in return was a devilish grin. No one wanted to give up on a good spectacle.

Martin stood up as well, adjusting the worn gray coat as his eyes pinned Evan's in challenge. In the back, the crowd dispersed somewhat, treating Julian to the nauseating image of a forearm bent where it should not have been. The ale he'd drunk choked his throat, and he struggled to keep it down, wordlessly watching his friends gather around Evan and Martin, who sat at the end of the table, already engaged in a fierce staring contest, as if they were about to fight to the death for their king and country.

Julian's head was light with nothingness when Martin roughly tossed off his coat, exposing a torn shirtsleeve. He was a massive man, possibly even stronger than Evan, with bright, piercing eyes and a beard that made him look like the angriest incarnation of Poseidon, about to pass his judgment on men of the sea.

Julian caught Martin's gaze, wordlessly asking him to stop this nonsense.

But Martin would not. He pulled up his sleeves and looked away.

Evan took off his coat, and sat opposite him, mirroring Martin's gestures in the way he rolled up his sleeve, revealing the veiny forearm covered with dark hair.

Julian stared, unable to go against his body when everything about Evan called out to it. Stories of men fighting over one woman had always seemed irrational to him, but now that he was the delicious ham desired by two equally vicious dogs, it made his heart soar in more ways than one. There was the guilt over feeling proud of being the object of such intense lust, but the other side of the coin was much darker. This might escalate into something ugly, and even if no bones ended up broken, he did not wish for Evan and Martin to become bitter enemies.

Why they somehow fancied themselves his keepers, he had no idea, and it made him angry, yet at the same time, he was proud. Love truly was a complicated beast.

Martin and Evan's hands entwined, muscles straining in their arms, and Julian had to fight for his place by the table to not be pushed back where he would not see the goings-on. He would intervene if necessary. He truly would.

Evan's body next to his smelled different somehow. Sharper, as if he'd rubbed himself in some exotic spice that would burn Julian's tongue, were he to taste it. His muscles bulged underneath the sleeve, his shoulders set, neck shortened as Evan pulled it between his shoulders, watching his opponent from beneath thick eyebrows.

Martin squeezed Evan's arm, as if already testing his grip. His hand was slightly bigger than Evan's, and it looked as if it belonged to a man older than Martin, with the heavy tan, rough skin on the knuckles, and thick veins running along the back.

His eyes briefly strayed from Evan's face and met Julian's gaze, pinning him in place as if he were a moth about to stay forever in Martin's collection. Martin's green gaze burned Julian's neck, which was left uncovered after he'd used the cravat to wipe himself clean, licking the exposed skin without touch.

Julian exhaled, hot as a furnace now that he looked at Martin in a completely new light. Under the clothes that clearly had not been made to measure was a strong body that could push Julian against the wall with ease, were he to want it. The sleeve of Martin's shirt slid to his elbow, revealing a thick forearm marred by a long, white scar, one more reminder of the rough life Martin had led. His brows were low over eyes that were deep-seated and intense in their anger.

Once the arm wrestling started, Julian was deafened by the yelling all around. After a single beat of his heart, he joined in, fiercely proclaiming that he cheered for Evan. It gave him a thrill to be so frank about his support, to yell about just how much he wanted his man to win. Even if Evan's sole focus was now on the struggle against Martin, sweat beading on his forehead, muscles bulging in his arm.

Julian touched his shoulder, just a brush of hand, but sensing how stiff Evan was made him imagine feeling all that hard flesh against him. He wanted to whisper into Evan's ear, tell him that he and Martin were being completely unreasonable, mad, but Evan seemed so determined he didn't even blink at the touch. It was as if the world ceased to exist apart from the tiny spot between him and Martin where their hands pushed against each other, with the odds changing favors within seconds.

Julian called out Evan's name and squeezed his arm again, sweating underneath his coat as all their friends, and some of the other patrons, gathered around the table, cheering on their favorites.

The masculine energy combined at the table was more intoxicating than the ale had been, but second by second, Evan's hand was being pushed down by the pure brawn of a hardened sailor. The image of a broken arm once more flashed through Julian's mind, and he stilled, clutching Evan's shoulder, suddenly not as excited anymore. This unreasonable jealousy had already gone too far. How long could two men measure their strength at the table, for God's sake?

Martin slammed Evan's hand against the wood with a growl of victory, and cheers resounded all around, with something even splashing onto Julian's neck as men raised their cups.

Evan's shoulders worked laboriously up and down as he watched his opponent, eventually nodding. "A round for all."

Martin leaned back, his powerful chest rising and falling underneath the old shirt, eyes burning in triumph, even though the cost of it was evident in the dark flush on his face and the damp sheen visible in the candlelight.

Julian never took his hand off Evan, mesmerized in the crowd that moved about them too quickly, eager to pick up their reward. He leaned in, took a deep breath, and said, as steadily as he could. "That was a decent game."

Evan angled his body over the table, so Martin could hear him in the racket around them. "I hope you enjoy the prize as I am enjoying mine," he said and slowly stood up, a towering figure of somber color in the crowded tavern.

Julian shuddered, calmly breathing in the stale air. This was a sign. They were done for the night, and for once he would not protest. He would say his good-byes and make his way to the lodgings he and Evan had hired for the night. And once they got there, he would show Evan just how much he was appreciated, whether he won or not.

"Good night," Evan said curtly to Martin, who frowned in return.

Julian did not wish to prolong this night anymore, so he took his coat and followed Evan out of the Crab, to the inn that provided rooms of quality a tad higher than the quarters in the second floor of the Crab.

The cool air outside hit Julian with a vengeance, and he needed to hold on to his hat for it not to fly away. He walked alongside Evan, toward the inn where they had already left their horses, feeling warm inside despite all the worry. Fortunately, the moon emerged from behind the clouds and it was not dark enough for them to need lamps in order to move down the main street.

"I am sorry you've lost," he said in the end, wanting to cheer Evan up. He could imagine it was humiliating to be bested in front of the person one wanted to impress and was determined not to have Evan feeling inferior. "I was more than impressed."

Evan glanced at him with a half smile, and wrapped his arm around Julian's shoulders. "Oh, no. It was good. They will now like me all the more for it. Besting Martin in front of his friends might have been unbearable for the man."

Julian gasped and slapped Evan's arm, frowning at him in the sparse light. "You did it on purpose?"

Evan's smile widened and he spread his arms. "You will never know."

Chapter 22

Evan

Evan wouldn't dare claim that highway robbery was now a routine act for him, but with Julian at his side, his confidence was high and his morale strong. Even the weather was not as adverse as last time, a pleasant evening with a cool breeze to disperse the summer heat. The road stretched over the hills, and they'd traveled a good three hours to make their move far away from home. But with the man surely intending to spend the night in a nearby inn, his carriage should be rolling their way at this hour.

Funds taken off Miles Hughes had been already eaten up by the monster that was Tredele, and it was high time an opportunity like this one fell into their laps. As Evan's need to please Julian grew, so did the expenses, and he'd be damned if he spared any for a man as sweet as him. Throughout his life, Julian had become used to conditions that Evan did not want him to give up on, especially not after he'd chosen to stay with Evan out of love and turned a blind eye on the inconveniences it brought upon him.

Evan looked at Julian's handsome face, unobscured by the scarf just yet, and still he couldn't believe that this charming man was now part of his life. Each day with Julian was a blessing. Even when they squabbled, Evan enjoyed knowing that his lover was willing to challenge him and wasn't blindly agreeing with everything Evan wanted. Moreso, Julian held strong opinions that made their debates challenging in a way that made them all the more pleasurable, and he held big dreams that could sweep men off their feet and into Julian's imagination filled with adventure and excitement in foreign lands that he craved to visit. If it weren't for the responsibility of Tredele, Evan would have been the first in line to mount Noir, and leave with only one bag at the saddle as long as he could follow Julian.

Oh, what adventures they could have. With Julian to hold his hand and steer conversations away from disaster, Evan would gladly drink in the wonders of the world—the old one, the East, maybe they could even venture to the isles of the Caribbean and bathe in waters as blue as the sky above them, as blue as the sea on the beaches of Scilly. As blue as Julian's eyes when he smiled at Evan in clear daylight.

But Evan liked them even more when they were darker—pupils huge within the bright rings of blue when Julian clutched Evan's flesh, making the sweetest, most obscene sounds. This was only his, only for him.

Evan loved Julian more every day.

Snow was calm, silently picking at leaves on the other side of the road, a white shape between the dark bushes that served as their hideout. A light breeze played in the leaves, making them sway in the bright moonlight. It took him and Julian a greater part of their second day at Looe to find out where and when exactly they could entrap the traveling goldsmith on his way from Liskeard, then several hours out of the present day to establish the most convenient location in case there was more than one vehicle in the traveling party.

Eventually, they settled on betting their luck on a spot where the road dipped between two hills, with steep ground on one side and a gentler slope on the other, where they could both successfully hide themselves between the trees when the time came. The carriage, however, or carriages for that matter, would be entrapped in the low land, unable to compete with riders in terms of speed.

"Part cow, part snake," said Julian carelessly, tossing Evan's way another of the guessing games they entertained themselves with to shorten the wait. The charades also took their minds off the violence to come, something neither Julian nor Evan were particularly excited about, yet whatever needed to be done, would be done.

Evan frowned, searching his mind for an animal that could in any way be a combination of both. A white snake with black spots? He didn't know of one like that. Neither had he ever heard of a scaled cow. Maybe it was more of a metaphor. "Are there snakes that produce milk?" he wondered out loud.

Julian smirked, wiggling his eyebrows. "I know of one," he said, his eyes unmistakably trailing down Evan's stomach, as if they could see through Noir's thick neck and Evan's breeches.

Evan shook his head, but laughed. "Lecher. I'm serious."

Julian shrugged. "Ah, possibly, somewhere in the Far East. If there are stories of men who turn into tigers, why wouldn't there be snakes that produce milk?"

"I've heard of men in Sibiria who have two souls. That of a man, and that of a wolf. Do you believe it could be true?"

Julian's smile softened. He turned his head toward a vine climbing up the tree and traced it with his hands. "If two men can love one another as we do, I can't see why wouldn't there be something like that as well, hidden away in the vast planes of Sibiria?"

Evan smiled back, and urged Noir to cross the road, just so that he could grab Julian's hand. His heart was more tender than ever, yet he knew Julian wouldn't mock him for his words. "Do you believe lovers' souls entwine?"

Julian blinked, and his mouth twitched in amusement. "By God, if you don't temper that mood of yours, you will ask the fellow for jewelry for your groom instead of taking away his gold." His first instinct seemed to be humoring Evan, but his hand squeezed around Evan's tightly.

Evan groaned and pulled away even though he knew Julian would only say such things in jest. "It's all your fault. I used to be a rock, and now I'm moss."

"No. You are still a rock. There's only a bit of moss softening your edges," said Julian, cradling Evan's hand in his palms and putting his fingers to work on his knuckles, gently massaging each one.

Evan sighed, already eager to be back in bed with Julian. Or on the tiny beach in the secluded cove they'd found recently. Julian's body naked in the pristine waters had been a thing of statuesque beauty until a crab pinched his heel and he rushed back to shore squealing in panic to Evan's never-ending mockery.

"Something's coming," Evan said at the sound of wheels and horses somewhere behind the hill. It wasn't time for games anymore. He pulled the scarf over his face, and the hat lower on his forehead.

Julian's face transformed, the smile dropped, replaced by sharp focus, though not without a glimmer of excitement in his eyes. He pulled up his scarf, fastening it at the back of his head almost too tightly and retreating behind the bushes. He needed to go deep, with Snow's white coat, which they had once again stained with coal. The sound of hooves tapping against the dry dirt was unmistakable, as was the clatter of the wheels.

They would have Evan approach the travelers from the front, and Julian search the carriage for jewels while the coachman was held at gunpoint, so Evan urged Noir forward, watching the shadowy horses emerge on the top of the hill. He dismounted and patted his stallion's neck, growing increasingly stiff in the shoulders. A man such as Mr. Sonora would surely not journey without protection, not when he was about to sell his wares in the great houses of Cornwall. The coachman had to be dealt with as well, but Evan had brought rope, and was proficient enough with it to make the process quick. No blood would have to be spilled if all went according to plan.

Julian was merely a shadow amidst the thick natural hedge by the road, ready to do his magic and convince the travellers it would be wiser to have their purses taken than die. Evan's job was to block the road, but that meant opening himself up for frontal attack. He needed to keep his head cool and not only watch for any signs of foul play with the sparse light, but also make sure Julian would not suffer any injuries.

He took several deep breaths, his body stiff with the stress of it all. Regardless of how excited he'd been about this opportunity when they first heard of it in Looe, this was merely his third attempt, the most ambitious one so far. He did have all the faith that Julian would act to the best of his abilities, but that could prove not good enough if their victims chose to fight back

But as the carriage rolled off the hill, with trunks piled under a protective sheet on top of it, time for deliberation ran out. The vehicle hurried down the slope, and Evan was glad to see it was not followed by yet another carriage. He took out two pistols, exhaled slowly to purge himself of the latent fright, and emerged out of the shadow just when the animals started losing pace upon the next incline.

His feet were heavy like anchors keeping him in the middle of the road.

"Stop if you want to live!"

There was something different about the two horses pulling the carriage. Their cantering seemed uneven, the lack of rhythm slowing them down. Evan blinked, seeing from up close that their backs had been covered, as if they were resting. One of them shook its head, whining loudly as the coachman stood up in his seat, his slim form on top of the bulky black carriage very much like that of a scarecrow.

Julian stepped out of the darkness, his gait recognizable to Evan even in the dark clothes that drowned his slim body, obscuring his smaller form.

Making him unrecognizable by padding the shoulders of the coat and creating the illusion of a more robust man had been the goal, and with the scarf tied around his face, he would be difficult to discern for anyone but a very close friend. But if so, why were there ants running amok up and down Evan's spine?

"Gentlemen. I do hope you will listen to reason, not to pride," said Julian loudly, his voice lowered for the purpose of obscuring his identity even further.

Evan inhaled, then exhaled. And then, as one of the horses moved, something glinted beneath the hem of the covering on its back.

It was a stirrup.

These were not animals used primarily for carting.

"Get back!" Evan yelled to Julian without a second's thought. If his instincts were wrong, they'd lose a bounty that could have turned their lives around, but if he was right, they'd run into a bear trap, and the iron teeth were about to break their bones.

Julian turned into a statue, shoulders stiffening under the coat. Like a cat caught stealing milk, he stared at Evan, eyes wide and hands clutching his small sword.

Something rustled above, and when Evan's gaze shot back to the coachman, his heart stirred with terror. The elongated shape of a pistol sat comfortably in the man's hand.

"Will! To the horse!" Evan yelled at the top of his lungs, using the fake name they'd agreed on. He took two steps forward, physically unable to run when Julian was within the reach of the predators inside the carriage, but once a shot thundered in the night from the coachman's pistol, Evan stopped caring about his resolve to not spill blood. At such close proximity, the bullet avoided him by chance only. Air evacuated from his lungs and he shot right back, the roar of it just as loud as the hammering in his chest.

The coachman gave a startled cry and stumbled to the road like a burlap sack filled with meat. The horses stirred, backing away, as if Evan were a lion pining for their delicious flesh, and in that same moment, when the coach rolled back slightly, its door burst open, spitting out a shadow with a sword in hand.

The long blade cut through the air, straight at Julian's unprotected chest. With a loud cry, Julian stumbled away and raised his right hand. Steel met steel, but the stranger used his advantage in height well and brought his sword down so hard Julian barely came out of it unscathed, spinning away with the too–large coat crippling his usual grace.

"Not so loud now, eh?" snarled the giant in pursuit of Julian.

"I want them both alive!"

A chill went down Evan's sweaty back at the voice. Pascoe. A setup by Pascoe. They needed to run now and arrive at Tredele before their absence could be discovered, or else they would both hang.

Evan darted forward when the giant swung his sword at Julian again, and their blades met with a spark between them. Evan would not be fighting the man. All he needed was an opening to pull Julian his way. Only God knew if the coachman had been hurt badly enough to stay down, or if he would remain a threat behind their backs.

Evan swung his own sword at his foe, no doubt a member of Pascoe's entourage of deputies, eager to receive a fraction of the prize Miles Hughes put on their heads. But money was not a motivation equal to life, and the giant wasn't fast enough this time. Evan cut into his forearm, making him scream and swear, but it was distraction enough for Julian to crawl away from where he'd fallen and be the first to make a run for it.

Evan was right behind him, urging Julian on when he spun around to look for him. "Run! Go!"

When the door on the other side of the carriage rattled, Evan rushed toward Noir's hideout in the bushes, his blood freezing when he spotted yet another shadow on top of the carriage, emerging from between the chests. He ran blindly, reaching into the deep shadows to grab first the mane, and only then the reins of his stallion.

The world became a blur. The air thickened, pulling on Evan's clothes and grabbing his limbs to keep him in place, but he fought through the stiffness in his joints and pulled himself up, seeing only Julian, who stopped Snow at the top of the hill and waited, so vulnerable to bullets and their fire.

Something exploded so close to Evan he felt a wave of heat touch his face, and a branch broke next to him, falling to the road.

It was the last trigger that needed pulling, and Evan yelled for Noir to dash forward, as the sound of the horses being freed from the carriage came from what seemed like inches behind his back. He was one with his horse, lowering his head to avoid branches as he put all his effort into reaching Julian.

The bloody fool shouldn't have waited, perched on the background of the sky like a live target for that bastard Pascoe and his men. Evan nudged Noir with his heels and lay low on his back when more pistols exploded behind him, like fireworks from hell. His mount whinnied helplessly, yet he all but flew through the air, galloping his way to Julian and Snow.

The air lost the burning quality of gunpowder, and he rushed past Julian, behind the curve of the road and beyond the reach of bullets. He looked back at his lover, who followed suit, hunched over Snow's back and slapping the reins against her neck.

Noir heaved, and while not running as fast as he could, he still tore through bushes and plains, with Snow in the lead once more.

"Go right, over the creek," Evan shouted when he grew certain no one would hear them anymore. At least two of the men could have followed them on horseback, so there was no time to rest.

Julian did like he was told without question, his face determined as he pulled down the scarf and rose in the stirrups. His coat floated behind him when he charged across an empty pasture, with a herd of cows watching them at a distance. Snow's gait was light even at the most rushed speed, and she leapt over the water as if Julian weighed nothing.

Noir made a strangled sound, slowing down, as if he were afraid of the glimmering water, but he jumped over the creek when Evan loudly smacked his lips. Evan took a deep breath, his insides twisting as the black beast carried him through the air, but they got no farther.

Noir's front legs did not break their fall, and they tumbled down into the moonlit grass. Air got stuck in Evan's throat, and as the ground sped toward him, he rapidly jumped to the side, half jumping, half rolling off Noir's back.

Evan barely avoided sliding back into the water, his mind dazed when he managed to stand up, instantly heading to Noir's side. The beast wheezed through the bit, his eyes wide and shiny in the light of the moon.

"What is it?" Evan spoke to Noir as if the horse could answer him, and he got to his knees, stroking the animal's back. Julian cast a shadow over him when he approached on Snow's back, but Evan couldn't hear his words when his fingers trailed through the stickiness on Noir's side.

Evan felt as if his heart was about to stop. Shaking his head, he wanted to deny the sensation, hope it was merely resin Noir must have picked up on the way, but when he looked closer, even in the dark he could see the red shade spreading over the stallion's black coat. Only then he noticed the gash where all the blood originated.

"They got him. The bastards shot him..." Evan could hardly catch a breath, and his fingers trembled. For years, Noir had been his most intimate confidant, the one being he came to for comfort. He could not simply bleed out like this. "Not now, friend," he whispered and his mind went dark, as if filled to the brim with hot tar. It was all his fault. He'd led this loyal beast into death, and yet Noir still found it in himself to carry Evan to safety. The poor thing deserved so much better.

Hands clutched his shoulders, and he barely kept himself from punching back, but then Julian's whisper swiped over his neck, breathless and comforting despite the crack that was slowly growing in Evan's chest.

"He won't go further. He's bleeding too bad. We need to run," said Julian, stiffening when distant voices rolled somewhere at the mouth of the valley.

His breath came in quick rasps, but Julian never stopped holding Evan, never tried to save his skin at all cost. "Get on Snow. I will deal with this, and we'll go."

Evan tore his eyes away from Noir, to face Julian, and despite the torment of hearing his dear horse whinnying in terror, a wave of gratitude rolled over him. He would eventually find the will to stomach helping Noir to the other side, but he was too rattled by what happened to push himself to do so just yet. He stroked Noir over the forehead one last time and got up on soft knees.

"Thank you," he whispered to Julian and gave him a quick kiss on the temple before walking off toward Snow, fighting against the heart that was weighing him down more than anything he'd ever carried.

His foot stomped down midstride when the loud wheezing came to an abrupt end, but he couldn't bring himself to look back and mounted the mare, so short and small in comparison to Noir it gave him a sense of otherness. He didn't dare look back as nausea climbed up his throat.

Julian ran up to him and briefly squeezed Evan's thigh before grabbing his hand and climbing on behind Evan. "Go, let's go," whispered Julian, clutching Evan's coat and digging his knees into the backs of Evan's thighs.

Evan urged Snow forward, but his heart was still bleeding over not being strong enough to do justice by his friend. His mind throbbed with the thoughts of consequences of what they'd just done. Where would they even go? Tredele was far away, and if Pascoe constructed such an elaborate ambush, he could surely have men on the lookout around the estate.

Evan kept Snow at an even pace, as he suspected she found them too heavy. Now that they were off the track, they needed to mind the noise as well, to not let their enemies know which way they went.

"Once they find Noir, they will know it's me. Us," he said, trying to find some comfort in Julian's arms wrapped around his waist. Only now it hit him that Julian had been bested and fell in the process. "Are you all right? Did he hurt you?"

Julian's breath trembled, and he tightened his fingers on the front of Evan's coat. "It was an elephant," he whimpered when Snow moved more abruptly, and he had nothing but Evan to hold on for balance.

Evan frowned, pulled back into reality by Julian's words. "Are you delirious?" he asked and wanted to smack himself right away. Julian would not know if he were, of course. So he added a question that could prove a more accurate diagnosis. "Are you dizzy?" he tried.

Julian swallowed and pulled closer, resting his forehead on Evan's shoulder. "In the charade. It was an elephant. Your turn."

Evan sighed, and welcomed the distraction as they rode down a narrow path next to a stream left behind by recent storms, in the shadow of a tall cliff. "It has a snake for a nose, and its young are called calves." He nodded. "But this is no time for games, canary. We need to choose a course of action. Fast."

Julian shuddered behind him. "You're right. They will know once they find Noir. They would smoke us out of Tredele like rats."

Evan raked his mind for any assets he owned, and no matter how many times he thought of Tredele as a dragon, which he needed to feed offerings if he didn't want to become its prey himself, it was still *his* dragon.

"No one would ever suspect I'd go to Fairfield Park. People like Pascoe would know we are merely acquainted. We'd be safe there at least until tomorrow."

Julian pushed his face against Evan's back. "Wouldn't it be safest to run now, when they have not yet organized greater numbers of men?" he whispered.

Evan swallowed, still not believing what he was about to say. "I will sell Tredele to Blackwell. He wanted it for a long time, so I'll let him have it. It would pay off my debt and leave much, much more to spare." He clutched the reins with new determination. "Pay for our travel to Italy, and give us much to live off, maybe pay for a modest home somewhere."

Julian's arms squeezed Evan so tight he needed to steady himself, but he didn't want to take this sense of safety from his frightened lover either. He'd led both Noir and Julian into the trap laid out for him, but he'd rather let Pascoe have his revenge than see Julian die.

"We will go? You will leave?" Julian wheezed and rubbed his face against Evan's back. "Yes… we could leave Cornwall and take the first ship to the continent. We'd be safe."

For years, Evan had considered Tredele his anchor, but now, once the decision to cut off its chain had been made, he wasn't afraid to be drifting. For the first time in his life, he could shed the weight that for so long had been cuffed to his ankle and go where he pleased. He would do as he wished, ancestors and duty be damned. If Peter could gamble away their mines and die in a puddle of his own sick, Evan could sell Tredele, take himself a male lover, and run away to Italy.

The lightness in his heart was only weighed down by the fact that he wasn't on a ship set for Naples just yet. But it was all right. Now, it was Julian who was his anchor.

"We need to leave. Tredele will be in good hands, even if Blackwell decides to tear it down and give it new walls, roofs, and façades, good riddance," he said through clenched teeth.

Julian nodded and molded himself to Evan's back so tightly as if he didn't want to leave any empty space in between. "Italy. It will be a safe heaven for us. Lead, and I will follow."

Evan stroked Julian's hand, clenched on his coat. "Let's find a way to Fairfield Park."

Julian kept looking behind his back when Blackwell's old butler led him away, but Evan kept his exterior completely stoic when he faced Blackwell. Clad in a banyan the color of red clay and a white cap, the elderly man regarded Evan from a chair by the fireplace. The house was still as a grave, with most of the household long in their beds. It was impertinence to call at anyone's house unannounced, much more so deep into the night, but Blackwell had still been working in his study and agreed to see him.

Without his brilliantly fitted clothes, Blackwell seemed much more like an old man, with the warm light of the fire deepening the wrinkles on his lively, intelligent face. He poured himself some wine.

"A robbery," he repeated after Evan.

"The criminals stole my horse. I don't know how they think to sell him without being caught. They'd have to take it out of Cornwall, I believe." Evan considered drinking some of the wine that had been offered, but he needed his mind sharp no matter how many times his memory offered the image of Noir dying in the darkness. His only hope was that the sentence Julian administered had been quick and painless.

Blackwell rubbed his nose. "It's a stroke of luck you both came out of this alive. Shall I send for the constable?"

"No need," Evan said, and swore at himself internally, because he was certain his words came too quickly. He leaned against the warm wall by the fireplace. "We will see him tomorrow. Between the two of us, Mr. Blackwell, there are no secrets about the state of my finances. If Noir isn't found, I will need to purchase a new horse, as one is not enough for an estate the side of Tredele.

"While rattled by the attack, I was faced with the reality of my position. I've had a few hours to think since the ambush, as well as months that have led me to this decision, but I would like to offer Tredele for sale. You are a good man, Mr. Blackwell, and as heartbreaking as it will be to let go of the house and land, it is time that I move on."

Blackwell was silent for a very long time, with only the ticking of the clock above the fireplace filling the atmosphere in the small, private office. "That... is not at all what I expected," said Blackwell in the end and finished his wine, as if it were a gulp of gin.

Evan sighed. "I imagine you thought I came up with a pity ploy to borrow yet more money. No, a man needs to know when to finish, and in all honesty, I believe I've dragged this out longer than I should have already."

Blackwell's eyes traced Evan's body, and it almost felt as if his gaze had the power to strip away the lies and see right through Evan. "It is a shame that we will not be family after all."

"It did not feel decent to pursue your daughter, when she so clearly despises the look of me," Evan joked, hoping to loosen up the atmosphere.

The corner of Blackwell's mouth twitched. "She has a difficult character, but a big enough dowry should buy her a decent husband."

"That I am sure of. Shall we draw up the contract? I do have a few clauses that I would like to write down for the good of the servants." Evan licked his lips, all too aware of how desperate and rushed this looked. All he had to count on was Blackwell's own eagerness to put his hands on Tredele. He would most likely rather seal a deal than risk a change of mind on Evan's part.

The old man poured himself more wine, and then slowly leaned forward until his elbows rested on his knees. "Forgive me, Sir Evan, but you do seem quite… desperate, for lack of a better word. Why now? You haven't even named a price yet."

"It's this brutal robbery that affected me so. Looking death in the eye has that effect on a man. And if I don't do this now, I know I will have second thoughts tomorrow."

Blackwell considered his words for a few moments. "Have I told you that my grandfather knew yours?"

Evan tilted his head in surprise. "No, I don't believe you have."

Blackwell smiled, glancing at the red wine gently moving inside the glass. "It is but a rumor, as I was just a child when he died. Who knows, it might have been delirium, but he told me that the two of them used to be friends way back, when Grandfather still had nothing, before he acquired his wealth. He told me of Tredele, and of the power he sensed within its walls. I have wanted it ever since. I wanted my grandfather's family to have that land and the house he kept in his thoughts until the day he died. I will not spoil the heritage of your family, Sir Evan. You have my word."

Evan sat down opposite Blackwell with a clear mind. "I have faith that you will do good by my servants as well then."

Blackwell licked his lips, lost in thought. "I do not know what truly happened tonight," he said in the end, raising his sharp gaze to Evan. "But you and your friend will be safe in my house until morning. Leave then, and I will not know a thing. Neither will my servants."

Evan closed his eyes for a second, then nodded. "Let's negotiate the conditions, then."

Chapter 23

Julian

There were armies of men marching through Julian's veins. Their boots thumped against his flesh, their bayonets picking at him from the inside until all he could do was curl up on the bed the maids had prepared for him on Blackwell's orders. It had become dark once he extinguished the single candle on the nightstand, a decision he now regretted.

Night terrors had passed with his childhood, but now they were back with a vengeance. Buried underneath the covers, he listened to the scratching of claws somewhere beyond the bed. Then, the scratching turned to clomping, and he pulled the sheet over his head, sweating into the clean nightshirt as his heart beat so fast his jugular was starting to block his windpipe.

Was the devil himself after him now? If so, he'd appear in the form of Noir, whose blood Julian could still sense on his hands, even after a thorough wash before bedtime.

If only Evan's arms were tightly around him, none of these nightmares would reach him. But the reality was just as terrifying as his imagination. They'd been as good as caught red-handed by the constable. They could both hang for what they'd done. How had it all seemed like a game before when both their lives now edged toward the cliff leading straight down to hell?

He opened his mouth against the sheet, sucking in air that was too hot, yet unable to make himself look beyond the coverings.

He was scared.

At any time, Pascoe could come here with his men and drag Julian out of this bed, straight into the cells of the gaol. With

Pascoe knowing of Evan's inclinations, there would be no pity for them. Not a soul would cry for them when their feet swung in the air.

What if Pascoe kept them apart, forcing them to hunger for touch and a gentle word until the end of their days? This possibility brought Julian's heart into a rush so fast he needed to come up for air after all, barely keeping back a sob.

How long had he been in bed? The maids had prepared one for Evan in the room next to his, so perhaps he was already back from his conversation with Blackwell? Then again, this house was brimming with servants. If Julian walked out into the corridor, someone could notice. What if they were apprehended by Pascoe and ended up sentenced for sodomy on the basis of a servant's testimony?

All these thoughts clamoring in his mind now had him hot all over, so he dared pull down the covers to breathe freely, but it gave him no peace. The cool air clung to his throat and made his stomach clench.

He looked toward the window. The curtains had not been drawn, and the sight beyond the glass pulled him off the mattress and then barefoot over the soft carpet. There was a balcony outside this window, and it seemed to extend toward Evan's room.

Julian grabbed the handle, freezing when he heard the silent clomping again, but he swallowed the anxiety rising in him and opened his room into the cool night. A breeze pushed Julian's linen shirt closer to his body when he made a step outside, shocked when his foot touched the stone floor that might have as well been ice.

But Evan's room was now so close and attainable he wanted to laugh out loud with sudden relief. If someone had told him a few months ago that he would be evading the law and sharing his bed with a man, he'd slapped the impertinent bastard—yet here he was, hungering for that man's touch as if it were clean water. It nourished him in ways he never thought possible, feeding Julian's talent with words and making him feel truly alive after years of sleeping with his eyes open.

He stumbled over something. It gave a metallic clang and rolled across the balcony, but it did not fall. He gave a sigh of relief and looked at the windows of Evan's room. The moonlight illuminated thick, white curtains that obscured the inside from view—a sure sign of someone's presence.

Julian clutched his shirt as the wind raised it with a vicious blow of air, eager to join his beloved and find out what happened in Blackwell's study. He needed Evan to tell him that they were safe. Julian was ready to believe him, even if promises of peace of mind would only be lies.

He put his hand on the handle and opened the door, silently maneuvering his body inside.

Something cold and hard pushed against his forehead, and only half a second later he realized it was the muzzle of a pistol.

Evan stared into his eyes with his own wide open, and quickly pulled back the weapon as if it burned him. "Julian," he hissed.

Julian couldn't move. The pistol might have as well blown a bullet straight through his skull, leaving him to bleed out at Evan's feet. His mind went cloudy, and his knees soft.

Evan grabbed Julian halfway to the floor, but Julian was already regaining consciousness when Evan picked him up with a loud grunt.

Julian grabbed Evan's nape and pulled himself closer, sealing Evan in a powerful embrace that left him feeling warm and safe, despite the damn pistol that now lay next to them on the floor. "Evan, what did he say?"

"It's done." Evan gave him a kiss and carried him to the bed where a single candle stood lit on the nightstand. "My debt is paid, I have an advance of banknotes, a few pieces of jewelry, and more will be paid into the hands of Blackwell's finance man in London. The last one is a gamble, but it might pay off once everything cools down, and we're settled in Italy. What about you? You're so pale.

Have you eaten?" He pointed to a tray with buns, scones, jam, cheese, and meats.

Julian shook his head, letting Evan's scent lull his senses to peace. "No, I couldn't possibly eat. The noose is waiting for my neck, and yours. Will Blackwell not alert Pascoe? Did he believe the story you told him?"

Evan sighed and pulled Julian into a hug on the bed. Those arms around him was exactly what Julian needed. So hot and strong as if they could hold up the world on Evan's shoulders. "We can stay until morning. He knows something is rotten about our arrival at night, but he's willing to overlook it. He wants the estate and doesn't want to be considered an accomplice to whatever he thinks we've done. We backdated the contract by a few days. It will be all right."

Julian gulped down his fear and curled up tighter against Evan. His thoughts raced like horses carrying the king out of danger. "He would not have told you if he intended to betray us."

"Precisely." Evan stroked Julian's shivering arms. "I've got this under control. Who knows whether the judge would not declare a contract void, were I apprehended. We will leave at dusk."

Julian relaxed and licked his lip, tasting the salt of fresh sweat. Evan's hands were warm and steady on him, their touch bringing much-needed peace. "Leave," he repeated and traced Evan's arm with his fingers. His heart thumped. It would be just the two of them, in a foreign land, escaping the law. Just he and Evan against a world that was out to get them. "I never thought we would. I thought we would stay at Tredele forever."

Evan pulled him into a tight hug, and rolled them over into the covers. "You liked it there so much?"

Julian gasped when Evan's firm body pressed against him, and he looked up, watching the illuminated contours of Evan's face. "It grew on me. Everything you touch grows on me."

"Looks like I am moss after all." Evan smiled and kissed Julian's neck, their bodies only separated by the linen of their shirts.

Julian's mouth twitched when his chest pressed against Evan's. He was quiet for a few moments, watching his lover's dark, gentle eyes settle on him. "I don't care what you are as long as you look at me like this," he whispered as blood swelled in his veins again, the invisible soldiers resuming their march, but this time without bayonets. They were caressing Julian's skin with soft, velvety hands.

Evan grabbed Julian's wrists, and pulled them over his head, slowly rolling on top. His eyes never left Julian's face. "Like this?" he asked, making a languid movement of his hips. Julian took a big gulp of air, mesmerized by the heat burning within Evan's eyes. He knew that all that lust, all that tenderness was there only for him. He wasn't merely a pretty face to have around anymore. Evan had risked his life for him more than once, he'd told him to leave the scene of the ambush despite them being outnumbered, but Julian did not need this kind of proof to know that he was cherished. Evan loved him and never hesitated to show it with those little things he did every day.

"You've changed me so. Have you noticed?" asked Julian, lifting his upper back to rub the tips of their noses.

"How so?" Evan reciprocated the caress. "I've noticed your throat takes a cock very well now," he whispered with a wide grin, as if they weren't one step away from the noose.

Julian laughed, the anxiety that had driven his darkest fantasies earlier gone. "That is your doing indeed. But... you uncovered this whole world before me. You showed me who I can be, and you made me happy. I might not have a shilling in my pocket, but I know what I am now."

Evan entwined their fingers, but he was still keeping Julian's hands in place, as if he were the anchor, and this bed a safe haven. "You are my joy. And since I am a very selfish man, I'd do everything to keep my joy around."

Julian curled his fingers over Evan's hand and massaged his knuckles with his fingertips, his chest swelling so much it took him forever to find his voice. "We might not have much privacy in the next few weeks, before we reach our destination."

Evan sighed and touched his forehead to Julian's. "We shouldn't even be together now. But I will steal any moment with you that I can."

Julian swallowed, briefly closing his eyes as emotion washed over him in burning hot waves. "I gave you permission, remember?" he said in the end, daring to look at Evan again, and his stomach twisted with nervous anticipation. He hadn't dared mention this since their quick encounter in the dark alleyway in Looe, but now his body started pulsing faster, all the way to his throat and eyelids. He sought a glimmer of understanding in Evan's eyes, but when he found none, his toes curled and rubbed against Evan's calves. "Please, will you be my storm tonight?"

Evan blinked, pausing for a long moment, but his grip on Julian's hands became stronger. "Didn't you say a storm was too much?" He lowered his face against Julian's neck. "That its lightning burned you?"

It was the heat of Evan's mouth burning Julian now, and he trembled, arching against the strong frame of Evan's body. Evan could have bent Julian to his will were he a different kind of man, but he'd been ready to forget about some of his needs for Julian's sake. That alone was enough to set Julian's skin on fire. He was important to Evan, way more than he'd ever been to anyone else in the world.

In that dark alley, Julian had felt the scorching heat of Evan's lust. He knew how badly it could hurt him, but he was ready to accept it and forfeit all control. He could still remember that rough touch, the fingers digging into his flesh and the teeth on the back of his neck, a transcendence to a whole array of emotions twisting Julian's flesh and molding it into something new. His body had never felt anything like that before or after.

He glanced at Evan openly, not wanting to feel any shame about what he was about to do. "I am ready for it now. Don't deny me."

Evan took a deep, raspy breath. "Oh, I will not, believe me." His eyes were black, with wide pupils, staring at Julian not only with adoration but with dark lust ready to be unleashed. They'd been together long enough for Julian to know Evan craved to take charge, tie him down, and leave marks on Julian's flesh, even if he then offered to bring Julian breakfast into bed. Giving in to Evan's desire would not constrict Julian. It would liberate him from having to choose or plead now that he'd declared what he wanted. Evan would not stop until he was told to.

"What if you change your mind?" Evan said with a toothy grin. "Shall I tie your wrists, so you cannot resist?"

Desire shot through Julian, eating into the very substance of him, deep into his bones. Unable to speak right away, he gave a frantic nod.

"Am I not despicable anymore for doing so? Where is the revenge you promised me all those months ago?" Evan straightened up and untied a fastening of a curtain around the bed. It obscured most of the room, but Evan now had a thick piece of rope in his hand, and Julian's breath hitched at the mere look of it.

"We are both despicable," said Julian, raising his hips just enough to pull the shirt from underneath his body as he started taking it off. He wanted to be completely naked for this. "But if someone thinks less of me because I want this, they can go to hell."

Evan's gaze trailed all the way from Julian's legs to his face. Slow and appreciative, as if Julian's body was the sweetest offering, even though it was Julian who felt like he was getting the prize when Evan pulled his shirt off as well, revealing the sturdy wide chest.

"Fuck anyone who thinks so. They don't know the pleasure of it, and they are poorer for it. When I imagine being between your legs, all I think of is that it would make you belong to me completely."

Julian's chest hollowed, and he quickly sat up, touching Evan's stomach, hard under the short dark hairs. He captured the warm lips of his lover and moved over the mattress to be even closer. "That is what I want. I want you inside me." It was the quietest whisper, barely there, but it hung between them with such force, as if Julian shouted it into Evan's ear.

Evan took a deep breath that made his nostrils flare, and just like that, Julian was back on the bed, Evan's lips on his, forcing Julian's mouth to take Evan's tongue as if it were a foretaste of his cock. Hot, hungry, and forceful, the kiss took Julian's breath away, but when he wanted to add hands to the equation and slide them onto Evan's strong back, Evan grabbed them, and started tying the wrists together blindly.

Julian wheezed with excitement and pulled on the rope, his eyes on Evan's in silent challenge. He loved being put in his place in bed. Any evidence of Evan's superior strength made his blood flow faster. He briefly wondered why his mind had never even considered for him to take Evan this way. Julian would not be opposed to this kind of play. In fact, he would gladly bury himself between Evan's buttocks, were his lover to want it, but this would have been play and pleasure, not the vibrant need that screamed at Julian to submit and let Evan do how he pleased.

He trusted Evan not to hurt him.

"Ah... pulling already? I need to tie them tighter then," Evan said, and made the fastening hug Julian's wrists. Seeing him this excited, his eyes glistening, his face flushing, and his cock filling, made Julian eager to please in any and all ways. There was a raw honesty in Evan's enthusiasm which told Julian exactly what he needed to know about Evan's intentions.

He grinned, drunk on the passion brimming between the two of them. "Make it tight so that I can't escape your thick rod," he uttered, briefly lowering his gaze when he remembered where exactly said rod was going.

Evan moved up and straddled Julian's chest once he attached the rope to the headboard. "Oh, you won't be able to. I will make your thighs tremble and your knees soft." He looked down at Julian's face and started slowly stroking his cock in front of it.

It offered the most perfect perspective of Evan's sac and the veiny shaft caressed with long fingers.

It was as if Julian's cock had filled with boiling milk. He could feel it stiffen and twitch without a chance for release. Julian moaned and pulled at the rope, shuddering as it rubbed against his wrists when he leaned forward, his mouth open for a taste. Evan was magnificent in his raw masculine energy. Thinking of the deed they agreed on was already making Julian's head fizzle.

"You'd like to kiss it before it drills into you?" Evan smirked and rubbed the cockhead over Julian's lower lip, leaving behind its delicious aroma, yet not letting Julian suck.

"You're a cruel master," whimpered Julian, licking the salty aftertaste and pulling himself up until an ache in his shoulder forced him down.

"Oh, no. You were much more cruel for making me think I would go on for an eternity without ever being allowed to possess your body completely." Evan reached down to Julian's throat and put his hand on it, gently pushing on Julian's Adam's apple. "You have me obsessed. I still shiver when I remember seeing my seed trickle out of your body." It was as if Evan could sense Julian's reaction before the dark flush reached his cheeks in the first place. "Don't be ashamed. Things that arouse are rarely those that are proper and genteel."

Julian pressed his teeth into his lip as memories came back to him. The seed spilling down his thighs had been a token of his humiliation, but Evan had watched it happen. It had excited him to see the evidence of Julian's body having yielded to his lust. "Your opinion is the only I care about in these matters," he said. He was vulnerable—yes—but he wanted to be so with Evan.

Evan petted Julian's hair. "Good. You're learning. I love to see you so bare in front of me." He slid off Julian's chest, and took his time simply watching him. "Spread your legs for me," he said in a voice thick with lust.

Julian took a deep breath and looked Evan's way. He kept his knees together at first, dragging his feet closer to his body, and only them parted his thighs. The cool air was like the touch of a ghost on his sensitive skin, but maybe it was just Evan's need manifesting itself this way. "Have you thought of this? Of taking me when I am so helpless?"

Evan's grunt was enough of an answer. "There is a demon inside me, Julian. I cannot explain it, nor do I try to anymore." He ran his fingertips over Julian's inner thigh, making all the little hairs bristle. "I don't know if the experiences with Peran have colored me this way, or if I was simply born wicked, but when I see a pretty bird like you, I want to devour and debauch. There hasn't been a day since I met you when I didn't think about having my cock buried deep inside you while I listen to your helpless moans and watch you twist under me."

Julian's whole body twitched and he uttered a low groan, arching his hips toward Evan. The picture painted before him was powerful enough to chase away any doubts Julian could possibly have about this act. If that was how madly Evan wanted this, Julian wanted to sate that need and make him forget any other man he'd wanted before. "I thought of that too. In the alley. Your cock was so hard, and it fucked me so roughly while you kept me still."

Evan's lips curled into a small smile. "Oh, yes, that was as close to the real act as I could get, and it was glorious. I came while feeling your arse go rigid against me. Did I ever tell you it is worth worshipping?" He reached to Julian's buttock and pinched it hard.

Warmth filled Julian's chest, and he smiled, all-too-widely for a captive. "You are welcome to worship all you want," he said, keeping his gaze on Evan even as he rolled to his stomach.

Evan let out a deep breath, and his hand instantly wandered to Julian's backside. "Yes. Up. Kneel and spread your legs for me. Show me how much you crave me."

Julian felt the flush climbing up his chest and tingling on his face, but he pushed his ass against Evan's palm, smiling when he thought of the two fitting together like two halves of an apple. His spine arched when he pulled himself to his knees, but with his front resting against a soft pillow, he just kept it there, enjoying the softness of down as Evan watched him.

Evan stroked Julian's ass before giving it a little pat. "This truly is worth dying for." He moved between Julian's spread knees, and not being able to see him made Julian's heart thud in the most delicious way. He now couldn't anticipate where the touch would come from or whether it would be a caress or a slap, but as tension grew inside him, so did the excitement that toyed with his balls. Evan had intimate knowledge of every part of him, and he found every single one beautiful.

"Don't say such things. You're not dying," whispered Julian and twisted his neck, looking back at Evan's muscled form, so close to Julian's most vulnerable parts. The last time had been a violation, but it would not be so now. Julian calmed his breathing, trying to listen to the rhythm inside his body, both relaxed and tense at the same time.

Evan smirked, and his fingers slid between Julian's buttocks, teasing the sensitive pucker of his anus. "I'm not. I've never felt more alive. Feel this?" He shifted closer and his hard cock poked against Julian's thigh. "This is all because of you."

Julian pushed back, rubbing against the stiff prick that was so ready to enter him, and yet Evan waited. His touch sent burning hot fingers ghosting over Julian's flesh, already softening up his hole. It was the same sensation he'd felt in Looe, this overwhelming need to be touched in the most intimate of ways.

"Oh, God…"

Evan chuckled darkly. "You're wanton. I never thought I'd see you this way. Sweaty, hot, and ready to take my cock, my seed, and all I have to give."

Desire rolled through Julian rapidly, and he curled his toes, rocking back against the fingers between his buttocks. He was hot. He was cold. He was done just waiting. "Yes. I will welcome the storm with open arms this time."

"It will swallow you whole." Evan reached for something from the tray by the bed, and moments later, his fingers were slippery when they pushed for entry into Julian's body.

Julian glanced to the side with a small frown, but then he knew what it was. He would never look at butter the same way ever again. His cheeks burned fiercely, but he chuckled nevertheless. "That's it. *Devour* me," he uttered despite his stomach clenching at the intrusion. But when the finger pushed in, he let out a sigh of relief. It was so much better than the damn candle. Even if not exactly comfortable, it was warm and alive as it moved, slowly screwing into the tight channel of Julian's body. He rolled his head to bury his face in the pillow again, trying not to tense up too much, but his muscles inevitably attempted to crush Evan's bones.

Evan's other hand tightened its grip on Julian's hip, holding him in place when two of his fingers pushed in all the way to the knuckle, past Julian's defenses. When they moved back and forth, all Julian could think of was that they were preparing him to yield to Evan's cock, to make him nice and slippery inside so that Evan could fuck him the way he liked.

He curled his shoulders, fighting the urge to pull away at the sting of pain. It dispersed quickly, leaving Julian to the unfamiliar sensation. He was not certain yet whether he enjoyed it in the same way he enjoyed kisses, but as Evan shifted closer behind him, groaning loudly, Julian moved his hips back without thinking, as if it were the most natural thing in the world.

"Let me know if it hurts," Evan whispered against Julian's back, moving his fingers back and forth in a spellbinding motion.

Julian closed his eyes and curled his shoulders, pushing back against the intrusion once the initial ache eased, leaving him with the alien sensation of something drilling its way inside him. His thoughts left his body and crawled over the covers, reaching Evan's thighs and wondering at how thick and strong they were. Julian could recall their magnificence in all detail, intimately familiar with the way Evan liked thrusting against his lips. He thought of the tense stomach pulsing with each rolling motion, and the thick stand emerging from the nest of dark curls between Evan's thighs. Below them, the heavy balls would be by now pulling closer to Evan's body as it readied for fucking.

"Oh, you will know," said Julian, trying to laugh off the uncertainty that was rapidly sinking its claws into his flesh. He'd made his decision and didn't have the need or desire to take it back, but he still recalled his first time in strange detail, and it terrified him that those memories could stay in his and Evan's bed forever.

Just as those thoughts were tearing him away from what was happening here and now, Evan pulled out his fingers and wrapped his arms around Julian's waist, to roll him over. Julian landed on his back, faced with what he'd seen in his imagination. Evan in all his naked glory, some of his hair sticking to his flushed face, his stomach moving up and down with every loud breath he took.

"I want to see your face when I drown in you," Evan said, and his eyes pinned Julian to the bed as effectively as the rope on Julian's hands.

Julian opened his mouth, unable to utter a sound as air stuck in his throat. Pulled by an overwhelming need, he arched closer and licked Evan's lips, shuddering at their touch. He hadn't known just how much he wanted this change of position until Evan rolled him over. Worry melted and mixed with the red blood in his veins, simmering for everything Evan was about to give him.

Evan deepened the kiss and grabbed Julian's legs, as if he could do with Julian's body whatever he pleased. Maybe he could? Maybe Julian was ready to bleed for Evan if that was required to have him.

Evan placed Julian's legs on his shoulders, pulling them closer together, and he let his prick slide to Julian's slippery hole, teasing it with the cockhead, yet refusing Julian the last thing that would make them one.

The touch was shocking even though expected, and Julian rocked his hips, longing to get away and push back at the same time. His skin felt tight, as if it couldn't accommodate his need anymore, and he twisted his hips, far too taken with Evan's glistening eyes to care about the undignified position or anyone's opinion of sodomy.

He moaned, rolling his head over the pillow when the head of Evan's prick dipped between his buttocks, pressing against the hole that tightened against Julian's will.

Evan moaned deeply, nipping on Julian's shivering lip. "Let me in, sweetie. You know you want to," he said with a devilish glint in his eyes, pushing at Julian's opening again and again.

Julian opened his mouth, sucking at his lover's warm, sweet breath as their lips barely moved. He shuddered, instinctively resisting each intrusion, but the resolve in his body seemed to be slowly dwindling, and he arched his chest, struggling for more touch. "I do. Oh, I do..."

"You're at my mercy now," Evan whispered into his lips, tormenting Julian so deliciously it was hard to bear. "What if I deny you my cock?" But despite the words he pushed a little harder, almost entering Julian, yet not doing it just yet.

Julian whined, shocked by the depth of raw emotion those words awoke inside him. For a moment, he believed he would die if it came to this, withering away from the absence of Evan's touch. His eyes stung, and he watched Evan in helpless shock, taking in deep breaths of air as his muscles went lax, and the thick cock nudged the entrance of Julian's body once more.

He shuddered violently, tightening the muscles in his legs and rapidly pulling Evan closer.

Evan's throbbing cock pushed deep into Julian's body, and it didn't feel like an intrusion anymore. It was as if a void in Julian's soul was finally being filled. Evan didn't stop at that either, rocking his hips and inching his thick prick in farther. Now that he got a taste of it, he wouldn't stop anymore, taking everything Julian was willing to give and more.

Julian made a low, guttural sound, tense as a string when Evan fought his resistance and pushed on until his cock was completely embedded in Julian's tight channel. He closed his eyes, breathing too quickly. His head spun like that of a man balancing on the edge of a cliff. He would either fall to his death or fly.

Julian was ready to spread his wings and take Evan with him. A numb sensation in his hands made him aware of just how vigorously he was tugging at the rope. It dug deep into his flesh, cutting the blood flow until it left Julian's fingers with a tingling that mirrored the wild currents in his heart.

Evan deepened the kiss, and his tongue exploring Julian's palate and the soft insides of his cheeks was all Julian needed to calm down.

He was loved.

Evan fucking him did not make him feel used, but cherished. The more he thought about that throbbing, stiff thing of beauty penetrating the depths of his body, the more rigid his own cock got.

He laughed, sensing the movement of the air between their faces. Evan lowered his body, encasing Julian underneath his chest, as if he were the most precious treasure that needed to be kept safe. There was still a bit of discomfort from being stretched so wide, but the sensation of accepting the man he loved into his body while they kissed and hugged was incomparable to anything Julian had ever experienced.

"I'm taking that your laughter is a good sign." Evan kissed Julian's cheek and he gave the side of Julian's thigh a slap. He made a pleased groan after Julian's ass tightened around his cock.

"Yes. It feels strange, but so good," whispered Julian, twisting his hips as he watched Evan's face for a reaction. The thick prick was such a warm presence inside him, and now that his muscles accepted their fate, he was tuning in to the tight fit between their flesh.

Evan nipped on Julian's cheek and slowly pulled his cock out, only to slam it back in. "What about now?" He was trapping Julian in the mixture of his scent and arousal, but Julian wouldn't even dream of running, about to drown in Evan's fiery passion.

The firm thrust stung a bit, but he relaxed, and the one that followed felt much more agreeable.

He was getting good at this.

Julian laughed again at that thought, watching Evan with a sense of completion rising in his chest. "Slowly," he whispered, stealing another kiss when he arched toward Evan, rubbing himself over hot, damp skin.

"You want to make it last longer," Evan teased. "I see…" The way he drove his cock in and out was creating a heat in Julian's prick that was hard to explain since it only got to brush against Evan every now and then.

Julian's balls pulled up with excitement every time Evan plunged his prick into him, and moment by moment, Julian was craving more of what he couldn't yet pinpoint. It felt almost as if Evan was rubbing Julian's cockhead through layers of fabric. Each thrust was smoother, more languid, and Julian's insides opened up to Evan's ministrations, accepting them without question.

He turned his head to kiss Evan's arm where it was lowered next to his head and looked at his lover, the fire inside him only fueled by the burning passion he could see reflected in Evan's gaze. "You look so happy."

"You have no idea." Evan murmured in reply and kissed Julian's lips, but his hips never stopped their movement, rocking against Julian faster by the second. "I want you to take my spend the same way you swallow it. You like it, don't you?"

Evan lifted Julian's ass off the sheets, changing the angle of his thrusts as he folded Julian's body underneath him, and this new position allowed Julian to see Evan's cock between their bodies, dipping in and out, faster, getting ready to spill into him.

A stab of sensation pierced Julian's body, and he thrashed against Evan, rapidly pulling him in with his legs. For the briefest moment, he was afraid it was pain, but then his mind pulsed with a pleasure so pure it might as well have been distilled out of all the times he'd spent in Evan's arms. "Oh, my Lord," whimpered Julian, pulling at the rope so rapidly the bed gave a creak of warning.

Evan's eyes widened, and he gave Julian a wicked grin. "Oh, yes. That's it," he hissed and grabbed on to Julian's hips, as he started a merciless rhythm, fucking Julian into the bedding. Faster, and faster, each time brushing against that spot inside of Julian that made him thrash against the fastenings on his wrists. Earlier, only a ghost of pleasure, now the pressure was like a hand touching his cock from the inside. If only his hands were free, he'd toss off like a madman, with Evan's cock still buried inside. He remembered how it had throbbed when Evan came inside of him last time.

But he wasn't free. He depended on Evan's generosity with touch, and his eyes watered when Evan's cock wouldn't stop teasing him from the inside. He would come without even having his prick touched. Was that possible? He was beginning to believe anything was possible with a lover like Evan.

Another involuntary moan was stifled by Evan's big hand covering Julian's lips, and forcing him to take air through his nose. "Be quiet," Evan ordered, his own voice raspy.

Julian rocked his whole body, already drenched with sweat as that wonderful cock filled the void inside him again and again, pleasuring Julian in ways he never thought possible. His shallow breath was slowly making his mind fly, but Evan was there to be his anchor, with his powerful frame keeping Julian in a firm grasp and his mouth uttering grunts that rolled over Julian's skin like yet another caress.

He opened his mouth and licked the middle of Evan's palm, the only thing that kept him from screaming into the night.

Evan closed his eyes at the touch and bit his lip to not moan. He made a few harsh thrusts that pushed Julian to the edge of pain, and then stilled on top of Julian, only slowly rocking his hips and panting. His cock throbbed intensely, and the bliss painted over Evan's face made Julian relax. Evan's seed was now filling Julian's body like a prize for a job well done.

Julian's own cock twitched for attention, but the raw need was only fueled by the euphoric tension on Evan's face. Julian's heart thumped fast, his blood rushing inside his veins. He wanted this moment to last forever. Just him and Evan, frozen in the state of utter bliss, safe from the clutches of anyone who wanted to hurt them.

Julian already knew he'd want Evan to come inside him again, and he could hardly believe he'd waited so long to love him this way. But his thoughts died down the moment Evan's hand wrapped tightly around Julian's cock and started pumping it with well-known precision and purpose.

"I want you to come while my cock's still hard inside of you. I love that." Evan watched him intently with half-lidded eyes and slowly removed his hand from Julian's mouth.

"Just don't move yet," whispered back Julian, suddenly greedy for the firm girth. He clenched his fingers on the tense rope and gave in to sensation while Evan's slick hand pulled over his prick, twirling the thumb around the head.

Evan rested his forehead against Julian's and watched him as the sharp movements brought Julian's arousal to a boiling point. Pleasure rippled over Julian like a tall wave, pushing him into the warm water and taking his seed.

He gasped, raising his chin to capture Evan's mouth again, and they pushed so close together, there remained no space for air between them. Julian rode his pleasure with Evan's prick buried deep inside him, and then collapsed into the covers, completely spent.

When Evan's cock slipped out, it was a loss Julian wasn't ready for, but Evan lying next to him and hugging him close made up for it. Evan's stubble scratched Julian's neck when Evan kissed him there, and despite having felt so anxious not long ago, Julian was now as peaceful as the sea on a sunny summer's day.

The slippery feeling between his buttocks and thighs was still making him shy, but it was also a token of what had just happened, and that brought a grin to his face, not allowing it to fade. Julian pushed himself up and cradled Evan's head between his neck and shoulder, smelling the unruly black hair. "That was... more enjoyable than I thought it would be," he said in the end.

Evan pulled away with pursed his lips and frowned. "Since when are you this lousy at giving compliments?"

Julian burst out laughing and kissed his forehead. "Well, it was quite spectacular, but in a different way than I expected. Now I know what you meant by saying that some men cannot get enough of this. There I was, merely thinking I would enjoy having you inside me, but you exceeded my expectations."

Evan grinned. "That's more like it." He stroked Julian's chest, and teased his nipple with his thumb. "Sadly, we need to get ourselves in order in case we need to leave sooner than anticipated. But..." He looked at Julian with a sigh. "I wouldn't have given up this time with you for anything."

Julian beamed, warmth radiating from the depths of his ribcage. He had a sudden urge for touch and loudly knocked his finger against the headboard, raising his brows at Evan. There would have been satisfaction in simply making Evan happy, giving him what he desired, but this act turned out to be so much more rewarding. "I love you too."

CHAPTER 24

JULIAN

In his dreams, Julian led Evan to the river that circled the hill atop which stood Tredele. They went barefoot down a narrow path through a shallow ravine, basking in the early summer sun as the fresh grass tickled their toes.

Julian knew it was a dream, because there was no breeze. The carpet of tiny blue flowers, very much like a shadow between the trees, was still, even in this odd space that seemed to have been torn from the flesh of the hill by an ancient giant. Evan was smiling at him, as if there were no care in his world. As if Tredele were not weighing him down, as if he were free to go where he pleased, with no responsibilities other than the ones to himself and Julian.

They ran past a tiny stone chapel that might as well have been in this place since the beginning of time and dove into the greenery at the shore.

Only now the wind started blowing. Leaves whispered against Julian's skin when he uncurled his fingers from Evan's, letting him lead the way. Above them, gray clouds appeared out of nowhere, blocking the sun, but what was a bit of rain when one intended to swim anyway? Julian could already hear the calls of the mermaids from the story he'd written about Evan before meeting him in person, and he followed his lover, who already disappeared between the reeds.

The mud at the shore was ice-cold on his feet. He emerged from the bushes, faced with the high water, and moved toward Evan, fighting against the wet ground that sucked his feet in.

Evan did not react to the touch, transfixed on the bathing maids whose skin shone just like fish scales. They were screaming, thrashing around beneath the surface like hungry carps in a pond, their voices low as those of men. One of them briefly jumped from the water, only to spiral toward the shore, like an arrow sent Evan and Julian's way.

In the murky depths, her skin lost some of its bluish glow. The screams erupted even louder until they drowned out the sound of the wind, and the mermaid pushed herself over the surface with a vicious bark, opening a mouth full of sharp teeth.

One by one, the other mermaids approached the shore as well, their mouths opening to growl like hellhounds. One grabbed Evan's wrist to pull him into deep water, another one bit into Evan's arm and shook her head violently.

Julian's heart skipped a beat, and he inhaled deeply before opening his eyes to the canopy above the bed.

He sat up, his gaze falling on the window, where bright lines on the edge of the curtains betrayed the start of day. His heart thudded when the loud, relentless barking from the dream assaulted him again, echoing from somewhere beyond their walls. Screams accompanied the howling, and although he could not understand any of it, hearing such racket early in the day was a sign they couldn't afford to ignore.

Evan looked sleepy for half a second when Julian shook him, but then his eyes went wide-open. "Put on your breeches and boots. Now." He rolled off the bed, frantically dressing in only the most basic items of clothing.

Julian followed his example and pulled on yesterday's shirt, but then a single voice turned his blood to ice.

Pascoe bellowed with such ferocity that Julian feared the windows would crack from that voice rising over the relentless barking. "You think us daft, Mr. Blackwell? I have seen his horse in the stable!"

Julian could not discern Blackwell's answer, his head pulsing with fear as he leapt for the door, knowing the balcony could not be used with hyenas waiting outside.

Sparse morning light slipped past the curtains on both ends of the corridor, making it appear gray, but it was enough to guide Julian to the right door and the neat pile of clothing he'd left there earlier. His trembling hands did not provide much aid in fastening his drawers and breeches, but he succeeded nevertheless, rushing back to Evan's room with boots worn over bare calves and feet. The highwayman's coat didn't provide him with enough freedom to move, so he pushed it into a chest on his way out, following the one way he knew of at this point. His mind was merely a white empty space, with no decoration or substance.

"Let's go," Evan whispered, dressed in only some of his clothes as well, the coat foregone.

Julian didn't even get a word in. Evan grabbed his hand, pulled him into the passage decorated with portraits, and led the way away from the staircase they'd come up last night.

Julian's lungs seemed to have expanded beyond the capacity of his chest, filling him with air that made his gait lighter, quicker. Evan turned his head left and right, as if he expected each of the paintings to be spying on them, but then he pushed Julian at the wall, as if he intended to move bricks with the sheer power of his muscles. But no, it was a door.

Julian stared into the complete darkness of that hole in the fine silk wallpaper until Evan pulled him in and shut the entrance behind them.

"Watch your step, the stairs are uneven," Evan whispered, pulling Julian down into the lightless abyss, but as they continued down the staircase, a glow emerged below.

Julian clutched the railing, shocked by how steep the way felt. His feet came down in the usual manner at first, but the steps were not only of different height, as Evan warned him, but also extraordinarily short, as if intended for a child. He forced himself to put his heel down while brushing it against the previous step, and only this way did he avoid the disastrous possibility of falling down and breaking his bones.

The scent of a freshly started fire bit into his nose, but he followed Evan farther down the narrow tube of the staircase.

They were in the servants' part of the house, he realized, but he did not care at this moment how Evan had found out where to go. All he knew was that they needed to run, and fast.

They entered a high-ceilinged kitchen with a new set of copper pots and pans on the wall, and food for the day laid out on a huge table in the middle. Evan led Julian toward a door on the other side, but a scream loud enough to alarm the whole estate made them both lose their rhythm. A scullery maid dropped the piece of wood she was holding and cowered behind the open fireplace, eyeing them as if she saw a ghost.

Voices erupted beyond the wall, and Evan staggered back from the door, squeezing Julian's hand so hard Julian's bones creaked. They ran past the cowering girl and into a barren walkway with many doors, each leading to a different part of the kitchens. Chased by the ever-present shouts and barking, they were like rabbits trying to escape from an ambush while smoke was already being poured into their den. All exits seemed to be manned, but there was always hope that the hunting party missed *something*.

Julian's heart clenched when the high-pitched voice of a young girl stuttered loudly behind them, a sharp contrast to the masculine roars, which now unmistakably came from inside. The hounds had gotten wind of prey and would not settle until they purged their fangs in blood.

Just as Julian realized they were at a dead end, Evan pushed him into a room so cold it felt like being shoved into the arms of winter. His nose filled with the scent of fresh meat and blood, the cause of it evident when he spun around to face carcasses and game hung from the hooks on the ceiling.

Evan pushed a small satchel into Julian's hands, confusing him even more. "Hide. If all goes to hell, go to Plymouth and buy passage to the continent," he whispered and urged Julian back, toward an open cupboard.

The voices were getting closer, heavy boots stomping over the floor like a crowd itching for a hanged man's parts. Julian stared at Evan, breathless and stiff in the joints, his fingers barely capable of holding up the satchel.

"Evan, what...?"

"Make it to the ship. I will find you," Evan whispered, his face determined despite the tremor to his voice. He shoved Julian into the cupboard, between sausages hanging down like fruit ripe for picking.

Julian fell inside, only now forcing himself to curl his legs to fit the cramped space. He grabbed Evan's wrist and pulled on it, but when a vicious barking clamored through the corridor, echoing as if it came from the depths of a well, Evan shook his fingers off and shut the door. The scent of herbs and smoked meat filled Julian's nose, and he gasped when the lock snapped closed right next to his face. Light trembled in the small keyhole, and he leaned in to look through it as soon as it was vacated. He forced air into his lungs, stiff with fear as he watched Evan shove the key into the carcass of a pheasant.

The thunder of footsteps suddenly stilled, and Julian did not need to see the men in pursuit to know the two of them had been discovered. He wished he could stop breathing altogether, and it was only the emptiness in his lungs that prevented him from making a noise when a vicious-looking bloodhound leaned in toward his hideout, eye against the empty keyhole.

Behind it, Evan raised his arms in surrender.

For a moment, a deathly silence filled the room, louder than the low growling across the wood from Julian, but then a familiar character stepped on stage, closely followed by a man holding the hound on a tight leash and pulling it away from the cupboard.

Pascoe seemed taller somehow, and his soft body that had been trained for sitting at people's bedsides seemed monumental in this moment of triumph. Julian covered his mouth when his teeth began to clatter.

"By the look of you, I imagine you know your crime?" Pascoe said, and even though Julian could not see the bastard's face, he could hear the smile in his words.

"What is the meaning of this?" Blackwell asked somewhere beyond Julian's narrow field of vision.

Pascoe made a low, laugh-like noise. "Sir Evan Penhart is our local highwayman, Mr. Blackwell. Shot one of my men dead yesterday. I managed to injure his horse, but he had an accomplice, and they escaped on the other animal. The one in your stables, sir. So, where is the other scoundrel?" Pascoe put his hand on the wooden table by the window, and leaned against it casually.

Blackwell inhaled sharply, emerging on the narrow scene of the keyhole in the same banyan and cap he'd worn the night before. "I do not believe this. Sir Evan is a gentleman, and he has never been anything but kind to my family. What a ludicrous idea."

Pascoe glanced at him sharply, and in the bright morning light the reddish hue of his skin was easy to discern. "As sad as this makes all of us, there is no doubt. The bloodhounds led us here based on the smell of the saddle on his fallen horse. The white mare still has dark stains from the coal used to change the appearance of her coat. I am afraid that you have put your trust in the wrong man, Mr. Blackwell." Pascoe made a step toward Evan, hunching forward like a bull about to attack, and Julian bit on his fingers so hard for a moment he thought he broke skin. "Where is he?"

"Not here, as you can see," Evan said in a stone-cold voice, standing straight, even though his hands clenched and opened constantly. "He was slowing me down on the one horse we had, so I left him in the woods."

"Is that so, Mr. Blackwell?" There was mockery in Pascoe's voice, and knowing of the bad blood between him and Evan, Julian was sure the bastard enjoyed this victory more than he ever enjoyed healing his patients.

Blackwell went silent for a moment, and Julian's heart thudded so hard he could barely hear his thoughts, let alone the people in the room.

"That is true. Sir Evan came here alone last night," Blackwell said in the end, to Pascoe's face souring.

"Damnation. Where is he? That goddamn fool. Reece?" Pascoe bellowed, raising his voice so high, Blackwell shushed him.

"Mr. Pascoe, my young daughter is present in this house. She could overhear you, and I do not want her to know of this kind of language!"

Pascoe clenched his teeth so hard Julian could spot the twitching of muscle around his jaw even from his hideout. The cupboard was slowly closing in on Julian, the little walls moving his way to chase him out. He had no right to hide and listen to Evan answering those questions. They went through with two robberies together, so why should Evan take all the blame?

And yet he couldn't make himself say anything, frozen in place like a mouse about to be eaten by the cat.

A man from Pascoe's entourage moved to tie Evan's hands, but Pascoe pushed him away. Only then Julian recognized him as Davies, one of the men who'd come to Tredele after their first robbery. "I'll do it myself," Pascoe hissed.

Evan's hand gravitated to a plate of cut meats on the table, unbeknownst to anyone but Julian. He took something and closed it in his fist just before Pascoe spun him around. "Reece is a writer, not a robber," Evan snarled. "My accomplice is of much lower standing. You will not find him."

Julian's body sagged, and he clawed his fingers into his cheeks not to scream. He knew he should say something, but his mouth remained mute, something at the back of his mind telling him to stay as he was. That Evan could somehow handle everything himself. But deep down he realized there would be no coming back from this for his lover. The constable had him, along with all the proof that was needed.

Pascoe showed his teeth and pulled Evan's arms back so rapidly Julian's muscles ached just from watching the scene play out.

Blackwell sighed. "I am certain there is an explanation for this."

"Aye, he's a good liar," said the man who held the hound in place, but the moment Julian followed the voice, his muscles became stiff as wood when he noticed the hound pinning him with its dark gaze. It stepped closer, pulling on the leash, and Julian's mind exploded with fear.

He could not go to jail. They would surely send him off to Bodmin, where the largest gaol in all of Cornwall had newly been opened. In a cell with hardened criminals, men who habitually murdered their lovers or stole cows, robbing entire families of their livelihood, he would be an easy target. And even if he befriended his cellmates somehow, his body and mind were not used to the hardships of cold walls and little to no food. He would wither away even before the hangman got his dirty hands on him.

"What's in the cupboard?" asked the master of the hound, stepping closer.

Blackwell groaned with annoyance. "Sausages. No wonder the beast's interested."

"Let us see," Pascoe ordered, and Blackwell stepped closer, making Julian's eyes water with anxiety.

"The cook holds the key. He must have locked it, as not all servants are honest, it seems," Blackwell said and pulled on the doors to the cupboard to show the others that it was in fact locked.

Two fat tears rolled down Julian's cheeks at the rattling.

Pascoe groaned, and stepped back from Evan, but then came at him with a fist to the stomach so hard Evan had to lean forward to stay on his feet. "And that's for the man you shot!"

"That's enough, Mr. Pascoe! The court will judge this man and provide a fair sentence!" Blackwell raised his voice as well.

A searing pain spread through Julian's body, as if he himself had been punched by this vicious man. He couldn't breathe, drowning in the vast, dark sea of panic. Just hours ago, Evan's face had been alight with a smile so sweet, so happy. At that moment, they'd both believed there was nothing that could possibly stop them, and watching him treated so roughly was torture.

And yet, Julian didn't make his presence known.

Pascoe smirked and tipped his hat at Blackwell, grabbing the back of Evan's shirt and shoving him toward the door. "I will not make your eyes bleed anymore, Mr. Blackwell. Justice will be served indeed."

Ignored by the search party, the hound tried to pull toward Julian's cupboard again.

"I will assist you with searching my house myself if you wish. As I said, there are ladies still sleeping upstairs," Blackwell said.

Julian watched Evan, convinced of the importance of this moment. Evan had been lying when he told Julian he'd find him in Plymouth, and Julian knew this but still remained in hiding, abandoning his lover to Pascoe and the men who'd lost a friend to Evan. Things would get ugly very soon.

Blackwell and Pascoe talked when one of Evan's palms opened slightly, dropping the piece of sausage he'd earlier collected. The hound's ears perked up, and it pulled toward the fallen piece of meat, making his handler curse loudly. Even now, captured by his mortal enemy, Evan thought of ways to save Julian when Julian's survival instincts refused him the will to make a similar sacrifice.

Completely stunned, he watched Pascoe take Evan away, and not a single glance ever fell to the cupboard where Julian was hiding, even Evan's. It was only when the loud footsteps started dying out somewhere at the other end of the kitchen area, a sharp whine left Julian's lips. He wheezed for air, choked by the smoky scent of homemade cold meats and by the guilt rapidly rising inside his chest.

What had he done? It had been him who convinced Evan to return to the highways for gold in the first place, so how could it be that he was still intact while his lover was taken by a man who'd awaited this moment for years?

Julian forced himself to breathe, taking in air with sheer willpower. There was still a chance for the judges to administer a punishment other than death, but then what? Transportation? Julian would never see Evan again.

Minutes stretched, and he had no idea how much time passed. It could have been minutes or hours with the stupor that overcame Julian's mind. A servant came in, went out, and Julian couldn't choke out a word. He clenched his fingers on the satchel containing all the money Evan had received as an advance from Blackwell, and even the jewels. All of it left in Julian's hands as if he deserved it solely for existing.

He pressed his face against the packed leather and smelled it, hoping to sense the faintest trace of Evan on it, but he couldn't find it. The pouch had only been his for the last few hours, and now he was gone.

Maybe Julian would slowly dry out in this cramped space, killed by the biting cold that made him shudder more and more. How long had he even been there? Time seemed to stretch beyond all imagination, but unless he fell asleep sometime, it was still the same day. Evan surely was on the way to gaol.

Every time someone entered, Julian was on pins and needles, but this time, someone in buckskin breeches stopped in front of the cupboard, rendering him stunned.

"Reece?" Blackwell asked in a voice without emotion.

Julian hid his face in his knees and put his hand against the wooden door, not trusting himself to speak.

Blackwell knocked on the sausage cupboard, making him gasp as if the whip were coming down on his back already.

Julian's teeth clattered loudly. "I–I'm here…"

Blackwell groaned and started shuffling around the room. "Where's that bloody key?" he muttered. "They've all gone now."

Julian leaned against the door, his chest swelling with sobs he dared not let out. "The pheasant… he put it in the pheasant."

"He locked you in there? I guess... it does make some sense." Blackwell groaned as he handled the dead bird.

Julian stayed still until the lock creaked, and Blackwell opened the door, towering over Julian's folded body. Slowly, Julian looked up, squinting to protect his eyes from the bright light coming through the windows. "Where have they taken him?"

Blackwell took a step back, his round body and fashionable clothes not taking anything away from the stern look on his face. "Gaol, I imagine. I wished to stay out of this, but I had given him my word that I would keep you safe. I did the best I could in the circumstances."

Julian watched him, not trusting himself to move just yet out of the place that had protected him from Pascoe and his dogs. In comparison, the room was unfamiliar and choking in its size. "Thank you," said Julian.

"Now get out of my house. They did not take the horse. I wish to never see you again, is that understood?"

Julian swallowed hard, flinching as if Blackwell had kicked him with his exquisitely polished hessian. Those words were what made him finally move, and he climbed out of the cupboard, pulling himself up and stretching his tense muscles. Everything around him was muted by the storm bellowing in his gut, the one that twisted and turned all his insides with guilt and pain. "Has he a chance?" he uttered.

"For a quick death. If the hangman knows his job." Blackwell's words sank in slowly, making Julian's insides ache even more. He shook his head. "May God protect me from friends like you. Hiding like a rat when they took him. What else would one expect from a criminal though, when even your own father doesn't want to hear from you."

Julian opened his mouth, fully intending to protect his honor and tell Blackwell they had been outnumbered, that one way or another Evan would have been in this situation, with or without Julian, but those were all lies. Were Julian not here, Evan might have been quicker, maybe he could have fled the dogs then. Maybe *he* would have hidden in the cupboard that had only enough room for one man.

Julian hung his head as the cold trickle of truth trailed down his body.

He was a truly despicable man. He'd always liked to think of himself as daring, but what good was that, if he had a coward in him when it mattered most?

His hands shook—he didn't know if from being so long in the cold or of emotion—as he pulled his hair back, not even daring to look up at Blackwell.

Slowly, he nodded. "I will be gone. Forget all about me, Mr. Blackwell."

Chapter 25

Evan

The darkness in the small cell and the stench coming from the bucket in the corner were nothing in comparison to the cold fear pooling in Evan's stomach when he wondered whether Julian had made it out of Fairfield Park safely, or if he was somewhere here in Bodmin, just a few cells away. Evan had no way of knowing, and he was sure it would drive him mad before the hangman got to him.

His body ached from the brutality of his capture, head spinning after hours with no water or food, but Julian was at least something to focus on. If he got away, the advance from Blackwell could provide him with a comfortable, if modest, living for years to come. Unless Julian couldn't handle his funds well and idled it all away on wine and Italian men. It was a bitter thought, but he could not demand of a man to remain chaste forever. Things would work out for Julian, he was sure.

His body gave an involuntary flinch when someone approached. This part of the gaol had seemed empty when he was brought in, so surely the man loudly approaching this way was heading for Evan's cell.

Evan licked his dry lips, analyzing what route to take. Silence? Denial? Was there anything that could save him at this point? Even the mouse rotting in the corner hadn't found a way out, even though it had not been chained to the wall by the neck and hands.

Evan let out a bark of a laughter when he imagined tiny shackles for the mouse, but it died on his lips as soon as the footsteps ceased.

The key clanged loudly in the iron frame of the door, and Pascoe walked in, shutting it behind him. In his hand he held what Evan first believed to be a walking stick, but as the man moved into the faint light coming from the grated window, Evan's lips dried.

It was a cane, much like the ones he remembered being used at school for discipline, only thicker and longer.

Pascoe was trying not to smile, but the sense of victory was radiating off his body like the odor of bodies decaying on a battlefield. He watched Evan, slowly walking around the cell that, despite its size, had been clearly designed to hold more men. With Evan kept in one corner with iron shackles fastened to the wall with a thick chain, Pascoe had nothing to fear despite being physically weaker.

Maybe Evan should bite him to prove him wrong? It would be worth a few licks of a cane just to see fear on Pascoe's face.

"Does your medical practice suffer because of the job you do? Most men of your position put all the work in the hands of their deputies, but not you," Evan said, gathering all his loathing for the man.

Pascoe smirked, raising the cane and caressing it with his fingers, as if he admired the quality of workmanship. "Some things are more important than others. This parish is rotting with vice, and I have an income that is not related to my profession. Don't worry, I will not starve."

Evan watched him from his place in the corner, burning with the need to cut Pascoe down, but there wasn't much he could do other than not allow the bastard to break him. "I've heard some men *enjoy* the cane. Is that a vice?"

Pascoe's eyes were sharp as he looked Evan's way. "Do you enjoy its licks? Is that what Julian Reece was doing to you all this time?" he asked, approaching Evan in slow steps. He tapped the cane against his palm, eyes never leaving Evan's.

Anger coursed through Evan's veins and made his hands ball into fists at the mention of Julian. "No," he said, all too aware that it came out snarly. "But maybe you enjoy holding the cane all too mu—."

The cane swished in the air and slapped him across the naked chest, leaving a burn that pushed a scream of pain at Evan's mouth. He refused to voice it, biting his lips instead.

"Better confess what you've done before it's too late," said Pascoe calmly.

Evan took a deep, raspy breath, watching the bastard's boots so close yet out of reach. "Back at Fairfield Park you made me believe you had all the evidence you need…"

The cane poked at his collarbone and trailed up his bare neck, pushing against the side of his Adam's apple, as if about to pierce Evan's neck and bleed him out.

"I know what kind of man you are, Penhart," said Pascoe almost fervently, leaning over him with a vicious snarl. "A sodomite. Rotten since his younger years. I still remember the utter disgust I felt when I found you with that whore of yours all those years ago. It is not far-fetched to suspect you capable of other vices."

Evan looked up at him, hot with the loathing bubbling up inside him and ready to spill out through his mouth. "Have you ever tried buggery? With your wife, I mean? She might enjoy it."

The sudden punch in the face threw Evan back at the wall, rattling his brains inside the skull. Who would have thought there was so much strength in that withered body? "Do not speak of my wife like this. She's a respectable woman."

Evan tried to speak, but the first word turned into a broken yell when Evan sensed a sudden pressure to his cock and balls. He closed his thighs but Pascoe's boot was already there, twisting against the tender flesh.

"We should give people like you a chance. Castration could turn you into honest men. You'd be like geldings—with no desire to chase tails," Pascoe said slowly, watching Evan squirm on the floor.

No matter how much Evan hated Pascoe, his own helplessness and the fear those words induced made him grow hot and cold at the same time. He bit into his lips before more cursing could fall out of them.

The swish of the cane came next, and he twisted away, rolling toward the wall once Pascoe's boot was gone from between his legs.

"I know who you are, you deviant beast. It is people like you who pull this country into the abyss. You will burn. Satan will be buggering you with burning irons for all eternity," hissed Pascoe.

Evan heaved, his body aflame with pain. At least Julian would be spared this treatment. Even if Julian's heart broke once he realized Evan would never join him on the ship to Italy, Julian would find a future for himself.

"Is that what you came for? To prey on me before I get a noose around my neck?"

Pascoe's nostrils flared and he raised his cane high, laughing when Evan flinched just looking at it. "You are learning, Penhart. I do not find pleasure in your pain. In fact, I am here to offer you something of value."

Evan glared at Pascoe with suspicion. What could this mockery possibly be?

"Salvation?"

Pascoe smirked. "No, I cannot give you that, but mercy? That I can. Penhart is an ancient name, and I would hate to see it more tarnished than it already has been."

Evan got back to his knees, eying Pascoe with a frown. "Is this supposed to be even more torment? Have your men not done enough?"

Pascoe leaned against the wall, just out of Evan's reach. "A man can only hang once, and as it is, I could... avoid mentioning your past again. Sir Evan Penhart would be merely a highwayman. I cannot see the possibility of the jury not holding you to blame for what you did. Mr. Miles Hughes will secure the right witnesses."

"What does it matter if I am to hang?"

Pascoe shook his head lightly. "Reece suddenly appearing at Tredele and becoming tight friends with the man who's known to be a recluse? I know what really happened. You took Reece as your catamite, which couldn't have been that hard, since he was already a known drunkard and rake. His kind will do anything for their wine, and Tredele has deep cellars, I imagine."

Evan's vision went spotty with white-hot fury. He lunged at Pascoe, but his teeth clattered an inch from the man's leg. "You know nothing about him! I wouldn't allow you to lick his boots!"

The cane fell on Evan's back, leaving a burning trail of pain.

"Oh, was he willing then? All the worse. Maybe the two of you will meet again in hell. But he was never known for this vice, so I find it believable that it was you who debauched him. It is all your fault that he could be arrested. I would examine him myself," said Pascoe slowly.

Evan shuddered with revulsion at the thought of Pascoe's dirty hands on Julian, both violating his lover and humiliating him in the very way Julian feared. Ignoring the cane that would undoubtedly fall on his back again, with sweat beading on his forehead, he threw himself at Pascoe, only for the chain around his neck to pull him back so hard that for a moment it seemed it broke his neck.

"Don't you dare!" he yelled in a frenzy of helplessness. "If you touch him, I will bloody kill you! And if you hang me, I will come back from hell to haunt you 'til the day you die, you bastard!"

Pascoe's foot flew at Evan's head and rattled his brain yet again, hitting him where hair covered the skull and bruises would not be seen. "Look at you, thrashing around like a rabid dog. The only man to blame is you. You pulled him from simple vice to crime. I know he was your partner on that highway. I'm not blind not to notice a body underneath a coat. If I had my way, he would hang alongside you, and I would have him die first, so that you could rethink your sins," whispered Pascoe, his voice echoing in the cell.

Wrath and pain melted together inside of Evan into a fire that would burn him alive. "He is innocent, and you have no way to prove otherwise," Evan said through his teeth, the metallic taste in his mouth making him dizzy.

"Is he? You seem quite adamant to protect him and defend his honor. Do you expect me to believe you are always as worried for your friends, or is this guilt?" Pascoe sighed and walked up to the window, leaving Evan hurting on the stone floor. "He is not worth your sacrifice. A man of his description was a passenger on a stagecoach heading for London. He's left you, and now that he has no one to supply his appetite for wine and expensive clothes, he is going to find a new man to provide those, I imagine."

Evan's heart ached, and he bit his lip so hard he drew blood. Could this be true? Julian didn't even try to get on the ship in Plymouth, as Evan told him to? Didn't he have the faintest hope that Evan would make it? He breathed hard through his nose, fighting back the itching under his eyelids. Maybe it was better this way. Maybe Julian was the one with the stronger mind after all and left to save himself, knowing there was nothing to be done for Evan. But no matter how desperately Evan wished to believe his own explanations, the sense of betrayal still burned his veins with every beat of his heart.

"You wouldn't be able to comprehend the kind of love I feel for him," Evan rasped without even looking up at Pascoe.

The worn boots moved over the floor, thumping against the cold stones. "And what kind is that? I have seen you. I know what kind of thing your so-called love entails," mocked Pascoe.

Evan watched the cane in Pascoe's hand, uncaring anymore how many more times it would land on his back. Julian was gone, and soon enough, Evan would hang.

"A love that transcends death, and lust that could sate hunger without eating."

Pascoe was silent for a long moment. "Have you fulfilled that lust at least?"

Evan chuckled to himself. With Julian already out of Cornwall, away from Pascoe's clutches, at least, in these last days, he would be able to make Pascoe uncomfortable. At a trial, it would have been Pascoe's word against Evan's. "Oh, so many times... When I was deep inside of him, he was the embodiment of all my cravings. And he took it so beautifully." He looked up at Pascoe with a smirk, ready to take a smack from the cane.

For a moment, Pascoe looked a little bit ill, but then, a smile tugged at the corners of his mouth. "Atkins, Davies, have you heard and noted? I am thoroughly disgusted."

Evan stilled, but curled his shoulders when the men outside laughed, and came into view, opening the door with a loud squeak. He had not heard them come. Had they been here all along? Listened to his every word?

"Aye, Mr. Pascoe. Pretty filthy if you ask me," said Davies, leaning against the wall.

Evan moved back, closer to his corner and the dead mouse, for once rendered speechless.

Pascoe took his time to savor this easy victory. "I would say that this time I do have enough witnesses while you don't have anyone to save you with bribes. I could convict you of this and make sure sometime in the future, this finally reaches Reece."

Evan swallowed the bile that rose to his throat. "No. No, no, no. He is innocent," he pleaded despite the mocking laughter of the two deputies. He shouldn't have toyed with Pascoe. He should have kept his love secret and taken it to the hangman. Why had he been so thoughtless? What would it have proved in the first place?

"Don't you backtrack, *sir*," said Atkins in a mocking tone. "We've heard all about you buried in him up to your bollocks."

Evan couldn't help the tremble in his fingers. "What do you want from me?" he whispered, deep down hoping that Pascoe had an agenda in all this, that Evan could still make things better for Julian, even if his beloved had already abandoned him.

Pascoe smirked. "I don't want you on the pillory, I don't want you transported, I want you to swing on the noose, as you should have years ago. You will not ask for any witnesses of your good character—if you could find such liars anywhere—and confess to the crimes you've committed on the highways." He straightened up, eyes shining with pleasure so obvious, it made Evan wonder who truly was the deviant man in this cell. "I do not have evidence for Reece being your accomplice. If you do as I say, I will not mention your perversion during the trial. He will be safe. Until he's caught with another man, of course, because I am sure that will be the case quite soon."

Evan looked down at Pascoe's boots, and the dirty stone floor. The humiliation was worse than any caning could have been. "I will confess," he muttered, unable to bear the thought of Julian being dragged into court because of him. He'd been the one to pull Julian into an illicit love affair, so he would take the blame.

"Is there anything else you'd like to tell us?" asked Pascoe, lovingly stroking the cane, while his men snickered, watching the scene without a word. It hit Evan that they were merely waiting for their chance at taunting him, which would surely come once their master left Evan in this lonely cell where no one could hear him scream.

Evan wanted to say many things. 'I will see you in hell', or 'You can never take away what I feel for Julian', maybe even 'I'd have hung for Peran had I been I given the chance', but these all seemed foolish when Pascoe could hurt Julian, so he kept his head low.

"No."

"Wise choice," said Pascoe, turning on his heel. "May God have mercy on your soul, Penhart."

Evan's gaze followed him all the way to the door, where he slowed down and passed the cane to Davies, whom Evan only now looked at properly. Both the deputies were rather tall and well fed, with arms that could surely lash a man until he bled all over.

Only once in his life had Evan felt so desperately helpless. On the day his father locked him in a chest, so he wouldn't be able to testify on Peran's behalf and save the man he loved. At least this time, he got the choice to do right by Julian.

The door closed, but the two men remained inside, now slowly approaching him from both sides. Evan put his forehead against the floor, as if in humility, but he was hoping it would only get his back caned.

As expected, the first stroke came down hard on his bare skin, and he couldn't help it, he screamed out in pain.

CHAPTER 26

JULIAN

The warm, fragrant air and the cloudless sky were laughing into Julian's face. For over an hour, he'd ridden to Bodmin, because he knew that was where Evan would have been taken. But after wasting all that time, his aching brain finally realized that his presence there would not matter at all. What would he have done once he arrived?—Bite his way through the thick walls of the gaol? Climb them and somehow pull Evan out through the grated windows?

He was a mindless coward who couldn't even find it in him to stand by his lover's side when it mattered. Blinders of pride had finally fallen off Julian's eyes, for the first time allowing him to see his true reflection. He'd led his life the way he wished to, without considering others. He'd done nothing to appease his father and yet expected a comfortable life from him. No wonder Father's patience finally ran out. How long could one keep a cow that wouldn't give any milk?

Crushed by that realization, Julian let Snow walk down the winding roads, empty like an expensive painted cup that had been stained on the inside and was no good to use anymore. Despite the dull ache in his chest that called out for him to follow Evan, he feared Pascoe would try to get his hands on him and use him against Evan. It was only out of gaol that Julian had the slightest chance of helping his lover's cause.

Or should he put trust in Evan's words and board a ship the way he'd been told to? Maybe Evan knew of something Julian did not?

No. No, he could not do such a thing. As far as Julian knew, Evan had no friends to speak of other than his servants, who at this point would have likely spat into Julian's face if he appeared in Tredele ever again. Blackwell did seem to have liked Evan in his own way, but Julian was certain he would not put resources into aiding a known criminal and getting further entangled in those matters.

Evan was alone in this, and Julian was the only man who could still give him a chance, but how? He had nothing. His wealthy friends had turned away from him, and those who had not would consider him guilty by association.

He pulled on the reins, stopping Snow in the middle of the road, breathing hard in the heat of the early summer. If Julian still had the influence he used to have, maybe he could have provided substantial assistance, but for this he would need his father and access to all the influential old men Father called friends.

No. He could not beg Father to aid him after so many weeks of enduring the disdainful silence on the side of Julian's entire family. Who else then?

Maybe Barnaby Rowland could be of some assistance, or... Julian remembered his mother was friends with the wife of a judge. He wanted to weep in anger and desperation alike. Everything came back to the rift in Julian's family caused by his selfish ploy to bypass the law and become financially independent. All that happened to Evan ultimately had been his fault.

But enough of the self-loathing. There had to be *some* way in which Julian could aid Evan, even if he didn't have the strength required to tear down Bodmin gaol and bury Pascoe under its rubble.

He would do whatever it took.

He urged Snow into a canter—the best he could do on those damn roads—and with the sun setting behind him, he made it to Looe in the orange light of dusk. Having just one shirt, he'd pulled it off for the ride not to sweat through it on the way, and only donned it again after a quick bath in the river close to town.

With the black jacket he'd worn last night, it was as presentable as he could be in such spartan conditions. Although without a waistcoat to keep the linen from pooling around his chest like a sack, it was hardly tolerable attire for a gentleman.

Merely weeks ago, Julian would have never shown himself this way to anyone but a whore, a servant, or a very close friend. Now there were greater reasons for shame in Julian's life for him to care about a matter so trivial.

He put on the oversized coat once he approached town and kept the hat low over his eyes for fear of being recognized and apprehended by a man sitting in Pascoe's purse. Caution led him down narrow alleys where people would be less likely to see him, glad for the darkness to obscure his features further.

Julian desperately tried to banish apprehension from his mind, calm himself with deep breaths and thoughts of this venture turning a dreadful situation for the better. Instead, his heart galloped every time a pair of eyes glided over him, but he'd made his decision and did not stop until the pale walls surrounding his family's representative garden emerged in the darkness. The house was just out of town, yet at night hardly anyone wandered the roads.

Snow was sweaty, her breath heavy from exertion, so he led her to the river just off the property and tied her to a tree by the shore, so she could freely satisfy her thirst.

Julian sighed and forced himself to face the wall again, feeling sickened by its imposing height and all it stood for. His family home was not nearly as big as Fairfield Park, but it was a modern building with sleek columns at the front façade and tall windows fitted with glass imported all the way from Italy. The representative garden was inspired by Father's stay in India, and contained palms and a conservatory housing tropical plants that were always a talking point at parties. Years ago, Father had purchased two monkeys to live in a cage outside, but both perished just months later. Their enclosure had since been converted into a romantic grotto. Julian's father was a fabulously wealthy man.

If anyone in Looe had the resources to intervene on Evan's behalf, it was him.

Knowing the butler would send him away if he arrived at the front door, Julian chose a different route. Unlike the people he employed, Father did have an emotional bond to Julian, no matter how upset he'd been with him. Surely something could be done.

Now that everything had gone to the dogs, Julian regretted the mean, demanding tone of the letters he'd sent to his family after he'd been publically rejected. No matter how much it had hurt him to be pushed away and asked not to contact his family ever again, he tried to keep up a brave face and not think about it too much. Now it all seemed like the petty reasons of a proud man, who really had not done much to be proud of.

He would not have done so for his own sake, but for Evan, Julian could grovel and beg.

He climbed the tree that grew just outside the wall surrounding Mother's rose garden and pulled himself up on one of the thick branches. Once he was up, getting on top of the wall built around the whole property was child's play. With the gardens bathed in the purple hue of dusk, he jumped in and landed behind a bush of yellow roses.

The bees were gone at this point, so he rushed between the flowers, heading for the house. He could already see the lights in the two large windows upstairs, where Father's study was located next to his bedchamber. Julian's breath caught, and he listened, making sure there was no one else in the garden to notice him and alarm the footmen. He rushed past the hedges cut to perfection around a fountain, only to slow down his pace as he approached the dark bulk of the house. He knew there was a downpipe running over the outer wall of his father's bedroom, and at this hour, with the house locked, it could be his sole way inside.

He watched the scene for a full minute, listening to any noises and looking for movement, but spotting none, he ran across the bare area between the flowerbeds and the house. Having reached the wall, he touched the lead pipe and listened, looking up along its snake-like body.

Julian was in luck, the balcony at his father's bedroom neighbored the pipe, but the second floor was far away. He took a few deep breaths and found the first pair of iron holders. He pressed on them, and they seemed solid enough, but his heart would not stop racing. Climbing the trunk of a tree could be a long and laborious process if there were no branches to hold on to, but bark was rough and grass much softer than the stone surrounding the house. Falling down from the pipe could prove disastrous for Julian.

He waited, his forehead pressed against the cool metal while he gathered courage for the steep incline. When he opened his eyes, no purple hue was to be seen in the sky. It was night, and he was left to depend on touch.

But if this could bring Julian any closer to obtaining help for Evan, it was worth the risk. He pushed the tip of his shoe on the support and lifted himself up. The iron did not give under his weight, so he searched for the next set of supports with his hand and put his other foot against it, grabbing the pipe. Forced into an uncomfortable frog-like position with one of his knees raised high enough to be level with his chest, and having to keep his feet turned inward to fit just their front part secure on the support, Julian felt far from comfortable. But he reached up and slowly climbed to the next pair of supports, freezing when the lead tube creaked under his weight. Maybe he should not hold on to the pipe itself after all?

A few moments later, Julian was heaving. Halfway to his goal, the emptiness behind him was screaming at him to call for help, have someone take him down with the aid of a ladder. But this would have ultimately ended in failing Evan, so Julian took all the time he needed before clutching yet another piece of rough metal that dug into his fingers with such ferocity he could almost smell blood already.

Once he finally reached the second floor, it became clear that his assessment of the proximity between the balustrade and the downpipe had been skewed by distance, and seeing the balcony so close, yet far enough away to suggest danger made Julian's throat ache. Clinging to the holders, he carefully separated his foot from the support it stood on and swung it to its goal but missed its mark. Time and time again, Julian found he could not put his foot on the edge and only ever brushed his toes against it.

Supporting most of his weight on bare hands and an uncomfortably twisted leg was taking its toll on Julian, and he choked on a sob, closer to honest prayer than he had ever been. The nothingness behind his back was licking his nape with its icy tongue, beckoning him into its cold arms, and out of desperation, he jumped.

His fingers missed their target and slipped down the iron balustrade of the balcony, sending a pang of sharp pain all over Julian's arm. He did not scream for the sole reason that his whole body was too focused on holding on, but when the hard, pale stone tiles underneath rushed to meet Julian, he grabbed the decorative metal bars of the balcony, which growled when his body weighed it down in a sharp tug. Julian stilled, keeping his eyes shut as his feet swung in the air, his wretched life hanging only on the strength of his arms, and that was running out fast.

He grunted, curling his legs and then stretching them out, to force himself into a swinging motion. There was only so much a man could stand using strength led by desperation, and he *would* come out of this alive and whole. Still actively avoiding the view below, Julian put his entire focus into tuning his body into a pendulum. After three swings, he raised his leg high but it couldn't quite reach the support he needed yet.

Julian's forearms cried out when the ledge of the balcony dug into his wrist from the motion, but then his heel pushed through the cast iron decoration of the balustrade. Shock made Julian stop for a few moments, the relief of relative safety so immense he could hardly breathe.

Getting on the balcony itself was a much easier feat now that he had the worst of it behind him. Once he stood on the marble floor, with the faint light from his father's study illuminating the scenery, the madness of the feat he'd just completed dawned on Julian with such force he folded in two with nausea. His fingers were so sore he could not uncurl them right away, but the shock was washed away by thoughts of Evan. The pain of having to see Pascoe smacking Evan so viciously flooded his mind, and he almost wished for more physical danger to keep his thoughts from wandering to things he could not change anymore.

It had been scorching hot all day, and the balcony door had been left open for more fresh air. Julian's feet carried him on their own through the empty bedroom. He could hardly believe that just days ago, he lived with the man he loved in an aged yet fine estate, and now he was breaking into his father's house, with not much more than the shirt on his back. There was the purse Evan left him, but Julian didn't exactly consider that his possession. It would be *theirs* once they were reunited.

He looked out into the main corridor, but when he spotted a servant replacing candles, he jumped right back into the bedroom and waited for her to leave. Wouldn't this be just like the story of the prodigal son? Wouldn't Father *have* to accept his apology if Julian put it like that, appealing to Father's sense of decency and faith in God? Julian would grovel, if necessary.

With his fingers slowly retaining their original blood flow, Julian slid into the corridor that he'd played in when he was still a little boy. A wave of memories washed over him in an aggressive tide, and he had to stop, swallowing the hurt at having been driven out of here. And worse yet, he only had himself to blame for all this misfortune.

On soft legs, he walked up to Father's study and knocked on the door, taking in a large quantity of air to calm his mind before the storm to come.

And there is was. Father's voice. "Come in."

Julian opened the door and stepped inside. His heart thrashed in his chest, and it almost felt as if it was about to box his ribs from the inside. The scent of tobacco was pungent in the small room, making Julian lose his breath slightly.

Father stared at him with a severe gaze. He looked younger without the wig, but he seemed to have lost weight in the recent months as well.

"Julian," he said and put down his quill, judging Julian from the tip of his boots to the top of his head. "You look appalling."

Julian felt a shudder of relief trail down his spine. Father hadn't ordered him out yet, which surely counted for *something*. He made himself smile, even though that was the last thing he felt like doing, and stepped toward the chestnut desk. "Those few months have made me rethink my behavior. I've suffered a lot of indignity, and it had me learn humility, Father."

"I don't remember inviting you to my house," Father said and leaned back in his chair. Yet still, he was attentive. "Now you have seen how much trouble and strife you have caused, and you dare to come back? And I am not surprised at all." Father stood up and put his palms on the desktop. "Because I hear your dear benefactor has been taken to Bodmin for highway robbery. Of course you would be looking for money. Is that right?"

Julian's face tingled, a sure sign of pallor coloring his cheeks. "Father... have you not missed me?" whimpered Julian, struck by the hateful look in his parent's eyes.

"No. Why would I? I suffered humiliation of having to expose my private affairs in public, but once it was settled, not having to deal with your greedy self was like a weight lifted off my shoulders. For once I did not have to worry about setting you straight anymore, and I could tell the whole world that we do not in fact associate with each other."

Julian's body sagged, and were he here just for his own benefit, the lash–like words would have already sent him through the door. But he was here for Evan's sake, so he swallowed his pride and the hurt that was pushing roots into his heart and kneeled in front of the desk. "Father, you need to understand... I was in bad company. Sir Evan set me straight."

Father frowned, taken aback, and seeing him listen made Julian's chest soar with hope. He'd never lowered himself this way before, and Father had to understand the meaning behind the gesture.

"Sir Evan Penhart? The man who beat Mr. Hughes into a pulp and shot a coachman? You have to be jesting."

Julian lowered his head, hunching forward on his knees. The images of the last day and night were coming back like a flood. Evan cradling him in his arms, their bodies joined in the most intense of embraces. Evan taken away in chains like a common criminal.

He could have hidden if he didn't have the burden of caring for Julian.

"Father, you need to understand. His brother left Tredele in ruin. The roof collapsed while I was there. He was just desperate to keep the legacy of his family alive. He is a good man, Father, he really is. It was but a mistake on his part. It was desperation."

Father seemed to be mulling it over, and finally said, "What is it that you want of me?"

Julian exhaled, clutching the front of his shirt. Pinned by the pale gaze, he felt small like a louse, and equally easy to crush. "He does not have friends of importance, and he needs help. The constable holds an old grudge against him and will fake evidence to have him hung. And Sir Evan does not deserve this at all. I owe him my help for all the kindness he's shown me."

Julian's heart sank when Father's eyes turned even icier, and he flinched from the pain of it. "So this is what it's about. You rejected everything this family stands for, but now you wish to profit from the association. You want to save that criminal, so he can pay your keep. Get out, Julian."

Julian's knees were heavy against the floor, but he dragged them toward Father, crawling over the plush carpet. "No, that is not true at all, Father. I know that I did you wrong, and I will make up for it. I will do whatever you wish," he whimpered, reaching out to touch Father's house shoes.

"I will not be helping that scoundrel. He will get what he deserves. Find a new friend with a purse fat enough if you still can. I washed my hands off you long ago. Out." Father took a step back, but Julian followed him, folding his hands over his heart.

"He is no such thing. He is a good man, who merely wanted to pay his servants fair wages. Father, this innocent will be put to death. How can your Christian soul take that?" he asked as panic rose within him at a rapid pace. He had no shame anymore. "I—I will marry that girl, if that's what you want. I will be useful to you."

"Do you think the world has waited for you to come to your senses? She's married. Who in their right mind would have entrusted their daughter to you after what you've done?"

Julian clenched his teeth, breathing heavily. "But I am here, and I will do as you say if you only help him. I know you have... men to do your bidding. Maybe they could intervene on your behalf?" uttered Julian breathlessly, clutching to this one chance with all he had.

Father squinted at him. "They could. But I will not ask them to. Leave, or I will have you thrown out."

But Julian wouldn't leave. He followed his father on his knees all the way to the door, in disbelief when help really was called. He heaved against the wall, his mind a spin of images that were there to torment him about all his failures. The footmen grabbed him by the arms roughly and forcefully took him out of the house, all the way to the gate, where they wordlessly pushed him outside.

Julian stared as they walked into the darkness, looking back at him as they indulged in conversation Julian could not hear, yet from the quiet laughter, he assumed he was the butt of their joke.

To think he used to be their master only months ago. Without Father's money or Evan's protection, he was no one. Worse still, he had nowhere to go and had to hide away in case Pascoe was looking for him.

Yet, were he in power to turn back time, he would have gotten into the carriage that took him to meet Evan a hundred times over. His life had been forever changed on that day.

Julian walked back to Snow, and it was as if a clock kept ticking inside his mind. He couldn't stop the seconds passing no matter how much he wanted to. Evan was trapped in Bodmin, he would be sentenced and hanged because Julian had burned all the bridges behind him, thinking he was invincible. Now he had no friends to answer his plea.

He slid his arms around the mare's neck, and she pulled on his coat with her teeth, so he squeezed her harder. If Evan died because of him, Julian would never forgive himself.

His eyes itched, but he blinked until it passed along with the choking weight in his throat. Crying was the last thing he required right now. It would bring him nothing but more sorrow, and he needed all the focus he could muster.

He searched his mind, looking for answers that just wouldn't come. There was enough worth in Evan's purse for Julian to hire henchmen who'd do his bidding, possibly break into the gaol and snatch Evan away. But he knew no one at Bodmin, so how could he put his trusts in unknown me—

And then it came to him as crystal clear as the sea on a sunny day. He had one more resource—his unsavory friends his father so despised. He had Martin, and Martin knew all the crooked people in Looe and beyond. Maybe he could help?

He mounted Snow in a hurry, and rushed her down the hill to Looe. He could only hope that Martin had swallowed his anger since his first encounter with Evan. Or that he didn't hate Evan as much as he seemed to for that matter. Martin could, of course, laugh into Julian's face and tell him that it served Evan right to hang, but as a smuggler, wouldn't he feel compassion for a fellow outlaw?

The two of them had been friends for years. Surely Julian's lack of romantic interest in Martin couldn't have made all that time void?

Julian rode Snow as fast as she was able to run, all the way to the cottage just within Looe's borders where Martin resided with no wife or other family. Now Julian knew why. He stopped outside and quickly tied Snow to an iron ring sticking out of the wall before walking for the door. There was candlelight shining through the gaps in the shutters, so Martin was definitely inside.

Julian stopped two steps away from the entrance, suddenly aware of his poor state. He hated thinking of this, but maybe he would have a bigger chance at this attempt were he as good–looking as always. He should have washed his face and hands in the river, but it was too late now, so he pulled up the tail of his shirt and rubbed his skin with the linen.

He combed his hair back with his fingers and tied it with a leather strap, then pushed the shirt carefully into his breeches to make up for the lack of waistcoat, and adjusted the coat.

Before he could knock, Martin opened the door wide, wearing only pantaloons and suspenders. He stilled at the sight of Julian.

"Ye alone, lad?"

Julian stared at Martin's firm chest, which had a long scar peeking through the hair growing at the centre, but he quickly regained his voice. "Yes."

"You can come out," Martin yelled inside, and opened the door wider.

Julian walked in, breathing in the stench of cheap tallow candles and sweat as he looked around the single room with a bed, an area for cooking, and other basic furnishings. "Are you… hiding a fugitive?" he asked, pulling the coat closer around himself before remembering that he'd come here with the intention of looking his best. He let it fall loosely around his body and uncover his shirt.

Martin snorted, looking Julian up and down when he closed the door. "Now I am. What brings ye?"

A young man with a bush of red hair came out from behind a few sheets hung in the middle of the room for dividing space. He was still pulling on his nightshirt, and flashed Julian with his ass. "Evenin'," the boy said with a silly grin, and grabbed himself a piece of bread with cheese from a plate sitting on a small table by the bed.

Julian stared between the boy and Martin, uncomfortable at having interrupted their intimacy. "I–I'm sorry. I can see it's a bad time," he said, wanting to be polite in order to have Martin more inclined to help him. That he was good at. Making friends and convincing people to aid him when it was needed. Unless it was the case of his stubborn father.

Martin shook his head. "Get some breeches, and wait outside," he said to the boy who pouted with his mouth full.

"How long?"

"It's warm. Until I tell ye to come back."

"But there's mosquitoes," the boy whined, but was already pulling on a pair of breeches.

"You'll live." Martin gently pushed him toward the door, with a slap to his ass.

Julian looked away and pulled off his coat, unable to stand its heat in a room that was so steamed-up it might as well have been a bathhouse. He put it on the backrest of a chair and unclenched his hands, stretching the stiff joints while he went through the things he intended to say.

Martin's life was none of his business, although clearly his relationship with the boy was more casual than what Julian shared with Evan, or he wouldn't have tried to win Julian's affections just last week.

"I've heard gossip..." Martin raised his eyebrows.

Julian swallowed hard but kept his gaze on Martin. "Pascoe has him," he whimpered, scowling at how weak his voice sounded.

Martin sighed deeply and leaned against the table with his arms crossed. "Risk of the trade, right?"

Julian tried to take a deep breath, but with his throat clenching, it was merely a wheeze that could not supply all the air he needed. How could Martin talk of this so casually? "He protected me. And now he's in Bodmin. Martin… you know people, I need to help him," he grabbed on to the footboard of Martin's bed.

"It's a lot yer askin', Julian." Martin pursed his lips with a frown.

Julian held on tight, shivering slightly. He was at loss. If Martin refused to help him, he'd have no other choice but to let Evan die or step forward and die with him. Both perspectives were equally unbearable. "I— I have money, I can pay the men. Oh, God, Martin, please, help me," he said in the end and rubbed his face, too terror-stricken to keep up the calm façade.

"Oy, come 'ere," Martin said in a voice so firm it had Julian's nerves screaming at a lower volume. He pulled Julian against his chest, closing him in an embrace of naked, beefy arms. Julian leaned into him, letting go of the strings that kept him whole.

He sobbed, pushing his face against Martin's neck. His whole body hurt, even his heart, and nothing would ever be good again if they couldn't save Evan from the noose. "It's all my fault. It was my idea."

Martin slowly pulled away after stroking Julian's hair a few times and went over to the other side of the table. "I was thinking it might have been you with 'im." He groaned and cut off a piece of bread.

Julian chewed on his lip, folding his arms across his chest, as if it could somehow hold him together when his body was on the verge of collapsing from stress and lack of sleep and food. His head spun, but despite the hunger, he could barely look at the bread. "It was."

"Was worried you was caught too, but I figured I'd had gotten word of it." Martin spread some butter on the thick slice of bread and covered it with cheese. "You said you've got money?"

Julian nodded, and the pouch burned him underneath the shirt, where he'd hidden it for protection. "I would be generous. I just want him out, and we will leave for Europe."

Martin watched him for a long hard moment, putting the bread on the plate for now. "The other men will ask for money, but I don't want any silver or gold. I got another thing on me mind..."

Julian stared at him, breathless as the truth behind that statement sank in, sending icy rivulets all over his body. They had been friends for years, and Martin still demanded something like this from Julian? Even after finding out of his feelings for Evan?

He glanced at the door, behind which the boy was still waiting for his place in Martin's bed, a place that Julian would be taking tonight. A sense of revulsion and betrayal sat on Julian's shoulders, making his fingers tremble when he untied the lacing at the cuff of his sleeve and pulled the tails of his shirt out of his breeches.

He could not believe Martin would do this to him. But if Julian was ready to marry for Evan, he could also spread his legs and endure serving a man he now loathed with a passion. Letting Evan have him again had been such a difficult decision, but here he was, about to let another man touch him and demand things Julian was not ready to give. His skin felt filthy already, greasy with sweat that wasn't Evan's or his.

"Oy! What ye doin'?" Martin's eyes went wide, and he walked up to Julian in two long strides. He grabbed his wrists and shook him. "I just wanted a kiss, ye dumb lad. We're friends. I don't want yer money, 'cause I help friends for nothin'. And if I'm too hideous for a kiss, then that's fine too." He groaned and shook his head.

Julian's heart exploded with relief, and he stepped forward, pulling Martin's face down by the beard until their lips met. The long hair was surprisingly soft, yet different than that on Martin's head, but the strangest sensation of all was the gentle scratching of the hair growing around Martin's mouth. Julian's head spun as he opened up to the kiss, putting all his gratitude into the caress.

Martin didn't abuse the privilege. He took his kiss, but when he was about to overstay his welcome, he backed away, stroking

Julian's neck with a sigh. "Bastard has it too good with ye." He pushed a plate with the bread toward Julian. "Now eat, and let's get some plannin' done."

Julian smiled as hunger finally hit him at full force. He sank into the chair and picked up the simple food. Evan could never know of this kiss, or he'd punch the man who was about to risk his life for Evan's. "He might be a scoundrel. But he is my scoundrel."

Chapter 27

Julian

On the day of the execution, clouds above Bodmin were thick as curdled milk. A storm was hanging in the air, making it damp and unpleasant as the spectators gathered in the streets, thirsty for blood. Julian was glad he'd made the journey from Looe the day before, because the roads were congested with carts and people coming on foot to watch the spectacle. The streets in town had never been quite so full, and with inns bursting at the seams, Julian slept at a friend of Martin's, although the word sleep was an overstatement when one spent the night tossing and turning on rags laid out on the floor.

At least the weather made it reasonable for them all to be wearing coats and hats. Martin, Daniel, and Julian mingled with the crowd on the way between the severe silhouette of the gaol and the gallows at Five Lanes, where Evan was to be hanged.

Only that he would not be. Julian had not been stingy and paid all the men Martin chose. Their plan was anything but noble, and at first, Julian needed to overcome his natural qualms. But in the end, he agreed that Evan's safety came first. And if setting a town on fire could help them accomplish that goal, Julian was ready to throw his morals to the gutter.

It was not very likely people would end up dead, as they all agreed on targeting public buildings. A fire would unleash enough chaos to delay the execution, and once almost everyone joined the efforts to control the inferno, leaving Evan with a sparse set of men on guard, Julian would make his move.

Until then, he needed to keep his head down and trust that paying handsomely for the loyalty of Martin's crew would bring about the outcome he so desperately needed.

Julian had felt ill when he watched the gallows—or the three-legged mare, as the locals called the instrument of amusement for all but its victim—being prepared this morning. Situated on the crossroads, where travellers from other towns and villages could easily reach it, the Five Lanes that averted their eyes from the daily gloom of their lives was a popular place to be.

Julian had attended two executions here in his younger years, and it had been yet another opportunity for drink and whoring, in the same way watching horse racing was. He hadn't thought too much about the fate of the executed back then, assuming justice had been done to the thief and murderer who had been hung.

But now that Evan was to be the main attraction, Julian watched the jeering crowds with what seemed like a new set of eyes. Gin and ale were sold by the gallon, and he'd seen men hiding in narrow streets for quick relief of their other needs with prostitutes, as if another man's death excited them so.

Julian had earlier forced himself to eat, as he knew he'd need focus and physical strength to execute the plan, but the meal was still heavy in his stomach when up the street leading up to the walls of the gaol, he heard the crowd shouting.

The people around Julian climbed to their toes, looking toward the bend of the road, like seagulls ready for scraps. All of the hair on his body stood up as the racket became louder, and small children in tattered clothes ran into his view, undoubtedly ahead of the cart that carried Evan.

A heavy hand squeezed Julian's shoulder. "Stay calm," Martin whispered, when the cart with Evan came into view.

Evan stood in the wobbly cart with his hands tied behind his back, barely managing to stay upright. Holding his face low, he couldn't possibly see that he was not alone anymore. That Julian was here and would find a way to save him, no matter the cost.

Julian had overheard earlier that the chaplain who had kept Evan company throughout the last weeks did not consider his charge repentful and refused to accompany Evan to the gallows. With no relatives or friends to say farewell, the execution itself would be a short one, were it to take place. Evan's loneliness in what he must consider his last moments made Julian unbearably sad.

There were yellow and blue bruises on his face, and the front of his shirt was already stained by something that looked like eggs, but he stayed calm, only the muscles by his jaw working as the crowd of good men and women turned into a tumble of beasts. He was deaf to all the obscenities and stood with as much pride as was still allowed him in the single horse cart of raw wood and with three men armed with pikes standing guard around the vehicle.

Julian bit the inside of his cheek until a salty, metallic taste spread in his mouth, but Martin's arm kept him in place, even though his hand was on the pistol hidden underneath the coat.

A noose was already placed around Evan's neck like a promise to the mob, and despite it still being loose, the sight made Julian's heart tear at the seams.

When Evan drove by, Julian saw his back and clenched his fists so hard his nails bit into his palms. The whole back of Evan's shirt was dark brown with old blood and red with fresh.

"Is it true he escaped the law before?" mumbled Daniel from behind Julian.

Julian's teeth clenched and were he not intent on following the cart, he'd tell the bastard his mind. Martin groaned, his hand still on Julian, as if he were afraid Julian wouldn't have the self-control to wait for their accomplices to go through with the next part of their plan.

"Did he?" Martin asked as the three of them snuck along the road, keeping close to the buildings.

Daniel snorted. "He did. Heard he 'ad his faathur's footman bugger him, but yew know 'ow it is with important men. Only the servant got what he deserved."

Martin scowled. "Shut your face. What does it matter now? You got paid or not?"

Daniel made a nondescript noise, but his comments only made the groove in Julian's heart deeper. He pushed two loud women apart and rushed behind the cart, intent to outrun it and show himself to Evan.

Guilt was like puss underneath his skin, making it tender and likely to break. Evan hadn't had any protection in gaol. He looked starved and pale. Julian had wanted to go to see him, or at least send someone with nourishing food for him, but Martin advised against it, to not raise suspicion that Evan in fact still had friends. Julian had grudgingly accepted that explanation, but seeing Evan like this made him realize how utterly alone his lover must have felt for the last weeks, locked up at Pascoe's mercy.

Julian wondered if Pascoe had tortured Evan, because men present at the trial claimed he'd admitted to his crime with no fight at all, which was so unlike Evan it twisted Julian's gut.

No matter how quickly Julian pushed through the masses of people, Evan wouldn't lift his gaze to the crowd, so it was a lost cause. And with the mob screaming obscenities, Julian didn't believe he could get Evan's attention by yelling.

He flinched when his lover was hit by scraps of food. It felt as if they had been aimed at Julian. He pushed his way to the wall, where there was a bit more space and rushed as fast as he could, to reach the gallows before Evan's arrival. If he was to execute his part in the plan once his new henchmen provided necessary distraction to the men of justice, he needed to be close.

They had a man with horses waiting just off the Five Ways, so if all went well, he and Evan could disappear very soon. With the town burning no one would be able to chase them until the crisis was resolved.

Julian was not proud of what he was about to be a part of. He did not want the good people of Bodmin to lose their homes and possessions, but with Evan's life on the line, he was ready to sacrifice them, as he had been ready to give up on his pride and the dreams he'd chased most of his life. It didn't make him a good man, but he'd stopped caring about that a long time ago. The people who dared throw rocks and rotten vegetables at Evan, the keepers who tormented him and hurt him inside the gaol—they all deserved to have their homes burn to the ground.

The closer he was to Evan, the thicker was the crowd, and one woman elbowed him in the stomach when he made an attempt to get ahead of her. He squeezed past her crying child instead. There was no time to lose, and the sight of that noose around Evan's neck was making Julian sicker than the stench of drunkards, rot, and sweaty bodies combined.

Close to the three legs of the gibbet stood several carriages, the wealthy and influential watching the proceedings apart from the poor after paying a handsome sum for the privilege. Men were gathered in groups and engaged in lively conversation, their eyes already set on the road from the gaol, but ladies were present as well, and Julian's stomach twisted when he noticed the fair face of Elizabeth Blackwell in one of the carriages. That she was more glad to watch Evan's demise than give him her hand in marriage was like a personal affront to Julian, and while he believed the young woman to be somewhat dim-witted, he'd never thought her this cruel.

Miles Hughes was present as well, already healed from the encounter with Julian and Evan, but now that he was waiting to watch the death of the man who humiliated and robbed him, there was no trace of shame left under the expensive clothes and powdered wig. He was waiting for the spectacle with his friends, face red from the fine wine they were all drinking. They were taking bets too. How long would Evan take to die perhaps?

Julian's throat constricted in raw, helpless anger, but he stood in the crowd, as close as he could without making his presence known to those who could recognize him. He was ready. All he needed was a sign.

As soon as one man left a spot in the crowd to get more ale, Julian was there to take his place and stand that one step closer to the gibbet. The fire would burn. People would panic. Julian would run up to steal Evan away, and they would ride all the way to the cove where Martin hid a boat for their use.

There was no room for mistakes, so why was there still no smoke?

A hand closed on Julian's shoulder, and he spun around, prepared to fight, but only found Martin's determined gaze to challenge him. "I... it's you," he uttered, trying not to attract attention, but with the people around him so drunk and cheerful, he was likely to remain anonymous.

"Ye could 'ave lost me. Don't ever do that. You need me following, so no one stops you and him when the time is right," Martin whispered into Julian's ear, but despite having much more experience in these matters, he seemed tense as well.

Julian didn't need to look back to know the cart with Evan was coming. Noise rose, the sweaty bodies rolled like pilchards in a barrel, and when he glanced toward the gaol, he saw Evan's lonely figure fighting to stay upright with his hands tied back. It pained him to see his lover so helpless. Since they'd met, Evan had always been a man of action, someone who knew what to do, and who Julian could depend on. But he was as human as any other man walking this earth, and with neither wealth nor friends, he had as much chance to be sentenced to death as any other highwayman.

A tall horse walked ahead of the cart, and Julian's blood froze when he recognized its rider as Pascoe. He was relaxed and sported a modest smile when he approached the wealthy gentlemen in their carriages. Hughes greeted him in a tubal voice, raising a glass of wine in celebration when others patted Pascoe on the back as soon as he dismounted.

It was sickening to see him so celebrated, and Julian knew he would never scrub this kind of dirt off him unless he tore his flesh all the way to the bone. Pascoe's and Hughes's flesh for that matter. All of them looked so smug over a man a thousand times better than them about to be executed. He'd spit in their faces were he close enough.

Martin's hand once again clenched around Julian's arm when the cart stopped under the wooden construction that could take Evan's life and the magistrate started reading out a statement about Evan's crimes. The crowd jeered, sending obscene comments in the air, and Julian's heart beat so hard he was afraid he'd faint. When he glanced at Martin, the fear began choking him as well. Martin didn't even know he was being watched, too concerned with the town left behind their backs.

Something was wrong. There was still no smoke coming. What could possibly be taking so long?

Helpless, Julian looked back toward the gallows, at the small cart and Evan on top of it, standing silently, as if he'd already made peace with what was about to happen. The hangman held the other end of the rope as he climbed the ladder, to put it over the thick beam that reputedly could hold the weight of eight men at a time.

Evan looked up into the crowd in silent challenge, his eyes expressionless when the magistrate approached on horseback and raised his hands to silence the mob, without much success.

Julian couldn't bear the wait and managed to pull out of Martin's grip, past a voluptuous woman, and that one step closer to Evan. He wanted to tell him it would be all right so badly he'd offer up his finger for the opportunity. What if the fire came too late? The hangman was about to fasten the rope to the beam. If the horse pulling Evan's cart got scared by fire, and, *oh, God,* it surely would, Evan would hang regardless of the magistrate's orders.

Julian stared at that beloved face, and it was as if he'd pulled Evan's gaze his way with sheer willpower. When their eyes met, life lit up on Evan's face. He straightened his shoulders, and smiled widely as a man about to see his babe for the first time, deaf to the cacophony of jeers and hisses followed by more rotten vegetables thrown his way. He flinched only briefly when a tomato assaulted the side of his head, spraying juice all over, but his gaze never left Julian's. It was as if Julian's sole presence here made death somehow agreeable for Evan.

For a moment, it was just the two of them, the crowd nonexistent, the noise they made insignificant in the face of such utter relief. Now that the connection had been made, Julian remembered all the times his skin itched for Evan's touch, his warm embrace at night, words that were so sparse yet pulled on the very cords of Julian's core. His life before Evan was an insignificant procession of images, and out of those he could still only remember the few that happened when he was sober. He was here to snatch his life back, to have his lover at his side again.

Where were the damn fires?

His eyes itched when the hangman started winding the rope around the beam above Evan's head, the horse nervously moving its legs surrounded by such aggressive crowds and the guardsmen. Julian mouthed, *I'm taking you,* but he had no way of knowing if Evan understood it from the movement of his lips.

The magistrate turned to Evan once he was done reading. "Does the prisoner have any last words?"

Even the rowdy crowd quieted down this time, their ears greedy for tomorrow's gossip. To Julian's relief, the hangman stopped winding the rope, too interested in the highwayman's words to hurry. He believed he had all the time in the world, after all.

Evan took a deep breath, and somehow even in the dirty linen shirt, with his face bruised and matted hair, he appeared authoritative, magnificent in his noble posture, "I once had a canary, and I caged it, which is one of my deepest regrets. When I finally let it free, it sang more beautifully than it ever had in captivity. And when I let it live in my garden, my lovely bird flew right back in through the window. I loved it then even more than before, because at last I knew it enjoyed my company. I have nothing left now, but I hope my songbird lives a good life on the seeds I left for it. There has never been a bird I loved more."

Evan's words echoed in Julian's ears, filling him with liquid gold, warm and soothing yet hard, a power that was now streaming through his limbs and making them steady. Tears blurred his eyes, but he blinked them away, watching Evan with fearful adoration. He might have been tortured and humiliated, but he was still as strong and proud as he'd always been. Maybe even more.

Up above, the hangman started making a loop with the rope, and when the horse threw its neck back and forth, eyes wide with stress, Julian pushed the man before him into the arms of the nearest guardsman, baring his sword as he rushed at the cart, jumping in from the open back before any of the three pikes could lick him.

"No!" Evan yelled, his eyes wide, but that did not stop Julian from cutting the noose. The risk of the horse getting startled and hauling the cart from beneath Evan's feet any second was too much.

The spectators only now woke up from the stupor after Evan's baffling words, and the magistrate stared at Julian with a scowl. "Apprehend this man!" he yelled, and there were more guards moving their way in an instant.

Julian raised his gun, in time to make the guardsmen step away. He pushed Evan toward the horse, his mind in a frenzy, lungs hurting as he squeezed his hands on the two weapons he had, alone against hundreds of spectators.

In that moment, he realized this would be their end.

And then, a loud ringing came from the town, and all the heads turned toward it. Shouts erupted all around as the shocked spectators fell on one another, some still watching the gallows, some already turning their attention to the thick smoke over Bodmin.

"Fire! Fire!"

Evan looked back at Julian, but then kneeled in the cart and pushed his head at the hindquarters of the horse with such ferocity it seemed he'd break his neck from the feat. The beast bucked and threw itself forward. Its handler leaped back in panic, but that was the extent of what Julian saw before the sudden movement of the shaking cart threw him to the wooden floor.

"You daft man! Run! Now!" Evan yelled at him despite the horse carrying them aimlessly into the crowd of wealthy men and women.

Julian sucked in a breath of cool air, arms stiff when he got to his knees, just in time to punch the face that appeared at the side of the cart. He forgot he was still holding the sword and hit the man's teeth with the hilt, but that was merely a detail in the chaotic reality that Julian now needed to master.

"With you!" he screamed, looking up, past the horse, which charged straight at Hughes and his friends. A wealthy lady Julian did not recognize stepped on her long gown and fell into the dirt, rolling away like a street runt to avoid the hoofs and wheels.

"You're mad!" Evan yelled, but looked out of the cart. Julian knew the expression Evan now carried. Sharp and calculating the odds, already wondering how to make them better.

A cry of pain and another tore through the air when the horse trampled someone, a deed made even more irreversible by the cart's wheels bumping over the body. The mob was no better than the panic-stricken gelding though, running disorderly like ants when their nest was being smoked, looking for their family and friends, as the smell of burnt wood and tar was becoming thick in the air. The highwayman could go to hell for all they cared when it was their possessions that were in danger.

Julian struggled to keep his balance on the uneven ground, but he stood up, stiff with determination when several men on horseback went in pursuit, one of them coming close from the side, teeth tight with determination as he stretched his arm out to grab the reins of the cart horse. Julian pulled the trigger, but the bullet missed its mark, and he cursed loudly, throwing the pistol the man's way. This time, he hit his mark, and the guard fell off his mount like a log.

Julian ducked when a guard in mud-soiled clothes swung a sword at them, but a crack of wood under his feet promised nothing good. The gelding screamed, and the floor rocked, then rapidly rose on one side, turning Julian's world around. The cart tipped to the side, and they both rolled out of it like dice out of a cup.

Julian fell into the mud, cold wetness soaking through his clothes as if it were blood, but he would not give up. There was still a chance. He needed to save Evan. He stood up, sword in hand, determined to protect his lover until Martin—

Something punched the back of his head so hard it felt as if the contents of his skull transferred the power behind the strike to his eyes, squeezing them uncomfortably as Julian's whole head radiated with pain. He fell to his knees, confused by the dull pulsing at its back, but was already struggling back to his feet when he saw a pair of hessians approach, at a pace that should not be attainable by humans.

He looked up, but all he saw was a fist that knocked him right back into the mud. He fell, head and arms sucked in by the wet ground when the bright silhouette of a man loomed over him. He pushed down on Julian's chest and slammed the enormous fist down to his face. Something cracked, and Julian started to choke, reaching up to protect himself but too dizzy to grab his opponent properly.

Evan screamed out in fury, and still on his knees, sank his teeth into the man's thigh so hard Julian's foe momentarily lost his balance. The bastard thought nothing of his new opponent still being bound at the hands and dedicated all his attention to Evan. He struck Evan on the head over and over, swearing despicably, but Evan would not let go, growling like a rabid dog when blood went down the man's breeches in rivulets.

Julian blinked, coughing up blood, but when he tried to drag his body up to help Evan, something thumped next to him, and he was unceremoniously rolled over, facedown into the mud. Rough hands pulled his arms back, and then came the rope, looped around his wrists so tightly he winced, turning his face to the side for a breath of air. The man behind him hauled him to his feet without any care for his comfort.

The taste of blood mixed with smoke that was already biting into his eyes, but it was the intense feeling of failure that tinted all of Julian's senses. Evan did not even have to be tied up, since his hands were still bound.

Julian had acted too fast, yet he didn't know if he could have allowed himself to wait. None of it mattered now, because the town was burning, and both of them were apprehended anyway. All the plans, the dreams of a future together, and hope for everything working out in the end—burned to ashes

They were both hauled away, but Evan still found a moment to bump his forehead against Julian's temple gently, like a cat happy to see its master.

CHAPTER 28

EVAN

The guardsman who hauled Julian all the way from the gallows did not spare him any insults or injury. Still soiled from falling into the mud after Julian pushed a man at him, he seemed to see his treatment of Julian as merely a prelude to a more suitable revenge, as the other guardsman forbade his companion from using his pistol in the chaos.

Evan's head was spinning from the abuse inflicted on him by the time they reached a large building of gray stone, which used to serve as a gaol before the new one had been build. Today it seemed desolate, and once the guardsman kicked its door open and pushed Evan inside, dust became a scraping presence at the back of Evan's throat.

With the fire spreading due to the wind, there was no time to spare to take Evan and Julian to the gaol all the way uphill, so the old lock-up would have to do, until the immediate danger to the whole community had been dealt with. With the noose still heavy around Evan's neck, he could not bring himself to care about a danger as abstract as the fire that was still too far away to touch him.

The building reeked of rotting wood and mold from not being aired frequently enough, with beams taking up most of the space below the roof. He did not get to see much, as he was pushed down the steep stairs so abruptly that for a moment he feared he'd fall. But Evan followed all orders and did not struggle, wary of the knife held against Julian's throat.

The old lock-ups were still there, illuminated by air busy with floating dust, though the stench of excrement and dirty flesh had been replaced by the odor of ink and old paper since the last prisoner had been held here.

A large key stuck out from one of the locks, and it creaked loudly when one of the guardsmen opened it and pushed Julian into the cage of moldy stone and iron. Inside, there was not even enough space to fit in a good-sized bed.

Julian stumbled, and fell to his knees fell to the wooden floor with a dull thud, but he quickly rolled to his ass, looking up, eyes clear above the swollen nose and the bloodbath that was his lips.

Evan managed to stay on his feet when he too was hauled inside, but the door locked behind them with an air of finality.

"Setting fires to the homes of honest people to save a convict? We will all enjoy pecking at your flesh, piece by piece," hissed the guard, spitting to the floor, his hands clenching on the bars as if he believed his touch could melt them and bury the two prisoners alive. He took the key with him and tossed it on the table, somewhere between piles of papers and old books before leading the way up the stairs. "Once we are done, you will both be begging for the noose."

The other guardsman stopped at the landing of the stairs, looking as if he wished he could cook them both in boiling oil, but when his companion urged him with hurried words, he rushed upstairs and closed the door with a loud thud.

Evan leaned against the wall with his shoulder and took a deep breath, still in disbelief over what had happened at the gallows. "Untie me, and I'll do yours," he said to Julian in a voice weaker than he expected it to be. His mind was a disorderly mass of joy and depths of sorrow over Julian being here with him. His body ached, he couldn't believe he was still alive, but it was the realization that Julian hadn't left him that occupied his mind most even though he knew he should be thinking of a way out of the lock-up instead.

Julian gasped, some of the bloody spit bubbling up around his nose, but he crawled to the wall and used it as leverage to pull himself up. He watched Evan with something akin to wonder when he stepped forward and buried his face in Evan's dirty old linen. His arms trembled, but he pushed on, hugging Evan without embracing him.

Evan sighed and put his chin on Julian's head. "They told me you left for London," he whispered, fighting the tremble in his voice and overwhelmed by the closeness of his beloved man. Since capture, he'd endured torment for the sake of Julian's safety, but he'd thought that despite his sacrifice, he would die alone, without a single friendly soul to console him. Oh, how wrong he had been.

Julian raised his head, shuddering. "What? No... I... organized people. I did my best. But I failed. I'm sorry..." He finished on a choked whimper and shook his head.

"You shouldn't have come." Evan kissed the side of Julian's face with his dry lips. "I made a bargain with Pascoe so that you could be safe. Untie me. We need to think while there is still fire." He turned around, painfully aware that the back of his shirt revealed the story of his torture.

Julian's breath was loud behind him, but he finally turned around as well, and his warm fingers tugged on the rope around Evan's wrists. "What did they do? You're still bleeding?"

"I was... lashed. It's just skin." The last thing he needed now was Julian worrying about him too much. "That sick bastard, Pascoe, baited me about you. I lost my nerve. I should have been quiet, but I'd been made to believe he and I we were alone. He brought people with him who could be potential witnesses to what I said, in case Pascoe wanted to pursue you. I didn't want my words to pull you down with me." As soon as Julian had untied his wrists, Evan turned around and hugged him tightly. He swallowed when Julian filled his arms in such a familiar way. "I wish to say you've been stupid to have come back, but I am so happy to see you. I was sure I would never kiss you again. They made me believe you left me to rot." Evan shut his eyes tight not to cry. Julian was the essence of his life, and knowing that he'd been there for him these past weeks made the suffering Evan had to endure somehow more bearable.

Julian flinched. "No. I have not. I would never. Why would you believe their lies?" he demanded, pushing himself deeper into Evan's arms, uncaring that his hands remained tied.

"I never truly believed them, but Pascoe has a way of punching a man's heart without ever touching him. Not that he didn't. His cruelty reached me in both ways." Evan pulled away and started untying Julian quickly. "Please tell me about your reckless plan." He groaned as his shirt rubbed against a raw wound on his back.

Julian hissed as soon as Evan freed his hands, and he shook them, scowling with pain when blood trickled back into his pale fingers. "I wanted to see you all this time, but Martin said we should surprise them. I'm sorry I left you alone with this," he said, watching Evan for a few moments before reaching out for him, as if he were afraid a simple touch could hurt Evan somehow. "I'm sorry you had to go through this. I shouldn't have hidden back at Fairfield Park. I'm a coward," he muttered with pain twisting his pretty face when he finally touched Evan's chest.

"A coward would have left for London. You're here with me. I think you have just proven you are recklessly brave. If not stupid." Evan smiled slightly and kissed Julian's bloodied lips.

The slim body sagged against him, and Julian cupped Evan's face. He was trembling from head to toe as he dove deeper into the hug. "I would have never left you," said Julian softly when he finally pulled back, keeping his forehead against Evan's. "Y–you're worth dying for. You're worth more than any other man."

Evan sighed, and closed his arms around Julian, all too painfully aware that he would soon need to let go. Who was he to deny Julian the protective feelings that he himself had for his lover? "You shouldn't have come, sweetie. But I know you're too stubborn to be convinced. You said Martin is behind the fire? Behind trying to save me? Doesn't the man hate my guts?"

Julian looked away briefly. "He's my friend first and foremost. He found men to help us, and I paid them from what Blackwell gave you. But they ran late with starting the fire, and I couldn't risk you. I lost my nerve. It was all in vain, and now we both—" His breath caught, and he glanced at the dirty floor. "We're done. We will die, won't we?" he asked in a voice so quiet Evan could barely hear him.

Evan took a wheezing breath at the thought of his beloved Julian slowly dying on the noose, a spectacle for the mob to see. "We will find a way," Evan said sternly, even though his mind was frantic. He needed to make Julian feel safe, or at least hopeful for as long as was possible. He pulled away to clean Julian's face off blood with the front of his shirt.

Julian flinched at the touch to his nose but closed his eyes and pulled on Evan's shirt. "No, we will not. It's over. Pascoe will hurt you again, and now he knows of us. He knows, doesn't he?" whimpered Julian, glancing at Evan with hazy eyes.

Evan nodded with a deep sigh, still angry that his own pride had led him to an outburst against Pascoe when he should have stayed quiet to do the least amount of damage. The image of Pascoe's cane against Julian's flesh was making Evan sick already. Julian was gentle. He couldn't handle the things that would be unleashed upon him now. He was young, stupidly brave, and scared. "I thought you were gone. I thought it wouldn't hurt you."

Julian clenched his jaw and nodded. It took him the longest moment to speak again as his face expressed the whole variety of emotion, each immediately passing into the other. "What will they do to me? Will they keep us apart?"

"If they take us back to the gaol, I believe they might." Evan's stomach twisted uncomfortably at all the ways in which Julian could be harmed in one of the cells in a distant part of the gaol. And he would not be able to do a thing about it. "Julian," Evan cupped Julian's cheeks and looked into his eyes, "I will find a way to keep you safe. I would do anything for you." No matter how empty the promise was, if they were to be shackled and taken away, the need to reassure Julian was stronger than the wish to share the burden of truth. Julian needed hope, especially now, when his eyes were glossing over.

"Can I help you? With your back?" asked Julian, suddenly changing the topic, even though he still held on to Evan's shirt, as if only an ax could sever them from one another.

"No, better not look at it. It needs to be washed, and there's no water here." Evan stroked Julian's face, yet again disbelieving that he'd come to Evan's rescue, that he hadn't left, that Pascoe had no idea about the depth of their love for each other.

Julian took a deep breath, his eyes keeping Evan in place with their complete devotion. "Please. Show me."

Evan sighed and kissed Julian's forehead before turning around, so that his back faced the small window. "It's not as bad as it looks," he said to reassure Julian. Evan did not have to see a mirror to know his back was a mess of bruises, cuts, and dried blood.

There was a moment of stillness before the fabric, stiff from the fluids that had soaked into it, moved against his skin. Julian seemed hesitant, but in the end, he raised the shirt, and the cool air teased Evan's back.

Julian's breathing became erratic as he brushed his very fingertips over the sore lines.

"See? It's nothing that bad," Evan said, not believing his own words. The need to keep Julian safe from such harm was becoming a throbbing presence under his skin that he could not get rid of.

Julian pulled on Evan's shirt gently, slowly molding himself against Evan's skin, his warm breath ghosting over the fresh scars. "I'm sorry. You must be in pain."

"I'd be in pain unimaginable if you got shot back there." Evan turned around to end the morbid spectacle that was his back. "I won't let that happen to you. Do you understand? I won't let you suffer." And if Julian's sentence for setting the town on fire to aid a convict were too cruel to bear, Evan would find a way to end

Julian's life sooner. To somehow take him in his arms, and only then end his suffering. With no pain, when Julian felt safe and joyful. Thinking about such horrors made Evan nauseated, yet if it needed to be done, he would do it.

Julian looked away, his nostrils flaring, yet another sign of distress on his handsome face. "How can you protect me? You are the strongest man I know, but there is so many of them." Julian's gaze trailed over Evan's face, finally meeting his eyes again. "I know what will happen to me. To us. And I don't regret coming for you, but... I confess I am scared," he whimpered.

Julian's words cut through Evan's heart like a flaying knife. "I *will* find a way." The ability to comfort Julian was all he had, but his senses became more alert the moment he heard the door to the old gaol open upstairs. Would they be parted, or taken to Bodmin gaol together?

Julian pushed into his arms, his fingers scraping at the still–fresh wounds through the linen. "Oh, God, Evan," he whispered, holding on as if intent not to let go at all cost.

"We can't be seen like this." Evan pulled out of Julian's grasp, no matter how much he wanted to stay in it despite the pain in his back. Being moved while the city was still in a state of chaos could be their one last chance at escape.

Julian pulled back his hands, unclawing them carefully as footsteps knocked against the wooden floor above. Evan swallowed, listening on. It did not sound like the heavy weight of a guardsman thumping against the floor. Had a thief taken his chance in the turmoil of the fire?

Julian stepped back when another pair of footsteps followed, one clearly resonating from the narrow staircase nearby.

Evan cocked his head at the sight emerging before him in the dusty, damp cellar. Crisp blue taffeta swept over the stairs. For a second, Evan could not comprehend what he was looking at, but when Elizabeth Blackwell looked into his eyes with a hungry, wide–eyed gaze, he knew this was the opportunity he'd been waiting for. The chit's stepmother followed inside in a hurry, but looked back to the stairs every now and then. She must have indulged Elizabeth's fancy despite knowing they should not be here.

Julian gasped silently when the ladies approached, both gathering their lush skirts not to drag them over the dust and grime. Elizabeth halted two steps away from the iron doors, just out of Evan's reach, were he to attempt a touch.

"Mrs. Blackwell. Miss Blackwell. These are not the circumstances in which I expected to see you again," Julian said with a rasp to his voice, and despite the swelling around his nose and the red streaks still present around his mouth and chin, he gave his finest bow.

Evan leaned against the bars, watching for opportunities and frantically pondering how to use the situation to his advantage.

"Was it you all along, Sir Evan? You were the highwayman?" Elizabeth choked out, barely breathing, and with her eyes glistening with attention.

She wanted a story worthy of her favorite novels, and Evan would give it to her.

He nodded. "There is no way to hide that now. But I would have never stolen from a lady."

Elizabeth took a deep breath, her bosom, uncovered in the July heat, moved inside the deep neckline of her dress like two trapped bunnies. She chewed on her lip and spread her fan, using it to chase away the dusty air. "How come no one knew your true heart?"

Mrs. Blackwell folded her arms underneath her breasts and watched them in silence, pristine like a statue with heavily powdered hair and the white muslin that enveloped her form.

"I planned to reveal it to the one I marry," Evan said with a soft sigh, captivating Elizabeth's eyes, and she wouldn't even blink to cut that connection. Her breasts moved in rapid waves now, cheeks rosy with excitement.

"Oh, Sir Evan. That is most romantic. Would you have taken your beloved wife with you, so that she too could have had a taste of adventure?"

Mrs. Blackwell sighed, and her eyes softened as well, tension leaving her shoulders. "I am sorry to see you like this, Sir Evan. If only we'd known sooner how desperate you were..."

"All is not lost," Evan said with his heart drumming faster in his chest. He reached out for Elizabeth's hand. "If you ladies have taste for adventure, today you could become part of a legend."

Elizabeth's eyes widened, and she stepped closer but Mrs. Blackwell rapidly pulled her back. "What would your father say?" she hissed, shaking her head. "You had your chance, but you cannot marry a convicted man."

Julian exhaled and joined Evan by the bars. "He was happy to see you both by the gallows. Two angels to bid him farewell. Faith and the affections of a beautiful woman is all a man needs in life, even more so in the face of imminent death."

Mrs. Blackwell frowned, but it did not make her serene features any less stunning. "We came against my husband's wishes. He would not like for us to see such a brutal spectacle, but we both felt we could not let Sir Evan die alone. It was the Christian thing to do in those circumstances."

Evan was still holding out his hand, hoping that the conversation would make the ladies feel more at ease. It was rude to request someone's touch this way outside of the ballroom, but he did not have any more honor to lose "I was happy to see you. I reckoned that at least in my last moments, you would see the true me, which I could have never expressed. I hope you will enjoy Tredele, as it is the heritage of it that inspired me to dreadful crime, not greed or a thirst for blood. An honorable man cannot allow the home of his ancestors to fall into such disrepair. I was ashamed. I thought I could never make an offer of marriage to a lady when all I could offer her was a desolate estate like Tredele. One can not live on love alone."

Mrs. Blackwell opened her lips and walked up to the bars, reaching inside and closing her warm fingers over Evan's palm. "And yet you acted so honorably and confessed to your crimes instead of spitting lies like a coward. You don't know how much your plight moves me and Elizabeth. It's a disgrace what that dreadful man Pascoe did to you."

Evan weighed his choices. Would he terrify them by showing his back, or would the horror move their compassionate hearts? He swallowed. "I was sentenced to hang, but that wasn't enough for John Pascoe. For the two weeks in Bodmin, he tortured me every day. Please, lift my shirt, Julian." He turned around, fearful that this could prove a misstep, but the gamble was worth it.

Elizabeth gave a sharp gasp, but Mrs. Blackwell did not move to cover her stepdaughter's eyes. Julian shook his head when he walked up to Evan, hands picking up the tails of his shirt, as if it were a curtain at a circus. Evan did not mind in the slightest. This was theatre meant to get them out of here.

"It is a personal vendetta, if you ask for my thoughts," said Julian, slowly raising the shirt, but whimpers came from behind the bars as soon as the first scars appeared. "Sir Evan told me once that they had loved the same woman. She married a man from London in the end, as her family wanted her to, but her affections stayed with Sir Evan. Pascoe was humiliated when she refused him a dance at the assembly rooms once after dancing with Sir Evan. Mr. Pascoe was on the lookout for any misstep in Sir Evan's conduct since, always accusing him of the worst things imaginable."

Mrs. Blackwell took a deep breath. "How despicable. That man has no honor."

Evan figured the show on his back was enough, and when Julian let go of the shirt, he turned around to find tears streaking down Elizabeth's face.

"I cannot imagine the suffering that man inflicted on you, sir," she said between one sob and another. This time, when she approached the bars, Mrs. Blackwell did not stop her.

Evan swallowed and squeezed her trembling fingers. "I would not ask this if I didn't see that you truly understood the dire nature of my situation, but would you help us, given the opportunity? Would you be willing to step that inch away from the guidance of the law, were it to help a friend?"

Elizabeth's cheeks darkened when she pushed closer to the bars, her lips opened slightly as she took every breath in a gasp, watching Evan like a long-lost lover. "Will you tell your bandit friends all about me if we do?"

"Elizabeth," muttered Mrs. Blackwell sharply, but she didn't seem as outraged as she should be, all things considered. Maybe she too was merely waiting for an opportunity to excuse providing help to criminals?

"Mrs. Blackwell. We hate to put you in this position, but our lives are in fact in your lovely white hands," said Julian softly.

Evan gave Elizabeth a cocky smile and squeezed her hand in a way that quickened her breathing even further. "I will only tell those I know to be honorable men."

Elizabeth wiped away another tear. "But what can we possibly do? We have no influence on the judge... maybe Father has?" She looked back at her stepmother, but Mrs. Blackwell shook her head slowly.

"He had a fondness for you, Sir Evan, but not after what has happened," she said in a trembling voice, as if she was ashamed to bear this bad news. "My husband is a good man. However, he never strays from what he believes is a just path. Sometimes, our opinions on the matter differ," she said, capturing Evan's gaze.

Evan exhaled slowly. If he understood her correctly, they might in fact leave Bodmin as free men, even if as fugitives. "If you only have the courage in you and throw away propriety for but a few hours, you could help us much more than even Mr. Blackwell." He swallowed, watching the tense faces in front of him. "You came here by carriage, did you not? Our jailors ran off to help put out the fire. They left the keys on the table right behind you. If you escorted us to your carriage, we could be out of Bodmin, and out of the hands of that brute Pascoe."

"Escorted? What if someone sees us with you?" asked Mrs. Blackwell, but Elizabeth was already running for the table. Her stepmother raised her hand, as if to stop her charge, but in the end, she let her willowy arm fall and watched Elizabeth return with the old key, an expression of triumph spread on her face, eyes seeking praise.

"Our skirts are lush, Mother."

Evan smiled at her, his heart soaring. "I would have never dared propose that myself, but it seems we are much more alike, Elizabeth, than we might have imagined."

Mrs. Blackwell flushed furiously, but went silent.

Julian's body was radiating a feverish heat just inches away from Evan when Elizabeth's small hands pushed the key in place, and she twisted it in the lock forcefully.

The door was open.

Evan was so overwhelmed with this turn of events, that when he went out, he grabbed Elizabeth by the waist, picked her up, and made a twirl with her in his arms before letting her back down again. "Let us be quick. The guardsmen might come back at any moment. You have my word that we are nothing but honorable, and no harm will come to you."

Mrs. Blackwell gave a sharp nod and urged Elizabeth to the staircase before following, like a guardian of Elizabeth's virtue. Julian's fingers briefly skimmed over Evan's hand, and their eyes met, both of them drunk on this unbelievable strike of good fortune, even though they were far from safety yet.

Diving underneath Elizabeth's dress was an unbearably awkward affair, and Evan wished he didn't have to disrespect a young lady like Elizabeth this way, but she was eager to help, so he would not hesitate. The most nerve-wracking aspect of the slow pace toward the carriage with Elizabeth and Constance pretending to chat, was not seeing Julian and not knowing how he was doing.

Not being able to protect him if Julian's boot slipped out from under Constance's skirt and alarmed someone.

The air smelled of smoke even with the screen of perfume that was soaked into Elizabeth's dress. He hoped the fire was close to being extinguished, for the sake of Bodmin, although he would not be sad to see the gaol burn down to the ground.

The fashionable skirts these days were not as extravagant in their size as they had been in the youth of Evan's mother, but there was still enough volume to hide underneath during the short walk.

Men were shouting in the background, something about more water being needed, but he stilled, alarmed when Mrs. Blackwell asked her coachman to prepare the steps. That would be the toughest test yet—disappear inside the carriage without being seen by the servant. But once the skirts lifted, revealing the portable wooden construction, he crawled inside like a cat leaping for a mouse.

Elizabeth threw a blanket down on him while Mrs. Blackwell was already sending the coachman away, telling him to hurry out of Bodmin, not worry about closing the door behind them.

The door locked, the curtains were drawn, and Evan was still shattered to pieces by what had just happened, in disbelief that he and Julian might actually get away when a few hours ago he was sure this would be the day he died.

"We need to be silent. William answers to Father," Elizabeth whispered as the carriage rolled forward. She shifted in her place right next to her stepmother, their broad skirts taking up most of the leg space, but Evan would not complain about anything right now, feeling drunker than he'd ever been.

Mrs. Blackwell watched Evan and Julian with worry marring her perfect forehead. "Where do you want us to take you?"

Evan glanced at Julian. They hadn't had time to discuss this in private, but he was sure Julian could come up with a perfect answer. He had said that Martin was involved, but not much beyond that. The two of them merely needed to stop close enough to walk to whatever destination Julian came up with, and far away from Bodmin to not raise suspicion if Pascoe went in pursuit.

Julian exhaled and rubbed his temples. "For now, let's head for Fairfield Park. I will know when we ought to part from you," he said in the end. "We will not endanger you after this. It's a promise, but both of you have our eternal gratitude."

Elizabeth swallowed hard. "What if I *wished* to see you?" she asked, casting a long look at Evan. It was astonishing how quickly she started finding him interesting after the truth about him came to light.

Mrs. Blackwell sighed and opened a silver box, showing colorful sweets placed in rows. "You cannot meet Sir Evan ever again, child. That really is enough excitement for a lifetime. Marzipan?" she asked, offering the food to Evan and Julian.

Evan sighed, wondering what husband would ever meet her love for adventure. "There is no other way, Miss Elizabeth. We need to leave Cornwall. Quite possibly, leave the British Isles altogether. If I ever find a way to do so, I will write to you about wherever I end up going. I hope that can be of some solace."

Elizabeth fanned herself and gave him a brilliant smile. Her hand dove beneath the hem of the muslin scarf in her neckline, and she slowly pulled out an embroidered handkerchief. Mrs. Blackwell watched it with a frown but did not intervene when Elizabeth presented the cloth to Evan. "So that you have something to remember me by, Highwayman."

Evan kissed the sweet-scented fabric with a smile, grateful to the two women who chose to defy the law for his and Julian's sake. But moments later, his gaze still drifted off to Julian in silent understanding. No words were needed to express the tenderness he felt, and the relief over escaping the clutches of death.

If Julian hadn't been there today, Evan might have not even wanted to be saved. A life without his precious canary would have been an empty cage.

Chapter 29

Evan

They were halfway from Bodmin to Fairfield Park when Mrs. Blackwell asked the coachman to stop the carriage between the trees to gather some of the flowers growing far from the road. The man did as he was told, although Evan could imagine he considered this a silly fancy.

With him gone, Julian opened the door on the other side of the carriage and rushed into the thick bushes. The fresh air, fragrant with ripe leaves and flowers, filled Evan's nose with a sweetness he'd never hoped to sense again. He squeezed Mrs. Blackwell's hand and kissed her fingers, eager to join his lover in the safety of the thick greenery. He grabbed the handle by the door, already lowering one foot when his gaze met Elizabeth's eyes.

She leaned forward, cupping his face as their lips met in an innocent, closed-mouthed kiss. He was shocked by her boldness, but if that was what she wanted for saving Evan and Julian's life, he was happy to give it to her.

"Farewell, Mrs. Blackwell. Miss Elizabeth," he said in the end, winking at Elizabeth, but once he lowered himself to the ground, no one could stop him from running to safety. He spun around and dove between the leaves, grimacing when a branchlet smacked his cheek.

Julian was waiting for him on the other side, flushed, smiling despite the swelling that hadn't receded since they left Bodmin. When their hands connected, it was like thunder spreading heat up Evan's arm, and he wouldn't let go, even if it made their escape through the woods less comfortable.

Julian's thumb swirled over Evan's fingers in a discrete caress when they rushed down the hill and into a valley that opened up just beyond the road. There were sheep dotting the green meadows on both sides, and with the sun so warm on his skin, with the trees smelling so good, with Julian at his side, Evan could hardly believe that he'd been at the gallows, waiting for death, just hours ago. It now all seemed like a bad dream.

They didn't talk much, walking closer with each step once they reached the protection of the trees at the bottom of the valley. Julian's arm rested at the small of Evan's back, and they were side to side, hips touching as they marched through the woods. In the end, they reached a shallow brook, and Julian decided there was more than enough time for them to make themselves presentable.

"The lugger is picking us up early in the morning, and marching all the way south shouldn't take more than four hours," said Julian, before dropping to his knees and picking up a handful of the clear water. He drank it greedily, then pulled off his neckcloth and used it to quickly wipe the blood and grime off his face. He moaned, touching his swollen nose, but there was nothing they could do about it without a doctor. Evan made an attempt to find out whether the bone was broken, but Julian would not let him touch it.

Evan washed his face but was too hungry to do anything else when he spotted a carpet of whortleberry plants dotted by ripe fruit just off the path. "I can't believe we've done it," he said with his mouth full and a frown. It all seemed too good to be true.

"You should have eaten that damn marzipan. We won't be able to afford such delicacies now," said Julian, approaching him. He lifted Evan's shirt, and before Evan could ask what was going on, the cool cloth softly brushed over his battered skin.

He let out a moan from the mixture of pain and relief, and closed his eyes, savoring the sweet and sour juice of the fruit. "That marzipan wouldn't have been enough to feed a cat. Don't worry. As long as we're free, I'll find a way to feed us... You didn't spend *all* the money, did you?"

Julian pulled closer and brushed his lips over Evan's skin as he went on with the gentle cleansing of his wounds. "No. I lied to them about how much I had. My father did teach me a thing or two about bargaining. We still have plenty if we live a thrifty life."

Evan smiled, hoping Julian wouldn't see it, as he was certain his mouth and teeth bore the evidence of the dark flesh of the whortleberries. "Now that's the Julian I know and love."

Julian rested his chin on Evan's shoulder, watching him from up close, eyes hazy. His face seemed on the crossroads between two emotions, but in the end, it relaxed, and Julian rubbed Evan's arm in appreciation. "I thought we wouldn't come out of there alive, and yet here we are. I'm sorry I doubted you. I never will again."

Evan reached up to pet Julian's hair. The acknowledgement made him all warm on the inside. "Gaol wouldn't suit you."

Julian sighed and closed his eyes, reaching back to the brook to clean the cloth before brushing it over Evan's skin. "I doubt I'd have spent much time there after attempting to free a convict so publically. And after having a hand in starting a fire."

Evan looked up at him and kissed Julian's chin. "You'd set the world on fire for me. How sweet of you."

Julian blinked and found Evan's hand, squeezing it hard. "I let them take you just hours after we lay in bed together. You have no idea of the things I would have done to have you back."

"You listened to what I asked of you. There is no blame in that." Evan hissed when the wet cloth touched a fresh wound.

Julian rubbed his cheekbone over Evan's shoulder, sighing loudly. "We're in this together. You can't protect me all the time. How could you expect me to live on after they hanged you?"

Evan bit the inside of his lips, struck by the depth of Julian's affection and finding it difficult to form the words to express his own. "I would have hoped that my love for you would live on somehow if you were alive..."

Julian nestled his head in the crook of Evan's neck as they both froze by the water, like statues. "I'm your bird. You said so yourself. I can't live on in the wild. I don't want any other master either."

Evan chuckled and kissed Julian's hand. "Well said, my sweet canary. I think I will bathe before we go farther after all, because you might decide 'the wild' is a better prospect than a man who spent two weeks chained to a wall."

Julian laughed and let go of Evan, settling in the grass. He rested his back against the tree and watched Evan wash, unusually quiet. They eventually set out again, after gathering some of the berries, and ate them on the way south. They did not meet any people, except for spotting some women and children at their homes far away.

The fortnight since Evan's capture seemed like months. With Evan not eager to share the horrors he'd been through, Julian spoke all about the things he accomplished in order to secure Evan's release. He talked about the men he hired, and about his sleepless nights, and a whole lot about Martin.

Evan couldn't help the tiny pang of jealousy, but it was more like a mouse squeaking in a forest than a lion roaring at his face. It would have been unreasonable to distrust Julian after what he'd done to save Evan, and Martin wouldn't be saving a potential rival if he wanted to snatch Julian away.

At sundown, they reached the shore at last, and Julian took some time investigating their surroundings before deciding they ought to head east. The gentle breeze was soothing on Evan's face, as was the steady whisper of the waves that crashed against the rocky cliffs. Freedom was within arm's reach now. Once he and Julian left Cornwall, they would be out of Pascoe's grasp, safe somewhere far away.

Julian became more animated when in the bright moonlight he noticed a rock sticking out of the sea some twenty yards away from the shore. By the time they reached the cove where a boat awaited them, hidden away, it was completely dark except for the silvery sheen of the full moon. It was gloriously round and bright, as if it wished them a safe journey on the calm waves. Yet another strike of luck.

They made their way down, and through a manmade path cut out in the rocks so that carts could enter the beach. Evan was sure that wherever they ended up, he would sleep for a week. Preferably with Julian in his arms and knowing they would both be safe from now on.

Julian's hand slid into his when they reached the sandy ground close to the beach. Walking became a bit of a nuisance, as the thick-grained sand was not only damp from the recent high tide, but also gave very easily under their weight.

Julian took Evan far from the entrance to the cove, which indeed seemed like the perfect place for a secluded departure with its steep walls, narrow mouth, and distance from the nearest village. They took their time walking along the beach, between large rocks, where at last he spotted the dark opening of a cave.

Evan walked in first, sure that he spotted the boat's bow in the faint moonlight, but deeper inside the cave, the darkness was impenetrable.

"You know how to navigate based on stars? In case I lose my way," said Julian, following Evan into the cave, hand steady on Evan's arm.

Evan chuckled. "I do actually. I will buy a new telescope one day, and—"

"Or so you think," came from the darkness, making Evan's blood run cold.

Metal hit rock, and a spark lit up a torch in an instant, illuminating the face of John Pascoe with its orange glow. It was as if he were the devil, and this cave was Evan's personal hell. More faces appeared behind Pascoe, and two more torches went aflame.

"Run," Evan said to Julian, already backing out.

Julian spun around, letting go of his hand. Evan turned back to the entrance, and to Julian, whose dark silhouette was such a sharp contrast to the pale glow outside. Three men. Evan and Julian stood a chance here, but not in the dark, not in close quarters. They needed to lure Pascoe into the open where at least Evan could see his opponents properly.

He was right behind Julian, inches away when they reached the exit, but then something knocked into Julian, tackling him into the sand with a wild roar.

Another man. And one more torch, close to the path out of the cove.

Five men.

"Go on, run!" yelled Pascoe, not far behind him. "You won't get far!"

Evan's focus was on Julian being held down in the sand by a massive man, but when he ran up to them to help, the two fighting men pushed him into the sand as he tried to force them apart.

There were six men. Another one approaching fast.

Evan needed to get a weapon off one of them, no matter the cost.

Someone—he had no idea whether Julian or the massive bull of a man on top of him—kicked Evan's thigh in the midst of wrestling. Julian cursed loudly, struggling against his opponent, but then the tide reversed with a dull thud that made Evan's skin crawl. Julian swung something at the man's head repeatedly, and the massive body fell into the sand, rolling off with a push from Julian.

"Stay where yew are!" yelled the young man running their way, but he seemed to struggle with pulling out a pistol while holding a torch. This could be Evan's opening. He didn't get up, instead lunging for the man's legs and throwing him headfirst into the sand. Both the torch and the pistol dropped to the beach.

The thug twisted in Evan's grasp, kicking him chaotically as he scrambled toward the fallen gun, casting a long shadow in the light of the burning torch, which now bathed the sand around them in its orange glow.

"Let him go, or your friend will lose his pretty head," said someone, and Evan's blood froze. He could not afford to ignore what might not be a bluff.

Evan's head snapped up, and though he still held one hand on the young man's face, the threat was real. The last man to reach them was panting from the run, but put his torch in the sand and aimed a pistol at Julian, who stayed still on his hands and knees, eyes cast down.

Evan swallowed and slowly backed away from the man he'd been fighting. He spat out some sand, and straightened up to kneel, barely keeping his fists in check when the young bastard dug his pistol out, showing off a pock-marked face in the glow of the torch, triumphant, as if he'd gained the upper hand by his own virtue.

"Good. Nice and slow," said the young man, pressing the barrel of the gun against Evan's back so hard it dug into the open wounds, making Evan grit his teeth.

Now that there was enough light, Evan recognized the man who held Julian at gunpoint. It was one of the deputies, who'd come to Tredele with Pascoe to investigate the horses way back, Atkins. The deputy spat into the sand and kicked the fallen giant, who groaned at the touch, but didn't move from where Julian rolled him over.

Tension covered Evan from head to toe as Julian looked up at him, with shadows forming on his face in the warm light of the burning torch.

"I told you, Penhart. You are not getting away this time," said Pascoe, approaching calmly in his usual black suit.

Evan discreetly looked around for weapons, noting a knife on one of the men, but there were also two swords, and three guns, if he included the one at Pascoe's hip. The man standing at the mouth of the cave was the other deputy, Davies. A slim man with long black hair.

But the man standing on Pascoe's other side, with his arms crossed and a smug smile, did not look like someone Pascoe would wish to be associated with. There were tattoos peeking out from beneath the man's shirt, and his face had seen too many fights to count. Yet there was something familiar about him.

Julian blinked, looking at the two men wide-eyed, breathing so fast he might start choking up soon with his nose still swollen.

Pascoe smirked and glanced at the tattooed man. "You might think you can secure someone's loyalty by offering them generous fangings, but it seems even men of dubious morals have rules they won't break for money."

Julian shuddered, but bared his teeth, and Evan saw that it was out of fury, not fear. "Daniel. You swine."

Then it came to Evan. He met the tattooed man during his and Julian's night in Looe. He was a friend of Martin's and drank with them all.

Daniel walked up to Julian with a mean smirk. "Yew thought I'd just do yewr biddin' so that yew can live with this man as his wife? Your lot makes me sick," he said, leaning down and slapping Julian's face so hard Evan's ached in compassion.

Julian erupted off the ground, knocking his head straight into Daniel's gut. The man opened his eyes wide, breathless from the punch, and once Julian was on his feet, it was too late for him to protect his face. Julian knocked him over with a roar that echoed off the cliffs, hands clawing at the bastard's face.

"Get off him!" Atkins yelled, looking between the fight and Pascoe, but in the end, he fired with a deafening finality.

"No!" Evan screamed, but it was Daniel who squealed like a slaughtered pig and fell to the ground with dark blood staining his pantaloons.

Pascoe sneered, as if this display of violence were beneath him. "Stop this at once!"

But Julian was deaf to the order and used the advantage given by the missed shot. He plunged his hand against Daniel's face. The man gave a breathless shout, thrashing beneath him as blood spilled from his eye like a sticky tear. He jerked his hand away from Julian's clothes, and something shiny swung in the air, disappearing in Julian's thigh before Evan could warn him.

Julian's desperate cry pushed Evan into action, and in that moment of horror and fear for his lover, he didn't even think of the pistol behind him. He needed to take Julian into safety more than he needed air. Twisting his upper body and ignoring the pain in his back, Evan grabbed the young man's hand before he could pull the trigger. With firearms out of the game, their enemies would be lesser threats, even if the one who'd accidentally shot that treacherous scum Daniel was already drawing his sword.

The young man's eyes went wide, and he tried to pull his wrist out of Evan's grip, but it was no use against Evan's strength. Evan gritted his teeth and rapidly twisted the bastard's hand. The pistol shot into the sand, raising a cloud of dust that tingled Evan's throat and eyes, but with the naked steel reflecting light all-too-close to Julian, Evan already decided on his next step. He pushed back the youngster and leaped at Atkins, grabbing the handle of his sword with one hand, and his bare throat with the other. They fell down, and with Julian's moan resonating in Evan's ear, he smashed his forehead against the deputy's for good measure.

Atkins loosened his hold on the sword, and Evan pulled it out of his hand, getting to his knees when the air once again filled with noise and the smell of gunpowder.

For a moment, the thundering sound made Evan's ears ring, and he could sense the hot breath of the pistol through his shirt. He needed to touch his chest to know he hadn't been shot. He spared Atkins no mercy, and kicked him straight in the groin, giving himself a precious second to look over his shoulder and make sure Julian was as safe as he could be right now.

Julian and Pascoe were down in the sand. Julian held on to Pascoe's legs and tried to crawl on top of him, with the handle of Daniel's knife still sticking out of his leg. His bruised face was all determination, but a sharp jab with the handle of the pistol sent him off Pascoe with a cry of pain.

Evan's opponent went down to his knees, disarmed and holding his crotch from the pain, but Evan didn't pay him any more attention than necessary. His feet were carrying him to Pascoe and Julian before that monster could do any more damage to Evan's beloved.

When the young man stood in his way, about to speak, Evan did not care to spare him anymore. He plunged the stolen sword straight into the man's soft middle and twisted it for good measure when the blade came out on the other side.

Evan's life with Julian was on the line. He was done playing games and holding off. For what?

Atkins chose this moment to come at Evan, pushing so hard Evan's starved, bruised body lost balance. He fell into the sand, scrambling to keep the weapon in his hand as the man's boot smashed against his wrist and pushed it down into the sand.

Evan swore and rolled his head away from the young man, who bled all over the sand like a calf prepared for skinning, only to spot the burning fire of the torch so close he could reach it. He closed his hand on the smooth wood and before that son of a whore Atkins realized how he'd meet his end, Evan pushed the torch against his side, setting his clothes aflame.

Atkins's scream echoed in the cove, and the bastard rolled off Evan, frantically running to the sea, where he threw himself into the waves.

In the yellow glow of the torch, the eyes of the dying young man widened, but he couldn't even move a finger anymore, his strength drained by blood loss. Evan pulled the sword out with new determination and dashed to where Pascoe was still fighting Julian. On the periphery of the torch glow Daniel was crawling away slowly, like the maggot that he was, but Evan could deal with him later.

Pascoe was on top of Julian, his back the perfect target, so Evan swung his sword at the devil's spawn.

Pascoe looked back just in time to react, as if demons whispered of danger into his ear, and he rolled off Julian, putting him in line of Evan's weapon. The sharp steel halted just inches above Julian, and Evan froze, shuddering when his mind offered the most gruesome of endings to this night. They looked at one another, sharing one thought when Davies emerged out of the darkness with his sword drawn. Behind him, Evan saw a red glow inside the cave.

Pascoe backed away to stand behind Davies, panting from the effort of the earlier fight. It was yet another reminder of just how pathetically mortal the bastard was. The man who'd haunted Evan's dreams for years could have been killed so much sooner if Evan had set his mind to it. It didn't matter anymore. Pascoe would die tonight.

Davies's eyes met Evan's, just the two of them about to duel to the death on this beach.

Davies's eyes caught the fiery glow of the torches as he paced between Evan and Pascoe, watching Evan like a wild animal looking for an opening to deliver the deathly strike. The sea hummed close by, not entangled by the events happening at the shore, powerful and constant. It would carry Evan and Julian to safety as long as they managed to tear themselves out of the hands of the law.

Davies kicked some sand, and Evan prepared to fight him, but the man just watched, as if it had merely been a ploy to assess Evan's reflexes. Evan didn't have time to waste. Nor was he afraid to attack, so he lunged at Davies with the sword, suddenly hit with the realization that he'd never been intent on killing his opponent when he fenced. When he'd sparred with acquaintances or taught Julian more advanced fencing, they used precautions not to hurt each other, but here and now with Davies? Evan would use any dirty trick in the book to stick his sword into the man's guts or gouge his eyes out. He'd cut his tendons or plunge the steel into Davies's back if necessary.

The clang of metal resonated through Evan's muscles, and he set his moves to the tone of it, ready for another strike, waiting for an opening to slash, push, or simply divert Davies's attention and punch him in the face instead.

The man was surprisingly good with the sword, and Evan found himself questioning whether he wasn't a former soldier of some kind. Steel met steel as they danced in the sand, keeping distance only to spar with a fury Evan never knew in an opponent. Davies likely knew what would be the end of this night for him if he made even the smallest mistake. Evan was, after all, a cornered animal. Behind Davies's broad back, Pascoe stood with his fists clenched, eyes darting to Julian, who stood opposite him with a red-streaked knife in hand close to the neck of unconscious giant he'd earlier knocked out with a stone.

It was when Pascoe finally moved toward the sprawled form that Evan rushed forward, lunging at Davies with a rage that was scorching the inside of his bones. He was about to strike when something cold, wet, and heavy pushed at him from the back, grabbing his neck. Atkins was back from the waves.

He yelped, instantly wary of exposing his chest and stomach to Davies, but his injured opponent was too slow, and Evan managed to use the force that pulled him back at first, and he leaned forward, using all his strength to lift Atkins before the man would try to strangle him. He didn't manage to free himself of the fish-smelling arms, but their grip loosened at least. Davies took a hesitant step back, and Evan used that moment to thrust his sword from below, through Davies's jaw, and straight into his skull.

Davies would not survive, but Evan didn't have the time to make sure. He let go of the sword stuck in the man's head and repeatedly punched back with his elbow, trying to hit Atkins's stomach, but the bastard was as resilient as a cockroach. He held on to Evan's neck with the crook of his arm and barely let any air pass through Evan's throat. Their feet sank into the wet sand, and as Atkins pulled Evan back, water washed over his feet.

Even with the icy wetness soaking through Evan's clothes and freezing his back, his vision was blurring from exertion and lack of air. He strained his back, grabbing the bastard's forearm to lessen the pressure to his throat, but when a sharp cry tore through the air, and the arms around Evan's neck twitched, he knew it was his chance.

He spun around, flexing his back and yanking his whole body forward so hard his spine and muscles moaned in protest. His opponent gave a shriek of panic as he glided through the air over Evan's head.

He fell into the shallow water with a loud splash, and Evan followed him like a harpy, ready to tear at flesh, but blood was not necessary here. All he needed was to keep Pascoe's hound underwater long enough. Droplets splashed into Evan's face, leaving his mouth tasting of salt. Very much like the blood of the men he'd killed tonight.

Even though confused, Atkins struggled. He tried to come up for air, looking like a carp with his mouth opening and closing fast, but Evan pushed him right back down with no mercy, holding down Atkins's head and shoulder no matter how much the bastard thrashed, or how frantically he kicked about in the water. Evan had lost all his scruples the moment those cunts had put their hands on Julian.

He was a predator set on survival, and Pascoe underestimated his will to live on. A much larger swarm of rabbits would have been needed to stop a wolf from breaking all their necks.

He'd been so set on keeping Atkins underwater that it took him a good moment to comprehend that the body he held down wasn't moving anymore. He straightened up, oddly numb, and clenched his fists as he turned around to leave the cool waves that had gotten him soaked and his back stinging all over where salty water had bitten into it.

Julian looked at him from his place by the fallen giant. And so did Pascoe, the gray-haired man in black who had destroyed Evan's life all those years ago and had been set on doing it again now. Pascoe was old and weak. He was no threat where there was no one to listen to his authoritative voice.

Their eyes met, and Pascoe ran.

The wolf in Evan snarled, and he went in pursuit without even questioning the decision his body made for him.

Pascoe would not be getting away. Not after pushing Evan this far. He did not get to simply walk away after coming here with five men who would gladly kill both Evan and Julian, were they given the chance.

For long years, Evan had been both afraid of what Pascoe might do to him and loathed him to his very core. He'd always avoided confrontation on Pascoe's turf, becoming the Ghost of Tredele instead of living his life to the fullest, always too afraid he would be exposed for sodomy if he took a lover. That Pascoe would track them down like two foxes and have them hanged, or ripped to pieces by the mob at the pillory.

Now it was Pascoe's turn to fear for his life.

Despite the wet clothes pulling Evan down and slowing his gait, he was still quicker, still stronger.

Pascoe ran like a man much younger than he was, even though the sand was keeping him from using his legs to the fullest, and he stumbled to his knees before pulling himself up.

"Just go. I will not pursue you. Be gone!" cried out Pascoe, stumbling again, his hair in disarray as he scrambled to his feet in desperation.

He knew what was coming. Evan would sink his claws and fangs into Pascoe's flesh and rip at it until enough blood was spilled to turn the beach red.

Evan reached out, closer to Pascoe by the second, and his fingertips brushed against the man's jacket. A few seconds later, Evan closed his grip on the fabric and pulled so hard Pascoe tumbled into the sand.

Evan was on top of him, with victory already drumming in his ears when his hands closed around Pascoe's neck. "You don't get to let me go, because you didn't catch me!" Evan stared into Pascoe's eyes, feeding his strength on the grief and hate that had been brewing inside him since Pascoe had destroyed his life. "You will never hurt anyone again! And I will think back to your death with satisfaction every time I fuck my man!"

Pascoe grabbed Evan's wrists, trying to kick, but Evan pushed down the unruly legs with his weight. His head pulsed with the need to end this farce. He craved to be free, and Peran deserved to at last be avenged. He had not deserved what Pascoe unleashed on him, and now was the time for Pascoe to pay for his sins against an innocent man.

Pascoe's throat twitched under the weight of Evan's hands, the Adam's apple pushing on his fingers to no effect as the sick bastard's eyes bulged, reddening in the silvery glow of the moon. The choking sounds that came with the torment gave Evan no pleasure, but he watched Pascoe, wanting to make sure his face would be the last the cruel whoreson would ever see.

The hold on Evan's wrists weakened, but he pushed down on the throat for a while longer, to make sure Pascoe was dead. He watched Pascoe's soul lift from his body inch by inch once the man couldn't access air anymore.

Evan leaned lower, looking into Pascoe's bloodshot eyes from up close, listening to catch any signs of life. There were none. "I hope your soul never knows peace," he hissed, finally letting go of the limp body. No matter what a relief it was to bring Pascoe's life to a just end, his hands felt dirty. Soiled from having touched someone so rotten.

"Evan? Are you fine?" called out Julian, and when Evan looked back, he saw him leaning against the entrance of the cave, torch in hand.

Pascoe's body seemed to cool in Evan's grasp at a rapid pace, as if the hellpit that was the man's soul had now truly abandoned his old bones.

Evan sneered and spat at Pascoe as he got up, strangely light-headed and soft-kneed despite having committed such horrific deeds tonight. He tried to speak, but his voice failed him when he opened his mouth, so he walked toward Julian, shocked by the serenity of the cove in which six men lay dead.

Was it six though? Daniel? Was he dead or still crawling around somewhere, trying to escape Evan instead of paying for what he'd done?

He spotted movement at the opening carved in rock where he and Julian had earlier passed on their way to the cove. Between the vertical, man-made walls crawled Daniel, so close to leaving with just flesh wounds and with a fat purse that it made Evan ill to think of such an end for that dog. Julian must have thought the same thing, as he made a careful step along the rock, holding on to it as he limped forward on his injured leg.

"Stay where you are," Evan said to Julian in a hollow voice that echoed against the walls protecting the cove from land. Daniel left a crimson trail on the ground, pushing on to the safety of shadows, away from the men he'd betrayed.

Evan could let him go now that imminent danger was gone. But he could have also let Pascoe live, yet had chosen revenge. This was the kind of man he really was on the inside, and it had taken him much too long to realize it.

Evan was careful on the sand, as it made rushed movement laborious, and took his time, picking up a fallen knife on the way.

"What did you say *my lot* makes you want to do?" he asked.

Daniel looked back, ghostly pale against the blood dribbling from underneath his closed eyelid. He whined and pushed forward, as if it could save him at this point. "Please... I have a family to feed," he mumbled without looking Evan's way.

Evan came close in slow, deliberately menacing steps, and put his wet boot on the man's back, pushing him against the ground. "You're lying. But if you're not, you should have thought about them before betraying your employer." He pulled on Daniel's hair to expose his neck, and slit his throat open in one sharp move.

Daniel's body convulsed. He choked on his own blood, twitching in the sand as he fruitlessly fought for air. Evan pushed his hand underneath Daniel's jacket and pulled out a purse heavy with coins the bastard had taken off both Julian and Pascoe.

Evan didn't stay to watch Daniel die and made his way back to the beach. Only now, the ache in his bones and tiredness reached him. In the soft silvery glow of the moon, dotted by spots of blood and the orange torchlight, Julian struggled to pull the small boat out of the cave.

Evan scooted by the man whom Julian had earlier hit on the head with a rock, but he was also dead. He could tell no soul what had happened here. Satisfied with that knowledge, Evan walked up to Julian and helped him pull.

"You were stabbed in the leg. Did the bleeding stop?" he asked, surprised that his own voice sounded strangely to the point, as if he weren't able to communicate the depth of both the relief and burden that lay on his heart.

Julian's breath trembled, but he nodded, pushing all his strength into the task, his face reddened from exertion. "I tied it with my stocking. Doesn't seem to bleed anymore. Maybe they have a surgeon on the ship."

Evan let go of the boat when they dragged it out halfway to the water. "Show me." He pulled Julian close by the wrist, keeping his eyes on his handsome lover rather than on the bodies scattered around them. It had been a different matter when he was in the heat of the moment, but now that things had calmed down, he wanted all signs of violence gone, as if Pascoe's men had never stepped on the beach.

Julian winced and leaned against the boat, turning so that his leg would not be in the shadow. He looked away, touching the black breeches he was wearing. There was a stocking tied around his upper thigh, stuffed on the inside with what looked like a handkerchief, with just a few spots of red visible on the surface.

Evan swallowed, calculating if they could afford to stay for a few more minutes. More armed men might come their way, and with both him and Julian weary after the last fight, they might not be so lucky this time.

"We will look at it on the island. Or do you feel he's cut you deep? Do you feel weak?" Evan stroked Julian's shoulder, but pulled his hand away when he realized he was smearing blood over Julian's shirt.

Julian looked down at the streak, licking his lips as he glanced at Evan, sinking farther against the boat. "We need to leave. I'll be fine. There was so much noise. Someone must have heard the pistols."

"Don't overexert yourself," Evan said and pulled on the boat himself, dragging it over the sand with sweat dripping down his neck and his body hurting all over. He *would* get Julian to safety. After the risks Julian had taken for him, taking care of him was the least he could do in return.

He could feel the cool touch of the water through his boots, and he looked back at the soft wave breaking over his calf. He quickly rushed to the other side and pulled off his boots, tossing them inside their vessel. Julian pushed on the boat, getting it slightly deeper into the water.

"I'll be fine."

Despite the waves being so still this night, the moon silvery and bright, somehow the feeling of calm was gone, and the beauty of the cove would be forever marred by the brutality that it had witnessed.

Evan took a deep breath of the cool air. "I love you. You know that, right?"

Julian stared at him over the empty boat, his Adam's apple bobbing up and down. "I know. Of course I do," he said in the end. "Why now? Are you... are you hurt?"

"No. I would be lying if told you that I am all right, but I will heal. I just want you to know that no matter where life takes us, and no matter what we have to do to get there, I will always be the same man when I am with you."

Julian watched him for a long moment, his lively face frozen in the cool light of the moon. He sighed and stroked the edge of the boat, as if he didn't know what to do with his hands. "I know. You're mine, and I'm not giving up on you, whatever happens."

Evan managed to force a smile and nodded. "Get in the boat."

Julian didn't argue with him. He took his place at the bow and looked around, touching the things he must have left here earlier. Evan could see bottles, a burlap sack, and something wrapped in paper. Food perhaps?

With one last push, the boat was floating, and Evan boarded it hastily, grabbing the oars just when Julian grabbed his. But Evan leaned in, seeking the comfort of closeness, even if only for a brief moment.

"Thank you for coming back for me," Evan said and gave Julian a kiss. Whatever lay ahead of them, he knew they both considered each other worth dying for and killing for.

Chapter 30

Julian

Julian pulled closer to Evan, taking step after step in the wet sand. The sun was slowly rising and blinded him with its pure, warm light, so he looked down at the ripples made by the waves. They were surprisingly hard against his bare feet, but it was a pleasure to stretch his legs and sense the cool water wash over his skin, penetrating between his toes and teasing his calves.

They were alone here, two lone lives on the tiny island by the shores of southern Cornwall. The bloodied bodies they'd left in the cove seemed so distant now it was almost as if they left them behind in a different country.

His wound turned out to be shallow, and they got a bit of sleep each as the other watched. Even in these circumstances, even cold, Julian felt safe when he fell asleep with his head in Evan's lap. The hands that had killed five men would never hurt him.

"Are you certain they will come?" Evan asked and squeezed Julian's hand.

Julian rolled his head over Evan's shoulder, much calmer now that they were off the shore. He knew they could not return, as the bodies had likely been discovered already. Someone would point out who Pascoe had been after, and there was no one about Looe who did not know Julian's face. "If they don't, we will go to Devon, and board a ship in Plymouth."

Evan nodded, with a frown of permanent worry marring his forehead. He was still a big, strong man, but the two weeks in gaol had taken their toll on him. Julian couldn't wait to make sure he ate more.

"We will find a way."

Julian smiled, watching the tiny wet dunes beneath his feet. Was this what the Sahara desert looked like, only dry as parchment? "You were very brave last night," he said, even though the sight of Evan pushing at Pascoe's throat until his hands broke something and dipped lower was a constant presence in the back of his mind. He understood why Evan had done it, and as horrific of a deed it was, he knew Evan's strength would always keep Julian safe, like he'd promised. Evan was not cruel by nature, even if easily angered.

Still, last night had changed something in both of them despite ultimately bringing them closer. Julian wasn't the same man who entered that cove, and he was sure Evan wasn't either.

"I did what needed to be done." Evan looked at Julian with his black eyes reflecting the morning light. "And I would do it again to keep you safe."

Over Evan's shoulder, Julian noticed a three-masted lugger approaching on the waves, and his heart skipped a beat, rushing until one of the men inside waved a red piece of cloth—the sign Julian had agreed on with Martin.

"Evan... Evan, look," he said, pushing Evan toward the beach, his whole body trembling with relief. They were scarred both in body and mind, but they would leave, and they would eventually heal.

Evan let go of Julian's hand quickly, but lent him his arm, so that Julian wouldn't have to strain his wounded leg. "You did it," he whispered to Julian with a small smile.

Julian smiled back, and for once, it felt like the gloom that had befallen him when Evan had been captured was pushed away. "I didn't finish my book. And now I won't be ever able to recover it from Tredele. But that's all right, I think there are more important things to write about than stories that express my confusion with men."

"I'll make sure you are much less confused from now on." Evan snorted, and they approached the boat they'd come in to push it back into water.

Julian chewed on his lip, jumping into the boat as soon as the time was right. "I've been thinking about this when we were apart. You unlocked something in me. Something I would have never known if I hadn't met you. There are more men like me, I'm sure. I would like to write for them."

Evan bit his lip, but quickly released it with a hiss. He most likely forgot it was bruised and swollen after the fight. "Men who don't know they like cock?" he teased, but started rowing quickly, the muscles of his bare arms a sight to behold in the morning sun.

Julian took a deep breath, sensing the cool breeze in his hair. "It will not be a memoir of our pleasures, you crude man. I aim to unlock the floodgates inside their minds bit by bit. They will want cock once they read the last chapter," he added, smirking even as he waved at the men awaiting them on board the lugger.

"I'm sure your skill with words can do that. It's a shame you can't attach your portrait to each copy of your book. It would have driven men wild all over the country."

Julian's chest swelled with joy, and he nudged Evan's leg with his foot. "I'm serious. You're not just flattering my writing to be sweet to me, surely?"

"Would I flatter you to get you to take off your breeches?" Evan whispered as they approached the ship. "Never. It would be despicable."

Julian shook his head and stood up, waving at the small crew of men inside the lugger. They were so close now he could see their faces, yet another step away from the horrors of gaol and the noose.

"I hear you made quite a run for it yesterday," Martin said as he reached out and helped Julian on board.

Julian grinned and watched him pull Evan in as well. "And now you, my friend, might be a part of our legendary flight."

Martin shook his head with a big grin and patted Julian on the back. "How did ye get out? I was sure ye were a goner after ye charged at the guards."

Julian glanced at Evan before settling his eyes on Martin's smiling face again. He would be forever grateful to this man, and so should Evan. Maybe he would finally swallow that silly jealousy of his. "I will tell you all about it later. It will be a tale of chase and excitement," he said, unsure how much he could say about the events at the beach. Martin was a freetrader, a man who roamed beyond the eyes of the law, but he was not a murderer, and Julian did not want to lose his friendship.

Evan looked at the land they were leaving behind. "Where are we headed?"

Martin pushed his thumbs behind the waistband of his pantaloons. "Scillies. Far enough from here for now."

Julian glanced at him, breathless even as he laughed at such a lucky coincidence. Italy could wait if he would get to see the place where Evan had been so happy once. "I've always wanted to go there."

Evan looked back at Julian with a smile.

The end

Thank you for reading our book! If you enjoyed your time with our story, we would really appreciate it if you took a few minutes to leave a review on your favorite platform. It is especially important for us as self-publishing authors, who don't have the backing of an established press.
Not to mention we simply love hearing from readers! :)

How about a free book? ;) You can choose one here:
https://www.kamerikan.com/freebies

If you want to stay in touch with us, follow us on Amazon and join our Facebook group, the **K.A. Merikan Playroom** or join our newsletter at http://kamerikan.com/newsletter .

And if you liked Dex, Frank's nephew, you can read about the start of his relationship with Hammer in Dickhead :)
Find it on Amazon.

THE MAN WHO LOVED
COLE FLORES
K.A. MERIKAN

The Man Who Loved Cole Flores

K.A. Merikan

You want revenge? Dig two graves.

Ten years ago, a vicious gang called the Gotham Boys descended on a homestead in the mountains like a pack of wolves, leaving nothing behind but death and destruction.

Ned O'Leary was the only one to survive the ordeal.

He lost hope for revenge long ago, but its flame erupts in his heart when the gang is spotted again. By a stroke of luck, he is recruited to infiltrate the Gotham Boys and bring them all to justice. Ripped out of his wholesome life on a ranch, he has to find his footing with a band of ruthless outlaws who challenge his morals every step of the way

But the one who tests him most of all is Cole Flores. Deadly, full of himself and unpredictable, the gang leader's adopted son should be a man easy to hate, but instead, he sparks illicit desires Ned has never felt before.

Cole Flores is forbidden.
Cole Flores is corruption.
Cole Flores is everything Ned O'Leary craves.

Torn between love and revenge, lust and loyalty, Ned has to face impossible choices that are bound to leave scars, no matter how hard he tries to do the right thing.

"I don't know what this means, or how to do this with you," he whispered as his heart broke into a gallop. *"But I want to. I need to."*

Dark, dangerous, yet desperately romantic, "The Man Who Loved Cole Flores" is a gritty western M/M romance novel. Prepare for violence, emotional turmoil, and scorching hot, explicit scenes, as well as a heart-pounding cliffhanger to book 1.

The epic love story of Ned O'Leary and Cole Flores gets its HEA in book 2 – "The Man Who Hated Ned O'Leary".

Themes: Enemies-to-lovers, first love, revenge, undercover, friends-to-lovers, forbidden romance, outlaws and cowboys, crime, gang, secrets, loyalty, betrayal, period-typical homophobia, Old West, survival, corruption of the innocent, self-discovery, opposites attract

Length: ~155,000 words (Book 1 in a duology)

WARNING: This story contains scenes of violence, offensive language and morally ambiguous characters as well as sensitive topics of child abuse and suicide

Available on Amazon

CRIMINAL DELIGHTS: TAKEN

WRONG
WAY HOME

K.A. MERIKAN

WRONG WAY HOME

K.A. MERIKAN

ONE WRONG TURN. ONE RIGHT MAN.

Colin. Rule-follower. Future doctor. Witness to murder. Captive
Taron. Survivalist. Mute. Murderer. Captor.

Like every other weekend, Colin is on his way home from university, but he's taunted by the notion that he never takes risks in life and always follows the beaten path. On impulse, he decides to take a different route. Just this one time. What he doesn't realize is that it's the last time he has a choice. He ends up taking a detour into the darkest pit of horror, abducted by a silent, imposing man with a blood-stained axe. But what seems like his worst nightmare might just prove to be a path to the kind of freedom Colin never knew existed.

Taron has lived alone for years. His land, his rules. He'd given up on company long ago. After all, attachment is a liability. He deals with his problems on his own, but the night he needs to dispose of an enemy, he ends up with a witness to his crime. The last thing Taron needs is a nuisance of a captive. Colin doesn't deserve death for setting foot on Taron's land, but keeping him isn't optimal either. It's only when he finds out the city boy is gay that an altogether different option arises. One that isn't right, yet tempts him every time Colin's pretty eyes glare at him from the cage.

⚠⚠⚠⚠⚠⚠⚠⚠⚠⚠

Themes: prepping, alternative lifestyles, disability, crime, loneliness, enemies to lovers, forced proximity, fish out of water, opposites attract, abduction, Stockholm syndrome, family issues.

Genre: Dark, thriller M/M romance
Length: ~ 70,000 words (Standalone)

AMAZON

About the Author

K.A. Merikan is a duo of queer writers who don't believe in following the well-trodden path. In their books you can dip your toe into dangerous romance with mafiosi, outlaw bikers and bad boys, all from the safety of your sofa. They love the weird and wonderful, stepping out of the box, and bending stereotypes both in life and in fiction. Their stories don't shy away from exploring the darker side of M/M romance, and feature a variety of anti-heroes, rebels, misfits, and underdogs who go against the grain.

Be prepared for shocking twists, dark humor, raw emotions, and sizzling hot scenes.

e-mail: **kamerikan@gmail.com**
http://kamerikan.com

More information about works in progress and publishing at:
Facebook: https://www.facebook.com/groups/181754107524o882
Patreon: https://www.patreon.com/kamerikan